LOVE'S PORTRAIT

What Reviewers Say About Anna Larner's Work

Highland Fling

"[This book] just kept surprising me at every turn! I had a few moments of 'Really did I just read that?' and 'Did she just say that?' I love when a book does this because you feel the writer is writing outside the box. …All in all, I loved *Highland Fling* and think Anna Larner will definitely be an author I'll be watching out for."—*Les Rêveur*

"…this is one of those books that breathes 'good reading.' The author Larner has the perfect ear for a certain type of LGBT space, and weaves a convincing queer & lesbian psychogeography into the narrative, and her own experiences and previous work with archiving and creating space for LGBT history to be shared gives this book an authentic feel, not just in tone, geography and accent but also the emotional honesty that marks this book out as such a charming read."—*Gscene Magazine*

Visit us at www.boldstrokesbooks.com

By the Author

Highland Fling

Love's Portrait

LOVE'S PORTRAIT

by

Anna Larner

2019

ISBN 13: 978-1-63555-057-3

THIS TRADE PAPERBACK ORIGINAL IS PUBLISHED BY
BOLD STROKES BOOKS, INC.
P.O. BOX 249
VALLEY FALLS, NY 12185

FIRST EDITION: APRIL 2019

CREDITS
EDITOR: RUTH STERNGLANTZ
PRODUCTION DESIGN: SUSAN RAMUNDO
COVER DESIGN BY TAMMY SEIDICK

Acknowledgments

A heartfelt thank you to the BSB team, in particular, Len Barot, Sandy Lowe, and Ruth Sternglantz.

To my awesome beta readers, Bridget, Jen, Kay, Lis, Rita, Sue G, Sue L, thank you from the bottom of my heart for your continued amazing support.

To my wonderful partner, family, and friends—thank you, as ever, for your love.

To readers—a huge thank you! For when you support one author, you support us all, helping lesbian fiction to grow ever stronger so that our lives can be shared and celebrated with the turn of each page.

Dedication

For Ang

CHAPTER ONE

"A m I *very* late?" Molly wrestled free of her coat and squinted at the office clock through the mist of her steamed-up glasses.

"Well, let's put it this way, you're not very on time. Was it Daisy May again?" Fran asked with a tone that suggested she already knew the answer.

"It's not her fault. She's just not at her best, first thing."

"You need to get rid of her."

Molly took off her glasses and glared at her colleague. "Fran Godfrey. How can you say that?"

"And how can *you* own a car that won't start in the morning, hates the cold, not to mention the wet, shudders at the merest suggestion of speed, and stalls at the hint of a hill?"

"Well, I find your remarks uncalled for and bordering on disloyal."

The strip light above their heads fizzed and flickered. Molly climbed with a wobble onto her chair, took off her shoe, and banged the end of the light fixture, which gave a last fizz before returning the room to its headachy ambiance.

She dropped down to the floor with a sigh. "Daisy May, I feel sure, would speak very highly of you. If she could speak, obviously."

"Obviously. The reason that car and I know each other so well is that I've spent more time than is decent pushing her backside. How long have you worked here?"

"Oh, let me think." Molly proceeded to silently count on her fingers. "Seven months. You know, it seems like longer."

"Seven months. And how many times have I had to push your car?"

Molly shrugged. "Once or twice maybe."

"Four times. And in case it had somehow escaped your notice, I am not in the first flush of youth and such exertions are not only ungainly, but they are decidedly inadvisable."

Molly winced with guilt at the memory of Fran, legs apart, bracing herself against the rear end of her vintage Mini. "Of course. And it goes without saying that Daisy May more than sympathizes and is very grateful for your assistance." Molly rifled through the files and folders on her desk. "Don't suppose you've seen my notes for the funding meeting? I'm certain I left them right here by my pencil pot." Her heart sank as a sickening flashback called to mind the image of the papers resting underneath a jar of peanut butter on her kitchen table. *Bugger.*

Fran shook her head. "Sorry, no, and speaking of grateful, Molly Goode, Daisy May's not the only one who should be thanking me. Evelyn was in here ten minutes ago asking for you."

"What? Oh no, we were meant to meet before the meeting. I've no time to print my notes out again."

Molly rummaged in the bin, picking through used teabags and browning apple cores for the last but one version of her notes. She flattened out the screwed-up ball of pages and brushed away the hole-punched paper circles that clung to the tea-stained sheets. "What did you tell her?"

"I told her"—Fran looked up and smiled sympathetically—"that you were probably held up by your work in the storeroom."

"Storeroom. Excellent. Thank you. I owe you big time." Molly took a deep breath. "Right." She looked at the door and then at Fran.

"What now?" Fran asked, her eyes raised wearily at Molly.

"Was she in a good mood by any chance? Or was her neck all prickly pink?"

"Let's just say I wouldn't keep her waiting any longer."

"That bad? Right."

"Go!" Fran pointed to the door. "Oh, and Molly. Remember to impress upon them that the renovated annex would be the perfect venue for our community space. It'll be a real push in the right direction."

"Will do. Wish me luck."

"Good luck."

Molly hurried along the first floor corridor that led from the windowless office she shared with Fran to Evelyn's suite of rooms resplendent in oak panelling and bathed in the soft caress of natural light.

The length of the corridor always seemed to shift, shrinking and expanding to fit the moment. If Molly was late, like this morning, it felt like miles. If she had reason to want to drag out her arrival, she always seemed to arrive at Evelyn's door with alarming speed. The polished brass nameplate which read *Ms. Evelyn Fox, Director* never ceased to fill her with dread.

"Morning, Molly." The efficient voice of Evelyn's secretary Marianne had a comforting familiarly to it. She was the first person

Molly had met when interviewing for her post as Curator of Fine Arts. It felt like yesterday that she had stood at Evelyn's door mustering the courage to knock.

Molly glanced across to Marianne seated neatly behind her computer in her immaculate office. "Morning. I'm a little behind. Is Evelyn in?"

Marianne shook her head. "She's in the conference room. The chairman arrived early."

"He did?" *Crap.*

Molly stared for a moment at the closed conference room door. She could just make out the dull hum of discussion and then Evelyn's joyless laughter that always, like her smile, seemed to end too abruptly.

Molly counted to three in her head before knocking politely and entering on command.

"Molly, wonderful. Please join us." Evelyn's words welcomed Molly, while her piercing eyes held the pointed question, Molly was sure, of her lateness. "And, of course, you've met Mark before."

"Yes, indeed. Good morning, Mr. Drew." Molly held out her hand and the chairman of the museum's trustees shook it in a perfunctory way that spoke of his disinterest in her. Molly couldn't decide whether his lack of interest was because she was not important enough to cause him concern or not glamorous enough to trigger his arousal. She suspected it might be both.

Evelyn gestured for Molly to take a seat opposite her at the large oval table.

"Mark, Molly has been bringing together ideas to develop the museum's reach." Evelyn's focus returned to note making. "Isn't that so?"

"Yes, absolutely." Molly cleared her throat and tapped her notes together against the table in readiness to read out her thoughts. At once a flutter of tiny white paper circles drifted across the table to rest at Evelyn's pen. One paper dot caught the air from God knows where and settled on the chairman's tie. It would have been a joyful moment had it been a wedding.

Molly quickly flattened her notes against the table. *Oh my God. Keep going.* "The Heritage Lottery Fund has been very supportive of initiatives which promote diversity. In February each year, for example, museums nationwide participate in LGBT history month—"

Evelyn raised her pen just slightly in the air. The signal was clear: she was about to speak and that meant Molly was not.

Evelyn lifted her glasses away from her face and fixed her gaze beyond Molly. Molly resisted the urge to turn to look where she was looking. "Granted, it was organized before your appointment, but if you remember, Molly, we hosted a most stimulating talk this last February on the plays of Joe Orton. We couldn't be more committed to celebrating L"—she replaced her glasses and checked her notes—"GBT history month."

You couldn't? "That's wonderful to hear," Molly said, not intending to sound so surprised. "And yes, I remember the talk, it was great." Why had she been so nervous? For clearly here they were as one voice, one vision. "So then I would like to suggest that we place even more emphasis on this special month and really embrace the opportunity to reach out. I propose that we apply for funding to delve into our collections and work to discover—and indeed *uncover*—forgotten histories. And not just LGBT histories but all minority histories and give voice to those voices as yet unheard in our museum. I'm very keen to see us become a symbol, a flag bearer, if you will, for diversity. A place where all communities can see themselves reflected—"

Evelyn raised her pen again. "Thank you, Molly. Leading the way is something this museum takes great pride in."

The chairman nodded almost as if he was personally accepting the praise for everyone else's efforts.

"But, sadly, we often find ourselves bound by limited resources. Our aspirations clipped. The collections team are working day and night to meet the accreditation backlogs. At the end of the day it's a question of balance."

Molly's heart sank. But then what about if she trimmed her plans? "Of course, I understand. Then perhaps we can invite the LGBT community, which is very vibrant here in Leicester, to create an exhibition highlighting their life experiences, their memories. They could even choose to express themselves through art or simply talking. Fran, I know, is keen to capture oral histories, and to hear people's voices in an exhibition is always so thrilling and emotive. I would be happy to lead this—"

"I'm glad you brought up the subject of your time."

You are? Molly could sense herself being drawn off track.

"Going forward I need your full attention to return to the Wright Foundation bequest. There have been developments." Evelyn glanced at the chairman whose own attention seemed to have been drawn by opening the biscuit for his coffee. "Mark, would you find an update of progress with this particular bequest helpful?"

The chairman looked up with a start. "Yes."

Evelyn widened her eyes at Molly. "Would you mind?"

"Oh, of course." Molly turned to the page in her notes headed *Benefactors and Funders.* "Where shall I—"

"From the beginning."

"Right. The"—Molly cleared her throat—"Wright Foundation have been supporting museums and education projects for many years—"

Evelyn raised a finger and looked at the chairman. "To be precise, the foundation was established in 1888 by the philanthropist and social campaigner Josephine Wright with the express purpose of promoting the endeavours of institutions of art and learning." She returned her focus to Molly. "Please remember, details are always important."

Molly's cheeks stung. How did Evelyn always manage to humiliate her so effortlessly? "Yes, of course." Molly gripped her notes. "Sadly, its head for the last thirty-two years, George Wright, passed away in March of this year. This is of course a great loss, as George Wright was an unstinting supporter of this museum."

Evelyn leaned forward. "George contacted me in August of last year. He confirmed his intention to transfer his personal art collection to the Wright Foundation with the express purpose of also gifting the foundation's fine art to this museum." Evelyn stabbed her finger into her notebook with the words *to this museum.*

The chairman released a low, satisfied grumble.

Evelyn sat yet further forward in her seat. "George was at pains to tell me that the foundation's collection was small. I was to understand that the foundation is primarily a monetary fund and has tended to discourage offers to it of artworks. And not only that, he said when they have received artworks they have immediately gifted them on to a museum. I have to admit I wondered at this point what we were being offered. Can I pour you some more coffee, Mark?"

The chairman sat up a little in his seat, offering his cup, which Evelyn filled while she continued, "Nonetheless, over the generations a select few of the great and the good of Leicester have slipped through the net, so to speak, and gifted to the foundation the work of celebrated artists to ease their tax burdens. Thank God for death duties—they are without question a museum's best friend. The foundation has held on to these works, and they have been loaned out to national institutions. That is, until now. I will just say this: Auguste Rodin, John Piper, Paul Nash, and Vanessa Bell. A select but notable collection of international significance, and to acquire it is quite the coup."

As if newly revived, the chairman said, "Yes, this was excellent news. The trustees were impressed that the museum had been chosen as the recipient of such a gift."

"To be truthful," Evelyn said, "I think George felt rather let down to discover that those national institutions who had works loaned to them by the foundation had stored them, as much as they'd displayed them. I promised to fulfil his express wish to keep the foundation's collection together and accessible at all times to the public. He was of course much relieved. And despite his failing health and the tiresome paperwork, the necessary bequest forms to this museum were completed and signed." Evelyn's triumphant glow faded to a look of concern. "Six months have now passed since George's death, and we are in possession of nearly all the foundation's items, and yet George's art collection remains in place in his house. Isn't that so?" Evelyn looked at Molly.

"Yes, we are just waiting for Rodin's *Little Eve* to come from the Tate."

"Honestly, they are gripping that poor sculpture so tightly I would not be surprised if she arrives with fingerprints on her behind. And talking of gripping—and I do not mean to be unsympathetic at her time of grief—but George's daughter seems intent on dragging her heels with the handover of the bequeathed pieces from the house. How many are we expecting?"

"In the house there are, let me see…" Molly counted down the list in her notes with the tip of her pencil. "Four paintings, one work in pencil, one bust, three pieces of early Staffordshire porcelain, and two photographs. So that's…"

Evelyn let out a withering sigh. "Eleven. Out of?"

"A bequest of fifteen works in total."

"I even sent a follow-up note after the funeral repeating my condolences and assuring her of our best intentions with regard to her father's bequest in the hope that this might prompt matters. Nothing." Evelyn took another sip of coffee. "However, this brings me to the development in question. I heard yesterday that grant of probate was completed early last week on George Wright's estate, so the work to distribute his assets and settle matters once and for all can begin. This is excellent news, as I really feared we might be looking at next year. My earnest hope is that this stirs Georgina Wright into action, or at least into visibility. I do not think she has visited Leicester since her father's funeral, let alone stepped into this museum. Could you open a window, Molly, and let some air in?"

Molly opened the window directly behind them and stood for a moment in the relief of the breeze.

"And that is not all I find unsettling." Evelyn rubbed at her brow. "There is a general sense of disquiet with regard to Georgina taking over as head of the foundation."

As she returned to her seat Molly heard herself say, "Why, is she dodgy?"

"What? *No.* She's a banker from London who has made no secret of her disinterest in all things art. It would not surprise me if George feared her selling his collection to the highest bidder. And as for her intentions for the foundation itself and the impact to museums..." Evelyn raised her hands in a *Who knows?* gesture.

The chairman intervened, "I understand what you're saying, Evelyn. On the odd occasions I've met Georgina Wright, I've found her...how shall I put it...non-committal on museum matters."

Evelyn drained the last of her coffee and rested the cup with a determined knock against its saucer. "So we need a plan. A plan that will invest Georgina in the museum so she will think of us first when it comes to future funding."

Evelyn drummed her fingertips on the table as the chairman brushed at his tie.

Molly tentatively suggested, "We could have a dedicated temporary exhibition of the foundation's bequest. Fran could even prepare a short history of the foundation. We could invite Georgina—"

Pushing her chair back, Evelyn began to pace the room. "Yes, of course. That's it. I had thought to disperse the bequest throughout the museum, but this is better. The key is to show her that we are ready and waiting to display her father's collection and fulfil his last wish. This will flush her out from London and oblige her to hurry along in handing over the final pieces. But we need more than a temporary display—we need something substantial and, ideally, enduring." Evelyn stood stiff as if a solution had possessed her like the devil. "We need a dedicated space, and I can't think of a more prestigious and forward-thinking use of the annex. We need a name. The *Wright Room* has the authority we are seeking. We need a date for the opening. I'm thinking the beginning of December. And perhaps most importantly we need a dedicated individual to bring everything to fruition. And by fruition, I mean someone who will impress and guide and remind Georgina Wright that not only are we the foundation's *chosen* museum, but we are also the natural choice for any future foundation funding."

Evelyn and the chairman turned in unison to look at Molly.

"Yes, we are looking to you, Molly. We have every faith and trust in you. Your assistance with this initiative will be vital. Vital." Evelyn glanced at her watch. "More coffee, Mark. And another biscuit, perhaps?"

You are? It is? "That's...thank you," Molly said. "Just one thing. Did you say the annex?"

Evelyn placed a hand on her flushing neck. "I really rather hoped you were listening. Yes. The annex."

"It's just, well, I don't think that will be possible. You see, there is an expectation that the annex is already reserved for community use. Fran—"

Evelyn shook her head. "Fran, more than anyone, understands the difficult choices a museum has to make. Thank you for your time this morning. We won't keep you any longer. Let's meet again in a day or so to take the plan further."

Evelyn turned away. The discussion was clearly concluded.

Molly left the meeting and stood in the corridor with her back to the closed conference room door. The low rumble of the chairman's voice and Evelyn's hollow laughter carried on without her.

"You okay, Molly?" Marianne placed Bourbon biscuits on a plate. "Here, have a biscuit."

"No, thank you." In that moment Molly had completely lost her appetite. She had surely let Fran down. What's more, was she about to let down the entire museum by failing to impress and persuade the elusive Georgina Wright?

❖

Molly returned to her office, dropped her notes back into the bin where they belonged, and slumped onto Fran's desk with a heavy sigh.

"You're sitting on my sandwich." Fran pushed at Molly's hip, encouraging her to stand.

"I've sat on your lunch? Oh my God, could this day get any worse?" Molly held Fran's baguette, squishy in her hands. It was now less buoyant baguette and more flatbread and pretty much summed up her morning.

Fran stood with a groan. "Want anything from the cafe?"

Molly looked down, crestfallen, and shook her head.

"I take it the meeting wasn't exactly a great success." Fran rested a motherly hand on Molly's shoulder.

She couldn't bring herself to mention the annex let alone that she had prompted the idea of a dedicated exhibition in the first place. "Honestly it was chilling to hear them. Everything's about money or status. I thought museums were for and about the people."

"You're sounding more like a social historian every day," Fran said, with an approving nod. "Although isn't the art world, your world, all about that—status?"

"Not for me."

"Good for you." Fran placed her hands on her hips. "I think we need cake."

"Have lunch in the square with me?"

"Sorry, no can do, I've a shopping list longer than David Attenborough's career. But I'll see you later. So what will it be—Victoria sponge or, better still, eclairs?"

Molly mustered a smile. "How about both?"

"Good choice." Fran turned back at the door. "Do you remember what I said to you when you first started at the museum? That you will always feel disheartened if your approach is to work against them?"

Molly nodded.

"The trick, if there is a trick"—Fran frowned slightly—"is somehow to find a way to achieve what you believe is right but that still delivers for the powers that be."

"So is this how you handle Evelyn?"

"On my good days, yes. On my bad days, lots of rude words shouted at the top of my lungs in the privacy of the ladies' loo."

Molly giggled. "Right. Noted."

The instant Fran closed the door, Molly was engulfed by images of the chairman with his expression of vacuous power, his mane-like hair swept back, his tie tight against his collar moving with his throat as he spoke. He was confident in a bullish way that suggested at his heart he was insecure. His insecurity made him dangerous, and if she was not mistaken, that was likely the source of his power and influence—not his knowledge, not his experience, but the fragility of his ego, charming when stroked, ferociously defensive when challenged.

Evelyn seemed to be a master at managing him, stroking to calm and cajole. She appealed to his competitive nature by presenting the museum as a place of excellence. A leading institution, indeed. She was the consummate manager of people.

Molly closed her eyes at the image of Evelyn with her pen raised to silence her. Her temper rose. She needed to find a place to shout rude words.

Leaving the frustrations of her meeting behind, she headed to her sanctuary, a small public garden next to the museum. Aptly named Museum Square, the simply designed patch of civic ground was bordered on two sides by parked cars. A collection of benches placed around the inside edge of the square separated the grass from wide borders. A diagonal path, broken up by tree roots, stretched across, splitting halfway along to encircle a large horse chestnut tree. This tree marked the seasons, signalling the changing patterns of the year. In winter, bare and stark against white skies, the tree seemed to shrink, huddled with those brave or crazy enough to stop awhile and sit. In spring, tentative buds relaxed in the welcome return of the first rays of sunshine. In summer, students rested against its weathered waist reading their books, cool in the shade of branches laden with the soft flutter of green leaves. And in autumn, the debris of crushed conkers bashed free from its branches, littering the ground with evidence of battles won and lost and of time passing as the empty husks curled and browned.

She cherished those moments spent sitting on her favourite bench eating her sandwiches, with her lunchbox at her side and with the sprawling horse chestnut her faithful companion.

Basking in the calm stillness of the beautiful September day, she took off her shoes and let the grass brush against the soles of her feet. She lifted her chin to the cloudless sky. The air was changing from the dry sandy notes of summer to the sweet musk of autumn. The leaves above her were fading, and their greens had softened to mossy shades from vibrant lime. Even the midday light beaming through the canopy seemed weaker now, less luminous, its strongest rays falling on another person sitting on another bench, in another square, in another land.

❖

Georgina Wright stood at the sitting room window of her father's house. Her thoughts drifted, tangled in the trance-like rhythm of the passers-by hurrying up and down the tree-lined promenade just a few steps from the front door. Her gaze broke free to settle on the square across the way, taking in the many shades of green and the glint upon the iron railings of the changing light of the day.

When she was young she would sit for hours staring out of the long windows, watching the comings and goings. The square had a routine all its own then. First the flushed-face joggers would run along the promenade followed by the pallid sternness of rushing commuters. Then young mums would sit perched on the edge of benches staring anxiously into prams, or the elderly would pause to rest with gnarled hands against the railings, their shopping bags just that bit too heavy yet again. That was twenty years ago, and yet everything and nothing had changed. The promenade was just as busy if not busier.

Standing out distinct from the crowd, a woman caught her eye. She was sitting on a bench staring up into the tree's canopy with her face bright with wonder. Georgina had seen her before. For she was the beautiful stranger she hadn't meant to look out for in those last dark weeks of her father's life. Noticing her wasn't deliberate, at least not at first—she just seemed to have fallen into the habit of it, as one falls into the habit of many things.

She could even remember the first time she saw her. It was a Friday lunchtime in mid-February. It had started to snow and soft flakes drifting past the window had called her attention to outside. She remembered how she had pressed her hand against the cold glass as if to catch the flakes that were dissolving against the windowpane, melting in the grey-white light of the winter day. She had looked out to the square across the way, empty but for one woman who stood with her arms out wide, her face tipped to the sky. She had watched, entranced, as the stranger proceeded to brush a bench free of snow and then sat eating her lunch, as if the hazy winter sun had mustered in that moment the strength of summer.

Georgina looked away. That was the same day she'd arrived to find her father's doctor at his bedside. How sorry the pale-faced clinician was to tell her that it was only a matter of weeks before she would likely lose her father. Never had a day felt bleaker and never had a person seemed so out of place.

Her heart ached. How long would the memory of him hurt so much? It had already seemed too long. But she would be brave, as always. Routine had definitely helped. Visiting her father most weekends following his diagnosis, arriving from London on a Friday lunchtime to help with matters that required weekday hours had worked, hadn't it? She'd even sought a familiar comfort by sleeping in her childhood bedroom as if she'd never been away. And now while she settled her father's estate, she would repeat a similar routine. She would start by taking this coming week off work and basing herself here to kick-start matters. That was her plan, if she had a plan at all, other than to make it through her grief somehow.

Looking back, it felt like the beautiful woman was there just for Georgina, sitting on the same bench in the square eating her sandwiches. She had been her light in the darkness, constant and reassuring with her presence.

And today, on the brink of autumn, nearly six months on after her father's death, there she was again. Georgina stared at the imprint of daisies on the woman's sundress, watching as they seemed to glow in the last rays of the year's sunshine. The woman's bare feet had slipped from sandals and the curls of her auburn hair fell onto her shoulders, setting off the cream of her pale skin. Georgina's gaze fell absently to the woman's neck, her throat tilted to the sky…

The woman suddenly glanced across to where Georgina stood at the window. Georgina stepped quickly back to stand shaded, unnoticed in the centre of her father's sitting room. Her heart pounded. She felt exposed. It was not like Georgina to stare. At least not usually. People rarely held her attention. She would try to engage in polite conversation should the situation demand it but they would lose her not much beyond their first brag of achievement or their grumble about that day's irritation.

Did people find her cold? Did they wonder at how different she was to her father, who always seemed so graceful and composed? Without effort he would find the right words to say at the perfect moment. There was warmth and an energy behind his eyes that flickered like a smile as he spoke.

Tears threatened and stung. She sought out her father's armchair and brushed at the faded arms, the leather softened and worn to a light shade of brown where sleeve and hand had rubbed. She gazed at the seat cushion, flattened where her father had sat. It was as if he had just left the room, and if she pressed her hand against the cushion she would feel it warm.

Was that his voice, his feet against the tiled floor? She glanced across at the door that led from the sitting room to the hall, holding her breath, imagining in that instant that she would see his frame appear in the doorway, tall, slender, imposing.

A hot tear gathered at the corner of her mouth. Georgina brushed it away. She would not cry. What use were tears, after all? They never seemed to help.

She willed herself to focus on something.

The faint rings of tea stain on the coaster on the side table caught her attention. When she visited from London, they would drink tea and talk for hours. He would ask her about her work, keen to hear about the latest economic tool to revive the weary fortunes of UK companies. What else had they talked about? Their conversation rarely strayed from work. They both enjoyed what they did, for work was not just their job but their purpose and focus. The law for him was not just his profession, not just empty rules, but structure, definition, the very politics and agency of life. Neither she nor her father dwelled on the fact that their work had become their world to the exclusion of everything and everyone. It was their choice, wasn't it? Feelings were incidental, passing, and superficial. Work was substance, material, tangible, and real.

Georgina turned back to the window and risked a final look to the woman bathing in the sun. She had struck up conversation with a homeless man, or he had struck up conversation with her, either way she was pouring him a drink from her flask and offering her sandwich. Georgina was taken with her generosity, this act of compassion. Beautiful *and* kind then. The woman then packed up her things and walked away in the direction of the museum.

Georgina was surprised to feel the pinch of loss at her leaving. How could you miss a stranger? And how long could she ignore the echoes of emptiness in her busy life?

CHAPTER TWO

Beams of sunlight broke and flickered against the walls of the sitting room as a cyclist swept past, startling Georgina out of her thoughts. Enough. She was sick of sadness and of memories cloying at her, dragging her down. This happened without fail every time she came back to this house. And every time she couldn't wait to leave.

With the grant of probate, things were on their way to being concluded, weren't they? The solicitors were following her father's instructions as directed in his will and methodically tying up each loose end. Her role was to oversee the sale of the house and the safe storage or sale of his belongings. Georgina glanced across again at her father's chair. *Father.* There was no way she could bear to pack up his personal belongings and to see his life shipped out in boxes. Not yet. Not ever. She bit at her lip, fighting tears. She had time surely to do this while everything else was being settled?

She took a deep breath, her gaze falling on the beautiful blue ware vase that rested on the sideboard, so delicate and in blissful ignorance of its fate. Her stomach tightened at the thought of handing over her father's beloved fine and decorative art, so loved in this house for so long, to the grasp of the museum. It might have been his wish and the museum entirely within their right, but something still felt distasteful about it. Was it the polite yet feverous clamour of the museum to get their hands on his collection? It made her want to resist their every advance. For their director had been pestering the moment her father had died. *Could we make a time to meet? Had Georgina found a moment to think about how she would like the task best done? Please be assured of our best intentions.* And it felt like every time she spoke with the foundation's solicitors, they ended each call with *and then there's the museum bequest to fulfil.*

The foundation. Nausea gripped her. Every Wright family member since the foundation's beginnings had known that one day the responsibility to lead the foundation would fall to them. And now it was her turn. She knew people were looking to her and waiting to hear the tone of her compassion and to understand the focus of her concern, and to feel the impact of her decisions. She would no doubt be compared with her father and measured only by their differences and judged by what she lacked.

And she would now have to endure the fawning and the flattery of those seeking funding and reassurance that their future was secure with her. They'd all attended her father's funeral dressed in black like sharp-beaked crows, hunched, plotting, waiting for the moment to swoop. Even the director of the local museum across the way had been there, twitchy, triumphant, and making a point of shaking her hand.

Her head throbbed with a headache that had been threatening to overwhelm her for days. She caught her reflection in the gilded oval mirror which hung above the fireplace. Grief was unbecoming. She looked so tired. She tucked her hair behind her ear, away from her face. *That's so weird.* Without intending, she'd positioned herself in the mirror so her face was at the same height as the row of faces in the family portraits that stared back at her from the opposite wall. She touched her cheek, noticing that her skin had a pale luminosity that peculiarly matched the pallor of those who'd gone before her.

There was no escaping she was the sole direct heir to the Wright line, and she couldn't have felt less deserving or less equipped to carry forward the hopes of generations before her. For she couldn't continue a line all alone, could she? You needed love to do that. That one person by your side. She had no one. It wasn't that she was gay or she hadn't met Miss Right, so to speak. No. You had to trust to love, and there was nothing about love she trusted.

It struck her in that moment that there would likely be no more portraits. No more stiff necks holding the pose, wondering when the painter would finish. Had any one of those painted imagined they would be the last? Had any one felt the burden of the responsibility of being a Wright as heavily as she did now?

She turned and moved towards the portraits. She slowly walked the length of the wall, absently counting the portraits one by one. There were four paintings in total, three oils and one watercolour, each hanging on a brass chain from the picture rail. For how long they had hung in that spot was the subject as much of folklore as fact, for her father rarely spoke about them and Georgina had only ever known them hanging there, staring out, inscrutable.

At the beginning of the row hung a painting depicting the marriage of her distant relatives William and Josephine Wright. The ornate gilt frame matched the formal composition of the piece. The porch of St. Martin's Church formed the backdrop. To the right of William, at his feet, his spaniel loyally looked up at his master. Georgina loved that dog. How she had begged her father for a spaniel just like great-great-great-great-grandfather William's. She shook her head. She'd forgotten that.

William Wright looked so proud, standing tall in his boots and breeches, his chest puffed out in his high collared coat with its long tail, and his square jaw jutting out from his white cravat circled at his neck. He was handsome and sincere if the affectionate way he looked at his bride, as he held her gloved hand gently in his, was anything to go by. Or was this just the painter's imagination? Josephine in contrast was looking ahead, her face serious, almost reverent. Her expression had the quality of devotion and service about it. Had marriage meant sacrifice somehow to her? She was dressed in a modest gown of what appeared to be white muslin. And were they satin flowers embroidered at the wide scoop of her collar? A rose-coloured ribbon pinched the material under her chest and matched the small bouquet of soft pink carnations held tight against her.

The painting always left Georgina in a reflective mood rather than one of celebration. Was that intended? She leaned in to read the scrawl of the painter's signature: *W. Brown.* On a small nameplate in block writing were the words *St. Martin's, Leicester. In celebration of the marriage of William Henry George Wright and Josephine Catherine Wright (née Brancaster), 26th December 1833.*

Next to this hung a similarly sober work to mark the christening of William and Josephine's second child, James Ambrose. The painting captured the Wright family huddled with the priest around the font. Coloured droplets of light fell upon them from the stained glass windows above. All eyes were on the baby wrapped in a shawl in Josephine's arms. As if forgotten, a small child was all but hidden in the billowing skirt of the priest's cassock. "I see you Adelaide," Georgina said. It seemed at any moment she would run and hide behind the looming stone columns supporting the sweeping arches above their heads. How many times had she been missed? The little girl faced outwards with her innocent eyes as if pleading with the viewer not to overlook her.

Georgina pressed her finger against the little girl's name listed in the words that spread the length of the maple frame. "Was your brother hogging the limelight, Adelaide Jane? Did you cause a scene?" The inscription was matter of fact and gave nothing away. *6th June 1838, St. Martin's. Baptism of James Ambrose Wright, son of William and*

Josephine and brother to Adelaide Jane, aged three years. Oil on canvas by W. Brown, 1838.

Why so serious again, Josephine? Even proud William wore an expression shaded in something troubled. Were they sad on this special day? Was that what the painter saw?

The third painting along couldn't have been more different. Georgina stood staring at it, just as she had stood staring, looking up at it, as a child. It was everything the other paintings weren't. It was life in all its informal joyful vibrancy, caught in the lightness of watercolour.

It was the face of a beautiful young woman painted close up, in profile. It was smaller than the other works, and yet so much more affecting. Only the woman's face and neck were depicted, with the pink and ivory of her skin set off against a background wash of dark blue. Ruby lips were parted as if the artist had captured the sitter just as words had left her lips.

For so many years Georgina had loved this painting and, moreover, the enchanting woman captured within its frame. It was her comfort as a child, her familiar solace as a teenager, and now a sense of certainty amongst the chaos. Everything about it was precious. And everything about this woman was so different to the woman in the other portraits. Could this really be Josephine? In small engraved type the name *Miss Josephine Brancaster, 1832* erased as ever all doubt.

Had love caught her off guard? Changed her? But then, how could anyone not fall in love with her? Georgina cast a fleeting glance at the final painting of William Wright as an old man. Had he loved Josephine well? William sat, silent, in a simple wooden chair, the fireplace lit by his side, with the background beyond a dark murk of oil paint, focusing the viewer upon the foreground details of his face. His furrowed forehead was set as if in thought, pressing forward his silver eyebrows to shade his eyes, still bright and alive in his old age. A book rested in his lap and round spectacles marked the page he was reading. A brass plate read *William Wright, LL.B. 1868. A. Scott.*

On the wall next to each painting was a coloured paper dot tucked against the frame so as to be only just visible from close up. Had this been the method to single out the works to be included in the museum bequest? If so, where was the dot for the watercolour? She checked the floor. Nothing. She reached for her iPad and sought out the email marked *City Museum bequest* and downloaded the scanned copy of the inventory attached to the completed bequest form. She scrolled down the list. Twice. Nothing.

Surely this was a mistake? Her father couldn't have intended for the watercolour just to be left unlisted with the items of house contents for

Georgina to deal with? If he'd wanted her to keep the watercolour, then why didn't he say?

Something wasn't right. She would check with the solicitors and with the museum. In fact she would do everything in her power to correct what could only be a terrible error.

"Josephine." Georgina rested her fingers lightly on the frame. "I won't let you be forgotten. I promise."

CHAPTER THREE

Molly was always late, or at least that's how it always felt. So much so she had taken to rushing as her default speed of travel. *Hurry, hurry.* As she all but ran down the stairs, sparks of excitement tingled on her skin at the thought that someone had brought a painting to the museum. She liked to try to imagine what the work could be and the story it would tell and to anticipate who might be waiting for her.

As she reached the final few steps, she could see a tall elegant woman holding a bubble wrapped painting at her side striding confidently across the foyer towards the reception. Whatever Molly had expected, it wasn't her. The woman glanced over at her, and if she was not mistaken, she saw a glimpse of recognition in the woman's eyes. Had they met before?

Molly skidded to a stop in front of the reception desk.

"Hi, Fred." Molly dumped a pile of folders onto the reception desk before resting her palm on her chest to catch her breath. "Can you give these to Fran? She'll be down a little later for them. And hello there." Molly turned to the visitor. "How can I…help?" She hadn't meant to stare. She just found she couldn't look away.

The woman was somewhere in her late twenties, early thirties perhaps. Her chestnut hair was shaped into a loose bob. One ear was exposed, and she'd tucked a loop of hair behind it in a manner that was informal and yet precise. Her long face with balanced, refined features had a noble quality to it that suggested a hereditary ease to her beauty. Her tailored dark grey suit hugged every inch of her perfectly toned body. Everything was in exquisite order. Was she real? It was almost impossible not to reach out and touch her.

Molly quickly closed her mouth. What must this woman think of her? Staring and all but drooling like a fool. She needed to say something. Quickly.

Molly stumbled over her words to continue, "I have had one of those days. I was late, for starters." Molly shook her head. "I don't know about you, but I find that starts the day all wrong. And then I had an *awful* meeting. Oh my God. Oh, and to top it all, I sat on Fran, my colleague's, sandwich." Fred laughed. "It's not funny. Well, okay, it's a little bit funny. And I'd woken up to birds singing, and it had been such a beautiful morning. And the church across the way from me seemed to glow. Really, it was in every way a daybreak to match Monet's *Rouen Cathedral* captured in the morning light."

The woman visibly tensed. She stared intently at Molly without betraying a flicker of expression. "I'm not familiar with the work." In an instant the coldness of the woman's reply frosted their chat to brittle fragments.

"Oh, I'm sure you'd like it," Molly said. "He was such a wonderful painter—"

"I'm sorry, I don't mean to be rude, but will this take long?" The woman directed this question at Fred. "It's just I was hoping that someone at the museum could take a look at my painting today."

Molly said, "Well, that someone would be me. I'm the fine art curator here." Molly thought it best to try and manage a smile of sorts.

The woman looked down at the painting by her side before returning a concerned look at Molly. She couldn't have gripped the painting any tighter.

Stifling a rising sense of offence, Molly explained, "We don't, as a rule, I'm afraid, simply take objects from the public." The woman's cheeks flushed at the phrase *the public*. "You will need to complete an object entry form. This is standard procedure across all museums to help us to properly assess your offer or request—"

The woman shook her head. "I'm not offering you anything. I just need someone who knows what they're looking at to assist with ascertaining the provenance of this work."

Someone who knows what they're looking at? *Well, frosty knickers, how about someone with a masters in art history and curating. How about top of their class. How about you stick that up...* "Oh no, of course, I'm not presuming that you're offering this work to the museum. It's just the object entry form is the first stage for all inquiries of this type." Molly looked at Fred for support. Fred looked at her blankly, prompting her to ask, "Could I have an object entry form, please, Fred?"

Fred rummaged around and then Molly joined in, leaning over the reception desk, her bottom in the air, her feet just touching the floor.

Molly tried to focus on finding the form rather than on her awareness that the woman was once again staring at her. What was it about her that the woman was finding so curious? The scrutiny was unnerving. Maybe her summer dress looked out of place in September. *Oh my God.* Had she remembered to shave her legs?

"I'm sorry, we appear to have run out of forms." Slightly breathless, Molly leaned yet further forward. "I'll ask Fred to pop upstairs and photocopy some."

"Look, please don't bother," the woman said, with unguarded frustration. "Is Evelyn Fox available? A little later today perhaps?"

"Evelyn?" Molly quickly slipped down from the desk and turned to face the woman once again. "I'll need to check with her secretary, but Evelyn doesn't tend to get involved at this stage—"

"On balance I think it's best I make an appointment with Evelyn myself. Thank you for your time."

Utterly confused, Molly simply nodded in reply. She watched the upright figure of the most baffling woman in the world walk towards the sliding doors that led outside. How could someone so beautiful be so cold?

"Georgina!"

Molly turned at Evelyn's voice to see her quickly walking towards the door, her arms wide in a gesture of evident surprise and welcome.

Georgina—where had she heard that name? Molly watched as Evelyn air-kissed Georgina's cheeks. Was that...? "You don't suppose that's Georgina Wright, do you, Fred?"

Fred blurted out, "Georgina Wright—that's it. Yes, I thought I recognized her face."

"You've met her before?" Molly asked, intrigued.

"Not exactly. There was a drinks reception about a year ago. She accompanied her father. I remember now, she seemed uncomfortable, like she wanted to leave before she got here."

Molly stared at Georgina, watching as the striking woman stiffened with Evelyn's embrace. Georgina seemed to be explaining something to Evelyn.

"Have you ever wanted to be able to lip read?" Molly strained to hear what Georgina and Evelyn were discussing.

"Never had the need. I can hear my wife's dulcet tones from two streets away."

"Right." Molly nodded, half listening to Fred, half not.

Her heart began to race as Georgina and Evelyn were both looking at the painting. Should she have made an exception and just taken the painting for assessment, as it was Georgina Wright? But then, how was she to know it was her? The woman hadn't given her name. Although, was that because *she* hadn't introduced herself? She should have introduced herself. She should have shaken her hand. But then there was nothing about the woman's demeanour that invited a handshake or, for that matter, conversation at all.

Evelyn cast Molly a look. It wasn't a good look.

Molly looked away, pretending not to notice as Evelyn led Georgina past reception up the stairs, no doubt to her office with the fresh air and the light and the cultural oeuvre she was certain would impress Georgina Wright.

"You okay, Molly?" Fred asked. "It's just, you've gone quite pale."

"What? Yes, I'm fine. Absolutely. I'll ask Fran to bring you some forms when she collects the files."

Molly lingered in reception, giving them plenty of time to have reached Evelyn's office. Ten minutes later she climbed the stairs, still consumed in thought as to why Evelyn seemed so cross with her. As she rounded the corner into the corridor, she collided straight into a hurrying Georgina Wright. Their bodies met with a bump. Molly's soft curves pressed momentarily against Georgina's firm frame.

"I'm sorry," Molly said, breathing heavily. "My fault. I wasn't watching where I was going." She then moved in the same direction at the same time as Georgina. "Oops." Molly giggled. She risked a glance at Georgina's face. She thought she saw her smile, but then it had passed so quickly she couldn't be sure.

"After you," Georgina said, without emotion or expression.

"Thanks."

Molly stepped aside, and then without another word, Georgina Wright was gone.

❖

"First impressions, Molly. We only have one chance to make a first impression." Evelyn was standing with her back to Molly looking out the window. Her corner office commanded views of both the square and the front of the museum, enabling her to survey all around her like a captain at the helm of an ocean liner.

Evelyn had called Molly in to her office just as she was leaving for home. Molly had only just put on her coat and was endeavouring to slip an arm out but every time Evelyn turned around Molly froze in her seat. She felt in every way trapped.

Molly glanced at the painting resting on Evelyn's desk. She recognized it as the painting Georgina Wright had brought to the museum. It had been partially unwrapped. She could just make out the features of a woman—her red lips, the gentle brush of watercolour defining cheek and chin and neck.

"The painter is unknown." Evelyn's voice startled Molly.

"Oh, I see."

"As you know, Georgina Wright, of the Wright Foundation, visited the museum this afternoon. If you recall we spoke about Georgina this morning." Molly nodded. "She wants to find out more about this work, in particular who painted it, for what occasion—the usual sort of thing. It belongs to her father. Well, belonged to her father, I should say. She was surprised to find that it wasn't included in the bequest. I don't know whether it's a value question or a sentimental question—either way, we need to find an answer for her." Evelyn took her seat opposite Molly. "This is just the opportunity we have been waiting for, even better than I hoped, because it gives us a natural way in to broach the subject of the Wright room. I did not mention our plans. I didn't even remind her of the awaited bequeathed works. No. This is something I want *you* to do. Here is your chance to bond with Georgina and to build new alliances with the Wright Foundation going forward." Evelyn paused. "I'm just going to say this once. Where Georgina Wright is concerned there are no forms, no procedures, no...barriers between her and us. Is that understood?"

Molly's cheeks burned and her chest tightened. She nodded. "Absolutely. No barriers. Understood." In an attempt to move their conversation away from how useless she clearly was, Molly asked, "Does she know who the sitter is or when it was painted?"

"The sitter, she is certain, is her distant relative Josephine Wright, or Brancaster as was her maiden name, and this is confirmed by the engraving on the frame." Evelyn leaned forward, slipped her glasses on, and carefully teased back some more of the painting's wrapping. "Yes, just there on the bottom right, which also records the date 1832. Certainly I would hazard the frame dates from that time."

"Okay, great. I'll see what I can find out." Molly moved to stand.

"Please sit." Evelyn leaned back in her chair and tilted her head, as if to study Molly. "Georgina and I didn't really talk that much about the painting. As it happened our brief conversation turned to you."

"Me?"

"Yes. You see, I suggested that I would be asking you to work with her on this particular research, and I got the sense that, well, she seemed to hesitate at my suggestion, almost as if she was uncomfortable with the idea."

"Uncomfortable?"

"Yes." Evelyn's eyes drifted up and down taking her in. It felt like she was being read, like a book. "Have you any idea why?"

"No. We've never met before. I mean, she doesn't know me—"

"And there's the point. We only get one chance to make a good first impression." Molly opened her mouth to speak. Evelyn raised her hand. "I want you to learn from your encounter with Georgina Wright. I want you to practice exuding confidence, oozing capableness, embodying professionalism."

What the chuff? "I was trying to help her."

"When people come to a museum, they are not looking for help—one can get that anywhere. They are seeking *authority*." Evelyn fixed both her stare and her next question with a pointed aim. "How old are you?"

"How old? I'm twenty-six." Molly had no idea where their conversation was headed but it was certainly a destination she had no wish to visit. She cast an eye at the door. Any possibility of escape seemed hopeless.

Evelyn sat forward and perched on the edge of her seat. "Twenty-six. Yes, that's what I thought. This is a pivotal time for you."

Molly swallowed. "It is?"

"Yes. In my experience young curators' careers diverge at just the stage you are at. They all have potential, Molly. It is not a question of background, or intelligence, or even work history."

Evelyn was looking her up and down again. Molly folded her arms, hoping they would somehow protect her from Evelyn's scrutiny. Evelyn's intense gaze broke and dispersed as she sat back in her chair.

"The difference between mediocrity and superiority are two things. Poise and preparation." Molly wondered whether she should be taking notes. "Give nothing away of your emotions, Molly, unruffled, shoulders back, chin lifted with a quiet certainty." Molly lifted her chin slightly. "You will enter a room with a poise that suggests that no conversation or encounter will fluster you. And you should always know who you are talking to before you begin to speak."

Molly winced at the thought of how unprepared she would have seemed in front of Georgina Wright. No forms. No handshake. No—

"Allow your preparation to anticipate the content of the discussion. For it is the detail of what you say that will mark you out and that will speak of your authority. Do you understand?"

Molly sat staring at her hands tucked in her lap. "Yes." She had never felt so humiliated.

"Do not look so despondent. I am giving you a second chance to make a good impression for yourself and for the museum. You see, I still believe you can win Georgina over. I want you to do everything you can to secure the support of the Wright Foundation. I have absolute faith in you."

"But you just said she didn't want to work with me."

"No, I said she seemed uncomfortable with the idea. Georgina left my office with my reassurance that there was no better person available to me right now than you."

Available to you? It was somehow always difficult to find the compliment in Evelyn's praise.

"So I'll see you Monday. Come to my office, say mid-morning, with a plan. Goodnight." Evelyn stood and opened her door.

The meeting was over and so, Molly concluded, was her career.

On returning home, Molly sat slumped at her kitchen table, nursing a glass of red wine. She gave a heavy sigh at the sight of her forgotten meeting notes. She opened the paper weight cum jar of peanut butter and stuck a spoon in, scooping out a large curl of salty comfort. She repeated this action several times, interspersing them with large mouthfuls of Malbec.

Thank God she was home. Her day began crappy and ended even crappier. Yes, this was officially a *crap* day.

She took another scoop of peanut butter. She could hear Evelyn. *I still believe that you can win Georgina over.* Maybe she didn't want to win her over. Maybe she didn't care. Who was she kidding—of course she cared. But about her job and the museum, certainly not about what Georgina Wright thought. No way. Who did she think she was? How dared she pass judgement like that?

She kicked off her sandals and ran her hands down her legs. Smooth. Then what was she staring at?

What's more how dared that stuck-up woman make her feel so small, and in front of her boss? Who did that? What on earth did she say about her that gave Evelyn the impression that she was uncomfortable working with her? And why shouldn't she fill in forms like everyone else? And she could keep her hotness to herself. No one at this table was impressed. No, sir. So she was beautiful. Big deal. And *lots* of women wore a suit really well. You just had to be tall and toned. Molly took a large mouthful of wine. And firm and strong and unyielding. She'd smiled, hadn't she, when they collided? Oh my God. *Stop.* She was the enemy, and Molly would defeat her with her astonishing plan of brilliance. Once she had one of course.

She reached into her bag for her laptop and typed in the words *Josephine Brancaster, 1800s*. At least, she'd meant to type that. Instead her fingers found the letters that formed the name *Georgina Wright*. She sat staring at the list of results.

After eliminating those that suggested she played the ukulele or cared for endangered rhinos or taught at St. Joseph's primary school,

Molly found an entry that read: *Georgina Wright, Senior Strategist, UK portfolio, Investment Manager, Staithe Street Investment Group.* Money. She was certain that would be her.

She clicked on the summary and was directed to the profile of Georgina. Economics first degree from LSE. Early career for Citigroup bank. A brief flirtation with Schroders before developing her resume and reputation with Staithe Street. She was based out of London and was as formidable on paper as she was in person. *Wow.*

Molly took a deep breath. Georgina somehow managed to make the tiny thumbnail photo look like a magazine advert. She was perfect. Her smile was warm and sincere, and she conveyed an effortless sense of poise and stature. There was something else. It was a natural confidence. Yes, that was it. Everything was safe in her capable hands. *Stop thinking about her capable hands.*

Molly refilled her glass. Although, wait, did she look happier in this shot than when they'd met, or less tired, perhaps? Her eyes definitely had more light in them in this picture. Come to think of it, these were kind eyes that peculiarly didn't match the behaviour of the woman she met that morning. But then, she'd just not long lost her father, hadn't she? She must feel so sad. It might be why she was so cold. Yes, that made sense.

Maybe she should cut her some slack. Could it have been that Evelyn had also misread her? Maybe Georgina hadn't been uncomfortable with the thought of working with her at all. She would probably never know for sure.

What she did know, however, was that she had to prepare a plan for the painting for Monday, and unless she wanted to be working on it all weekend, she needed to make a start.

She stared one last time at Georgina Wright's photo, pausing to wonder whether being that good-looking was a burden, before closing the page's tab and typing *Josephine Brancaster, 1800s.*

Chapter Four

E verything okay?" Fran cast a surprised glance to the clock and then to Molly.

Molly yawned. "Yes."

"You're early."

Molly slipped off her coat and hung it behind the door. "I've been awake since four worrying about the fact that apparently I'm at a pivotal point in my career, according to Evelyn."

"She's right."

"Oh my God, don't you start. Oh, is that…?" Molly spotted Georgina Wright's painting leaning up against a chest of drawers. She lifted it to rest on top of her desk. "When did Evelyn call by?"

"You've literally just missed her. She told me to tell you to bring your research plan for the portrait to her office at about eleven. That's when Georgina could make it."

Molly's chest tightened. "Georgina? What, she'll be at the meeting?"

Fran shrugged. "Looks like it."

"Oh." Molly looked down and then gave a resolute shake of her head. "It'll be fine."

"Fred told me you'd had a bit of a run in with her. Georgina, I mean."

Molly nodded. "Let's put it this way—five minutes in her company does nothing for a girl's ego. I just asked her to fill in a form so we could help her with her painting, and it was like I'd asked her to poke herself in the eye. She was so dismissive of me and colder than a hypothermic snowman. And if that wasn't bad enough, my entire career hinges on me impressing her. How on earth am I supposed to do that?"

"By being you," Fran said with an affectionate tone. "And you're not to worry about Georgina. My guess is she's grieving for her father. They were very close."

"You know them?"

"I went to school with George. He was a couple of years above me. There was a group of us that used to hang out. But of course we all moved away after school to different colleges and so forth. I think he worked in London in his twenties, and when he returned to Leicester he was engaged to be married. Sixty-two is no age to die. Although his own father died at about the same age, and his mother even younger, so I guess it's a gene thing." Fran sighed and shook her head. "I know his daughter less, of course. Quite a sad family situation really."

Molly leaned against her desk. "In what way?"

"There was a messy divorce. Georgina's mother, Lydia, cheated on George and then left and never came back. Artistic temperament and all that. Everything changed from that moment on. I remember him coming in to the museum one afternoon not long after the divorce. I think he just wanted someone to talk to. So we had a chat and a coffee. He was clearly very hurt and angry. It utterly devastated him, and he worked all hours to forget about everything, no doubt, and poor Georgina was packed off to boarding school."

"Blimey."

"In fact, the last time I heard about Lydia Wright, she was still in Paris. She'd been tipped as the next Georgia O'Keeffe."

"Okay, wow. I confess I've never heard of her."

"Her early work is collected and has some value, although she remains relatively unknown. I think she managed the odd show here and there, but it's said she never fulfilled her potential, some say because of her unhappy marriage to George. Pretty sad all round. But to reassure you, I've always found Georgina under normal circumstances to be extremely polite, if a little reserved perhaps."

"Right. That's a relief."

"Do you know what would also help to impress her?"

"What, cutting her some slack?"

"Being on time to the meeting."

Molly looked at the clock. She had just over two hours.

"Bugger. Yes." Molly cleared her throat. "Right, Josephine, let's take a look at you." With a sense of purpose Molly carefully peeled away the wrapping to reveal the full beauty of the delicate watercolour.

Fran joined Molly at her side. "I've always loved this painting." She brushed her hand along the edge of the frame.

"You've seen this painting before?" Molly asked, intrigued. Fran seemed distracted. Molly touched her arm. "Fran? How do you know this work? It's just…if the painting's been brought in before, then that would be really helpful to know."

"No." Fran returned to her desk. "This is the first time to my knowledge this painting has been in the museum. I saw it at George's, hanging with the other paintings in his sitting room."

"George Wright's house?"

Fran nodded. "Yes, now and then he would host soirées, intimate benefit suppers at his place. He would call such evenings his persuaders. *I shall host a persuader*, he would say, if the museum was trying to raise money or something like that." Fran slipped her cardigan from her shoulders and absently folded it. "They always felt like such glamorous evenings, with the influential figures of the day."

"Sounds amazing." Molly shared a smile with Fran. Molly imagined silver trays laden with champagne flutes sparkling in the light from chandeliers. She pictured men dressed in dinner suits congregating by the piano or mantelpiece, their sharp white shirts crisp and bright, like their wits. And she imagined women poised at the edges of the conversation, as if holding their breath, their fingers looped around the threads of pearls at their necks. The air would be heady with cigarette smoke, cologne, and ambition. "Although, you know, I think I would have found it a bit stressful, trying to say the right things to the right people. Evelyn would have been in her element."

Fran shook her head. "This was much before her time. The late eighties, it must have been."

Molly raised her eyebrows. "You've been at the museum that long?"

"Not exactly. I began my career here. Then I worked in a few museums across the region, but somehow I always find myself back here, every time."

"Well, this is obviously where you belong." Molly followed Fran's gaze back to the painting. "So given what you're saying, it's not unreasonable to suppose that's where this portrait has hung all this time, where *it* belonged, on George Wright's wall."

"Yes, that would be my guess. You know…" Fran paused and frowned.

"What?"

"This painting always felt personal."

"Personal?"

"Yes, to George, to the Wrights. I can't quite pin down what I mean. All the other paintings felt like markers in the Wrights' history. Whereas the portrait of Josephine…I don't know. I wish I'd asked George about it now. I know that's not much use to you."

"Not at all. It all helps create a context for the work." Molly leaned over the painting. Her eyes traced the edges of the frame. The frame showed no obvious sign of problems such as mould growth or infestation.

The varnish on the right hand edge had faded slightly, suggesting that it might have caught at least for part of the day a sliver of sunlight. The glass had served its purpose well, protecting the canvas from dirt, which in turn had helped keep the paint colours distinct and bright. The red of Josephine's lips retained its evocative power and the dark of her eyes remained deep and true. The skin of her cheeks and neck had lost none of its radiance. The informal, almost sketchy style lent a sense of intimacy. It was like Molly was in the moment with the sitter looking just this way, holding the pose for the painter. She could follow the painter's strokes, the caress of brush against canvas. There was no doubting this was a painting of effortless, timeless beauty. It certainly betrayed nothing of its years, suggested nothing of the triumph it had won over the rigours of passing time.

Only the mount, discolouring slightly, caused Molly a little concern. "I think I'll suggest we temporarily remove the frame so we can replace the mount. I'm worried it might have degraded." Molly let out a sigh of relief. "Other than that, you're in good shape, Josephine Brancaster. You've done your family proud." Molly's chest tightened again at the word *family*. Soon she would be face-to-face with Georgina Wright.

"Sounds like a plan to me." Fran gathered her things to leave. "Now, make sure you are completely ready. And then for God's sake don't be late. I'll be in the storeroom if you need me."

Molly forced a nervous smile. "Wish me luck."

❖

"Come in, Molly," Evelyn said at the sound of voices followed by polite knocking at the conference room door.

Georgina glanced up in expectation. She stared at the handle waiting for it to turn.

All weekend she'd worried about seeing Molly again. She couldn't remember the last time she'd felt so confronted, so exposed, and so off balance by the sight of someone. For there she was, the woman from the square, rushing down the stairs, her arms full of folders, her face full of welcome.

And her name was Molly. *Molly.* She was real and standing just touching distance away. Every detail of her once imagined was brought to life, from the freckles across her nose, to the sound of her voice, to the way the light caught in her questioning eyes.

With Molly's gaze upon her, she'd panicked. And then, Molly spoke about art. She was an art curator. Did that mean she'd be like her mother? Everything in that moment felt at odds. She hadn't known what to do or what to think. Where was her composure? Where were the defences that had always kept her so cool and so calm?

What must Molly have thought? What must she be thinking now?

The door opened and Marianne led the way, pushing the conference room door fully open and flat against the wall.

"Thanks, Marianne. Morning, everyone," Molly said, her expression one of total concentration as she carefully carried the wrapped portrait of Josephine to the far end of the table and rested it gently in place.

Georgina stood. The weight of her chair pressed against her legs. She struggled to find her breath. Molly looked so natural and beautiful once again. Her denim pinafore dress and cream blazer couldn't have suited her more.

"Of course, you've met Molly before, Georgina," Evelyn said, with a breezy tone that implied *all is well*.

"Yes, indeed. Good morning," Georgina said, hoping her cheeks were not as flushed as they felt.

Molly held out her hand. "Good morning."

Molly's hand felt warm and soft in hers.

Molly then took her place next to Evelyn. She slipped her jacket off and scooped soft curls of auburn hair away from her shoulders to rest at her back.

"Georgina, as agreed, I have asked Molly to come up with a plan to help you to learn more about the"—Evelyn leaned forward, freeing her glasses from her hair to squint through them to read her notes—"1832 watercolour portrait of Josephine Wright. Artist unknown. Now—"

"Brancaster," Molly corrected. "Oh, I'm sorry, Evelyn, I didn't mean to interrupt you."

Evelyn placed her pen on the table and leaned back in her chair. "Not at all. This is your project. We are very much relying on you for the details of things."

Molly swallowed.

Was Molly feeling under pressure? "You're correct," Georgina said. "She became Josephine Wright when she married William Wright." Georgina opened her iPad and held up the screen for both Evelyn and Molly to see. "This is hanging at my father's place. It is of Josephine and William Wright's wedding day. Interestingly it's dated 1833. Do you see? Her maiden name of Brancaster is recorded in brackets." Both Evelyn and Molly leaned forward to take in the detail. "This tells us that they are the same woman. It also tells us the watercolour of Josephine was painted in the year before her marriage." Was she saying too much? "I'm sorry, all this detail has been swirling in my head. I don't mean to bombard you—"

"No, it's great. Thanks." Molly's encouraging smile couldn't have been more kind and reassuring.

Evelyn gave a slow nod. "So it might have been that William commissioned a painting of his fiancée. Yes, that makes sense."

Molly moved to stand again with the painting and eased the wrapping free to reveal the painting beneath the glass. She began to examine it. With a tone full of thought, she said, "Except, well, where we have paintings commissioned by men of their fiancées, they tend to portray the woman concerned as an ideal of femininity, virginal almost. I always think these paintings are symbols of ownership and of masculine power over women."

Evelyn cautioned, "But then we must take care not to read a work with personal bias."

"No, it's not so much my feminism clouding my judgement, although I recognize that at times it might." Molly glanced at Georgina.

As their eyes met, Georgina encouraged, "Go on. Please."

Molly sat again and continued, "What particularly struck me about the work was the informality of style which breaks down barriers to the viewing of it. By that I mean it encourages you to look. It has a non-possessive openness to it. It is like the painter was celebrating Josephine, not owning her. And it is sensual, yes, but without inviting judgement. Does that make sense?"

"Yes, yes it does," Georgina said in firm agreement. "I've always found this painting captivating. As a child I would spend hours looking at her. She's…"

"She's beautiful." Molly held Georgina's gaze.

"Yes."

"Well, we've certainly got a very interesting painting to explore," Evelyn intervened, a hint of impatience in her voice.

"There's something else that doesn't quite make sense. That I wanted to mention." Georgina glanced at Evelyn before turning her attention back to Molly. "My father has four portraits in total on his wall. They are all in chronological order except this painting. You see, it is hung third in line before a portrait of William as an old man. Would it not have made more sense for our painting to be first? Obviously it could have been mis-hung during redecoration and so forth."

Molly studiously made notes as she listened.

"I have images I can send you." Georgina lifted her iPad once again and thumbed through her photos. "If that's useful?"

"That's enormously helpful. Thank you."

"No worries. I'll do it right now."

"Great." Molly flicked to the last page of her notepad and scribbled down her email address. "That's a capital *M* and capital *G* in my name. Although, you know, I never understand whether capitals make a difference or not."

Georgina quickly attached the photos and pressed send. "Done."

"Awesome—I mean, thanks."

"So, your plan, Molly," Evelyn prompted, with eyes that had grown wide.

"Yes." Molly quickly returned to her notes. "So as with all investigations we'll start with what we already know." She looked at Georgina. "Anything else that comes to mind, just let me know. We'll go forward on the basis that the watercolour reflects Josephine as a young woman, just before she married. We'll check exhibition and auction catalogues as well as our museum records for any mention of the work. We'll keep our searches centred in the UK for now. There's a possibility that the painting was displayed at some point in this museum. Although Fran, our social historian, can't recall the painting from the 1980s onward, but before then—"

Evelyn said, "I think that unlikely. It's a little naive in style, amateurish."

"Amateurish?" Georgina asked, looking at Molly.

"My initial review of the work doesn't automatically suggest a well-known artist of that period."

Georgina sighed. "I hope I'm not wasting your time."

"Not at all. And all is definitely not lost because we do have a certain amount of information about Josephine herself. This is unusual because women as a rule tend to get lost in history." Molly flicked through her notes. "My initial online research has given us basic timeline information, date of birth, family, et cetera, but even more interestingly, several articles mentioned that she was an important figure in the abolitionist movement. They even describe her as a radical."

"A radical? Yes, actually now you say, I have a vague memory of my father saying that Josephine campaigned against injustice."

"Yep. She sounds really kick-ass. Pioneering, I mean. And it's perfectly possible that her various causes might produce some leads. The county's records office might be important for us—"

Evelyn raised her pen. "This sounds a little more like something our social historian would deal with." A rash of pink had begun to creep up Evelyn's neck.

Molly said carefully, "But it's about identifying the painting's provenance, surely."

"I'm just a little concerned about Molly's time, Georgina. I'm sure you understand."

"Of course I understand. My own time for this is limited too."

Evelyn closed her notebook. "Well then, within our resources, we promise to give this our utmost attention."

Evelyn and Georgina stood at the same time.

"Let me walk you out." Evelyn opened the conference room door.

"Thank you. And Molly, thank you also. I look forward to hearing about what you have discovered."

Molly stood. "Yes, of course, if I find anything, I'll let you know straight away."

"Great. Oh, before I forget. Can I have one of those forms you need me to fill in?"

"You want a form?" Molly couldn't have sounded more surprised. "You don't have to—I mean, where you're concerned…"

"I'm not sure I understand why you'd make an exception for me. It seemed important to you for your records."

"Yes, it is. Thank you. I'll make sure you get one."

"Wonderful, then everything's in order." Evelyn gestured into the corridor.

"Oh," Molly said, "before you both go, I'm sorry, just one last thing, I promise. I wanted to seek your permission to remove the frame. There's no sign of infestation. On the contrary, the frame appears sound."

With a face of imperious judgement, Evelyn inspected the painting.

Molly added, "It's just, I'm concerned about the slight discoloration of the mount."

"You think the painting might be damaged?" Georgina rested a protective hand on the frame.

Molly quickly replied, "No, not at all. Removing the mount is just a precautionary measure. You see, mount boards can become acidic over time and potentially harmful to the work. But really the watercolour itself is in good condition. The colours are distinct and bright, and the canvas is without foxing."

"That's a relief. So yes, please go ahead and undertake whatever preventative measures you think necessary. My father would be pleased to hear that the watercolour is otherwise in good order. He greatly cared about his collection."

"And please rest assured that we share your father's concern, and we very much look forward to receiving his treasured works into our care." Evelyn tucked the wrapping over one edge of the frame as a mother would replace a blanket over a child.

There it was. Georgina had wondered how long it would be before Evelyn made her move. Before she swept in, wings wide, claws out, her eyes fixed on her prey of the artwork in the house.

Georgina's defences rose in an instant. "I'm sure you understand that my father's concerns and my concerns differ. Greatly."

"Of course." Evelyn turned deathly pale.

Molly looked down at the floor, clearly embarrassed.

"I'll see myself out." Georgina turned and walked away, suppressing every urge to run.

❖

"Hi, Fred. I've brought you a tea." Molly placed a mug and a plate of biscuits on the reception desk.

"Much appreciated. I'll have to forego those devils, though, as my wife's got me on a diet." Fred patted his stomach where his shirt buttons strained to the point of popping.

"Tricky. Well, I'll step into the breach and relieve you from temptation." Molly took a large bite of a chocolate digestive.

"That Georgina Wright of yours just came past. I've only just finished picking up the museum leaflets that blew off the desk in the gust of her rush to leave." Fred shook his head.

Molly swallowed down a giggle. "Yeah, that might have been our fault. She's just come from a meeting with Evelyn and me." Molly shrugged. "It seems we have that effect on her."

"I wouldn't take it personal. Some people are just in too much of a hurry to be friendly."

"Maybe." But she had been friendly. In fact, Molly had enjoyed the meeting and chatting with Georgina so much, she'd forgotten it was Georgina Wright.

"Oh, and here, don't forget to take your post." Fred handed Molly a stack of letters along with a tan Jiffy bag.

"Okey-dokey, thanks." Molly pulled the bag open and tipped it so its contents slipped into her palm. She stared at the oblong red and white key ring which read *I heart New York*. There was no accompanying note.

"Everything okay, Molly?"

"What? Yep." Molly shoved the envelope into the pocket of her blazer. "Absolutely. I'm just going to pop out for a bit. Thanks, Fred."

Nothing felt okay.

Arriving in the square, she pulled the Jiffy bag from her pocket and rested it on the bench beside her. Had it really been nearly a year since it had ended with Erica? So much had changed. A new job, for starters, with new responsibilities. Molly risked a glance across to George Wright's house. All seemed quiet.

She'd forgotten that Erica still had her house keys, let alone that she would one day return them out of the blue. She hadn't forgotten, however, how much she had been hurt.

Tears traced their way to her neck. She did her best but failed to brush them away.

"Oh, Molly, what is it?" Fran arrived at her side and slipped an arm around Molly's shoulder causing her to cry even more. "Fred said you'd had a funny turn."

"Sorry I'm being pathetic. I can't remember the last time I cried." Molly took the tissue Fran offered and dried her eyes.

"Well, you do not have to say any more. Tears are a private matter."

"It's my ex," Molly said, fighting the urge to cry again.

"Oh. I'm sorry to hear that. Don't feel you have to—"

"I got dumped nearly a year ago. I came home to a note and an empty house."

"Goodness, that's brutal."

Molly blew her nose. "Yep. She was pretty cold. I had house keys returned to me today. Looking back, it had been over for a while before it ended, and I guess we were surviving on the vapours of good times."

"Well take heart that when you meet *the one*, you will know."

Molly sniffed hard. "How?"

"How? I'm not sure I can offer much advice on lesbian dating."

"No. I meant, how will I know? Because I want to. I want to find *the one*."

"Well what's that old saying—you'll meet them when you're least expecting it. Anyway, forget about your ex. She's an ex for a reason. Here have another tissue."

"Thanks." Molly wiped at her wet cheek.

"Your job is to remember that you're beautiful, funny, intelligent, and wonderfully compassionate. You will note, I didn't mention your appalling timekeeping, out of kindness."

Molly laughed.

"That's better. To be honest, when Fred also mentioned that a certain Miss Wright had rushed out of the museum, I feared the worst. I'm relieved she wasn't responsible for your tears."

They both looked over at George Wright's house.

"Actually, she was less weird than before. I even enjoyed chatting with her. We shared loads of ideas. She did however bite back at Evelyn when she mentioned her father's art collection. I had to look away."

"I can imagine. I suspect Evelyn's met her match."

"It's clear she really cares about her father's art and the watercolour in particular. When I mentioned removing the frame, she looked so concerned. Actually, out of respect, I should have asked if she wanted to be there when the frame was removed. I may do that after lunch."

"Yes, do. I think a bit of compassion in that young woman's direction wouldn't hurt."

Molly nodded as their conservation slipped into silence and they both stared across again at the house. She recalled the first time Evelyn had shown her the house from her office window. Molly's breath had caught at the sight of it. And the very thought that the Wrights had owned the house from the 1840s had filled her with awe. For everything about the house was beautiful. Ornate columns sunk flush into its facade evoked an air of classical formality. Light danced, caught like the stares of the passers-by, in the tall sash windows.

The house was the very embodiment of dignity, refinement, and grief. For if houses had a temperament, a mood, and Molly believed they did, then this house would say *I am sad, I am alone, I am masterless.*

The shaped hedges in the front garden, while still tidy, were losing their definition, their crispness. Soon, no doubt like people's memories of George Wright, they would blend with the background blur of everything and become indistinct. After all, gardens were always the first sign of the emotions inside a house, the barometers of feeling. Molly imagined that if this garden could cry, it would, and the birds would bathe in the tears, their wings carrying the droplets of loss far away.

CHAPTER FIVE

Georgina dropped her running shoes onto the floor and scooped up the post. Beads of sweat ran down her back and itched at the curve of her jaw. Two hours earlier and wound up by the meeting with the museum, she'd had to force herself to concentrate on making lunch and then on calls and emails. But the only thing that would settle her was to run, and to run hard.

Exhausted, she sank onto the bottom but one step of the hallway stairs and sifted through the stack of correspondence, discarding the debris of pizza leaflets, fliers for local jobs for cash, and the cellophaned horror of the starving plastered over the charity bags.

The last letter stopped her short with its all too familiar handwriting which was more a scrawl of ink than individual letters. How the postman read it, she never knew. How many times had she'd hoped these letters would go astray.

She ripped the envelope open, not caring if it caught the letter inside.

Dear Georgina,

I hope this letter finds you well, my darling girl.

I'm sorry that I have not written since your father's death, but as much as I tried, it seemed nothing could free my stilted heart to find the will to write. And now so many months have passed, slipping away like nymphs in the night. But you have been in my thoughts as ever every day.

I hear the funeral was a success. I am pleased for you. Funerals are such awful occasions, and one does not wish to remember them for any mishap. I could not bring myself to attend and felt in any case that I would have been an unwelcome guest. I was holed up in Paris that day and found amongst the chaos of my life a quiet moment on the steps of the Sacré-Coeur, and would you believe, the bell tolled just at the time the funeral began. You were with me in that moment, darling, in my hopes and prayers.

I never know whether you read my letters, but I still look for your reply and resist the defeated sense that I am writing a diary of my thoughts rather than corresponding with you.

I know how busy you must be, but if time, that silent thief, allows please reply. The thing is, we need to talk. Or better still, I have taken an apartment in Paris for the autumn season—why don't you come and visit? Any time at all.

Your mother,
Lydia Wright X

Georgina always read her mother's letters. She'd received three a year since her mother left, each sent to her father's house. They arrived with the change of season. In spring the tone of the letter would be bright and optimistic. *What high hopes, Georgina, what hopes.* In summer the letter would speak of her mother's fatigue at the heat and the tiring length of the days. In the autumn, they would strike a reflective note and a mood of melancholy with the dark approach of winter. *These short days it feels like one's life is contracting, leaving one gasping for air.*

She would hear nothing from her at Christmas. She'd always thought it cruel. The thought instilled a hatred which grew as she grew from a teenager to an adult. She had hated her mother for so long that the sharp edge of pain had become blunt, dull, the emotions a mere patina on the surface of her life.

But now with her father's death, everything seemed to sharpen and her memories resurfaced with painful clarity.

She looked into the living room through the half-open door. She could swear she could hear them quarrelling.

They did not see her there, seated on the top step of the hallway stairs, listening. The door swung closed and now it was just muffled voices and odd words spat out with venom intended to wound and scar. Words flamed up again like sparks of hate, burning bright in the air. And then an awful silence. The sitting room door banged open, and Georgina watched her mother leave without looking back, her scarf billowing at her neck. Georgina followed the sound of soft sobbing as she went into the sitting room. Her father was standing with the portrait of Josephine held tightly in his arms.

A bustle of schoolchildren passing by outside called her from her daydreams to the reality of the moment. She blinked several times trying to focus on now. Dark clouds gathered over the square and litter blew against the abandoned benches and the trees swayed in the gust of approaching rain.

She turned the light on casting an urgent glance to the paintings. A peculiar panic rose in her chest at the sight of the empty space with the rectangle of grey dust marking the outline of where Josephine's portrait had once hung. A sudden urge willed her to hold the painting tight in her arms just as her father had done.

Rain tapped against the window. Georgina shivered. A hot shower would help. But just as she turned to go upstairs her phone lit with an email. It was work, wasn't it? It was always work. She should leave it. *Oh, for fuck's sake.*

It wasn't work. "Molly?"

Dear Ms. Wright,

Thank you for your time today and for your help with the research of your father's painting. I wanted to ask if you wish to attend the deframing? I anticipate that it will take place at some point later this week, either Thursday or Friday morning.

I look forward to hearing from you,
Molly (Goode)
Curator, (Fine Art), City Museum

Had she said goodbye to Molly? In the heat of the farewell with Evelyn she couldn't remember. But things between them had ended well enough, hadn't they? Molly had promised to be in touch, and here she was keeping her promise. Yes, that matched every sense Georgina had about her. That she was faithful and honest, not to mention intelligent and good at her job if their meeting was anything to go by. She couldn't have been more impressed. For it was like Molly really *got* the painting at an intuitive level. She hadn't tried to impress or blind her with the science of her work or make excuses for why they might fail. No. Instead she had listened and worked with Georgina to find ways that might lead to discoveries. She'd left her with the sense that she would not give up on the painting. But most importantly of all she'd left her with hope.

She replied, *Dear Molly, Yes. Thank you. Thursday morning, say 11am? Georgina Wright*

The response came back in an instant: *Great—come straight to the Victorian gallery. See you then. Molly.*

The rain that had threatened seemed to pass, and in that moment the darkness lifted and not just in the square.

CHAPTER SIX

The Victorian gallery with its high ceilings and Regency period grandeur was reserved for the museum's fine art collection. Depictions of rural and industrial landscapes hung side by side with portraits of the great and the good. It was as if all humanity had been squeezed into one room and Molly loved it. Even the imminent arrival of Georgina Wright couldn't dampen the delight in Molly's heart the space evoked.

"Morning, General," Molly said with a salute to the oil painting of General Lansdowne, of the Leicester Regiment. "Ladies, you are rocking those parasols." Molly gave a thumbs up to the scene depicting a gathering of young Victorian era women at a picnic. She paused at the portrait of Saint Peter in a fishing boat. "Here's hoping you catch something, fella. Oh, and any help this morning would be much appreciated."

Molly shook her head and stood face-to-face with the heavily varnished 1839 portrait of Josephine Wright painted by George O. Thorpe. She'd given no particular thought to the donor before but now the inscribed words, *Donated by Lydia and George Wright, 1985*, seemed to resonate out from the frame.

The Hunt epitomized the country life of Leicestershire's gentry. Josephine was dressed in a long black riding coat with her cream leather riding gloves and crop resting in her lap. She sat side-saddle on a chestnut stallion whose muscular flanks shone and rippled, his head bowed at her command. Everything about the character of the painting was formal and seemed as if in shadow. The heavy varnishing swallowed the light, and any glimpse of joy was enveloped in the gloom.

Josephine stared steadfast past the painter and past the viewer to somewhere else in the distance beyond. Yet her expression was not thoughtful—if anything, it was vacant, empty.

"You seem so sad. Don't be sad, Josephine, you're too beautiful for that." Molly felt her own past hurts pressing against her chest.

"It's a very different painting, isn't it?"

Startled, Molly turned around to find Georgina standing at the entrance to the gallery, leaning against the doorframe with her head tilted to one side. Gone was the formal suit from Monday's meeting. Georgina was now dressed in snug tan chinos set off with a tailored white shirt with the sleeves rolled up a little way, revealing her slim, toned forearms.

Oh my God. How long had she been there? She was early. Of course she was early. Molly was now certain beyond doubt that any smidgen of respect or credibility she might have earned at their last meeting was now lost—just like her marbles. Talking to paintings…that settled it—she was certainly making an impression, *exuding* authority.

Molly stumbled over her words, managing, "Yes."

Georgina walked confidently to her, holding out her hand and smiling. "Thank you for inviting me."

As Molly shook Georgina's hand, she said diplomatically, "Thank you for accompanying me." To Molly's surprise Georgina blushed. How had she embarrassed her already?

"I want to say straight off"—Georgina rested her hand for the briefest of seconds on Molly's shoulder—"if at any point during this I look anxious, I'm just being overprotective."

"And I want to say straight off, that's perfectly understandable. After all why wouldn't you feel protective—the painting's precious to you. Shall we head over? I've laid everything out on this table here."

Georgina stood staring at the image of Josephine captured in tender strokes of colour.

"Okay. So, gloves." Molly handed Georgina a box of blue vinyl gloves. She made a point of not looking at Georgina pulling hers on.

The painting rested on a thin foam board that had been covered with several layers of tissue. "I had a chat with our conservator yesterday afternoon, and he was in agreement with the decision to replace the mount. I'll remove the frame releasing the mount today, and he'll take the next steps to undertake any further remedial preservation work as he sees fit. Work should be complete by the end of next week at the latest. Is that okay with you?"

Georgina nodded. "Yes. That's great, thank you."

"Okey-dokey. We're of the opinion that the frame is original and most likely made of a material called compo which was popular at this time. The gild is tarnishing slightly, so it's likely to be of an alternative metal origin, rather than gold leaf."

Molly gently turned the painting over. "Frames often tell us more about the work than the painting itself. For example if you look, there are no residual tape marks fixing the backing board to the frame."

Georgina leaned forward, tucking a stray piece of hair behind her ear.

Molly forced herself to concentrate on the painting, not on how close Georgina's chest was to her arm. "This suggests that the work hasn't been subject to repeated reframing, and it strengthens the likelihood that not only the frame but the board and fixings are original as well. But what particularly struck me was that there are no labels or stamp marks."

"And that's unusual?"

"Not for an artwork that hasn't been exhibited or auctioned."

Georgina stood back a little. "So are you telling me that it hasn't left my father's house?"

"I can only suggest what the work seems to indicate. Beyond that"—Molly shrugged—"we can't be sure."

"Of course, I understand. I don't mean to press you for answers. To be honest even though I manage risk every day, I'm not very good with uncertainty. I imagine you must have to work with uncertainty all the time."

"Well, it's a balance really, between what we know and what we think reasonably likely based on evidence. And as for uncertainty, I tend to think of it as more *possibility*, if that makes sense."

Georgina held Molly's gaze and smiled. "Yes."

Even her smile was perfect. And those smooth even lips that must be heaven to kiss. *Get a grip. Stop staring at her.* "Okay. Deep breaths. Here we go." Molly teased out the thin metal fastenings and lifted the backing board carefully away to rest on the tissue. She had expected to see a plain canvas with a smudge or two of paint, maybe. "Yes, this is just what we would expect to find, nothing un—"

An ink inscription had been preserved, clear and visible at the right hand corner of the canvas.

"Have you seen something?" Leaning in, Georgina read out the words Molly was reading. "*All my love always, Edith.*" Georgina frowned at the inscription.

Molly asked with a voice soft with intrigue, "Does the name Edith ring a bell to you at all?"

With her gaze fixed on the painting, Georgina shook her head. "No, I'm sorry, I don't recognize it." She then looked at Molly. "Why would someone called Edith sign the back of Josephine's portrait *All my love always?*"

"That's a very good question." Molly reached for her phone and took several photos of the inscription. "And we will definitely add this finding to our research."

"Unless…you don't suppose…?" Georgina paused.

Molly's chest tightened. Oh God, they were about to talk about girl-on-girl action, weren't they? Molly glanced at Georgina, who seemed remarkably unflustered. Of course she'd be calm—she wasn't the one battling with an inappropriate sexual attraction for the museum's key funder.

Molly tentatively suggested, "That they were…" How should she put it?

Without hesitation Georgina suggested, "Lovers? It's just a rather heartfelt note, isn't it, for a platonic gesture?"

Okay, straight to the point. "It's possible. Definitely. There's certainly nothing new about being gay. Although given the absence of mention of lesbians in history, you might think so." Molly stared at the inscription, so full of meaning and so empty of explanation. "What I would say though is that, in truth, the note could have been written by anyone. Edith could be anybody, family member, best friend. And don't forget passionate friendships, romantic friendships, were not uncommon during this period. Except a romantic friendship, if that's what this note indicates, and we don't know that it does, must not be confused with a lesbian relationship."

Georgina frowned. "No?"

Molly shook her head. "We need to understand this history within its context, not misread it with our modern sensibilities. And moreover we may be at risk here of confusing speculation with facts."

"But surely the note is a fact, isn't it? A piece of evidence?"

"Yes, but sadly evidence of only what we don't know. I'm sorry."

Georgina shook her head. "It just goes to show how little I know about Josephine. I wish I could be more helpful."

"You're helping being here," Molly said. "I've enjoyed your company. Thank you."

Georgina gave a nod in acknowledgement, and Molly's cheeks tingled with the intensity of Georgina's gaze upon her. Everything in that moment, including her heart, seemed to stop.

And then Georgina turned away. It was like the sun had gone behind a cloud, as an instant chill descended and Molly winced with the sting of rejection.

Oh no. She shouldn't have said that, should she? But then, it wasn't like she'd confessed, *I fancy you so much*. Although how she *hadn't* said it, she had no idea.

"I have to go now, Molly." Georgina looked at her phone. "Work commitments. Sorry. Keep me updated?"

Molly caught a glimpse of the full inbox of Georgina's emails.

"Yes, certainly." Molly tried and failed to muster a nonchalant tone. Did she sound as hurt as she felt? "Goodbye then."

"Yes, goodbye and thanks again."

Molly watched Georgina leave, and then she was gone. She turned to the painting lying there utterly dismantled and exposed, just like her.

Get a grip. Georgina Wright was an important stakeholder and she was meant to impress her, not pine after her or feel wounded when she didn't…didn't what? What on earth was she hoping for? For Georgina to ask her out, was that it? Or did she expect her to kiss her with those perfect lips. *You are making a fool of yourself.* What on earth would Evelyn think? *Enough.*

She took a deep breath and with care she lifted the mount away from the canvas. She wrapped each separate piece in tissue, supporting them with tissue wads to rest safe within a large plastic container.

"The conservator will look after you now, Josephine. You'll like him, although you'll have to overlook his taste in jumpers." A flicker of laughter in her heart burnt out immediately as disappointment, merciless and instant, stamped on the spark of her smile.

Chapter Seven

Georgina woke Friday lunchtime with a start. How had she overslept? It was noon, for God's sake. *Noon.*

Her night's sleep had been fitful and disturbed by dreamlike thoughts about Josephine's portrait and about *All my love always* and about the woman who had written it.

Who was she? Why such passionate words? What did it tell them about the painting and about Josephine herself? What was it they were missing? Only the thought that research just might reveal the truth had stilled the persistent questions. And in the silence that followed, it was the thought of Molly caring so capably and so tenderly for Josephine that brought Georgina to somewhere near sleep. Yes, Molly would find the answers. *Molly.* She'd been right to leave the meeting then and there, hadn't she? For what if Molly had seen in her eyes how much she meant to her? How much she'd enjoyed her company too. What then? Their work for that day was done and everything had been agreed. She had no right to keep Molly, and she had no right not to want to leave.

She'd worried herself to sleep and now she was awake—awake and late.

Rubbing her eyes, Georgina went downstairs and into the sitting room. The closed deep burgundy velvet curtains shrouded the room in a mournful darkness. Georgina drew the heavy material back to let in the day and watched as fine dust particles floated in the air. There was an ever-growing stifling emptiness to the space. The room, the house, was losing the presence of her father with every day, every week, and every month that passed. She'd kept on her father's housekeeper to call, now and then, to clean and keep an eye on the house, but she knew with a quiet dread that each time she returned the smell she'd cherished of her father's cologne and of his laundered shirts and suits, and the sweet herbal notes of tea just poured, would have faded to something stale, musty, and lifeless.

Georgina looked out at the busy square and at the passers-by hurrying to work or school. Outside the walls of her grief, life was continuing. *I need a coffee and a run.*

❖

"I think Josephine Wright might have been gay." Molly turned to face Fran who was wearing a woollen hat and scarf tightly wrapped around her neck. A sly cold breeze unsettled the square and blew Molly's hair across her eyes, and she brushed it away.

Fran tucked her jacket closer around her and sneezed. "I thought two days off would sort this cold. I blame my weakened state entirely on the storeroom. It's all very well and good preserving the objects at a stable chilly degrees C, but what about preserving the health of staff? Anyway. I'm sorry, what were you saying…Georgina's a lesbian?"

"*No.* I mean. I don't know. No. *Josephine.* You know, Josephine Wright, the woman in the watercolour."

"Oh. That's quite a development. I almost don't like to ask how you have formed that conclusion."

Molly turned in towards Fran, tucking her legs up to sit cross-legged. "There's a handwritten inscription on the back of the canvas of Josephine's portrait. *All my love always, Edith.*"

"Really?"

"Yes, I know. I was thinking about it in bed last night, and the more I thought about it, the more I got this intense feeling that we might have been the first to see this message for many years, if not generations. That's really amazing, isn't it?"

"Yes. And Georgina? I imagine she didn't know what to think."

"Funnily enough she took it in her stride—at least that's how it came across. She was the one, in fact, who brought up the lovers possibility. I explained to her that it was possible this Edith, whoever she is, had a romantic friendship with Josephine but cautioned we hadn't necessarily discovered a lesbian romance. Or at least, we couldn't be sure either way or indeed read it that way with our modern eyes. Would you like some of my corn on the cob?"

"No, certainly not. Thank you anyway."

Molly bit into the corn and between mouthfuls she said, "I mean the chances of us even finding out who Edith is or, for that matter, whether even finding Edith will help us know who painted the—" Molly fell silent at the sight of Georgina emerging from her father's house dressed in a running outfit of tight leggings and T-shirt. A dribble of herby sauce trickled down Molly's chin. Georgina paused at the top of the steps to place her earphones in and to fiddle with her phone strapped to her arm. She then proceeded to jog along City Walk in the direction of Victoria Park. Molly watched her until she disappeared out of sight.

"It could be Edith Hewitt," Fran said matter-of-factly. "She's very fit, isn't she, Georgina?"

"Sorry? You know who Edith is?" Molly mopped at her mouth and chin with a napkin.

"Her father was fit as well, kept himself trim. "

"What? I'm not remotely interested in Georgina's Wright's fitness levels."

"Uh-huh. If you say so."

"I do. I am, however, interested in the fact you know who Edith is."

"I know who Edith *might* be. There was an Edith Hewitt who worked alongside Josephine when they were both in their early twenties. They were ardent abolitionists and actively encouraged women to take part in their campaigns. They ruffled feathers."

"I love the idea of that."

"We did a temporary exhibition, some years ago now, on Leicester's political radicals, and Josephine's treatises and tracts featured. It was very popular. If my memory serves me right, Edith and Josephine worked from a borrowed office in Josephine's father's chambers in town. Charles Brancaster was a solicitor, and so of course was Josephine's husband, William Wright. Indeed the Wrights go forward to breed generations of solicitors. Apart, of course, from Georgina, who seems to have broken the mould."

Molly glanced in the direction of the park. "Political radicals. That's so fab, isn't it? I'm imagining them marching the streets, demanding the freedom of all slaves in the British Empire."

"Yes and no. They were resourceful, educated women, and they did so much more than march. Josephine in particular wrote tirelessly, lobbying politicians and anyone and everyone of influence. Not only that, but they rallied the support of local businesses to stop selling sugar from the West Indies, putting pressure on the plantation owners by threatening their market."

"Clever."

"But most effectively they galvanized women by getting them to boycott resistant businesses and to sign petitions. They collected thousands of signatures. They were effective and ignored, at least largely, by history. When we think about the abolition of slavery, we think Wilberforce." Fran tucked her scarf more closely around her. "It's frankly chilling."

"That's so unfair."

"It's even worse for your Edith, I'm afraid."

"It is?"

"You see, Josephine's family, I suspect, were better off and her status has helped her gain some visibility in history. It would sadly not surprise me if Edith's work has been swept up in Josephine's archives. They were both remarkable women. It just goes to show that history neglects as much as it preserves." Fran poured tomato soup from a flask into a cup.

"I absolutely hate the thought of that. It's so helpful, Fran, that you know all this."

"Steady on, I don't know much. The exhibition only scratched the surface. It was just outlines and discovered very little about Edith. You should try the records office. You'll probably have more time to spend there than I had—in fact, I remember now, time was so tight for me I sent a volunteer in my place. Sadly, if she missed anything I wouldn't have known."

"Yes, a visit to the records office is my next step. Although, to be honest, talking of time, I don't know how much of my time Evelyn wants to invest. She got a bit tense at the mention of research beyond the museum itself. I don't suppose you kept the research for the exhibition, did you?"

"Yes, it'll be somewhere. I'll have a look for you."

"Thanks."

"So dare I ask how you and the woman you're not remotely interested in are getting on? Have you wooed her with the many curatorial talents of Molly Goode?"

"That's the thing. I haven't got a clue. Take yesterday, for example— the meeting was going really well, and then out of the blue it's like these barriers go up and she becomes instantly distant and I feel instantly incapable. Maybe it's me? Maybe I'm being too familiar with her?"

"Too familiar? In what way?"

"I told her I enjoyed her company."

"Surely that's just lovely, and I'm sure Georgina would have thought so too. My take, for what it's worth, is that you're being oversensitive to her, over-reading every little reaction. Evelyn is expecting you to impress her, and you're constantly worried about *not* impressing her, and therefore you are left wondering what Georgina Wright is thinking."

Was that what was happening? "Yeah, that makes sense and explains why I can't stop thinking about her. It's really annoying."

"I can imagine."

"I mean, who is that immaculate? Her perfect face and voice. The way she tucks her hair over her ears. I bet you her tousled is most people's tidy."

Fran raised her eyebrows. "Tousled? I see. And of course, there's those long legs of hers, particularly in those leggings. I mean, how dare she."

"Yes, exactly." Molly paused. "I mean, no. Oh God, I don't know what I mean. I think it's best I try to somehow wriggle out of spending time with her. I'll pop to the records office, do a quick summary of findings. We've done a little bit of remedial work on the painting. Job done." Molly brushed her hands together. "Over."

"I think you'll find it's not quite over yet, as Georgina is heading our way."

"No, really?" Molly's napkin blew off her lap as she turned, at the same time awkwardly untangling her legs, to see Georgina slowing from a running pace to a walk towards them. Molly jumped to her feet to prevent the napkin from becoming yet another piece of litter. The napkin rested to a stop at Georgina's feet.

As Molly bent down to pick it up, she breathlessly said, "I think litter's terrible. I pick it up when I see it. Unless it's covered in something horrible—then I leave it. Obviously. Hello." Molly shoved her napkin in her pocket.

"Hello," Georgina said with a smile. She raised her hand to acknowledge Fran who waved back.

"Fran and I are just having lunch. We're keen picnickers." *Okay, that just sounded...weird.*

"Right. Yes. It's a beautiful square to be in." Georgina gazed up into the tree. "I can see why you'd want to take your breaks here." A peculiar expression washed over her face.

Had Georgina just blushed, or were her cheeks pink just from running? Running very hard...Molly watched a bead of sweat as it travelled down the edge of Georgina's cheek to the curve of her jaw to the sweep of her neck to...*Stop staring.*

Molly cleared her throat. "Please join us. If you want."

"I won't. I mean, I need to keep moving or I'll seize up and get cold."

"Of course. I understand."

"You run too, then?"

"Run? No. Well, when I'm late, I sometimes have to. The other day I overtook a group of joggers trying to get to a meeting. My meeting, not theirs. I was in flip-flops too."

Georgina laughed. "I'm impressed."

"Thank you." Molly giggled and then fell silent. She braced herself for the cold look away, but it didn't come. The barriers, for whatever reason, remained down.

"I came over because I've been thinking about Josephine's portrait—the inscription we found yesterday."

"Oh yes? Funnily enough, Fran and I were just chatting, and I have news about who Edith might be." Molly saw that Georgina had begun to shiver.

"That's great. Can we meet again then? For an update? The only thing is, I'm back to work from next week. I'm London based, you see. I suppose we could Skype or FaceTime?"

"London?" Molly hadn't meant to sound so disappointed.

"Yes. I've had time off to deal with my father's estate. You don't think Skype will work?"

"What? No, I mean…" Molly tried to gather her thoughts. She was obviously confusing Georgina and making her wonder what was wrong.

"Or"—Georgina looked back at her father's house—"I'm due to return again next Friday afternoon. My father's colleagues have had a plaque made in his memory. It's being put into the Cathedral. It should be over by three, half three. If I came to you at four, would that fit at all?"

Georgina began to jog on the spot which, quite frankly, wasn't helping Molly to concentrate on the question in hand. *Don't look at her boobs.*

Molly looked down and, speaking at the ground, said, "Next Friday. Let me see, yes, that would fit."

"Perfect. Look forward to seeing you then."

She was looking forward to seeing her again? Or was she just being polite? Molly looked up to see Georgina smiling. Returning her smile Molly said, "Okay. Great."

"Excellent. I'm off for a hot shower. Goodbye Fran."

A hot shower? Molly's thoughts began to stray to steamy shower cubicles. She pinched at her leg. *Where the chuff is your self-control.*

"Yes, goodbye, Georgina," Fran replied, an amused smile teasing at her lips.

And with that Georgina jogged away and up the steps to her father's door. She paused with the key in the lock, only to then turn and wave. Molly's cheeks tingled as she and Fran waved back.

"Yes, how annoying," Fran said with barely concealed sarcasm. "And the way you wriggled out of that meeting."

"She caught me off guard."

"Uh-huh."

"She *did*."

❖

"Come in!"

Molly opened the door to Evelyn's office and stepped just inside its threshold. "Hi," she said breathlessly. Somehow she never felt she had quite enough breath whenever she arrived at Evelyn's door.

"Molly," Evelyn said, removing her glasses.

"I hoped to have a quick chat with you before you left for the weekend," Molly said. "Do you have a moment?"

"Of course. Please, take a seat."

Molly sat down and gripped at the edge of the chair. "I wanted to update you on progress with the Josephine Brancaster portrait."

"Very good. And what has your research revealed? Do we know who painted it?"

"No. But we did discover an inscription written on the back of the canvas during the process of removing the frame."

"Really?"

"Yes. It reads *All my love always, Edith.*"

"Edith?" Evelyn sat back in her chair. "I see."

"Yes. Georgina didn't recognize the name. Fran, however, has suggested that it might be Edith Hewitt, who worked alongside Josephine at the time the painting was painted or commissioned."

"Edith Hewitt." Evelyn looked beyond Molly, her gaze no doubt fixed elsewhere along with her thoughts. When she returned from wherever she'd gone, she asked, "And so you're keeping Georgina Wright up to date then with your findings?"

"Actually she was with me when the inscription was discovered so—"

"You invited her to watch you work? Good thinking—keep her invested. Take every opportunity to impress her. Excellent."

Molly's heart fluttered with pride. "She certainly seems very connected to the painting and very interested in our research."

"Really? That's wonderful. It's so important the museum has made this connection with Georgina." Evelyn sat on the edge of her seat. "Now our focus must be on moving this connection forward. Yes, now is the perfect time to mention to her our plans for the Wright room. Understood?"

"Yes, of course."

"Great. Thank you for the update. Close the door on your way out." Evelyn reopened her notebook and began making notes. It was as if Molly had already left.

Molly didn't move. Evelyn eventually looked up.

"Was there something else?"

"Yes. So the portrait—"

Evelyn raised her pen and said, "I think we've given that project all the time we can. We'll have completed the remedial work for the painting itself. Is that right?"

Molly nodded.

"And you've done some background research illuminating more about Josephine, and we've even been able to identify the individual who likely gifted the painting—"

"We don't know for sure it was Edith Hewitt. That's why I'd like to visit the records office—"

"No, no, no. That's really not appropriate. I admire your enthusiasm, your keenness, indeed. But like I said, it is time to move on."

"But we haven't answered the one question Georgina asked us to. We still don't know who painted the portrait. I'm due to meet with Georgina again—"

"And do you think you will be able to find out? I mean, for certain? Do you think you will find in the records office that piece of paper, that item of correspondence that says, I, Edith, let's say Hewitt, commission you *whoever* to paint Josephine Brancaster? Tell me honestly."

Molly looked down and shook her head.

"Then goodnight. Fresh pastures now, Molly. When you meet with Georgina next, I want your focus to be the Wright room. Deliver me Georgina's commitment."

Without another word Molly left Evelyn's office feeling dazed. She numbly waved goodnight to Fred in the foyer and walked the few hundred yards across the square in a daydream and climbed into Daisy May.

Was Evelyn right? Had they probably discovered all they were ever going to find out about the painting? Fran certainly hadn't seemed confident that she would find out much more about Edith. *Fran.* How on earth would Molly tell her about the Wright room? She couldn't put it off any longer. What could she say? *I tried and failed.* Surely all Fran would hear is *I'm art and status* not *integrity and community.*

Molly dropped her forehead to rest on Daisy May's steering wheel.

If the prospect of raising the subject of the Wright room with Fran was bad, then trying to find the words to use to talk about it with Georgina was surely impossible. She'd seen her reaction when Evelyn just mentioned her father's art, and it wasn't pretty. Was it still somehow just too soon for Georgina to talk about the things her father cared about? It took no imagining to understand that would hurt, and Molly didn't want to do that to her.

And in any case, she still had to break the news about the decision to draw a line under the research for Josephine's portrait. What could she say? Could she tell her it just wasn't meant to be, and that the beautiful watercolour was destined to keep her secrets hidden under her frame? And the inscription? Could that be just a romantic question unanswered, and Edith would remain the mysterious, passionate woman who once had loved Josephine *for always*?

Molly lifted her head and turned the engine over. Daisy May started with just a hint of complaint from her carburettor.

Across the square the chandelier light flickered on in George Wright's sitting room.

"Let's go home, Daisy May," Molly said with a sigh. "Take me to the peanut butter."

Chapter Eight

M olly was determined to be ready for her next meeting with Georgina. She knew by now that Georgina would be on time if not at least five minutes early. She'd decided that she would be there at the museum entrance to greet her on her arrival. She would be poised and prepared.

So when Friday arrived and the clock in the office ticked past quarter to four, Molly raced downstairs and sat waiting in the foyer on the hard wooden visitor bench, expectant, everything tensed with anticipation.

"Hiya!" Molly leaped to her feet at the sight of Georgina strolling in through the sliding doors. Wait, did that just sound disrespectful? After all Georgina had just been to a church ceremony in honour of her father. She needed to calm down.

"Hello, Molly." Georgina brushed at the rain that had speckled the shoulders of her coat. "The weather's terrible. Oh God, look at me."

Molly did her best not to. She tried and failed—just as she had tried and failed not to think about Georgina all week and not to imagine this very moment when they would meet again. Georgina was dressed formally this time. Her tan mackintosh looked so elegant with its collar turned up and the front falling open to reveal the hint of a tailored suit. She'd arrived no doubt from the chic bustle of London straight to the sombre formality of the cathedral, and now she'd come here directly after, as promised. She wasn't dressing to impress in an empty way. No. She was dressed to be who she was: impressive and in demand.

Should she ask how the ceremony went? Or say, perhaps, how sorry she was about her father's death and that she understood how hard it must be? But would that be too familiar? She should keep her focus on work. Yes, that was best surely. "Shall we go to my office? It's this way up the stairs."

"Sure. After you." Georgina looked past Molly to the sweep of the stairs that curved away above their heads. "It's a grand building, isn't it."

"Yes, definitely. It's early Victorian in origin, built in 1836, so it also has that late Regency neoclassical feel to it which I *love*. The entrance porch is just amazing, isn't it, with those imposing columns. Fran reliably informed me on my first day that the porch is a pedimented portico."

"Impressive."

"Yep. The architect was that chap Hansom, who was of course responsible for the Hansom cab."

Georgina fell into step beside Molly. "Yes, I think my father mentioned something about that once."

Molly followed Georgina's gaze as she stared up to the ceiling with its ornate gold leaf mouldings framing the features of the arched glass roof.

Molly paused halfway up the stairs. "It started its life as a school, would you believe, and became a museum in 1849. It is without question a public building built to inspire an obedient awe."

She glimpsed Georgina's hand resting flat on the banister just inches from hers. A thin orange rubber bracelet rested around Georgina's wrist. Wasn't that the logo of the Young Women's Trust?

"I ran a half-marathon for them." Georgina lifted the bracelet for Molly to see.

"Sorry, it just caught my eye. I'd love to do more community outreach here at the museum, particularly for young women. In fact next March for women's history month, Fran and I are hoping—or rather *were* hoping—to invite an inspiring local female figure to speak."

"*Were* hoping?"

"We may have to scale down our plans due to limited resources and all that."

"That's a shame."

"I won't be beaten though—I'll come up with something."

"Good for you."

"And you'd be amazed at how the community rallies round when you reach out to them." Molly pointed across to a far wall of faces filling the entire space that stretched from the ground to the first floor. One hundred photographs of Leicester citizens young and old, from all nations and all creeds, looked back at them, smiling.

"Wow," Georgina said, her mouth falling slightly open. "I can't believe I didn't notice this before."

Molly stole another glance at Georgina's hand still resting on the banister. If she moved her little finger just an inch…

"One of the things I respect about my father's city is its diversity," Georgina said, her focus flitting from one face to another.

Did she say her father's city? But didn't she grow up here? Why would she distance herself like that? *It's none of your business.* "We invited local people to welcome visitors to the museum with a smile," Molly said, her heart swelling with pride at the memory. "I called it *A Hundred Smiles.* You know, I just put a notice in the foyer and invited people to join in. I didn't think many people would sign up. We had nearly one hundred people wanting to participate. It was truly awesome. There are three walls of photos in different areas of the museum. One of the walls…"

"One of the walls?" Georgina gently repeated.

"Well, one of the walls is at the entrance of the new annex." She had to raise the subject of the Wright room with her. This was the time, Evelyn had said, hadn't she? She could do this. Molly took a deep breath.

"That's exciting," Georgina said with a nod. "It's good to see the museum developing. Wait, is that…?" Georgina stood motionless staring out at the faces.

Molly gripped the banister. She couldn't do it. She couldn't tell her. Nothing about this moment felt right.

"Fran? Yes," Molly said. "To be honest it was nearly ninety-nine smiles and one grimace. I could only get her to smile by reminding her of one of the lunchtime concerts we hosted here where the pianist turned up late. We had to improvise, and by *we*, I mean me and Fran. I'd only been at the museum a week, and I found myself playing an impromptu variation of 'Chopsticks,' with Fran as my co-pianist. I think it's fair to say Fran and I bonded that day, and really everyone was disappointed when the concert pianist eventually turned up."

Georgina's smile tipped over to become laughter. "I'm sorry to have missed it."

"Happy to re-enact for you anytime—just ask."

"I'll bear that in mind." As Georgina turned to continue climbing the stairs, she said, "You seem to have a very person-centred view of your work."

"Person-centred? I guess so. No, I definitely have."

"And does that philosophy of approach extend to the whole museum?"

"Uh-huh. Absolutely." Molly guided Georgina towards her office with Evelyn's suite of rooms at a safe distance at the other end of the corridor. As they reached her office Molly stopped. "Okay, so I share my office with Fran, and we like to work on an intimate level."

"By that Molly means this room's bloody small," Fran said through the door propped open with a replica of an Aztec artefact. The erection of the tribal figure symbolizing fertility was as it happened a very useful door stop. "Please come in. And don't expect to sit," Fran said, with a welcome that lacked, well, a welcome.

"After you," Molly said cheerily.

"Thank you. Hello, Fran," Georgina said. "Good to see you again."

"Likewise. How are you holding up? I imagine settling your father's estate is about as enjoyable as a tooth extraction without anaesthetic."

Georgina nodded. "That's pretty accurate."

"Well, shout if we can help," Fran said. "As you can see, our door's always open."

Molly suppressed a giggle and lifted a pile of paper wallets from her chair and gestured for Georgina to take a seat. "I'm sorry our office is a bit full at the moment. The objects we work with are kept in the storeroom as a rule. Now and then pieces stay with us here temporarily, like Josephine."

"She's here?" Georgina asked, her tone reminding Molly of the reaction of someone to the unexpected arrival of a loved one.

"She's still with the conservator." Molly tried to clear leg space for their guest. "He's working on her as we speak."

"And Edith's inscription?" Georgina asked, her voice tight with concern. "What will he do with that?"

Molly rested her hand lightly on Georgina's arm. "Don't worry. The inscription will be left untouched and protected again by the backing board and the glazed frame, just as it has been. Her message was not intended for us, after all. I have those photos of it which I can send you."

"Yes, I'd like that. Thank you."

Molly followed Georgina's gaze as it flitted around the room. What was Georgina thinking? Had she been expecting a vast suite of lab-like offices dedicated to the pursuit of excellence in their craft?

Molly always thought of their office as an Aladdin's cave of wonder. A dressing up box with period costumes spilling out lay in one corner. A stuffed cat striking an alarming pouncing pose and adorned with a feather hat sat on the radiator that never worked. A haphazard collection of empty frames and mounts rested against a wide chest with thin drawers for paper objects to be laid flat in. Reference books, catalogues, and A4 lever arch folders balanced, defying all laws of gravity, on top of a filing cabinet, and a poster identifying every type of museum pest adorned the only wall space. Molly could only hope Georgina's expression of surprise was in fact childlike wonder.

Was this the time to tell Georgina that the museum would be returning the painting and that they had done all they could do? Yes. It was time. Molly took a deep breath. "So—"

"I've been—"

Georgina and Molly tried to speak at once.

"Oops," Molly said. "You go first."

"I've been thinking about the painting. To be honest, I can't seem to stop thinking about it." Georgina gave a slight shake of her head. "In particular about what you said in our first meeting—that the painting didn't seem to fit traditional works commissioned by a man for his wife to be. In this case, William for Josephine."

"Yes, that's right. I remember." Molly perched a hip on her desk.

Georgina continued in earnest. "And then when we found the note from Edith, I began to wonder whether there was a possibility that the painting was not just a gift from Edith but that she actually painted it."

Fran turned her chair in towards them.

Molly looked at Fran. "I don't suppose you can recall if Edith painted, or perhaps if your volunteer mentioned that she'd noticed anything, I don't know, remotely craft related in her research?"

Fran frowned in what was clearly a painful act of remembering. "I seem to have a half memory of a scrapbook listed."

"There's a scrapbook?" Molly reached for her notebook.

"Yes. In the records office. I presume it's still there. I don't recall mention of either Josephine or Edith as artists though."

"I appreciate I'm speculating," Georgina said, an air of defeat in her voice.

Molly shook her head. "It's definitely possible that Edith painted as a hobby. In fact, come to think of it, at this time watercolour was becoming popular with amateur artists. "

"So where do we go from here?" Georgina asked, looking intently at Molly. "Is there any way we can find out?"

Molly looked into Georgina's eyes. She cleared her throat. "We could go to the records office."

"Great." Georgina was smiling broadly. "I could make this time next week."

Molly nodded. "Yep."

"Nope." Fran turned back to her work. "The records office is closed on a Friday."

Georgina said quickly, "This Monday then?" She opened her phone scrolling through to her diary. "Mid-morning? This gives me time to make some calls and get things going at work. And then I'll go back to London after our meeting. So, ten thirty? Would that fit?"

"Monday?" Tricky. *Oh, what the hell.* "Yes, that could fit. Shall we meet in the foyer?"

"Yes, that's fine. Thank you both for your time." Georgina stood and carefully picked her way through the clutter to leave. She turned at the door and said, "I wanted to say that I really appreciate the distraction that working on this is giving me."

"I can imagine. It's our pleasure, Georgina," Fran said, glancing at Molly.

"Gosh, yes. Absolutely," Molly said, standing. "I'm looking forward to Monday already."

"Me too. Goodbye, both." And with that Georgina was gone.

Me too? Fran was staring at her. "*What?*"

Fran turned away back to her work. "Nothing."

Never had *nothing* sounded less like nothing.

❖

Molly had successfully managed to avoid Evelyn in the first hour or so of Monday morning. Not that it had been easy. She had been forced to hide in the loo at the sound of Evelyn's stiletto heels clipping their way just round the corner towards her.

And now Molly sat on the same bench with the same knot in her stomach. This time, however, her nerves had less to do with the imminent arrival of Georgina and far more to do with Evelyn catching her just off on a lovely trip to the records office. It didn't help that they would be going in Daisy May who was unable to leave or arrive anywhere without causing a stir.

Molly took a shifty glance around the foyer. Fred was trying to explain something to a visitor. By Fred's animated hand gestures, the visitor was either hard of hearing or unacquainted with his Birmingham accent. Just beyond the foyer in the gift shop, a child and mother were locked in a battle of wills over a plastic dinosaur. It was clear that no one was remotely interested in Molly or her illicit meeting. *Okay, this is good.*

With every question the beautiful watercolour posed, Molly felt more determined that if there was a chance that Edith had painted the portrait, then she deserved surely to have her name associated with it. It was a matter of right. The omission of Edith, not only from the painting's provenance but by all accounts from history itself, Molly knew in her heart should be corrected. Was this the occasion to put into practice Fran's advice, to achieve what you believed was right but that still delivered for the powers that be? Should she find the moment the trip to the records office would afford to mention the Wright room? It felt wrong—a duplicitous breach of trust. And Molly wanted Georgina to trust her, she wanted—

"You seem deep in thought," Georgina said, with an amused smile. Molly stood to her feet in surprise. "Hi. Sorry, I didn't see you arrive. I was just, you know, caught up in thinking about…the portrait."

How did Georgina manage to always look so hot? She was dressed in black tailored trousers combined with a fine charcoal-grey polo neck jumper. Her coat rested over her arm in an effortlessly casual way. It took all of Molly's reserve not to run her hand along Georgina's arm to touch what she guessed was the softest of cashmere wool.

"Shall we go?" Georgina gestured for Molly to lead the way.

"Yes." Molly cast a final glance to the top of the empty staircase, half expecting Evelyn to suddenly appear, apparition-like. She held her breath all the way out of the museum. She looked across the square to where Daisy May waited patiently, if not discreetly, with her yellow paint shining out rather than blending in. Molly could only hope that Evelyn hadn't chosen this moment to admire the view from her office window. "Okay, so, about my car, Daisy May—"

"Daisy May?" Georgina looked across at Molly and smiled. "That's cute."

Cute? Was she flirting? Of course she's not flirting. "Yes. I inherited her from my gran. Needless to say, she's super precious to me. She is cute, absolutely, but also rather elderly and I think at times a little oversensitive maybe. When I first inherited her, I took a night course in beginner's mechanics to care for her. Looking back, that was such a smart move."

"She breaks down a lot?" Georgina asked, looking at the bright yellow Mini in front of her.

Molly dug in her bag for her car keys. "Let's put it this way—over the years she has earned herself the not very flattering nickname Daisy May Start, Daisy May Not."

Georgina laughed. "She's very cool. She suits you."

Molly's heart surged with the compliment. For if she was not mistaken, Georgina had just in a roundabout way told her she was cool. At least that's what it felt like. "Thank you. Although you may want to reserve your compliments when you hear that we have only a fifty-fifty chance that she will start, and if she does start only a fifty-fifty chance that we'll make it all the way there. And"—Molly opened the passenger door—"if we make it there, only a fifty-fifty chance that we'll make it back."

"Goodness."

Molly climbed in next to Georgina who was finding it difficult to settle as she tried to find a place for her legs.

"Sorry." Molly wiped condensation from the windscreen. "I would suggest we move the seat back but then—"

"There would only be a fifty-fifty chance it would move," Georgina said, smiling.

"Yes," Molly giggled. "You're close. I was going to say that the last time I attempted to adjust the passenger seat was when Fran complained. For some reason the lever, yes, that one by your leg, adjusts just the seat back. Fran spent half an hour lying completely flat."

Georgina burst out laughing. Catching her breath she said, "You're not joking, are you?"

"Nope. So maybe rest your legs to the side." Molly accidentally checked she was in neutral gear with Georgina's knee. "Oh God, sorry, I didn't mean to. So that's not going to work—"

Georgina laughed again. "It's fine, Molly. Let's go."

"Okay, fingers crossed. Daisy May, we have an important guest. No antics." Daisy May started first time and, to her credit, made it to the records office with only one kangaroo hill start.

Chapter Nine

The records office, housed in a red brick former junior school on the edge of the city, was not Molly's most favourite go-to destination. It was such a tense and serious environment. It certainly didn't feel like the kind of place where you'd excitedly discover things. It felt more the kind of place where things were left behind, destined to be stored away and forgotten.

Molly watched as the receptionist wrote in immaculate handwriting the key words of Molly's request on to a slip of paper.

"Edith…Hewitt…Abolitionist," the receptionist said, as if deliberating over every letter.

"Yes, that's right." Molly suppressed the urge to ask *Can we hurry, please.* She looked at her watch. If she was to stand a chance to make it back without her absence being noticed and in time for Georgina to catch her train to London, then she figured they had less than an hour with Edith's archive. She glanced across to Georgina who was standing in the reception lounge typing on her phone. Molly could only imagine how busy Georgina was and how every minute of her time had a financial cost, and here was Molly spending her time with what felt like reckless abandon. She dreaded to think of the bill she might send Evelyn. Should she have rung ahead and had everything waiting for them? *Bugger.*

"Through the door on the left. Hand this slip to the assistant who will bring your material to you. No bags, no coats, no photos, and all phones on mute."

Georgina approached the reception desk and with a smile asked, "Are we being let in?"

"Almost. We're not allowed coats and bags. Just the stationery we need." Molly slipped off her coat, and to her surprise, Georgina took it from her and handed their coats to the woman at reception. "Thanks."

"No problem. I tend to travel light. I find it's easier that way. Although that's only thanks to technology. But the downside of being connected is that it's hard to disconnect. So thanks for today. I meant what I said Friday—it's a relief to have a distraction."

Molly basked in Georgina's warm and appreciative smile. "That's okay, and thanks for keeping me company again."

"My pleasure. I hope Edith's archive will have the answers for us."

Molly followed Georgina's gaze to the door that led to the reading room. "Yes, me too."

They found a table at the back which looked out towards the reception and the tall shelves filled with books and folders. The sweeping burr of the photocopier broke the silence in the otherwise deathly quiet room.

"It feels like I'm about to take an exam," Georgina said.

Molly whispered, "Yes, it's a bit formal isn't it? Oh, wait, here he comes."

A tall thin man, whose jumper matched the washed-out pallor of someone who needed more sun, rested three slim bound volumes onto the table.

"I'm sorry," Molly lifted a volume and glanced inside at the collection of handwritten verses. "But is this all there is?"

"This is everything that came up under your search terms."

Molly's heart sank. "But are you sure you didn't come across a scrapbook or something like that?"

The man shook his head. "Like I said, this is everything."

"Okay, well, thanks anyway." The man walked away. Fran was right. Either Edith had pretty much been overlooked, or at best miscatalogued and absorbed within Josephine's archive. Molly looked at her watch. There was no time to request Josephine's archives. She felt utterly sick at the thought that she had brought Georgina here for no reason. A pleasant distraction was one thing, but a complete waste of time was another, surely.

She glanced at Georgina who'd begun to gently leaf through a volume.

She looked up at Molly. "Looks like Edith was religious, as there are lots of what read like prayers spanning several years."

"Really? I thought it was poetry? Does it confirm anywhere that these are her prayer books? Is there anything in the front matter, on the title page perhaps?"

"Yes. She's written Edith Hewitt, Leicester, and the date. This one's August 1831. On first glance there's one volume per year until 1833."

"Okay, good. Everything helps us build a picture. I was just thinking—"

"That Edith's archive might have gotten mixed up with Josephine's? After all, Fran mentioned a scrapbook, didn't she? And it's not here."

"Yes, exactly. I'm very sorry if I've wasted your morning."

Georgina briefly rested a hand lightly on Molly's back. "It's been fun. Let's see what we can discover in the next half hour. Then why don't we come back when we both have more time. Yes?"

"That sounds like a plan. It's just…"

"Just what?"

She needed to tell her that Evelyn had asked her to draw a line under the research for the painting. And every minute she sat here with Georgina without discussing the Wright room she was surely risking the wrath of her boss. But then she didn't want their research to end—not for Edith and not for them. Because then they would have to talk about the Wright room and everything would change, wouldn't it? She didn't want things to change. She wanted Georgina to look at her as she was looking at her now, with no barriers between them. "Nothing. Yes, let's come back."

"Great. Although to be honest, Friday afternoons are still best for me. I'm guessing they won't open on request?"

"Sadly, I wouldn't think so. I tell you what, I'll come again at some point this week. I'll request all of Josephine's archive to review and we can meet up at the museum on Friday for me to report back. Four, again? What do you think? Unless you're not due back—"

"No, I can come back then. Excellent. Thank you." Georgina looked directly into Molly's eyes.

Molly got the sense Georgina wanted to say something else, but she let her gaze fall away back to the prayer book.

As Georgina began to leaf through the pages again a piece of paper folded into three along its length slipped out from between the cover and the title page. She picked it up and unfolded it. "Could this be something?"

Molly carefully inspected the loose paper. Just as with the discovery of Edith's inscription, she had the most peculiar sensation that she might have been the first person to open the paper since it had been folded and tucked away.

The creases were ingrained so deeply Molly was aware that she needed to take the utmost care not to cause the fragile paper to tear at its folded edges.

"Can you tell what it is?" Georgina asked.

Speaking at just above a whisper, Molly said, "It's a page from some sort of petition for the, quote, *immediate abolition of the institution of slavery conducted for the*"—Molly lightly traced her forefinger underneath the words—"*London Female Anti-Slavery Society.*" A note had been written in pencil at the top right hand side. It read, *3,025 signatures, time not allowing more. 1833. E.H.* "E. H.—Edith Hewitt." Molly cast her eye down the page to see a whole list of women's names, with Leicester addresses. "Edith collected about three thousand signatures from women in Leicester petitioning for the abolition of slavery. Wow."

"Can I see?" Georgina gently took the page from Molly. "That's a lot of signatures, although it looks like someone changed their mind." Georgina tipped the page towards Molly. Sure enough, one name, Mrs. Charlton, Granby Street, Occupation: frame-knitter, had been scored through.

Molly stared at the woman's name crossed out.

Spring 1833
Josephine and Edith's office
Chambers of Brancaster and Lane Solicitors, New Street, Leicester

"How dare she change her mind. Can the poor enslaved souls change their minds? No."

"Edith, please calm down."

"*I'd like to think more on the subject. I fear I have acted in haste.* That's what she said when I challenged her. In *haste*?"

"You challenged her. Edith, no, we spoke about this. Only this morning."

"Haste? If we do not act with haste. If we do not demand the immediate abolition, then those, and we both know who I mean, will be content to drag their heels to satisfy the will of plantation owners. It is a farce to suggest that slavery will die a natural death—a gradual end is no end. We must sign slavery's death warrant once and for all." Edith raised the pages of the petition in the air. "Mrs. Charlton notwithstanding." Edith flopped onto the chair at the table where Josephine sat quietly writing a letter.

"Have you finished?" Josephine asked, fighting the smile pressing at her lips.

Edith plucked the letter from Josephine. "I have only just begun. Why are you writing to that prisoner yet again?"

"I am minded to believe that my letters offer succour in between my visits."

"How you can face to be in those places is beyond me."

"He has no one, Edith. No one cares."

"Could that not be a good thing? Surely it is a mercy if no one is waiting for the release and pardon that will never come. Too often more than just the prisoner find themselves incarcerated by hopeless hope."

"I for one will never abandon hope. It is all we have. How you can have such tireless compassion for the slaves of the West Indies and such little sympathy for the prisoner on your doorstep? Now give me back my letter, Edith. Give."

Edith stood holding the letter high in the air. "Because the slaves' only crime was the misfortune of their birth."

"And my father argues the same each and every day for the prisoners here." Josephine reached up, only for Edith to stand on tiptoe. "I do not have the time for your games. Edith, for pity's sake."

Edith moved the paper from hand to hand, just avoiding Josephine's grasp.

"Well, if that is how it is to be." Josephine pinched at Edith's waist causing her to scream laughter into the air and to bend double, allowing Josephine to grasp the paper. She moved to turn away and Edith held her by the wrist.

"Wait," Edith said softly. "Please." Edith pulled Josephine into her and wrapped her arms around her and buried her face in her neck.

"Please let me go, Edith. Don't you understand it is an intolerable agony to be close to you."

"And don't *you* understand that not touching you and endeavouring just to be colleagues and no more than best friends is an agony I cannot tolerate."

Josephine held Edith away from her. "But we agreed and we have done so well—"

"I did not agree. Why would anyone in their right mind agree to lose a love? But how could I not continue to see you?"

"You have not lost me. You will never lose me."

"But that is not true is it? Is it?"

Josephine shook her head. "I will not lie to you."

"But yet you are content to deceive your own heart?"

As Molly carefully refolded the petition, Georgina flicked to the last few pages in the volume of prayers. "Goodness."

"What?" Molly looked at Georgina's face creased with a frown.

Georgina shared the open page with Molly, showing her the prayer she had stumbled upon. With a hushed voice Georgina read, *"Lord, today I have been burdened with such sadness that I cannot bear to utter even my own name. To speak, to write is to feel pain. I ask no more than tomorrow my burden will be lighter and my grief more tolerable. I ask this in your name.*"

Molly sat silently with Georgina. They were so close now she could feel the brush of Georgina's sleeve against her arm.

Georgina eventually said, "That's so sad."

"What was the date for this volume? Yes, there." Molly found the title page for Georgina.

Georgina leaned in. "Twenty-eighth of August, 1833. So that was the year after Josephine's portrait was painted." Georgina paused and quickly rechecked the dates in the other two volumes. "This was the last volume. It makes you wonder what made Edith so sad, doesn't it?"

Molly silently nodded as she reread the prayer. "That's so strange. Don't hold me to it, but I'm pretty sure that this prayer is more or less the same time that the Act of Abolition received royal assent. Surely she would have been celebrating?"

Georgina gave a heavy sigh and leaned back in her chair. "We're certainly missing something, aren't we? We know so little about her. We don't even know how old she was. Is there any way we can find out?"

"Yes, I may be able to. I'm guessing she'll feature in the local parish registers. I'll try to get a sense of her for us." Molly stood. "So...do you want to risk a lift home? There's a taxi rank just over the road if you'd prefer to grab a taxi."

"Won't Daisy May be offended?" Georgina rested the prayer book back with the others.

Molly laughed. "Yes, possibly."

"Well, Daisy May it is then." Georgina's smile lit somewhere deep in Molly's heart and she could feel it burning bright. It took all of her self-control to turn away to catch the assistant's eye and signal they were finished.

Within a matter of moments the prayer books had gone again, back into the store, back to where they kept the past dark and silent.

❖

"So how long does it normally take to get her going?" Georgina asked, amused at Molly's mortified expression.

"I am so, so sorry." Molly was looking around her. Rain had forced her back into the car from having her head stuck under the bonnet. "Normally I blow on something or oil something or tighten something or say something encouraging, and we're off again. She does have a thing about rain, though." Molly shrugged. "I'll ring the AA. I'll understand if you want to call a taxi."

The last thing Georgina thought to do was leave Molly stranded alone. "As I see it, we're in it together."

"Thanks, and thanks for being so cool about everything."

"You didn't think I would be?" Georgina wanted to know what Molly thought of her. This question felt, in that moment, so important. Was Molly enjoying being with her as much as she delighted in the mere mention of Molly's name?

"Funnily enough, I haven't given any previous thought to the scenario where I've broken down in my car, all but hijacking one of the museum's most important funders. And I've no prawn vol-au-vent or glass of chilled Sauvignon blanc to offer." Molly shook her head. She could only imagine what Evelyn would say.

As Molly made her call, Georgina wanted to ask, *Is that how you see me—as an important museum funder and nothing more?* But then, she was an important museum funder, and how else could Molly think of her? Right there and then, she just wanted to be a woman in the car with the woman from the square, telling her how beautiful she thought she was. Telling her how much she had meant to her this last year and, moreover, how much she meant to her now.

"All done," Molly said with a bounce in her seat. Her movement disturbed an empty frame, which slipped from the back seat to rest between them. "Oops. I'll just shove that back again."

Georgina felt the warmth of Molly's body briefly press against her as Molly stretched to slot it back into place.

Molly's car shared the same appearance as her office. It was crammed full with the extraordinary and the ordinary. Several large unfinished paintings rested against the back seat, propped up by an apple crate containing unfired clay pottery of all shapes and sizes. Plastic boxes were crammed with art materials, particularly half-squeezed tubes of paint of all colours and types. Molly just caught a wicker picnic basket that threatened to slide into Georgina's lap.

"You weren't kidding"—Georgina looked at the basket newly wedged behind the back seat—"when you said you were a keen picnicker."

Molly laughed. "Nope. I'm impressed you remembered."

Georgina felt her cheeks burn. She felt as if she'd be found out. As if Molly could tell that she could remember pretty much word for word every conversation they'd had. It wasn't as if she was even deliberately remembering—it was more she found them impossible to forget.

Molly's curls had frizzed a little in the humidity and her freckled cheeks were matched with a few remaining speckles of rainwater. She looked simply beautiful. How Georgina managed not to reach across and brush Molly's fallen hair from her face she did not know. How she stopped herself from stroking the droplets of rain from her cheeks she could not say. And how she didn't tell Molly that she was simply the most natural and beautiful woman she'd ever met, goodness only knew. Instead she sat there smiling back at Molly as Molly smiled at her.

Molly's smile faded.

"What is it?" Georgina asked.

"Oh, nothing," Molly replied, with a shake of the head.

Georgina could tell Molly was lying and that something was on her mind. But it wasn't any of her business. She should change the subject. "You certainly have a full car." Georgina gestured to the back seat.

"It's not usually quite that full. I'm running some art education sessions at a local school who tend not to visit the museum. I don't know whether it's the teachers or the parents who are resistant to visiting, but I figured it wasn't fair on the kids to miss out on the benefits of art. So I've invited myself round, so to speak. They kind of couldn't say no."

"I imagine you're hard to refuse." Georgina stopped herself short. That definitely sounded like a flirtatious comment, but before she had chance to qualify what she meant, Molly replied with a mischievous glint in her eye.

"I can be very persuasive."

But then Georgina noticed that the glint faded quickly along with Molly's smile once more.

"What is it? After all, you have me captured. My full attention is yours." And it struck Georgina that for the first time in however many years she hadn't looked at her phone or drifted off mid-conversation to more important thoughts. She was utterly captivated and it felt really good. "Molly? It's okay. Just say what's on your mind. Only if you want to of course."

"Well, there is something. Something…" Molly began to fiddle with the seat belt. "It's something Evelyn wanted me to raise with you. For what it's worth, I think it's a good something."

Georgina's stomach tightened. "Evelyn? Go on."

"It was important, as you know, to your father that the artwork bequeathed by the Wright Foundation to the museum should be accessible to the public. We promised this to him and we earnestly want to keep that promise."

"Okay."

"We want to dedicate a permanent exhibition space in the museum for the bequest. Evelyn wants to call it the Wright room."

"I see. And this of course requires me to hand over the remaining bequeathed works in the house so the museum can fulfil their promise to my father."

"Possibly. Well, yes. But I can only imagine how hard it is to let go of his things. I'm not sure if I was in your position that I would want to either."

Molly looked really uncomfortable. It was not the expression of someone trying to manipulate someone.

"Clever woman." Georgina's father had met with Evelyn on many occasions. He described her to Georgina as shrewd. He'd respected her as one respects the guile and cunning of a fox. Fox by name, fox by nature. It was a plan she couldn't say no to, and what's more it had been asked of her by Molly. Had Evelyn seen something in Georgina's reaction to Molly? Had she been read like a book? Her tell revealed?

"I find her intimidating." Molly shrugged.

"I can imagine. So the time you're giving to the portrait and today at the records office—all part of her master plan?"

Molly shook her head. "No, today was something I wanted to do for Edith and for…well because it's the right thing to do, isn't it?" Molly turned in her seat to face Georgina with her knees resting towards her. "Imagine painting a portrait that has hung on a family wall and no one knowing that you painted it. And if, for argument's sake, she was Josephine's lover, then Edith has been just blanked out, erased as if she'd never mattered. And she would have mattered—she would have mattered to Josephine." Molly cheeks flushed. "And it's not just Edith. There are so many minority histories that have been lost, and their voices silenced. And do you know what's really crap, sinister even? Museums know this. They pay lip service, with temporary exhibitions and so forth, but do they embed real change, real awareness in their permanent displays, are they going back into records and actively looking for these histories? No. Or at least, very rarely. They blame resources. I blame them." Molly brushed back her hair from her face. "I'm sorry. I'm ranting."

Georgina shook her head. "Don't apologize for caring."

"I do care—very much. It's something that I want to focus on with my work. Do you know what worries me the most? It's that they're not taking rigorous enough measures to prevent this invisibility from persisting into the future."

Georgina sat up further in her seat. "What measures should they be taking?"

"Well, one measure going forward would be for the Arts Council to make gender, sexuality, race, and religion specific and required fields in the records database. Simple, effective, achievable. As things stand at the moment, if a museum chooses not to specify and enforce the collection of this sensitive data"—Molly shrugged—"then ultimately, beyond the skeleton information required to be recorded for an object, what is collected or rather omitted is entirely at the discretion of the individual museum."

"So this measure would enforce some sort of positive discrimination?"

"Not quite. Cataloguers can note down white, male, Christian, and heterosexual if it fits the history. But *only* if it fits the history."

"So I take it you despair at the focus remaining on the privileged history of white males?"

"Yes. Absolutely."

"And so the plans for a room dedicated to art gifted by generations of wealthy white men to the Wright Foundation to reduce death duties are at odds with what you believe?" Molly swallowed hard and her cheeks drained of colour. "I'm sorry, I wasn't trying to catch you out. I can see it's not fair of me to put you in this position."

"It's okay. I'm not naive. I understand that the museum needs the support of important benefactors." Molly paused. "Your support. And that bequests are fundamentally important to a museum. But it upsets me that other initiatives, such as community orientated projects, can sometimes not be seen as a priority. You see, they want to put the Wright room in the annex which was originally earmarked as a community space."

"I see."

"But then of course it was your father's wish to gift his collection, and that's important too."

Georgina nodded. "Well, I think our first meeting on the subject of the Wright room has been very useful. Thank you."

"That's great."

"And for what it's worth"—Georgina's breath caught in her throat as an urge to cry surprised her—"my sense is that my father's collection will be in good hands."

Molly blushed deeply. "Thank you."

A loud bang on the window made them both jump. The windows had steamed up and Molly wound down her window and squinted into the rain.

A large man in a fluorescent jacket leaned down to look into the car. "You don't see many of these on the roads any more," he said, patting the roof. "Any idea what's wrong, love? Control said it just stopped."

Molly shouted, "She's not very keen on the rain and cold!"

The man laughed. "I'll warm my hands then, shall I?"

Molly said, with an expression of complete seriousness. "Yes, I think that would help."

❖

As Georgina's train to London drew away from the platform, she couldn't help but notice that her chest felt lighter. It almost seemed easier to breathe. Spending time with Molly felt like such a relief and a complete breath of fresh air. And more than that, Molly's passion for justice had renewed an energy in Georgina. It was the same energy that had dissipated the very moment her father had told her he was dying. She'd lost so much that day, including hope and positivity and even the reason for everything she once cared about. Nothing seemed to matter until perhaps now.

She looked out at the eclectic city diluting to the mundane suburban sprawl. She turned away from the window, opened her laptop, and began tapping a quick reminder note. She paused for a second and sat staring at the screen. Her thoughts drifted again to Molly and to her earnest expression as she had confessed her worries and hopes.

"Tickets, please."

The sweep of the door to first class closed behind the approaching conductor. She typed a few words before he arrived at her side.

Instinctively she half closed her screen from view, casting into shadow the words *the Wright Community Room and Gallery.*

❖

"I'm very late, aren't I?"

Fran looked up at Molly and then at the clock. It was just before two o'clock.

"Surely your question to me should be has anyone noticed your absence for the last three and a bit hours?"

"Yes, answer that one. I'm starved."

"No."

"Phew." Molly sat heavily down on the edge of Fran's desk.

Fran reached down with a groan and rummaged in her bag. She retrieved an apple and handed it to Molly.

Through a large bite of apple, Molly mumbled, "Thanks."

"So I take it that it went well at the records office, given how long you were there?"

"Define *well.*"

"You found everything you needed to know about Edith, including the painter of Josephine's portrait, and at the same time you won over Georgina Wright."

"Sort of. We did come across a random page from a petition on behalf of the London Female Anti-Slavery Society which was really interesting and confirmed Edith's part in campaigning."

"Did you? That's excellent. I don't remember anything like that."

"That's probably because it was tucked inside one of Edith's prayer books. It literally all but fell into Georgina's lap. But honestly, Fran, although the petition was great, it was a prayer that Georgina came across which was so incredibly sad. It stopped us in our tracks."

Fran nodded. "Yes, that happens. Once you start to explore an archive and become invested, I've often found it can be incredibly moving and, be warned, darned addictive. You have to be clear what you are trying to achieve to prevent yourself from getting lost amongst its treasures."

"Yep. I get that. Don't worry, I'm absolutely focused."

"And absolutely covered in oil." Fran pointed to Molly's oil-stained dress. Molly watched as Fran's eyes grew wide. "Oh, Molly, please don't tell me you took Georgina Wright in Daisy May and then broke down."

"No, no, no. It was a good thing, as it happened." Molly began hunting for a cloth to clean her dress.

"I'm struggling to see how Georgina Wright stranded in Daisy May was a good thing. Try in that box."

"It was good because it gave me a chance to talk to Georgina about the plans for a Wright room, and I think I may have helped Evelyn. At least I hope I have." Molly's stomach dropped at the recollection of all the critical things she'd said about the museum. "I got on my hobby horse about equality and museums and might have suggested that the museum should be doing more."

"Well, yes, they should."

"But what if it gets back to Evelyn?" Molly dug out a square of material left over from a medieval monk's habit and dabbed at her dress, only to give up and rest again on Fran's desk.

"Let's hope it does. So there's going to be a Wright room then?"

Bugger. Was it too late to say no? "Yes. I've been trying to build up the courage to mention it."

"I don't understand why would you need to build up the courage." Fran's expression fell into a stony fixed glare. "Unless of course—"

"I tried to say the annex had been reserved for community use. I promise I did."

"I believe you. I don't for a minute blame *you* Molly. So did Georgina approve of the idea of a Wright room?"

"I think so. I ranted on so much it's hard to tell what she thought."

"Well her father's bequeathed his art to the museum, so she might as well hurry up and hand it over, whether she likes it or not."

"Actually she said she thought her father's collection would be in good hands."

"Really?" A smile broke through Fran's frown. "Then I think you'll find you've won Georgina Wright over. So what's the next step?"

"I'll go back to the records office sometime this week. I have half a memory they open late one night. I think it was Tuesday."

"Wednesday. They're open until seven thirty."

"Really? Excellent. I was thinking after work would be better, less...complicated. And then I'll be ready to update Georgina when we meet again on Friday."

Fran raised her eyebrows. "She caught you off guard again then?"

"*No*, I mean we—What are you implying?"

"I'm not implying anything. I'm merely observing that you're spending a lot of time with someone you don't want to spend time with. And it has not escaped my notice that Georgina is also giving a lot of time to this *research*." Molly shrugged. Fran continued, "I would have thought she'd want it all wrapped up as soon as possible—all of it, the portrait, the bequest. Job done. And then she could return to her life in London."

"I suppose." Molly folded her arms, suppressing a sudden ache in her chest sparked by the thought of not seeing Georgina again. "She does seem really keen on our work together."

"Yes, she does, doesn't she?" Fran's eyes twinkled with suggestion. Molly stood up. "It's just work."

"Of course. Although I am wondering how you plan to keep working on the portrait when if I remember correctly you said that further research made Evelyn tense."

Molly looked at the ground. "She's told me to stop work on the portrait."

"*Molly*. Evelyn has expressly asked you not to, and you've carried on anyway? What are you thinking? You know you can't keep avoiding her."

"I'm not avoiding her."

"You all but ran down the corridor earlier. I thought there was a fire."

"I was late." Molly put her hands on her hips. "Anyway, I figure I can do what I want with my own time. Hence Wednesday night."

"Oh, Molly, please tread carefully. Whilst I'm all for acts of defiant rebellion, you need to be honest with yourself what this is all about and whether it's worth the standoff."

"It's for Edith. And of course it is."

"Are you sure it's just for Edith?"

Molly went quiet. She wasn't sure. Since meeting Georgina, she wasn't sure of anything.

"I'm going to say something else." Fran folded her arms. "You need to remember that Georgina Wright is an important funder for this museum. There's a lot at stake."

"I know."

"Good."

Molly moved the pile of paper wallets and slumped down in her chair. There staring her right in the face, resting wrapped on her desk, was Josephine's portrait.

"Josephine's portrait is back from the conservator," Molly said. "Did you know?"

"We pretty much share the same air molecules. I know everything that happens in this office whether I wish to or not."

"I don't like to unwrap it." Molly hovered her hands over the outside.

"Then my advice is to return it as is to Georgina. You know it's time."

Molly shook her head. "But I haven't finished my research." She began to feel a terrible panic. Returning the painting would feel like saying goodbye. But goodbye to who? Josephine and Edith, or Georgina? Either way Molly wasn't ready to let go.

CHAPTER TEN

What had changed? At what point had her perception of Georgina shifted from the frosty woman who had undermined her in front of Evelyn, to the woman her heart now ached for? Molly tapped her pencil against her bottom lip.

At what point did someone enter your heart and become so precious to you that you panicked at the thought you might not see them again or you might somehow let them down or disappoint them? When did they become the default person for your fantasies and hopes? And when did a stranger become the person you suddenly decided to take risks for?

Molly had so many questions fogging her thoughts that acting without thinking too much about what she was doing was helping.

It helped her to form a rudimentary plan. If Evelyn confronted her about progress with Georgina, then she would say that she had spoken to Georgina about the Wright room and that she was hopeful of the outcome. Furthermore, if pressed about the painting, Molly would reply that the matter was in hand, which it was after all.

It helped her to make the call to the records office to book this evening for her research and to request Josephine's and Edith's archives ahead of her visit.

Sadly, there was nothing to help her not feel a little daunted by the pile of paper that sat waiting on the long desk in front of her.

She glanced around the deserted reading room. She'd chosen the same seat that she had occupied just a few days ago. She couldn't bring herself to look at the empty chair next to her.

Right, focus. She would look for anything that might link Edith to the painting. Every small detail would matter.

But where on earth should she begin?

Sifting through the archive, her attention was immediately caught by a small tan leather notebook. A thin piece of cream ribbon frayed at its end bound the notebook closed. Could she open it? Should she? Teasing the ribbon apart and releasing the pages to flutter free was like releasing an undergarment. It felt illicit and deeply intimate.

It seemed to be some sort of logbook. Her breath caught at the sight of the initials *EH* marked in pencil on the back of the front cover. Why had this just been swept up in Josephine's archive? This was Edith's book. *Edith's*, not Josephine's. How easily and how indiscriminately Edith's past had been absorbed away.

She took a long deliberate breath. Her anger wasn't helping Edith.

She returned her focus to the contents, where every now and then a page was given a date and the dates seemed to run sequentially. Molly turned a page to find a drawing of a man with a really big nose. *WW* was written in small letters underneath. William Wilberforce? It was more a cartoon than a piece of art. She couldn't help but smile. By the side of the man were the words *And you say we are brazen faced?* On the opposite side was the drafting of a poem, declaring female resistance and call to duty. It was titled "Onward Defiance." It was a good drawing. Wait, Edith could draw?

Where was the scrapbook Fran mentioned? With renewed purpose Molly began to leaf through the archives once more, setting each item carefully aside. And then, half buried, revealing itself like the seabed in the ebbing tide, was the unmistakable shape of a scrapbook.

Molly's heart thumped.

She looked at her watch. It was seven o'clock. In half an hour the records office would close. *Please let there be something in here.*

She carefully opened the scrapbook, and a world opened before her. There were programs for events and rallies along with pressed dried grasses and flowers. A note, a line of memory had been written with each item fixed to the stiff textured paper. A blade of pressed dried grass was accompanied with the line *A wonderful picnic and walk with Jo in Bradgate Park. Chanced upon a sleeping doe.* This was Edith's scrapbook. These were *her* treasured memories.

Clippings from newspapers had been pasted next to each other. Molly leaned in further and read the *Leicester Chronicle*'s passage on the lighting of the first gas lamps on City Walk. *Crowds had gathered*, the article said. *The future had been lit before them.* She checked the date. The faded ink read September 1832. For some reason the clipping had been scored with a heavy pencil border. Molly knew that every mark and every underline meant something, but what? Evelyn was right. What on earth did she think she would find?

Dispirited, she eased the scrapbook to her side, and with a heavy heart she bent her elbows and sank her arms flat against the table, resting her head against her hands with her cheek pressing against the cold wood. She stared at the scrapbook, now level with her eyes. Wait a minute. What was that? Towards the back, a corner of a page protruded, and there was something marked out on it. It couldn't be. Could it?

Molly sat up straight and drew the scrapbook to her once more. At the point of the protruding edge of paper and tucked so deeply in as to be invisible to the casual glance was a collection of charcoal sketches. A couple of the sketches had become unfixed and Molly lifted them gently to rest in front of her.

"Josephine." She lightly traced her fingers just above the soft dust of charcoal lines that defined neck, chin, and the blush of lips.

Was this Edith's work?

Molly searched each sketch for Edith's characteristic *EH*. Nothing. This was her scrapbook—there was no question that its contents contained her life with Josephine. It had to be her work. It just had to be. If only she could find some evidence.

Think, Molly Goode. Think. Her gaze drifted with her thoughts once more to the logbook open at the drawing of Wilberforce. She lifted the logbook to rest in her palm and turned each page slowly sensing as much as reading and alive to the shape of the letters that formed the word portrait. Where was the loop of the P or the curl of the R? Or the word Josephine with its gentle sweep downward of the J.

Josephine's name was on nearly every page. It was as if Edith had noted every day they were together and every day they were apart.

Molly looked at her watch. It was twenty past seven.

She urgently scanned every page, and then on almost the last turn of the last page, logged with the date 4th April 1832, was the entry Molly doubted she would ever find.

Words today burn at my lips to speak and smoulder in ink on the page as I write. For I have captured our love in every shade. The sweet stroke of brush upon canvas, the exquisite memory of us. I long to paint you again and know you yet more with every new glance until no part of you is foreign to me.

"Blimey." Molly stared once more at the sketches as doubt in the heat of evidence evaporated away.

April 1832
Chambers of Brancaster and Lane Solicitors, New Street, Leicester

"Please tell me you have finished, Edith. My neck is stiff, not to mention other parts of me which are quite bereft of feeling."

"Just wait and let patience soothe your pain. I'm nearly done." Edith stood back and shook her head.

"I take no confidence from your words when they are undermined by your gestures."

"It is the background. It is too dark. I need something, a wash of white perhaps, to offset the depths of blue. There, yes. Yes."

"Good, then we are done." Josephine slipped from the stool and stretched, holding the small of her back, her chest expanding, while she found new rest in Edith's arms.

"We will never be done." Edith drew Josephine into her body, pressing as if to never let go. "Tell me that much, Jo." She breathed her words between soft kisses brushing against the delicate curve of Josephine's neck.

"Are we quite content that we locked the door?"

"How you worry."

"And how you don't. We will surely invite speculation if we spend too many evenings working late. Please, Edith. We must take care, lest these passions overwhelm us. The choice for our future is not ours to make—you know that as well as I, if not more. It is time for us to see reason. Surely it is time. We must…" Josephine's words were lost with her breath in the moment.

Edith guided Josephine to the floor and her dress soaked up the drips of paint expanding in wet circles of colour. She untied the ribbons of soft corset, releasing a gasp from Josephine to escape into the evening air.

"I hate that I need you so." Josephine's words, sharp with pain, cut at her lips to speak.

"And I hate your words. They wound me, and one day"—Edith slipped her hands underneath Josephine's skirt—"they will end my life more surer than a knife or gun or burning pyre."

Josephine let out a cry as Edith found the place which spoke more clearly than words could ever do.

"Are you finished?" The archive assistant arrived to fidget at her side.

"Yes, thank you." Molly managed a tired half smile. "What time is it?"

The assistant gathered the papers together. "Seven thirty."

"Right." Molly reached for her things, casting a last look at the scrapbook that held fast within its pages, tight-lipped, a secret passion that history with all its casual omissions had complicitly kept.

CHAPTER ELEVEN

Molly sat at her kitchen table poking spaghetti bolognese around her plate. She was finding it hard to focus on her tea, in fact, on anything other than Edith. She kept imagining how hard it would have been to love another woman at that time. To feel obliged to hide true love underneath the pretence of romantic friendship or passionate comradeship. How narrow your choices, if they felt like choices at all.

What would Georgina think of her findings? When should she tell her? She looked at her watch. It was nine o'clock. Was it too late to send an email?

The tang of the ragu sauce tingled at her mouth. Georgina wouldn't be obliged to reply tonight, would she? Molly reached across for her laptop and opened her email. She scrolled down to their correspondence from just over a fortnight ago and hovered her cursor over Georgina's name. It brought up the empty outline of a person. Molly felt a twinge of disappointment that she could not see Georgina's face. When had she started to need to see her face? This was not good. She must keep a grip on her feelings before she embarrassed herself and everyone else.

Keep it professional. Taking a deep breath she began to type.

Dear Georgina,

As agreed, I have returned to the records office and conducted further research of archives related to both Edith Hewitt and Josephine Wright. I am pleased to inform you that I have been able to identify the painter of Josephine's portrait as Edith Hewitt. A number of preliminary sketches for the work were found within a scrapbook. I was further able to corroborate Edith as the artist by a passage in a logbook entry.

I am really pleased to give you this news and I look forward to discussing this and other matters on Friday.

With kind regards,
Molly

Molly reread the words to ensure they spoke of detached professionalism. With a final check, she pressed send. Her heart fluttered with the thought of Georgina reading her message and thinking of her, if only for the briefest of moments. *Oh, for God's sake. That's enough.* She'd done what she needed to do, and Georgina would likely not even respond, as she was seeing her in a few days anyway.

Molly stared at the inbox. She hit refresh. Nothing. She waited another minute and pressed refresh again. Still nothing.

Standing with a self-recriminating shake of the head, she firmly shut the laptop with the same determination as someone keeping a lid on something wild that might escape.

She picked up her dinner plate and went to the sink, where she filled a bowl with soapy water. "Yeah, it's official you're the saddest loser—"

Her phone beeped from deep within her bag. She turned off the tap. It was a work email notification. She looked at her laptop. She had intended to count to one hundred but barely managed five before she rushed back to her seat and opened her mail.

That's great news. Thanks! G

Molly looked at the brief reply. There was no *Hi Molly. Look forward to seeing you Friday, Molly. I really fancy you, how about a date, Molly?* Nope. And why would there be? She pushed the chair from under her, grabbed a wine glass, and reached into the fridge for a bottle of Sauvignon blanc. She'd just turned off the kitchen light to head into the sitting room to drown her irrational disappointment in something trashy on the television when her phone beeped again and her laptop screen lit up.

Molly peered back into the kitchen and glared at the screen suspiciously. Nope, she would not look. It was not from Georgina. Was it? No, of course it wasn't. She'd given her reply. Hadn't she?

Molly glanced into the sitting room and then back at the laptop. *Oh, for goodness' sake, just look.*

Molly sat at the kitchen table in the dark. She blinked several times at the message she'd received.

May I ask a favour? Friday is looking horrendous and it is unlikely that I'll make it back to Leicester until late evening. I checked the RO's website and they are open Saturday mornings. Would there be any chance at all that we could meet then? I would love to see the sketches and talk more. Completely understand of course if this is asking too much.

She would love to talk more? It would be specifically about the matter in hand though, right? Yes, and then their conversation no doubt would turn from the painting to the Wright room. And then that conversation in time would be complete. There would be no more reason for them to meet and nothing else to be said.

How could replying to an email make her feel so happy and yet so sad?

Dear Georgina,
Yes, Saturday should be fine. Would ten thirty suit? And shall I meet you there?
Molly

Molly quickly pressed send this time, resisting the urge to second-guess every word.

Georgina's reply was pretty much instant: *Yes. Great!*

Instant and brief.

Should she reply? But there was nothing left to be said. The plan had been made. In the light from her laptop, Molly rummaged in her bag for her diary and found her pencil and marked *Georgina Wright RO 10.30am* in Saturday's entry.

She sat back in her chair tapping at the diary's page and staring at the hypnotic blink of the cursor. Mists of daydreams about Saturday drifted in to cloud the reality of the moment. Georgina would be waiting outside the records office, and Molly would rush up to her and hug her and say *I've missed you.* And Georgina's reply would be a kiss. A perfect kiss from perfect lips…

The tap dripped a series of short plinks into the washing-up bowl, rudely bringing Molly back to the here and now. She looked down at her diary to find that she had doodled a heart around Georgina's name.

Chapter Twelve

"Molly, do you have a moment?" Evelyn stood in the doorway of the Victorian gallery and watched as Molly's school group filed out past her. "I hope you've enjoyed your time with us today, everyone," Evelyn said, her fixed smile flitting from one child's head to another. The teacher, who had spent the entire class chatting to her colleague, gave a sheepish nod in response.

"Yes, of course," Molly said. "How can I help?" Molly had the thirty seconds that crossing the room gave her to try to decide what Evelyn wanted to talk about. She desperately tried to remember what she had planned to say if Evelyn tackled her on the painting, when a young girl from the class came rushing up to her. "Hello again," Molly said. "Jude, isn't it?"

The girl nodded and blushed. "Here." She thrust a small plain brown gift bag towards Molly.

"Oh." Molly took the bag and peered in to find a small red stone in the shape of a heart. "Thank you. But I'm not sure—"

"I think you're awesome." It looked for all the world like the girl wanted to say so much more as she stood fixed in the tight grip of admiration. Before Molly could say anything the girl ran off.

"It seems you have an admirer." Evelyn gave a wry smile.

"Poor thing. Crushes are so crushing aren't they? I remember I had a crush on my art teacher. She could do no wrong in my eyes. Come to think of it, she's probably the reason I became a curator."

"Molly." Evelyn's voice bristled with impatience.

"Oh yes, I'm sorry. You wanted to ask me something."

"Walk with me." Without waiting, Evelyn left the room.

Every encounter Molly had with Evelyn seemed to be filled with mystery and, therefore, trepidation. Every conversation felt loaded with something other than the simple matter at hand.

Molly hurried after Evelyn, catching her up at reception.

"Fred, do you have the keys to the annex?" Evelyn nodded regally at an elderly couple who were sitting on the foyer's bench. "I do hope you can join us at our lunchtime concert tomorrow," Evelyn said, with a smile of almost pious agony. There was no doubt that Evelyn could turn it on.

Molly waved a quick goodbye to them as she fell into step with Evelyn.

"There has been a development with the Wright room. I wanted to update you." Evelyn's tone gave nothing away.

"A development?"

"Yes." They had reached the annex, and Evelyn unlocked the entrance doors, flinging them back with effortless aplomb.

The room smelled strongly of paint and freshly cut wood. Wedgwood-blue walls offset with ivory picture rails lent the room an imperial grandeur. Slate-grey benches had been pushed temporarily aside to allow for the honey-coloured varnishing of newly laid hardwood floors. *Wow.*

Molly had been in the annex less than a week ago, and it had been an empty space of plaster walls and concrete floors. Did this mean that Evelyn had heard from Georgina? Was it full steam ahead? But then surely Evelyn would have said. No. If the room was ready, that was extra pressure on Georgina, wasn't it? Of course. Evelyn was a woman on a mission—that much was clear.

"The room's beautiful." Molly went to the French doors and pressed her hand against the paper sheets taped to the glass, protecting the room from prying eyes. "May I ask, does this mean…"

Evelyn was distracted by an errant paint drip of blue on the white skirting, before her attention turned to other hazards. "I've ordered blinds in addition to the UV light protector film for the windows and doors. Thoughts please, on other measures."

"Yes to blinds. Sensible for both security and environmental control." Molly spun around. "Of course, we'll need to monitor the space to get a sense of humidity, temperature, and so forth. With three outside walls and so much glazing, as the seasons change there's a chance we may need a dehumidifier."

"Good. Investigate and action, please. Anything else?"

"We'll need to look at security and insurance. We will need plinths for the sculptures and possibly glass cabinets to keep the porcelain protected."

"Good. I agree. There is nothing more hazardous than fine bone china in the vicinity of a visitor's elbow. So where were we?"

"You were about to tell me of a development?"

"That's right. I spoke with Georgina Wright this morning, and she updated me about the meeting you had together on Monday."

Molly's legs went instantly weak. She squeezed out, "Monday?"

"Really it's like having a conversation with a parrot. Yes, Monday. Georgina said that she was pleased to have had the opportunity to talk with you, and that she was happy with our plans for a dedicated room for the foundation's bequest. Your conversation had been so helpful it seems that it even inspired her *own* choice of name for the room."

"That's great."

"No, Molly. It's not *great*. The name the Wright room had a certain... clarity of vision. One collection, one purpose, one exclusive experience."

Molly wasn't about to ask what name change Georgina might have requested.

Evelyn shook her head. "The Wright Community Room and Gallery lacks...status. It makes me wonder what it was about your conversation that made Georgina come up with that alternative."

No way. The Wright Community Room and Gallery. Georgina had listened to her? And more than that, she'd heard her. She'd felt it and sensed it and seen it in Georgina's eyes and in her voice. And it seemed that she'd respected her ideas to such an extent that she'd acted on them. Wow.

Evelyn clearly gave up waiting for Molly's explanation. "I have no concept now for the space. If it's mixed purpose..." The phrase *mixed purpose* caused Evelyn to suck her cheeks in as if sucking on a lemon. "I do not appreciate *surprises*. Is that clear?" And with a glare that chilled Molly to the bone, Evelyn left.

Molly slumped to the floor.

"Why does Evelyn look like she's chewing on a wasp?" Fran stood at the door of the annex with her hands on her hips, casting an unmistakably suspicious glance around the room. "So this is the Wright room then?"

"Well—"

"I managed to pin Evelyn down yesterday—sadly only metaphorically—and she was obliged to admit the necessity for a change of focus, as she put it, for the annex."

"Fran—"

"I absolutely hate that I like the room."

"It looks great, doesn't it? I honestly think that the Wright Community Room and Gallery is going to be awesome."

"What?"

"Yep. Name change." Molly leaped to her feet, rushed to Fran, and gave her a hug.

"For goodness' sake, let go of me. And tell me everything." Fran gingerly took a seat on a newly painted bench. "Come sit."

"Actually I have two awesome pieces of news."

"Excellent. Start with the name change."

"Okay. Well, obviously, you know about Monday's meeting and that I spoke to Georgina about the need for the museum to do more for equality and diversity et cetera."

"Yes, yes. Go on."

"Well, this morning Georgina spoke to Evelyn and confirmed that she was happy with the idea of a Wright room. What's more, she said that chatting with me had inspired her to come up with the revised name. She listened to me Fran. She *really* listened."

"And I'm *really* impressed. What a classy thing to do—but then her father was like that. I am now very excited about your other news."

"I know who painted Josephine's portrait."

"No—so you found this out last night?"

"Yes. It's Edith Hewitt."

"Edith? So Georgina's hunch was spot on?"

"Yep. You see, I requested Josephine's archive alongside Edith's. I found sketches for the portrait all but hidden away in the scrapbook, and then an entry in a logbook made a direct and explicitly passionate reference to Edith painting Josephine. I know there's still an element of speculation perhaps, but the room for doubt is far less. Edith was the artist and her lover."

"What a twenty-four hours." Fran stood and examined her skirt for paint. "Does Georgina know?"

"I emailed her last night to provide her with an update and she asked if we could meet again at the records office for her to see the sketches. So we're meeting there Saturday."

"Saturday?"

"Yes. Don't look at me like that. It was her idea."

"So Evelyn's sour face was because you told her you were carrying on researching the painting with Georgina?"

"Not exactly. That was the name change. Before you say anything, I know there's a lot at stake."

"I've said everything I care to on the matter." Fran gestured for them to head back to their office. "I can't help seeing that your unconventional methods are achieving results."

"Thank you."

"It's just…don't let the cost of those achievements be at the expense of your heart."

"I won't, I promise."

CHAPTER THIRTEEN

Georgina was uncharacteristically late. Molly had received an email about an hour earlier to say that Georgina had been held up but was on her way. She'd replied, *No problem, thanks for letting me know*. She'd done her best not to reveal in her email any hint of disappointment. After all, what was it that Evelyn had said—*Give nothing away of your emotions*.

Molly leaned against the bus stop outside the records office, casting her eye up and down the busy street. She checked her watch. It was ten forty. Her nerves tingled with excitement. Her meeting with Georgina had all the qualities of a date. She had spent last night mithering about what to wear. In the end she had settled on her denim pinafore dress accompanied by a light blue blazer and finished off with a bright pink neck scarf. She wanted her meeting with Georgina to feel as relaxed as they had been together in Daisy May. Moreover she wanted Georgina to smile at her the way she had done then. And she wanted to make Georgina laugh again, to see her face light up with joy.

But Georgina was late. She fought back the memory of the many times her ex had kept her waiting standing awkwardly outside restaurants or at parties where she knew no one, or worse still at home all dressed up sitting at the kitchen table waiting for the text that said, *Delayed at work, meet you there?* It was always work—every time. Work came first and Molly, well, was expected to understand. But all she understood was that she hadn't mattered.

A cool breeze nipped at her cheeks and the dust from the street whipped and stung against her legs. She looked at the warm glow of lights emanating from the records office. If she was sensible, she would go in and begin her work. After all she wanted to have the opportunity to check the parish registers. She glanced one last time in the direction of town before turning away with a heavy heart and her head warning her to take care.

She pulled off her scarf and slipped her jacket from her shoulders to rest on the seat back of the same chair at the same long desk. She glanced quickly around the reading room. Nearly all of the tables were occupied with stern-faced people, heads bent in concentration. And she must concentrate too.

Her heart tugged with affection at the sight of Josephine's and Edith's archives laid out once more, ready as requested in front of her. She rested her palm flat against the scrapbook as one would rest their hand against a loved one's chest to comfort and reassure them. At the same time it was impossible to ignore the three large leather-bound volumes of registers from the parish of St. Martin's which sat at the far end of her desk like a forbidding granite mound.

She took a large breath and pulled the first volume towards her. It was the record of baptisms. The gold imprinted title on the cover read *Register of Baptisms, Parish of St. Martin's, 1800-1810.* Her online research had confirmed Josephine's date of birth as the 18th April 1808. She'd hoped that it would not be unreasonable to assume that Edith and Josephine were more or less the same age.

She rested the heavy volume onto a reading cushion and gingerly opened its front cover. A musk of aging paper and the sweet tang of the leather binding filled the air around her. She resisted the urge to sneeze as she stared at the list of faded brown ink smudges shaping letters which formed the names of each individual. She felt a shiver at the immediacy of this physical object from the past, so tangible against her skin. It was thrilling to feel so connected to the moment many years ago when the clerk put ink to paper and to vicariously share in the recording of the beginning of an individual's life.

She turned each page, scanning down the list of names. She found the page with Josephine's record and ran her finger along the line of text that read: *Baptism 18th May 1808. Josephine Catherine, daughter of Charles Brancaster, Solicitor, and his wife, Anne. Born 18th April 1808.*

She stared at the line of ink that spoke of a life just beginning. She imagined Josephine as a baby held cradled in the priest's arms and half-buried in the white billowing lace of her baptism gown, her parents looking down at her with their faces lit with pride at this new life with such potential.

And how proud her parents would have been—for there were so many writings by Josephine spread across the desk. Each piece of work a testimony to a life dedicated to the service of those less fortunate than her.

When she closed the register, Molly's thoughts turned to her own mum and dad who were always there for her with love unconditional and unreserved. They were the first to console her when Erica had left, and they were the first to tell her that she could do better and what a fool Erica had been. They always saw the potential in her, even when she struggled to believe it for herself. The thought of letting her parents down hurt her, and it took no imagining to suppose that Josephine would likely have felt the same. It was certainly not difficult to understand what pressure Josephine must have felt. Had she married out of love for them as much as a sense of duty?

She returned the baptism register to the pile and swapped it with the register of marriages. The register spanned the years 1830 to 1840, and she quickly found the section that recorded unions that took place in 1833. She leafed through the pages to December, and her heart caught at the sight of the entry she was searching for: *Married 26th December 1833 William Henry George Wright, age 30, bachelor, solicitor and Josephine Catherine Brancaster, age 25, spinster of this parish, by licence and with the consent of those whose consent is required.*

She read the entry several times noting down the detail in her notepad. She couldn't help but think of Edith. Had Edith consented? Had *she* understood?

28th August 1833

"Yes! Yes!" Edith ran with all her might through the city streets, dodging market stall holders' baskets, skipping over stagnant puddles, narrowly avoiding the wheels of carts and the hoofs of horses. The church bells of St. Martin's rang out in celebration, their peel of notes carried on the wind up and over rooftops and out beyond the city to the workers in the fields.

Edith would not stop running. She lifted her skirt up from the floor with her right hand and she held a copy of the Leicester Chronicle tightly in the other. Her legs had all but given way, and her chest burned as she reached the steps of Brancaster and Lane.

Edith leaned her back against the door with exhaustion and knocked at it with the heel of her shoe. She felt a gust of warm air at her legs and the pungent smell of ink as the door opened. With a last gasp of breath, she said, "Good morning, Mr. Brancaster. I have just heard the news!"

Charles beamed at Edith and held the door open for her to enter. "Good morning, Edith. Yes, truly a day to remember indeed."

When Edith found her breath once more she said in one hurried string of questions, "And has Jo heard? Does she know? What has she said? I have already composed what our response should be. I think we shall not boast. No. Our words will be modest, as the facts will speak in proud ever-increasing volume for themselves. So has she? Heard? Mr. Brancaster?"

Charles looked at Edith, his face creased with confusion. "I rather think I am misunderstanding you."

"In what way? Surely it is not every day that such an Act receives royal assent. Today we have defeated cruelty and we have set humanity on a kinder, more just course." Edith held the newspaper in the air. "It has made the first edition."

Charles burst into a loud hearty laugh. "You mean the abolition of slavery. Ah, yes. I wondered at the bells. It is today then?"

"Yes." Edith leaned in to smell Charles's breath. "I rather hope, sir, you have not felt the need for sustenance of the alcoholic kind this early in the day?"

Charles laughed again. Edith was now convinced that he had quite lost his senses.

"And Jo?" Edith asked, with growing unease. "Will I find her at her desk?" Edith turned and walked towards the door of the office they shared.

"No, Edith." Charles raised his hand in opposition. "I'm not sure—"

Edith burst in without knocking. "It is official—your father is a mystery unto men and we are the two most triumphant souls. I hope I am the first to tell you—" Edith stopped short, stunned to silence by the sight of William Wright holding Josephine's left hand. She stared in horror at the sparkle of an engagement ring reflected in William's ruddy cheeks.

"Edith," Josephine said, her voice tight and breathless. "I am so pleased it's you. I wanted you to be the first to know. Although my father of course…Anyway, I wanted…That is, I hoped…" Josephine looked down.

"Edith." William gazed at Josephine with a face glowing with triumphant affection. "What our dear Jo is trying to say is that she has made me the happiest of fellows by agreeing this very day, in this very hour, to be my wife."

Edith looked away towards the ground at the sound of the newspaper slipping from her hand to the floor. The blood emptied from her head and her mouth became dust dry as the room shrank and then expanded around her.

Josephine rushed to her wrapping her arm around Edith's middle. "William, please, a chair. Quickly."

"No." Edith pushed herself free from Josephine's hold. "No."

"Oh, Edith, I had meant to tell you on my own. I had not intended the cruelty of this moment. William, will you leave us."

"No." Edith shook her head and turned for the door, only to collide into Charles.

"Edith?" Charles loosely held Edith by the arms.

"No," Edith said into his eyes.

And then she left, half hearing the confused reply, "I think it is the August sun. She will insist on running with no regard for the toll upon her of such exertion."

Edith ran with all her might, stumbling through the puddles, catching her legs and ripping her skirt on the baskets of the market holders, all but deaf to the cries of the drivers of the carriages brought to a halt to avoid her. With no breath, just adrenaline, to carry her up the steep flight of stairs to her room.

She collapsed onto her bed and lay there staring at the ceiling. For how long she could not tell. When the world returned to her, she could not feel her limbs, and all she could taste was the iron of blood in her mouth from the raw dryness in her throat. Nausea gripped her when she attempted to sit up, but lying down seemed worse. She felt the most awful bone-aching chill.

With legs that trembled, she made it to the fireplace. It took several goes to light the kindling in the grate. Numbly she lifted wood from a basket into the fire and stood, swaying slightly, and watched the edges of the wood char and begin to glow.

The heat stung at her eyes and cheeks, forcing her to turn away with her palm against her face. As she stood back her ankle caught at the table, causing a canvas stretcher that rested on top of it to wobble. She reached out to steady it. Josephine stared back at her from the canvas that stretched across the wooden frame. How many months she'd spent working on the painting, discarding canvas after canvas, beginning again and again, struggling to quite finish it. For how could she truly ever capture the depth of their love?

"No." She shook her head vehemently at the memory of the ring upon Josephine's hand. She then screamed, "No!" not caring who might hear.

She gripped the frame and stood with it held over the fire. Her fingers burned, matched only by the stinging at her cheeks of acid tears.

She collapsed into a heap, sobbing, with the portrait resting in her lap. She looked down at Josephine and her tears fell upon the canvas, smudging the paint at the edge of Josephine's eyes, so it looked for all the world to see that it was Josephine whose heart had broken, *and Josephine who had nothing left to do but cry.*

Molly sank back into her chair. Had Edith married too? To search the marriage records just like the baptism records with only her name would be like trying to find a needle in a haystack. It would take hours and something in Molly's gut told her that Edith hadn't married. It was the passion and the pure devotion that rippled through her archives that left Molly with a sense that Edith wouldn't compromise on love.

She looked at her watch. It was just before eleven thirty and there was still no sign of Georgina. Should she send an email to check if she was okay? Or should she wait as if she wasn't waiting at all? As if she didn't care?

❖

Georgina had spent early Saturday morning making calls and sending emails related to the settlement of her father's estate. Frustratingly, why Josephine's portrait had been excluded from the bequest remained unanswered.

It made no sense. There was no way her father wouldn't have made explicit provision for the painting. What was she missing? Thank goodness for Molly and for her tireless efforts to help Georgina find some answers about Josephine's portrait, when all other avenues had drawn a blank.

Just an hour before she was due to meet Molly at the records office, a work email arrived. Normally she would take this in her stride. It hadn't bothered her particularly in the past when her weekend or evening was interrupted. Work was quite simply her priority. But now things seemed different. She deeply resented the time she would have to give to the matter and that work would make her late for the one person she did not want to be late for. The one person she did not want to let down.

When she eventually arrived at the records office at half past eleven, she couldn't have felt more flustered.

"Molly, I'm really sorry."

Molly stood. "No worries." She gestured for her to take a seat beside her. "In fact, I've had a chance to explore the parish registers as we discussed."

Surrounded by books and papers, Molly looked beautiful, as always. The white of her long-sleeved T-shirt and the blue of the denim straps of her dress set off the soft pinkness of her skin. The sight of Molly never ceased to flood Georgina with joy.

She would not be the only one who felt that way of course. Molly had such a natural, warm, and open presence that surely even a complete stranger could not resist the chance to be with her, if only for a passing moment. Someone would be waiting at home for her, wouldn't they? They were probably wondering at the cheek of the woman who had demanded Molly's presence on a Saturday. And Molly would have felt obliged to say yes, when she had no doubt wanted to say no.

"Thank you for today," Georgina said quietly, aware of those around them. "I hope that being here isn't ruining your weekend plans."

"Being here with you *is* my plan. I'm excited to share my findings."

Being with me is your plan? Molly was just being kind, wasn't she? "That's great. And I'm excited to see them. Is this Edith's scrapbook that has the sketches?"

"Yes, that's right." Molly lifted the scrapbook to rest in front of Georgina. "I found four drawings in total." Georgina felt the warmth of Molly at her side as Molly leaned in to turn the pages to the place where the sketches were tucked, hidden from sight. "A couple have become loose, but if you look closely, they all have the same profile of Josephine that can be recognized in the final painting. You will see that two have her ear sketched and a third reveals slightly more of her shoulder."

They were so beautiful. "Can I touch them?" Georgina asked. "Or do I need gloves or something?"

Molly shook her head and handed Georgina one of the sketches. "No, your hands should be fine. Unless of course you've just been eating Kentucky Fried Chicken?" Georgina laughed. "The only thing to be mindful of is the edges where the paper has been folded. You can see how thin the paper has become over time."

"Yes, I see." The intensity of the moment pressed at Georgina's chest. Molly was so close to her now that she could smell the hint of something...not perfume, but could it be lavender? Yes, it was the fragrance captured in the purple-blue nodding flower heads waving on long stems in the summer breeze. She could have breathed Molly in all day...

"It's really awesome, isn't it?"

"Yes." Georgina simply couldn't bring herself to look at Molly, as if the merest glance would give away her every thought. And if she turned, their faces would be side by side and Molly's cheeks, her neck, her lips too close, just too close.

Georgina closed her eyes and squeezed her lids tight.

"Do you have a headache?" Molly's voice sounded gentle and concerned.

Georgina opened her eyes. A lie fell in surprise from her lips. "It's been a long week."

"Of course, I understand. I can always finish up here for us if you want."

Georgina said, "No. This is amazing, being here, so close to… to history." Georgina willed her focus to return. She fixed her gaze on the paper she lifted to inspect. She followed the pattern of the lines of charcoal sweeping across the page and noticed a faint pencil line here and there, half rubbed out. The paper felt so light and fragile in her hands, as if it was made entirely of memories and emotion. Had Josephine held this sheet of paper too? To admire progress or to comment on a stray line, perhaps? Or to ask if she should raise her chin just a little to catch the light on her cheek?

The sensation of suddenly remembering something important she had forgotten to say rushed at Georgina. In her head she declared, *I am your relative, Josephine. I am Georgina Wright.* "I can't quite believe that I'm holding the same paper that Josephine might have held."

"Yes, I know—it's crazy, isn't it." Molly beamed a smile that seemed to say *I understand and I feel the same.* "When I was looking at the registers, I was mesmerized by the handwriting of the clerk and by his intimate marks upon the page. I felt I was with him and sharing in that moment." But then Molly's expression of wonder faded to a frown as she looked away towards the registers. "I couldn't find out what you wanted to know about Edith. There are so many Edith Hewitts that I couldn't pinpoint her, at least not with any certainty, and she remains lost in the long list of names. I'm sorry."

Georgina reached out to rest her hand briefly on Molly's arm. "Thank you for trying for me."

Molly blushed. "Of course."

"And in fairness, you did warn me that all we know is what we don't know."

"Yes, I suppose. Although…wait." Molly's eyes grew wide with a spark of something. "There's this." Molly reached for Edith's logbook amongst the pile of archive material. "At first I thought it might be another prayer book. But then it became clear that it was a series of diary entries, logs, if you like."

Georgina gently held the other edge of the page Molly was holding.

"It's this entry, dated 4th April 1832." Molly removed a slip of paper she had inserted to mark the place. "Edith is talking about a painting she is working on. Just here, can you see?"

Speaking softly through the words like a chant, Georgina read, *"Words today burn at my lips to speak and smoulder in ink on the page as I write. For I have captured our love in every shade.* Our love?" Molly nodded. *"The sweet stroke of brush upon canvas, the exquisite memory of us. I long to paint you again and know you yet more with every new glance until no part of you is foreign to me."*

"Wow." Georgina stared at the page. "Okay, I don't know about you, but I read that in very clear terms that they were lovers."

"Yes, that's my take on it too."

"But, hold on, so they were a couple in 1832 and yet Josephine married the following year?"

"Yes." Molly turned the register that rested open in front of her at an angle so Georgina could see. "This is the marriage register, and just here"—she lightly ran her finger underneath the relevant line—"this is the record that confirms that Josephine was married on 26th December 1833."

"That's Boxing Day. For some reason, that's never occurred to me before. Is that usual?"

"I'll check with Fran, but my sense is this wouldn't be unusual, as Boxing Day was and is an established holiday. It would have been easier to take time off work. A rather less than romantic explanation, I'm afraid."

"Romantic?" Georgina said, scepticism shading her words. "Have you found evidence that she loved him?"

"No."

"But we do have evidence that Edith loved Josephine in the note."

"Yes."

Anger, hot and insistent, flared up in Georgina's blood at the injustice she imagined Edith had suffered. She reread the marriage record. "It doesn't say who was present at the ceremony. Do you think Edith attended?"

"I...I don't know."

"Sorry, of course you wouldn't know. What a stupid question to have asked you." Georgina closed her eyes. Tiredness pressed at her lids. "It's just...how could she do it?" Georgina opened her eyes and looked at Molly.

Tentatively Molly said, "It's likely she would have felt she had no choice, and...we can't dismiss the possibility that she did love him."

"And not Edith?" Georgina hadn't meant to raise her voice. A man gave a deliberate irritated cough, and another woman, whose glares Georgina had been ignoring, put down a pen. She whispered, "Sorry. Again. I'm tired and I tend to get a bit...well, let's just say being tired is not a mood improver for me."

Molly said, her voice equally hushed, "No worries, being tired makes me grumpy too. Not of course that I think you're grumpy, really I don't. *Anyway.* Why don't we wrap things up here?"

"Is that what you want? Of course it's what you want. You have to go home."

Molly shook her head. "It's not so much what I want. It's more if we don't leave soon, then I reckon the woman behind us—don't look!—will either throw something at us or complain. I think we've been a bit too noisy."

Georgina laughed. "I see. Quick exit it is then."

They made their way out on the street and into the bluster of the present-day.

"It's good to be outside again." Molly squinted, looking up to the silvery clouds blowing across the late September sky.

People pushed past them, and the traffic rumbled by in metallic glints. Georgina's gaze followed the shrug of Molly's shoulders as she slipped on her jacket. Her nose scrunched slightly as she wrapped her scarf around her neck, the material brushing up against her skin.

"Yes, it is. I like your scarf, by the way." The compliment was out before Georgina had the chance to decide whether it was too personal. Molly blushed. It obviously was too personal.

"Thank you." Molly rearranged her scarf. "I found it in a local charity shop. I did wonder whether it was a little too pink, but then I thought, Molly Goode, just carry it off." Molly shrugged. "Colour makes me happy."

And you make me happy. Georgina's heart stopped. Had she said that out loud?

Glancing in the direction of the taxi rank, Molly asked, "I'm guessing you came by taxi?"

"You guess correctly. I'm sorry again for keeping you waiting. It was work." Georgina sighed. "It's always work."

"That's okay." Molly's sad tone suggested it was anything but okay.

Georgina hadn't meant to turn the conversation back to work and to remind them that all they were was colleagues. But she obviously had when Molly straightened herself as if she was calling her professional self to attention.

"I'll write up my notes from the records office visits and do a sweep-up report for you." Molly cleared her throat. "The conservator has finished his work on Josephine's painting. So I think that's this particular project complete." Molly looked down and folded her arms across her chest. "I've enjoyed working with you. Thank you for the opportunity."

"*No,* thank *you,* for everything. And I really hope it's not the last time we work together." For Georgina nothing felt complete. She should arrange to collect the painting, shouldn't she? But she just couldn't bring herself to. The painting was her precious link to Molly and she couldn't bear to break it. Unless…"Perhaps our paths will cross in the preparations for the Wright room?" *Stop putting pressure on her.* Georgina could only imagine how desperate and pathetic she sounded.

Molly looked up and said, "Yes, definitely. In fact the room's—" Molly paused midsentence. "When you feel ready to talk more about the room and perhaps about the next steps for the bequeathed works in your father's house, just let me know."

What had Molly stopped herself from saying?

"Thanks. I will. I'm snowed under at work for the next couple of weeks, but as soon as I resurface, I'll get in touch. I promise." Georgina held Molly's gaze.

"That would be fab," Molly said softly. "Thank you."

"So did you approve of the name change for the room?"

"Yes, very much. I meant to say how much I liked it," Molly said, with a beaming smile. "Inspired, I thought."

"Well, what can I say, I felt very inspired when I came up with it. And was Evelyn as pleased as I thought she'd be?" Georgina said without an iota of guilt.

"I'm not sure *pleased* is quite the right word."

They laughed and the seriousness of all things work drifted away with their laughter.

Molly took a deep unsteady breath. "Shall we make our way? I'm parked pretty much next to the taxi rank." Georgina walked at Molly's side as they sauntered towards Daisy May and the waiting taxis. "Well, this is us." Molly nodded at her bright yellow companion.

Georgina couldn't help but smile at the sight of Daisy May. She was so much Molly. "Hi again, Daisy May. I hope you're feeling better." Molly patted Daisy May's bonnet. "She is indeed in fine fettle."

Georgina couldn't bring herself to leave. They could have lunch. Couldn't they? What was she thinking? Why on earth would Molly want to have lunch with her? She'd taken enough of her time already, and she would only feel obliged to say yes, wouldn't she? *Leave the poor woman alone.* She shook her head.

"Were you going to say something?"

"Just thank you again for today, Molly, and safe journey home. Goodbye for now."

If Georgina was not mistaken or reading too much into everything, she could have sworn Molly's face had dropped with what could be disappointment as she said, "Goodbye then."

Georgina turned and walked towards the taxi rank. Every step away from Molly seemed a step away from everything that felt right.

CHAPTER FOURTEEN

"I f you don't stop humming, I will be obliged to beat you to death with the commemorative bust of Richard III." Fran nodded to the replica bust perched on a potter's stool tucked up in a far corner of their office. She scraped her chair in closer to her desk.

"I'm sorry. It's just I woke up happy. But I also feel foolish to be happy." Molly shrugged.

"Don't worry—happiness doesn't last."

"Oh, that's…good to know." Molly perched on the edge of Fran's desk and began playing with her stapler.

Fran grabbed it from her. "Spit it out. Whatever you're fidgeting to say. Or none of us will get any work done."

"It's sort of personal."

"You've fallen for Georgina Wright and you don't know what to do about it."

"*Oh my God.* Is it that obvious?"

"Let's put it this way—I don't think I've had a conversation with you in the last month where you haven't mentioned her. And choosing to ignore my advice, you have persisted in going behind Evelyn's back to help Georgina with the portrait. So despite your denials, you haven't exactly been exuding disinterest."

"You think I'm a fool."

"Well, you know I worry for your heart. But you're not a fool. Georgina Wright's smart, wealthy, influential, and striking to look at. Quite frankly if you hadn't fallen for her, then I think you should have questioned your lesbian credentials."

"She was so lovely on Saturday. Do you remember, she asked to see the sketches for the portrait?" Fran gave a reluctant nod. "It was so amazing to see how enthralled she was. It felt a real privilege to be there.

There was even a moment when we parted where I thought she might have suggested lunch or something. But she didn't, because of course she wouldn't, would she. It was just foolish wishful thinking on my part."

"Mixing business with pleasure is notoriously complicated, and there's a reason it's not recommended."

"It tends not to end well?"

"I'm afraid so. And as I've said before, you'll tie yourself in knots trying to second-guess Georgina."

"I suppose."

"*So* moving on, is that it, then, for your research on the painting?"

"I guess so. I'd hoped to learn more about Edith. I even thought I might somehow come across her in the parish registers. Once again, wishful thinking. I did confirm to Georgina that the conservation work on the portrait had been completed and that was probably it for the research. She didn't mention picking the portrait up. She did, however, mention hoping to work with me on the Wright room. But then that's work, isn't it? So as you can see, I've no reason to be happy."

"Well I was going to give you this. But as there's nothing specifically on Edith it's probably not going to offer much cheer, and as you've moved on, it may be a bit late in any case." Fran lifted a slim wallet of papers from underneath a stack under her desk. "I was in the process of digging out some examples of the temporary exhibitions we've displayed over the years to encourage Evelyn to see women's history month as an opportunity to highlight local women, and I came across these. They're my notes and research from that Radicals exhibition I told you about. As I said before, there's not much. I've selected out the items related to Josephine Wright."

"That's awesome—thanks so much, Fran."

Fran handed the wallet to Molly, briefly holding it with her. "This is just FYI, because of course your insubordination—sorry, work on the portrait—is concluded."

Molly dropped her eyes from Fran's to the floor and crossed her fingers behind her back. "Absolutely."

Fran let go of the wallet. "Good."

Molly rested it on her desk and began to leaf through its contents. On the top there was a typed bibliography of Josephine's collected works. "Wow, this list is really detailed and gives a fab overview of Josephine's work."

"It was drawn up some years ago now by the volunteer who helped me." Fran frowned at the pages laid out in front of Molly. "But I can't imagine there have been additions to her archive."

"It's totally amazing, isn't it, to see how tirelessly Josephine wrote in support of those causes close to her heart." Molly looked across at Fran who gave a slow nod.

"Yes," Fran said wistfully. "She was quite a woman."

Despite how enthralling it was to glimpse into Josephine's world through her writings, Molly couldn't suppress the sensation of disappointment at the absence of anything related to Edith. If Josephine and Edith had corresponded, the letters were not listed.

Molly gave a heavy sigh. What was she expecting to find, anyway? A picture of Edith and Josephine arm in arm? A love note?

She slowly gathered the pages together and rested the bibliography back on top. *Hold on.* She ran her fingers down the list. "There's a gap of about two years where Josephine writes nothing. No letters, no treatises. Not even correspondence with the various societies she supported. Here, can you see?" Molly held up the list. "Is that what this question mark by the side was for?"

Fran leaned forward and squinted. "Possibly."

She looked at Fran. "Why?"

Fran shrugged. "Concentrating on her new responsibilities as a wife and mother perhaps? It seems most likely. In fact that's probably why I didn't question it further. Often the most obvious answer is the answer."

"It doesn't seem in keeping though with her nature, to just give up on what she cared about. Does it?"

"I'm sorry, if I could give you the answers, I would."

"It's okay. I understand." Molly stared at the papers in front of her. *So what happened in August 1834, Josephine, that made you stop writing? Was it marrying and becoming a mum? Was that it? Or had all those years campaigning exhausted you?* A soft knocking at their door drew Molly's attention from the unknown to the certainty of a visitor.

Marianne stood in the doorway smiling. "Hi, both. Molly, if you have a moment, Evelyn and the chairman would like a word."

"They would?"

"Yes. Now if possible."

"I'll be right there." Molly grabbed her notebook and pen and rushed, half tripping over the doorstop's manhood, as she hurried in the direction of Evelyn's office.

Evelyn's door was ajar. She could hear voices. Molly tentatively knocked.

"Come in," Evelyn said without pausing her conversation with the chairman. "I couldn't agree more, invitations must go out as soon as possible. Molly, please take a seat. Mark and I are just discussing progress with the Wright room."

"Yes, of course, the space is looking wonderful," Molly said breathlessly, slipping off her glasses which had misted from her run down the corridor.

"Yes, it's a credit to you, Evelyn." The chairman's neck and cheeks glowed red, Molly supposed with the sting of his excessive aftershave.

"Molly, Evelyn and I are concerned to understand Georgina's expectations for the space." As he spoke, the chairman was looking down at his half-empty cup of coffee. "I'm not sure the trustees had in mind a community dimension as such. It came as an unexpected...reframing of the room's purpose. I understand from Evelyn that you have now spent some time in Georgina Wright's company. We need to know— did she give you any sense of her plans going forward in respect to her relationship with the museum?"

Molly's chest tightened. "Well, to be honest, she hasn't explicitly suggested to me any particular expectation for the room or, indeed, plans for the future as such." Molly risked a quick glance at Evelyn who seemed concentrated on note making. "But our recent project together—"

"Yes"—the Chairman nodded—"the portrait of Josephine Brancaster. Evelyn has told me of Georgina's particular interest in that regard."

"Yes," Molly said, her voice lifting in harmony with the note of his interest. "It's a fascinating history—"

"Molly"—Evelyn lifted her hand—"we need to know if you have been able to progress matters with Georgina with regard to the handover of the outstanding items in George's house. Time is ticking."

"Yes. Georgina has agreed to get to grips with the handover as soon as she can."

"As soon as she can?"

"I understand that this next couple of weeks are difficult for her but after that—"

Evelyn released an exasperated sigh. "You *must* hold her to that. It is already nearing the end of September. We've pencilled in Friday 8th December for the opening. Please check this date with Georgina. Invitations must go out at the beginning of next month. Are we agreed?"

"Yes," Molly said with the most affirmative tone she could muster.

"And Molly." The chairman set aside his cup and leaned in a little. "See if you can't pin Georgina down on future matters."

"Yes, I'll do my best but..." The chairman and Evelyn were both looking at her. And not in a good way. "I'll do my best."

"Excellent." Evelyn returned her attention to her notes. "Thank you, Molly. That's all for now."

Molly walked slowly back to her office. Pin down Georgina on future matters? She could barely pin down her own heart from fluttering in her chest at the merest mention of Georgina Wright's name.

Chapter Fifteen

One of the things Georgina dreaded most about her routine of returning to her father's home on a Friday wasn't the deafening emptiness that greeted her, echoing from ceiling to floor. No. It was the post that had defied the redirection request that spilled out across the entrance mat. For there seemed nothing crueller than the unexpected sight of letters addressed to Mr. George Wright. And then of course there were those letters addressed to her that demanded her attention and that reminded her of all that she was trying to forget.

Georgina dropped her weekend holdall onto the floor. Stifling the shiver that came every time she opened a letter relating to her father's estate, she pulled open a brown envelope from the estate agent. The Finest of Country and Town had a plan—at least, that's what their covering letter said. *A vision befitting of a home of such stature, in such an envied position for business and pleasure.* Georgina flicked through the glossy brochure they had attached. The text was complete but there were no pictures. Georgina had been clear on this. She wanted the house empty of her father's belongings before marketing photos were taken.

The thought that her father's belongings would be used to market his home felt intrusive and disrespectful and akin to an act of betrayal. Georgina hadn't cared whether the estate agent minded or not. Given the commission they would earn, she doubted they would mind at all.

With a heavy heart she rested the brochure on her father's chair. She could not avoid the inevitable. Very soon she would sell her father's home and the memories formed within these walls would be dislocated and lost.

But then there was the museum, wasn't there? Was this what his bequest meant to him? Was it the difference between remembered and forgotten, dignity and disorder? Just the thought of her father's bequest upset her. She couldn't shake off the sense that the Wright room was in every way the physical manifestation of her loss. The vibrant warmth and energy of her father's life distilled away to black ink marking the dates of his birth and death. The collection of objects he cherished would soon become the sum of the man, when the individual aspects of her father were so much more.

A flash of yellow glinted from the square. Her heart caught at the sight of Molly bending in to Daisy May and placing belongings on to the back seat. *Molly.* A peculiar panic gripped Georgina. In that moment Molly seemed like the answer to everything, and she was no doubt leaving for home. She was leaving.

Without another thought, Georgina hurriedly texted, *Do you have time to come over? Sometime soon? Now even?* She pressed send before she had a chance to rethink or regret. She stood motionless, staring out towards Molly. Had she received her email? Please let her have caught her in time.

Wait, was Molly now looking in the direction of the house?

Georgina took a deep breath and stepped towards the window. She raised her hand tentatively, uncertain whether Molly could see. When Molly waved back, something in Georgina, something that had been tightly bound inside, unwound. Her heart surged with the sight of Molly walking across the square towards her.

She rushed into the hallway and gripped the cold round brass door handle, listening for Molly's feet on the steps, and then, not waiting for Molly to knock, she opened the front door and with a mixture of relief and joy said, "Hi. Come in. Please."

❖

Georgina gestured into the hallway that stretched out behind her. "Thanks so much for coming over. It's good to see you."

"It's good to see you too," Molly said. "I promise you literally just beat me to it. I swear I was about to email and check in with you. So this is great. I mean really great."

Molly stepped inside, utterly overwhelmed by the building she had admired from afar. "Wow." She had always wondered what lay beyond its formal black door. She had daydreamed of Regency grandeur, imagining a long tiled hallway with corniced ceilings and ornate plaster mouldings. Perhaps a heavy hall mirror would hang on a brass chain against the wall, casting the light and one's gaze along the hallway to the bottom of the stairs, to the fine spindles and curl of the banister.

And in one captivated glance, Molly realized that her imagination had been outdone by the imposing beauty of George Wright's home.

The octagon pattern of black and white tiles made Molly want to skip from one to the other. The tall ceilings made her dizzy, and the elegant staircase with its low wide steps begged her to dance up and down them.

The history of the house rushed at Molly to greet her. Was this how Josephine would have felt every time she walked through the door? Did her heart skip a beat? Did she dance on the steps with Edith, perhaps? Or had Josephine's marriage changed everything, and they'd simply moved on from each other as time ceaselessly moved on with the future its only destination.

Molly gazed further along the hallway towards a marble bust of Thomas Cook which rested on a console table. A vase of lilies which bowed their heads as if in reverence of George's passing had been placed next to the bust and lent the house a sober, contemplative feel.

Georgina nodded towards the lilies. "My father's housekeeper leaves them."

"They're beautiful, and so is your father's home." Molly tilted her chin to the ceiling and her hungry gaze feasted upon every ornate feature.

"Yes," Georgina said into the echo of the hall. "My father was very particular to maintain it."

"He's done an awesome job." Molly's compliment was met by Georgina's warm smile that sent a soft flutter like the brush of the wings of butterflies all the way through her.

Georgina cleared her throat. "So, welcome. If you have time—"

"I have time." She'd answered too quickly, hadn't she? She should have pretended to check her diary at least.

Georgina laughed and blushed.

Yes, she'd definitely answered too quickly.

"Great. Well then, can I offer you a coffee—or we could even risk a glass of something dusty from my father's cellar?"

Molly hesitated. A glass of wine? Okay. Why not? But what if she got drunk? *I mustn't get drunk.*

"Oh, I'm sorry, Molly," Georgina quickly said. "Of course, you're driving. Coffee it is."

"I could leave Daisy May and take a taxi home. I always try to park her under a street light just in case she doesn't start. Although I'm not sure how she feels about being top lit."

Georgina laughed again. "Excellent. Come with me and choose the wine you fancy."

Molly followed Georgina into the basement. "This is so impressive." Molly's gaze fell upon racks custom built into the cellar's arches and filled with bottles of wine. "Oh, a temperature gauge. This place totally appeals to the geek in me."

"My father would be pleased to hear that. He was serious about his wine. Wine and work were absolutely his two loves. So we have a dilemma. There are a couple of whites which are cold although not fridge chilled. Let's grab them anyway. Here."

Molly took the bottles Georgina handed her.

"And there are loads of reds. Shall I just pick a couple at random?"

"Yes." Molly laughed. "Random is good."

"Okay, I'm not going to go for anything too old. I'm afraid I'm yet to be convinced all things improve with age. Of course, I know you're about to disagree." A teasing smile played on Georgina's lips.

Molly hugged the wine bottles against her chest, dreading the thought that she might drop them. "No, I think you're right. The worst mistake anyone can make is to assume something has value simply because it's old. I work on the basis that a thing's value actually comes from what it means to someone."

Georgina was bending, trying to pick out a bottle from the many confronting her. Molly looked fixedly at the concrete floor determined not to let her gaze wander to somewhere it politely shouldn't.

Georgina stood up with two bottles in her arms. "Yes, that makes sense. Value, even in my work, is determined by opinion, and those opinions shift with often questionable rationale." Georgina rested against a rack for a moment. "I am constantly forced to restate positions to those seeking to shift them. Fixing opinions is quite frankly tiring."

Molly felt the bottles slipping and lifted her knee to hitch the bottles back into her arms. "Oops," she said. "Okay, all safe again."

"I'm sorry I've strayed on to work and kept you in the cellar. Let's go, please, after you. The sitting room's on the left."

Molly led the way up the stairs. "No, it's okay, I'm interested in what you were saying." Everything about Georgina fascinated her. She looked back briefly over her shoulder as she asked, "So what do you do exactly?" Molly braced herself for Georgina to talk about profit margins and capital growth.

"I'm one of a team of people working to develop investment strategies which have strict ethical criteria." Reaching the hallway, Georgina held the sitting room door open for Molly. "More and more investors want their money to do good while earning them a profit. So we wouldn't, for example, recommend companies to invest in who deal in arms or are known to damage the environment—that sort of thing. I'm quite strict, which doesn't always go down well."

"What you do sounds amazing."

Georgina rested the bottles of red wine on a small side table by an armchair, and Molly carefully handed Georgina the white wine.

"Thanks. One sec, I'll just put these in the fridge. Make yourself at home."

The last thing Molly had expected was mention of ethics when it came to investment banking. Were their values more closely aligned than she had even dared hope for?

"Bottle opener?" Georgina returned and began searching in the sideboard drawers. "I hate awful corks. Thank God for screw tops."

The surface of the dark wood sideboard was adorned with a beautiful blue ware vase accompanied by two fine Spode figurines of a boy and girl at play. Molly suppressed the impolite urge to touch their smooth cold surfaces and feel their delicate soft weight in her hands. The painting hanging above the sideboard stole Molly's attention from the china. She moved to stand in front of it to take a closer look. It was a detailed pencil sketch of the square, which seemed to have been composed through the sitting room window.

"It was drawn by my great-grandfather's brother Hugo a few months before he was called to the front, where he died."

"Goodness, that's heartbreaking."

"I know. It makes you see the sketch differently knowing that, doesn't it?"

"Yep, the life story behind the painting adds a whole new dimension, as you and I know."

Georgina nodded and Molly followed Georgina's gaze across to the far side of the sitting room and the wall which featured the Wright family paintings from the 1800s. Molly's heart caught at the sight of the empty space where Edith's painting of Josephine once hung.

Speaking just above a whisper Georgina said, "What do you think happened to her?"

"Edith?"

"Yes."

"I want to think she went on to love again and lived to a ripe old age campaigning against every human wrong."

"But you don't think so?"

"I don't know." Molly could not help but turn away dejected by the thought of what they knew about Edith and Josephine, and by the reality of everything they would never know.

In the hope of lifting the mood from reflection to something a little more joyful, Molly said, "I love your father's furniture. It's properly gorgeous, and it couldn't suit the room more."

Georgina had become distracted again by the hunt for a bottle opener. She scratched her head, frowning and glancing around the room said, "Yes, he had good taste."

A luxurious red velvet sofa adorned with a decorative throw over one arm and three large overstuffed cushions graced one side of the room. Even the piles of magazines heavy upon it could not diminish its impact. Opposite the sofa, a rich brown leather armchair was positioned by the fireplace to capture the view of the square. The sumptuous furnishings spoke of style and dignity.

The glint of the glass chandelier caught her eye and she stared up at the ornate ceiling rose from which the chandelier hung and instantly thought of Fran and of the parties she described. The room reminded Molly of a grande dame all dressed up in velvet with her jewellery heavy upon her and her talk of days gone by, better days when men were men and wars were real, and she'd danced with the duke all night long and never once tired, upright in his arms.

"This room makes me want to dance." Molly twirled round with her arms out wide and her gaze catching at the beautiful cornices that framed the ceiling like trims of icing on a cake.

"Let's just say it doesn't have that effect on me." Georgina sounded decidedly unamused. It was like the music stopped. "I may have to nip out and get us some wine after all. Sorry."

"Oh no, wait—there's a chance I have a corkscrew thing on a key ring." Molly rummaged in her bag. "Yes, here you go. Okay, so I know it's in the shape of a penguin, but you use its wings like this to lift the cork out. It's very effective."

Georgina smiled. Molly loved that she could make her smile.

"You're a lifesaver. Please have a seat. I'm afraid I've buried the sofa under a weight of my father's law journals." Georgina moved the sales brochure from her father's chair.

Molly's heart caught and ached at the sight of the brochure. The house would soon be sold, and the Wright room up and running, and Georgina would be gone with no reason to return.

"You okay?" Georgina asked, frowning a little with her question.

"Yes, although it doesn't seem very fair that I have the only seat. I have an idea. Here." Molly proceeded to tug the throw from the sofa. Holding one edge, she flung it into the air for it to spread itself wide and come to rest flat on the floor. She grabbed the cushions, scattering them across the throw. "Ta-da. A picnic. Not that I'm presuming you're going to feed me."

"We could eat. I could order in?"

We could? "Yes, I'd love that."

"Done. What sort of thing do you like?"

"I'm not fussy honestly—there is literally nothing I don't like."

"Easy to please, eh?" Georgina said with a teasing tone.

"Nope. Just greedy."

"How about pizza then? It may be simpler to eat as we're picnicking." Smiling, Georgina shook her head. "Right, I need to get us plates, glasses, and napkins."

"Okey-dokey. While you do that, I'll order the pizza. I was thinking anchovy, capers, black olives, and red onion, on a margherita base."

"I'm thinking easy on the capers, and you've got yourself a deal."

"Gotcha," Molly said. "On reflection, I think you're right. When I had that combo the other day, it was a little bit salty, and when I say a little bit salty, I'm pretty sure I would have been less thirsty crossing the Gobi Desert." Molly's cheeks tingled as Georgina smiled warmly back at her, with amusement dancing in the light of her eyes.

By the time the pizza had arrived it was six thirty and they were halfway through their first bottle of wine.

"Cheers, Molly Goode. Thank you for joining me this evening for this most magnificent picnic."

"Cheers to you too." Molly raised her wine glass in the air to glisten in the light from the chandelier. She sat on the throw with her legs crossed, chatting happily away, sharing stories and laughing. Georgina sat on the edge of the throw with her back resting against her father's armchair with her long legs sprawled out in front of her. She couldn't have looked more relaxed and more different from the woman Molly had first met, who had stood in the foyer so cold and aloof. Was Georgina's grief easing just a little? Had her broken heart begun to heal?

While they'd waited for the pizza, Georgina had changed from her work clothes into jeans and a figure-hugging grey T-shirt. She'd apologized that it was her sports T-shirt. Molly hadn't minded. Not one bit.

Molly bit into her pizza. *Don't stare at her.* She must concentrate on something else—something at least vaguely professional. She fixed her gaze instead across to the far wall and to the Wright family paintings, working her way from left to right. "I see what you were saying about the order being odd, and that by right Edith's watercolour of Josephine should be first. Not only that, there's something else that's odd. We have Josephine's wedding portrait to William, 1833."

"Yep," Georgina said. "And then the next is the christening portrait of their second child James, completed in 1838."

Molly moved to stand with the painting of James's christening. "So why no painting of the christening of their daughter?" Molly leaned forward to read the inscription, then looked back at Georgina. "It's weird, isn't it?"

Georgina shrugged. "Lost, maybe?"

"Maybe." Molly sighed. Every time she discovered something new or puzzling relating to either Josephine or Edith, it raised questions with no answers. And even when they did have answers of sorts, they didn't feel completely right. Molly returned to sit on the throw. "You know, even though I remember these paintings from the photos you sent me, they almost look different." Molly met Georgina's questioning gaze. "And for some reason, it's funny—all through our research, I never thought of Josephine as a mum."

"How do you think of her?" Georgina sat staring at the portrait of Josephine's wedding day.

"I suppose I think of her as Edith's partner."

"Me too. Can I be honest and say I'm struggling to get past the fact that Josephine gave up Edith to marry William Wright. It feels like such a betrayal." Georgina took another slug of wine tinting the edges of her mouth red.

"Oh, okay."

"Why do people say they love someone and then betray them?" Georgina turned fully to face Molly. Her expression seemed so serious and earnest. "Why do people do that? And then why would anyone trust love at all?"

Molly's chest tightened at the intensity of Georgina's unexpected question. She gripped the stem of her wine glass. "Surely not everyone's like that."

"Yes, but enough people."

Molly delicately said, "Yes, but equally enough people don't."

"And it's the people you least expect it from." Georgina drained her wine glass dry.

Molly didn't know what to say. Was Georgina speaking from personal experience? Was this about her parents, or had someone cheated on her?

"I'm sorry Molly—I'm rambling, and I'm being maudlin. It's the wine talking. And tiredness. Booze and fatigue equals nonsense."

"It's not nonsense. It's how you feel." Molly shrugged. "Perhaps I should go home and let you get some rest."

"No, really, I'm fine. Unless you want to go?"

Molly shook her head. "No. I'm having a lovely time. Thank you."

Georgina's tired eyes shone. "Good. Me too."

Molly lay down on the throw, tucked her cushion under her head, and stared up to the ceiling at the glinting chandelier. "If I lived here, I would do this every night. Lie here looking up and letting all my worries dissolve into the sparkling light."

Without another word Georgina moved across and lay next to Molly, and they fell silent staring up at the ceiling together.

Georgina's arm rested next to Molly's. *Oh my God.* It was pure agony for Molly for their bodies to be so close. It was sugar on her lips that she couldn't lick. It was the tickling tear she couldn't wipe away. It was the empty water glass on a sun-drenched day. It was everything she wanted and nothing she could have.

Fantasies hot and urgent rushed in to torture her. In her fantasy Georgina was leaning over kissing her, moving her body on top of hers with her hair falling against her cheek and neck. Why? Why? What was Georgina thinking, to lie so close? But that was just it. Georgina wasn't thinking anything, was she? It was just her being sexually frustrated and a complete fool.

Molly sat up, resettling herself to sit on her cushion. She needed to distract herself. She needed to think of something to say. She stared across at the paintings once again. She cleared her throat and asked, "It must be hard to see your family's artwork leave this house after so many years."

Georgina turned onto her side and leaned up on her elbow with her head resting in her palm. "Yes and no. We had no choice, of course, but to address my father's inheritance tax bill, and gifting his artworks helped with that. But for me"—Georgina sat up and turned herself to face Molly—"it was more that when my father first mentioned his wish to see his art and the foundation's collection on public display, I simply agreed with his decision. It made sense. The collection should be enjoyed by many, and in any case, there'd be simply no point to me inheriting it."

No point? "In what way? I'm sorry—I'm being nosy. It's none of my business."

"That's okay. In truth, art's not really my thing, and in any case I just can't envisage myself..." Georgina looked down.

"Please, like I said, you don't have to explain."

"I don't know how much you've sensed..."

Molly held her breath. Just a moment ago she'd sensed quite a lot.

Georgina said quietly, "It's just, well, I'm gay."

Molly's heart skipped a beat with uncontrollable joy. "That's great news." *That's great news?* Georgina looked up. What possessed her to say that? "I mean, great news you felt you could tell me. And as it happens, I'm gay too. Want to risk more wine?" Before Georgina could reply, Molly scrambled from the floor, grabbed both glasses, and refilled them. "Here you go. So cheers to that." Molly drank down her glass until the fumes of the peppery red overwhelmed her and made her cough.

Georgina laughed. "Cheers. So you're not dating anyone at the moment then?"

"Nope. I am officially clueless when it comes to dating. Come to think of it, that might explain why I've been single for a year now. But despite everything, I still hold out hope that I will one day meet the one." Could she ask Georgina the same question? Was Georgina looking for her *one* too? *Oh, bugger it, why not.* "How about you? Oh, and by the way, being gay doesn't mean you won't start a family and have lots of little Wrights running around to inherit the Wright dynasty, if that's what you were implying a moment ago."

Georgina shook her head and looked at the floor once more. "I know. It's not that. It's, frankly, I'm not great with emotions." Molly heard the sad blankness in Georgina's reply. "I struggle to let people in, and that's not great for relationships. To be honest, I try not to think about it. Work and—funnily enough—wine help with the not thinking." She took a large mouthful of wine as if to underline her point.

Okay. No more questions. "Understood, no thinking. Let's change the subject." The last thing Molly wanted to do was change the subject.

"I'm surprised you find dating hard. You seem very open." Georgina tilted her head and stared at Molly. Clearly Georgina didn't want their chat to stray too far from them either.

"Yep, I inherited my friendly gene from my mum. Honestly when I was a kid, we couldn't actually make it down the street without my mum stopping and chatting to someone. I remember this one time we had ten people for Sunday lunch. I only knew half of them. My poor dad just stood confused, carving the chicken as thinly as he could. They were so trusting. Looking back, I thank them that they helped me to see the good in people first, you know?"

Georgina nodded. "I'm thankful that I don't seem to possess any of my mother's genes." She moved once more to rest with her back against her father's chair and sat hugging her knees to her chest.

Molly didn't say anything. After all, what could she say to that?

"I'm sorry—I've managed to make you feel uncomfortable again. I seem to have a gift for it. Georgina Wright. Skills: investment banking and mood devastation."

"I'm not devastated. Actually I'm very comfortable." Molly returned to lying on her back. "Apparently, you're meant to tuck your shoulder blades under to lie properly."

"You do yoga?"

"Well, remember you once asked me whether I ran?"

Georgina laughed. It was a proper full wholehearted laugh. Had talking helped?

"I went to one class," Molly said. "We got to the pelvic floor exercises, and well, let's just say I embarrassed myself. I couldn't go back."

Georgina was wiping at her eyes and smiling broadly. "All that clenching and releasing, eh?"

"Uh-huh." Molly burst into laughter, joined again by Georgina.

It was nearing midnight before they managed to say anything without laughing and when the second bottle of wine ran out. Molly reluctantly moved to leave. "I should go home. That is, if I can stand."

"Here, I've got you." Georgina pulled Molly up from the floor and their bodies pressed unsteadily together. "I'll call you a taxi."

Molly stood at the window with Georgina waiting for the headlights of the taxi.

"The square's so quiet, isn't it?" Georgina looked out to Daisy May. "Daisy May will sleep well."

"My sense is that she's a fitful sleeper given that she's not great first thing."

"I know how she feels. I'll be lucky to get a few hours."

"Really?" Molly wanted to ask why, but then it was late, and she'd pried enough, hadn't she? "Well, you've got Daisy May to keep you company. Oh, headlights."

At the door Molly pulled on her coat.

"Let me pay for your taxi. I'm the one who plied you with alcohol and kept you up this late."

"And I'm the one who hasn't minded one bit. So thank you, but no thank you." Georgina was standing so close that she could feel the heat of Georgina's body against hers. She looked up into Georgina's eyes, and if her own eyes could speak she wished they would say, *You can kiss me if you want.*

"Goodnight, Molly."

"Goodnight." Molly opened the door. *Oh, bugger it.* She turned quickly and leaned up and kissed Georgina on the cheek. And with that she skipped down the steps and climbed into the taxi.

Molly woke the next morning with excitement bubbling over into laughter. What a night it had been and how crazy that she couldn't even remember the journey home or taking off her coat or shoes. She glanced at her phone resting at her side and her heart flooded with delight as she recalled the email she had sent from her bed to Georgina, saying, *I had a fabulous evening. Thank you.* And how could she ever forget that Georgina had replied, *Me too X*

CHAPTER SIXTEEN

Dear Georgina,

I had hoped to hear back from you, darling girl. But then there is nothing more cruel than hope, is there? And if you are hoping that ignoring my letters will cause me to give up on you, on us, then, my dear daughter, your hopes, I'm afraid, will also be dashed. Please can we meet? You choose the place? I just want to talk. We need to talk. Please get in touch.

With cursed hope and love,
Your mother,
Lydia Wright X

Georgina thought the worst she would wake up to the next day was a hangover. She was partly right. She had a hangover from hell *and* a letter from her mother.

After her father's death, she had stared at the post office's redirection request form. Just stared. Eventually, numb to everything, she had sent off the form with just her father's name. The next occupant of the house would receive the letters from her mother and no doubt cross out the name *Georgina Wright* and scribble *Return to sender*, something Georgina could never quite bring herself to do.

She sipped at a mug steaming with strong coffee and stood looking out at the square with her mother's letter tucked in her trouser pocket. Thankfully Daisy May seemed none the worse for her night out. Would Molly collect her today? Would she call? Should Georgina invite her over for a late breakfast maybe—make it clear that she wanted to see her again? Was that too eager? After all there was nothing worse than emotions spilling out unchecked with no regard for their effect on those in their wake.

She pulled her mother's letter out of her pocket and reread it before slipping the page back into its envelope. She then ripped it several times and tossed it on top of the pizza box to be thrown away.

Why a second letter so soon after the first? What was she so desperate to talk about, or rather, what on earth did she imagine she could say that would change the fact that she left and never came back? As for her hope, so what? Georgina had given her no reason to hold out for anything. And as for her own hopes, what did they have to do with her mother anyway? Nothing. Georgina's feelings were her own and her heart belonged to no one else. That was how it had always been and would be, wouldn't it?

She looked at the throw on the floor and at the scattered cushions and the dusting of pizza crust crumbs. *Molly.* She smiled at the memory of the night before, recalling their laughter and the intimacy of their chat. How easy Molly was to talk to, and how easy it would be to trust her and to share things with her that she had never felt able or wanted to share with anyone else before. And Molly had wanted to be with her, as she found another topic or poured another glass of wine, anything for the evening not to end. And then when it ended, Molly had kissed her, pressing soft lips lightly against her cheek. Georgina had fallen asleep with the sensation of Molly's kiss on her skin and the sound of Molly's laughter in her head, and she had slept not for a few hours but all night long.

She gathered the throw and held it against her heart before resting it to cover the arm of the sofa once more. As she did so something dropped to the floor. She picked it up and laughed at the sight of the sweetest of flightless birds.

Should she? Could she? Georgina took a photo of the corkscrew. She then attached it to an email which read, *Forgotten anyone?*

She pressed send and looked out at Daisy May. The reply came back by return.

Morning!

Georgina typed, *Your phone number or it's straight back to the zoo!*

There was no immediate reply. Was that email too forward? Had she misread something, everything? She sat on the edge of her father's chair with the phone resting in her lap. She pressed refresh. Nothing.

And then the shadow of the movement of a shape outside half caught her eye. She startled at the sudden knock at the door. It would be the estate agent no doubt. She sat motionless. Could she ignore it? The second knock drummed out a melody of sorts. Surely too familiar for an estate agent?

She hesitantly opened the front door only to find Molly standing on the steps with a brown bag crammed with what smelled like breakfast. *Molly?*

Molly was wearing flared blue denim jeans and a coffee coloured T-shirt with the image of Animal from *The Muppet Show*. A large multicoloured woollen jumper was tied around her waist. Her hair was scooped underneath a blue fisherman's cap and large sunglasses shaded her eyes.

Georgina let out a gasp of laughter, in every way an outpouring of relief and delight.

Molly held up a defensive hand. "Don't judge me. When I have a hangover, the only thing that seems to help is a full monty breakfast roll from Mr. Brown's around the corner. It literally has *everything*. I figured if I needed one, then you probably did too. Oh, I made an executive decision and went brown sauce and runny yolk. Good morning."

"Thank God for you." Georgina meant every word. "I'll make you a strong coffee to go with it. I've already had two. I frankly feel like death warmed up."

Molly beamed a smile in reply. She took off her hat and her hair fell loose at her shoulders and back. "Yep. I get that. I'm dosed up on paracetamol." Molly gingerly lowered her sunglasses. "And still everything's a bit too bright and a bit too loud."

Georgina whispered, "Follow me."

Molly followed Georgina to the kitchen at the end of the hall. "So did Daisy May's company help you sleep? Wow, was this here yesterday? This may be my dream kitchen." Molly ran her hand along custom oak worktops, her fingertips sliding against a white porcelain sink with carved-in drainer. Patting a huge fridge she blew out her cheeks and asked, "Does this make ice?"

"Three types of ice to be precise: large cubes, small cubes, and slush. It also filters your water, and I wouldn't be surprised if it drank it for you too. And this glorious device mercifully makes coffee." Georgina placed a mug under the Gaggia coffee machine, capturing the brown nectar. "Here."

"Thank you *so* much." Molly took the coffee and perched on a kitchen stool. She unwrapped her breakfast roll and, taking a huge bite, mumbled "Oh my God, this is so good. So did you sleep okay then?"

"Oh, sorry, yes, I did as it happens. In fact I may have to request to borrow Daisy May every night." Georgina perched on the stool opposite Molly.

Molly chuckled. "Sure." She then licked her fingers and held her palm at her chest. "I swear if you could marry food, then me and this roll would be a hot item."

Georgina teased, "Your forever one?"

Molly blinked at Georgina and then looked down.

"Molly, I'm so sorry. That was an insensitive thing to say."

"Don't worry about it." Molly shrugged. Her voice struck a newly detached note.

Oh God, I've hurt you, haven't I? Georgina searched Molly's face. "I really am sorry."

"You need to eat your breakfast before it goes cold," Molly said without emotion.

Georgina unwrapped the roll. In that moment, she had no appetite at all. Her heart ached at the sudden distance between them.

"I know it's old fashioned to have those values," Molly said. "And that you probably think I'm ridiculous."

"No, Molly. I'm the ridiculous commitment-phobe."

Molly asked quietly, "You don't think you'll ever marry, or partner with someone long-term?"

"The honest answer is I've never let myself think about it. You see, my mother…" Georgina swallowed hard, the words sticking in her throat.

Molly shook her head. "You don't have to—"

"I do. I want to explain. Look, let's go into the sitting room—maybe even reclaim that sofa. I can't believe I made you sit on the floor last night."

"You didn't make me. It was my idea, remember? It was fun." Molly slipped from her stool, picked up her empty wrapper, and threw it in the bin. "And you have exactly thirty seconds before I eat the rest of that roll for you."

Laying her feelings bare and opening up to Molly seemed to be working, as Molly seemed to relax again. And what was most surprising, Georgina wanted to open up. She wanted to tell Molly everything.

❖

A soft autumn light fell across Georgina's face and illuminated the white of her shirt and the blue of her denim jeans. She sat with a leg crossed over a knee, and her mug rested in her lap, as she looked out to the square. There was something far away in her expression. Where was she? What maze of thought was she lost in? Or which memory, phantom-like, had revisited her?

Nervousness tinged the edge of her curiosity. What was Georgina about to say, and what would it mean for her and for the possibility of a *them*?

They sat in silence for several minutes before Georgina turned to look at Molly and said, "When I was eleven, I witnessed my mother

kissing a man who was not my father. Right there in the museum's foyer."
Georgina nodded towards the museum.

You saw it? Molly followed Georgina's gaze.

"The man was some Svengali figure who wanted to manage my
mother's career. She was an artist. He was all charm, and my father never
trusted him, and it turned out he was right not to." Georgina looked at
Molly. "I told my father what I'd seen."

Blimey. Molly hugged her mug against her.

"My father was naturally devastated. Every evening when I came
home from school, I would hear them rowing. And then my father broke
the news that they were divorcing and my mother would be moving out.
He said that if I wanted, I could stay with him, and that he thought that
would be best for me. So I chose to live with my father." Georgina took a
sip of her coffee. "I was so cross with her. I refused to see her. I honestly
hated her, Molly, for what she had done."

Molly rested her hand briefly on Georgina's arm. "That's
understandable. Who wouldn't feel that way?"

"And then a year or so later, just a few months after divorce
proceedings had concluded, it was on Christmas Eve in fact, my mother
returned to the house to collect her remaining things. I overheard them
rowing again for what would be the last time." Georgina's attention
drifted to the paintings on the wall. "She left without looking back. I still
see her leaving in my nightmares."

"I don't know what to say," Molly said softly. "Except I understand
now why you feel the way you do…about everything." Molly wanted to
put her arms around Georgina, but she couldn't. She felt too much for
Georgina for it to be the innocent hug of a friend.

Georgina fell silent again. She sat staring into her lap with her
fingers wrapped around her mug.

"Not that it's in any way comparable." Molly gave a small shrug.
"But my ex Erica left without saying goodbye too." Georgina looked at
Molly. "I thought it was the most cowardly hurtful thing you could do to
someone. And she had been my friend as well as my lover. It felt like a
double rejection. Other than returning my house keys a month ago I've
heard nothing from her. Not that I'm sorry about that."

"She sounds charming."

"She's an art dealer, so funnily enough, charm is her stock-in-trade.
I don't know, maybe Erica thought there was nothing to say."

Georgina shook her head and her cheeks flushed an angry pink.
"But there's always something that should be said, though, isn't there?
Otherwise you're left waiting for the words that never come. Whether
you want to wait or not. It's cruel." Georgina stared away to the square

again. "As it happens, I received a letter from my mother this morning. She writes a few times a year."

"Really? It's good that you keep in touch despite—"

"We don't. I mean, I never reply."

But then why would she reply? Her mother broke her trust, and by the sadness swimming in Georgina's eyes, her heart.

Georgina looked down. "I know that seems cold of me."

"No. It seems human."

"She destroyed our family. After she left, I was sent to boarding school. I left my friends and my father and everything behind. In all the letters she sent, she never once said sorry. And now this letter—the second in just over a month. She says she wants us to talk. Does she think my father's death will change anything? She simply has no shame."

With the care of someone disarming a bomb, Molly said, "It may help you to talk to her."

"No. I can't."

Molly wanted to stroke Georgina's flushed cheeks and press a soothing cool palm against them. It was clear she had suffered such pain. There was nothing much worse than a wound inflicted by a parent to their child. "I'm sorry she hurt you."

Georgina took a deep shaky breath. "Thank you." She cleared her throat. "I'm sorry too. It was wrong of me to drag you into such a discussion." Georgina sat up straight.

"Don't worry about it. Honestly. Everybody needs to talk about serious stuff now and then. And I'm flattered that you feel you can talk to me." Molly risked a smile encouraging the sadness to disperse to the edge of things.

Georgina rested her arm across the top of the sofa, bridging the gap between them. "To be honest, you're the first person I've told any of this to."

"I am?" Molly's heart inflated to bursting. "Well then, I'm doubly flattered." If she was not mistaken, Georgina was looking at her with the intensity of someone who wanted to kiss her.

But then Georgina shook her head as if she'd said something foolish. "I've burdened you with my nonsense enough. Let's change topic." Georgina dropped her arm to rest at her side. "To a subject I'm hoping will be a little more straightforward. At least with your help."

Molly tucked her legs up under her to face Georgina. She took a deep breath, willing herself to concentrate. "Okey-dokey—fire away."

"At the risk of sounding pathetic, I'm struggling to muster a clear head to hand over the bequeathed works. Even though I understand it's best, it's just…" Georgina's voice broke and she swallowed several times. "I'm sorry."

Molly rested her hand gently on Georgina's arm. "Don't be."

"It's just, can you help me? I know it's been many months since my father died, and it's well overdue, and it makes no sense." Georgina bit her lip and took a sip of her coffee.

"It makes complete sense," Molly said. "How could you feel any differently?" How could she help Georgina when words would only ever be words? She needed to *do* something. But what? Wait. Would seeing the space where her father's art would be help? "I have an idea."

"Okay."

"You'll need to put your shoes on and come with me."

Georgina laughed. "I'm not sure what to think."

"Then don't think, just follow."

Molly led them outside and across the square to the museum. The weekend front-of-house assistant gave a distracted nod in Molly's direction as Molly reached behind the reception desk and grabbed the keys for the annex.

She opened the annex doors to be greeted by the peaceful empty space so in contrast to the rest of the hectic museum. The paper at the windows had been removed, and daylight flooded in, falling on the polished flooring and fading away into the whiteness of the skirting.

"So here we are. It's only just been finished, so you'll need to watch your clothes as I'm not sure what's dry and what's not."

"It's beautiful." Georgina stood in the centre of the room, casting glances from one corner to the other.

Molly closed the door behind them. "It's Evelyn's work."

Georgina raised her eyebrows. "Really? She's done an excellent job. Will you thank her for me?"

"Of course."

Georgina wandered over to the French doors. She stared in the direction of her father's house.

Molly sat on a bench by the back wall, determined to give Georgina the space she needed to take everything in.

After a few minutes of being together in silence Georgina said, "The way the room looks out to the house has a real poignancy to it, doesn't it? It almost feels like, I don't know, less a change of location for the artworks and more a shift of focus."

"Yes, that's a really good way of looking at it," Molly said, impressed at how quickly Georgina had grasped a sense of things.

Georgina turned to Molly. "Thank you for showing me this."

Molly stood. "No worries. Even with the art in place, it will retain this lovely feel."

Georgina gazed around the room once more. "It's hard to imagine it full of art."

"Right, yes. Well, we know there'll be plinths for the Rodin and for the bust of Thomas Cook. And we'll need to put the Staffordshire ware out of harm's way in a glass display cabinet. All it takes is a stray elbow or an unfortunate trip. You only have to ask the Fitzwilliam."

Georgina laughed. "Yes. Sensible."

"Then, let me think, there'll be an introduction panel giving a brief history of the foundation over time and of course an overview of your father's work and life. The paintings, the cartoon, the photographs, and the sketch will occupy the wall space. I was thinking of suggesting to Evelyn that we hang the family portraits from the 1800s together in a series just as they've been hung in your father's house for all those years." Molly pointed to the back wall that faced towards the square. "Just here, maybe? I thought we could even make them a talking point."

Georgina gave a hesitant, "Okay."

"You see, I always think with exhibitions, that people relate best to other people. To human stories. We could really engage visitors with the lives behind the paintings."

Georgina moved to stand beside Molly, staring with her at the bare wall.

"I know it will be a fab space," Molly continued. The sensation of Georgina so close was making it almost impossible to breathe. She struggled to compose herself to say, "Do you, I mean, if you're ready, shall we make our way back to the house?"

Georgina cleared her throat. "Yes."

As they reached the door, Georgina looked back into the room. "I can almost imagine him standing at the window, looking out to the square."

"I promise we'll care for your father's art," Molly said. "And do everything we can to respect his memory."

Georgina returned her gaze to Molly. "I know that. I trust you."

"Thank you." Molly swallowed down an urge to cry. "That means a lot."

❖

"Here you go." Georgina handed Molly a glass of water.

Molly sat forward on the sofa and pressed the glass to her forehead. "Ooh, thanks. That really helps *and* I may even drink it."

Georgina laughed. "I feel bad that you're having to help me, with a hangover and on your day off as well. Are you sure I can't get you something more to eat? Or another coffee?"

"Nope, I'm fine, thank you, though. And as days off go, this is fun. I like getting things done."

"Yes, me too. And if you're sure—"

"Totally."

"So what's the next step in the process of the handover?"

"Just let me know the date that suits, so we can schedule things, or if it's easier for you and you're happy to trust us, we could have a key and get on with the transfer on your behalf."

"Yes, the latter would be great. I've got to get extra house keys cut for the estate agent later today, and then I'll get them to drop a key in at the museum. Thanks for making everything less...overwhelming."

"My pleasure. And thanks to your father and to you for such a fantastic gift. I confess I'm really excited by the Wright room—sorry, the Wright Community Room and Gallery."

Georgina beamed a smile. "Good."

"And on the subject of being excited, and at the risk of sounding like a total geek, I couldn't be more impressed that the bequest includes a Leibovitz, but even more than that, my head spins at the thought of the Rodin."

Georgina nodded. "Ah, yes. Even I'm impressed by the Leibovitz photo. And you're not the only one interested in the Rodin. It's certainly been attracting a lot of attention. It's got quite an interesting history actually. It's been with the foundation since its beginnings in 1888. There is some speculation as to how the foundation acquired something so valuable. But the gist is that William Wright was the solicitor and confidant to a very wealthy industrialist here in Leicester. On hearing that Josephine had set up the foundation, his son, to reduce death duties following his father's death, gifted the Rodin. The more scurrilous rumour is that he didn't want his estranged wife to have it."

"Really? I love it."

Georgina burst into laughter. "It's good to know that the Wright history is entertaining."

"Absolutely. Never a dull moment."

A loaded silence soon replaced their laughter.

"I should probably go," Molly said. "And let you get on." Leaving had never felt harder. She gathered her things and followed Georgina into the hall. "Oh, I nearly forgot." Molly shook her head. "I meant to mention that Evelyn has in mind the evening of Friday 8th December for the opening. Would this fit? If this date is okay with you, then we'll proceed with issuing invitations."

"Let me just check." Georgina retrieved her phone from the pocket of her jeans and thumbed through to her diary. "Yep, I've pencilled it in, so to speak."

"Great."

Blushing, Georgina asked, "Is it still okay to have your number?"

Molly could have cried with relief. "Oh yes. In exchange for Penguin, obviously."

"Obviously."

Georgina went to fetch Molly's corkscrew while Molly typed her number in to Georgina's phone.

"One free bird." Georgina handed Penguin over with a wide smile.

"Thank you, although, on second thoughts, why don't you keep it for now. After all, a house without a corkscrew is a scary place to be."

Georgina laughed. "I'll buy one, I promise, and return Penguin to you."

Without debating the rights and wrongs or the personal versus the professional, Molly leaned up and kissed Georgina on the cheek, just as she had done the night before. She lingered a moment, brushing her lips softly against Georgina's skin, and then she stepped away. Georgina was looking at her face and studying every feature. Why wouldn't she kiss her? She could tell Georgina wanted to. Or was she imagining it somehow? Could it be that Georgina really didn't want a relationship with anyone? But then, why ask for her number? Or was it just for work? A chill rose like floodwater to her chest. That must be it—she considered her a colleague and nothing more. Molly swallowed hard and said, "Goodbye then."

Georgina nodded. "Yes, goodbye for now. And thank you again for everything."

Molly forced herself to turn the door handle and to walk away towards Daisy May, who as ever waited patiently for her return. She wasn't sure whether it was hearing the heartbreaking tale of Georgina's sad childhood and seeing her terrible grief, or the simple pain of not being kissed goodbye, but either way, tears began to stream down her cheeks that she feared might never stop.

CHAPTER SEVENTEEN

Georgina stood in the middle of the sitting room and watched Molly walk away towards Daisy May. She waited, wondering why Molly wasn't starting the engine. Had Daisy May broken down? Or was it Molly? She could just make out that Molly's head was bowed. Was she reading her phone? Or was she upset? Was Molly okay? Should she check?

No. What if she was the cause of her upset? Then going to her would only make things worse, surely?

Was she hurting her by confusing her? Was that it? By not knowing what to do about the girl she had no right to fall for. For there were expectations of her behaviour. There were professional boundaries. She was Georgina Wright, for God's sake. And yet all she wanted to be in that moment was Georgina, a girl who was falling for another girl who seemed to like her too.

What must Molly be thinking now? One minute she was telling Molly how she had never even thought about the possibility of a long-term partner, and then the next minute she was asking for her number.

It was cruel, for she could sense Molly falling for her just as she was falling for Molly. It was there in the nervous excitement in the air whenever they met and in the glances and the words that meant too much, but most of all it was in the palpable wrench of saying goodbye.

When they were together, she could feel Molly's gaze upon her and see the affection in Molly's eyes when she looked at her. And she had encouraged it. She wanted more than anything for Molly to want her. She was responsible for how Molly seemed to be feeling, wasn't she? She was the reason Molly had just kissed her cheek for the second time and looked at her with an expression that seemed to say, *I want more. I want you.*

London was only an hour away. They could date. But then what? How was she to know? She'd never got beyond dating. But then, Molly was different in every way. She already felt more for Molly, far more than those women she had dated for many months. Not only did she feel more, she felt differently. She instinctively wanted to protect her and care for her and make her dreams come true. She wanted to be her knight in shining armour and to rescue her from dragons. She wanted to come home to Molly. Only Molly. She wanted to hear her laugh and to admire her passion and to wake and plan a day with her and to fall asleep at night in her arms.

Maybe Molly was her *one*? Maybe there was such a thing? But then, hadn't her father thought that? Hadn't Edith thought that?

September 1832
City Walk, Leicester

"Edith! Edith, wait!" Josephine pulled at Edith's sleeve. "For pity's sake."

"Pity? How can you speak of pity?" Edith tugged her sleeve free from Josephine's hold. "You have none."

"And you have no sense! Wait!" Josephine followed after Edith, trying her best for her walking not to become running. Ladies did not run, after all. Edith, on the other hand, seemed to find walking at a genteel pace a torture she would not endure. Josephine could just see her ahead, running, weaving through the crowds that had gathered on City Walk for the much anticipated lighting of the first gas lamps.

"Edith?" Josephine looked for Edith's shape amongst the pressing throng, so familiar, so loved. She felt a hand slip into hers. She felt Edith's lips warm against her ear.

"I do not need sense when my heart tells me all I need to know." Edith lifted Josephine's hand against her chest.

"Please, Edith. I cannot be strong for both of us. We need to let each other go."

Edith gripped Josephine's hand tighter. "Why? Why must we? We can build a life together."

With her lips pressed in turn to Edith's ear lest someone in the crowd about them should hear, Josephine gasped, "How?"

"With love."

"Love does not feed us or pay our bills. It does not keep the cruel scrutiny of others at bay. Love will not protect our reputations, Edith. Love is not enough. And let us not forget, you have your mother to care for. Your writing will barely be sufficient, as it is."

"I have an endowment. Small it may be, but we could make it stretch. We can do anything. Be anything."

"Miss Brancaster. Good evening! I thought it was you." William Wright, ruddy cheeked, and eyes bright as if lit by the lamplighter himself, beamed a smile at Josephine. If he had seen Edith or for that matter caught sight of her dropping Josephine's hand to her side, he did not comment. "What a night! Can you see? I have a spot nearer to where the lamplighter will rest his ladder for this lamp here. Would you care to join me?"

"Good evening, Mr. Wright." Josephine gave a courteous nod. "I'm fine just where I am. But thank you for the kind offer to stand with you."

"Very well, as you wish. Should you change your mind, I am just there. Good evening to you." William lifted his hat and gave a small bow with his heels clicking softly together before he turned to stand a few feet away.

"How do you know him?" Edith narrowed her eyes, watching him leave as if chasing off the keen beau.

"I don't know him. He has been working with my father. I believe he is a solicitor."

"Well, I believe you are causing him to be quite distracted. He has missed that lamp being lit right at his ear, for his attention cannot be drawn from you."

"I have done nothing to attract his attention. You have my word."

"Men do not require a woman to *do* anything. There is a presumption, and I think he is presuming."

"And he is not the only one. For you are presuming too much—for us, for the future."

"I am not presuming you love me. I know you do."

"That is not the point. How many times must I say that?" Tears forced their way over Josephine's lips, squeezed tight in an attempt to hold back a sob. "I will not say it again. We cannot be together as we've been any more. We must stop this. This evening, in fact. Right now. And begin again as friends and colleagues. We must at least try."

With a heartbreaking blankness to her voice, Edith said with her gaze dropped to the floor, "I can no more stop my feelings for you than I can stop my heart from beating."

Josephine felt Edith move away. "Edith." She reached out and found no hand to hold, just air. Empty air bathed in a golden street light.

Georgina heard Daisy May's engine start. Her heart ached as she watched Daisy May disappear around the corner. Molly had left, and nothing about her leaving felt right.

❖

Molly sat in her kitchen with her cheek resting against the table's surface. A half-empty Nutella jar sat in front of her. October's *Museums Association* magazine was open to her side. She had stuck neon Post-it notes to sections and tabbed pages to mark interesting information or ideas. As Saturday evenings went, hers was, well, less rock and roll and more geektastic.

She tapped out a repetitive note against the glass jar. Trust her to fall for someone who didn't do relationships. Trust her to open her heart, unguarded. How did she imagine that someone like Georgina Wright would fall for her, anyway? What was she thinking? It was total madness. She was totally crazy.

She scooped out a large spoonful of Nutella. She held the spoon in her mouth and mumbled, "Maybe I'm destined to be single. I should get a cat for company. Or a dog. Or a parrot, or a—"

Molly jumped at the burr of her phone from her bag. She stared suspiciously in the direction of the noise. Who called at ten o'clock on a Saturday night? She'd not long come off the phone from her mum. It was nobody. "Or an alpaca? Nope, garden too small." The phone stopped burring. "A goldfish. Yes. That would work. What would I call it? Jaws? Moby Dick? FisheyMacFishface? Yes. That's settled then."

A beep sounded from within her bag, signalling that the caller had left a message. Molly dug to the bottom of her bag and felt for her phone.

Hi Molly, it's Georgina. Georgina Wright.

Molly dropped the spoon and sat up straight. She moved the phone quickly to her other ear as if somehow she could concentrate more with that ear.

I'm sorry to call so late. I've only just got back to London. The trains were delayed. Anyway. I'm just ringing to thank you again for your work and your company last night and today. It, you, made a real difference. So anyway, I was wondering...

Molly held her breath.

Well, the thing is, each year my employer hosts an evening for important clients. Sometimes it's the theatre or a gala evening, but this year it's a reception and talk at the National Portrait Gallery. It includes dinner. It's in a couple of weeks' time. I'm obliged to go to these things. So I was wondering if you would like to be my guest for the night?

Was she asking her out? No, it was a work thing. Right?

Anyway, so I'll leave it with you. Okay. Thanks again. Bye.

Molly pressed dial.

"Hello."

"Hi, Georgina, it's Molly."

"Molly. Hi."

"Sorry I missed your call. I was thinking of names for a goldfish I probably won't buy."

Georgina laughed. "Okay. And what did you settle on?"

"FisheyMacFishface."

Georgina laughed even louder. "Perfect."

"I thought so. And yes, please to being your guest at the do at the National Portrait Gallery. It's without question my favourite museum and not just in London but anywhere. Thank you for inviting me."

"That's great. Thank you for coming with me."

"I'm already really looking forward to it."

"To be honest, I wasn't, but I am now."

She was? *Play it cool.* "So do you know what the talk will be on?" She could hear a rustle of paper.

"Cezanne. It's by the curator of the temporary exhibition on Cezanne's portraits, John Elderfield."

"*Really.* Interesting. You know, I don't know much about Cezanne. At least not his portraits. I'll make sure I research for us."

"Excellent. Well I'll let you get back to your goldfish naming. I'll send through the details about the evening. Goodnight."

"Goodnight, sleep well." Molly listened for the phone to go silent.

In that moment, in her kitchen, at her table, Molly wanted to cry and sing and skip and dance and open her window, and not care who might hear her shout, *Georgina Wright* into the night.

CHAPTER EIGHTEEN

The following fortnight went by in a blur. No sooner had the estate agents dropped off the keys to the house, than Evelyn had scheduled a date less than a week later for the transfer of George's collection to the museum.

Dazed, Molly couldn't quite believe that this important step had been achieved. She'd sent a text to Georgina to ask how she felt and if she was okay. She replied, *Absolutely fine and really looking forward to seeing you.*

Evelyn had been so utterly consumed on first hearing of the imminent receipt of George's art, that she had not even blinked at Molly's request to attend the evening at the National Portrait Gallery. Evelyn's distracted words of advice—to take the opportunity to network and to mention in conversation the museum's ambitious program and the strength of its collections—had done nothing to settle Molly's nerves.

How quickly the day arrived for her to go to London. She couldn't have felt less prepared or, for that matter, more excited.

Her heart raced as she stepped off the train and hurried along the platform at St. Pancras Station onto the escalator that led her down to the main concourse and towards the exit onto Euston Road. She stared up in wonder at the beautiful glazing and ironwork arches that formed the station roof. The renovated red-brick Victorian building was simply awesome. It was always thrilling to arrive in London.

The air was a heady blend of diesel, food, and coffee. People gathered on the concourse in groups talking loudly and urgently in languages she half recognized. Others knocked past her, hurrying in a purposeful, intense way with their eyes fixed beyond to their direction of travel. And she was part of the hustle and bustle and energy that bristled in the air.

The large round station clock reminded her that time was tight. The train had been delayed by fifteen minutes. It was six o'clock. If she didn't loiter, she should be okay. But there was so much to see and so much to catch her eye and delay her.

But she was determined not to be late. Not today. Not for Georgina.

When she emerged from the station, a fine mist of rain dampened her hair and cheeks, and the lights of passing traffic lit the dew sparkling on her glasses. She half ran towards a waiting black cab and climbed in.

"Where to, love?" The cab driver turned off his light.

"National Portrait Gallery, please. I'm going to a function there." Molly's heart all but burst with pride.

"Right you are, then." The driver weaved his way through the streets, past wobbling cyclists and hissing buses. The reflection of streetlights streamed up and over the shiny black bonnet in a riotous river of colour.

The closer she got to the gallery, the faster the beat of her heart. Would she say the right things to the right people? Could she make Georgina proud? Would people wonder why she had been invited? Would Georgina regret inviting her—the local girl, so out of place in London and so out of place in Georgina Wright's life? Why on earth was she there?

By the time the taxi drew up outside the gallery, Molly could hardly catch her breath. Attempts to deep breathe were faltered by the sight of the imposing Portland stone facade looming up with its inset pillars and arches so synonymous with the iconography of London. The setting, in every way the heart of cultural power, never failed to send chills right through to her core. She leaned forward as the taxi braked to a halt and paid her fare.

"Ta, darlin'. Have a good one."

"Thank you. I hope to."

She opened the door, struggling at first to find the handle. As she stepped onto the street, she looked up to see through the drizzle of rain a figure walking with an umbrella towards her. *Georgina?*

"Molly, hi," Georgina said, with a warm confidence to her voice. "I'm so sorry—what awful weather to have to contend with."

"Hi. It's okay. Thanks for meeting me and indeed for getting wet for me." *Did I just say that?* Molly let out an embarrassed giggle. "I've been in your company for literally a second and I've already lowered the tone."

Georgina laughed and leaned in to Molly's ear. "It's my pleasure. Let's go inside."

Molly tucked in close to Georgina, her shoulder pressing against Georgina's side. They hurried up the steps under the entrance's arched doorway adorned with a heraldic coat of arms.

When they reached the porch, Georgina shook the rain from the brolly and, closing it, said, "After you." She held her arm out towards a revolving door.

There were two things in life Molly hated above all things. Injustice and revolving doors. Georgina must have seen her hesitate as she quickly opened the side door. "Just as quick," she kindly said.

"I literally have nightmares about them. In one, it won't stop, and I am left like a hamster on a wheel for hours running in circles."

"That's awful."

"Yes, I know. And in the other—"

"I'm sorry, one moment. Jeremy, hi." Georgina shook the hand of a tall man in a sharp suit with hair so immaculate it looked like it was sprayed on. His floral cologne engulfed them in an aroma of wild flowers.

"Georgina. Hello." Jeremy's cheeks flushed pink. Clearly, not just women felt the impact of Georgina Wright.

"The Oberons are running late. I would like us to wait for them. Please let the speaker know," Georgina said without dropping a beat. "I would also like a quick word with the de Clancys this evening, if you can wrestle them free from Martin."

And with a nod the man was gone.

"Sorry, Molly. You were saying?"

Molly's heart sank. Soon the reception would draw Georgina completely from her and she would be left standing in a corner with just a glass of warm white wine and a wilting crudité for company.

Molly shook her head. "Oh no, you don't want to hear my silly stories." She shrugged her coat from her shoulders, and before both arms were released from their sleeves, a young man was at her side offering to hang it up for her. "Thank you." The man headed towards what she hoped was the cloakroom with both their coats and Georgina's brolly.

"You look beautiful," Georgina said.

Molly turned to find Georgina smiling at her. She looked down at her sleeveless little black dress and adjusted the large bow of the bright yellow scarf tied at the side of her neck. "Do I look like a sunflower?"

Georgina laughed. "Not at all. You look very arty. In other words, like you belong. You are perfect."

Perfect? "You look beautiful too." Molly's cheeks tingled with the exchange of compliments that meant so much.

"Thank you. In truth, I've come from work. I figured a suit's a suit."

A suit's a suit? Did she not know how hot she looked? Everything about Georgina was tailored and refined, as usual. A crisp white shirt set off her blue pinstriped jacket and trousers cut to perfection and worn with an upright ease. She was quite simply dreamy.

"Let's find the reception." Georgina glanced around the space. "We're in the Lerner Gallery for drinks and to take in the modern artwork, and then of course we have the lecture followed by the Cezanne exhibition."

Molly walked by Georgina's side. "I'm really excited, although please forgive my lack of preparation as work has been hectic."

"Forgiven. And dinner, I am led to understand, will be in the Weldon Galleries."

Molly slowed to ask, "The Weldon Galleries?"

"Yes. I take it from your *wow* expression that's impressive."

"Have you never been?"

"Nope."

"It's an awesome gallery with this beautiful silk wallpaper, *but* they're also the Regency galleries. We'll be dining in the company of reformers and abolitionists. The very people Edith and Josephine campaigned with. I think we can safely say they would have approved."

"Excellent. Meant to be, then?"

Molly nodded. "Yes." Everything about being with Georgina felt meant to be.

"Georgina, the Oberons have arrived." Jeremy reappeared gesturing discreetly to an elderly couple who were looking around, rather lost.

"I understand if you have to leave to mingle," Molly said, trying her best to sound self-sufficient and nonchalant. "To network."

"Thank you. Although ask anyone who works with me—I am not usually one for small talk. I've been client manager for the Oberons and the de Clancys for several years now. I brought them with me from Schroders. They have put a lot of trust in me, so to ignore them would be unforgivable."

"Absolutely."

"As for others"—Georgina glanced around the room—"I'm pretty sure I'll be more successful at engaging with them with you by my side."

Molly felt a pinch of hurt. Was that the only reason she invited her? She wanted someone arty by her side to be able to quote art to impress her clients?

"And particularly here." Molly looked down.

"Particularly *anywhere*," Georgina said with a quiet certainty to her voice.

Molly looked up at the sensation of Georgina's hand resting softly on her arm.

"So if you can bear it at all, Molly Goode, I shall leave your side as little as possible."

Delight and relief surged within her, spilling over into a smile at her lips. "I think I can just about bear it."

"Phew. I'll say hello to the Oberons, and then I'll grab us both a drink. Champagne?"

"Definitely." Molly laughed with Georgina and saw her joy reflected back in Georgina's eyes.

"I won't be a moment."

In that instant, it almost seemed as if Georgina would kiss her, as a lover kisses—goodbye for now.

But Georgina looked away to the Oberons and Molly quickly gathered herself to say, "Go."

Georgina greeted the Oberons with genuine warmth and affection, and their faces lit up. Molly felt so proud to be in the company—no, the guest—of someone who could have that effect on another human being.

With exquisite happiness, Molly casually wandered around the Lerner Gallery. She paused briefly at each contemporary portrait of a famous face hung against the stark white walls. The sitters stared back at her spotlighted, as if in shock by the glare of the track lighting above. The painted out arches that divided each viewing space ensured that the clean lines of *now* remained crisp and uncluttered by the architecture of *then*, unfettered by the tangled past.

In one corner of the space dedicated to self-portraits, Molly's attention was drawn to a painting of a woman at an easel. The woman wore an artist's smock and had her hair gathered loosely under a headscarf. Behind her was a sleeping child, tucked up in a wicker chair. It was entitled "Artiste, Mere, Femme." Molly leaned in closer to read the signature. *Lydia Wright?*

"One out of three may be correct." Georgina handed Molly her drink and a small plate of nibbles. "Here. I bring champagne and a pastry filled with something herby and lovely. Although I have no idea what it is." She stared with a blank expression at the painting. "My mother painted it."

"Then…is that you?" Molly studied Georgina to compare the child Georgina and the woman in front of her, so impressive, so grown up.

Georgina glumly nodded. "I suspect it will be the closest you'll get to meeting my mother. The painting was done at the villa in the south of France. When they divorced, my mother got the villa and my father the art. I was the only one left with nothing."

Molly didn't quite know what to say. She tentatively suggested, "The painting has a real sense of place. It has a distinctly French feel about it."

"I rather think it has a pretentious feel. But then everything about her was a pretence after all."

Georgina looked so sad. That was it. She would never mention Lydia Wright again.

"Look, the Queen, over there." Molly pointed to the far corner of the room.

Georgina turned away from the painting and Molly stole the last pastry from Georgina's plate. She shrugged at Georgina's amused if indignant expression. "Snooze, you lose. I'm pretty sure the herby loveliness is lambs lettuce spiked with chervil."

"And I'm pretty sure I'm never taking my eye off my plate again."

"Very wise." Molly could see the light had returned to Georgina's eyes. The next half an hour or so with Cezanne would surely snuff it out again. "Do you think your clients would notice if we skipped the talk?"

"More to the point, would you mind? You said you were excited by it."

"I can see it another time. And we can always sneak in for the end."

"Then I have an idea. Just a sec." Georgina moved towards the other side of the gallery and began speaking to one of the staff who looked across at Molly before seeming to agree to something.

"Molly. Molly Goode? I thought it was you."

Molly turned round, straight into the puzzled face of Erica Bell. Erica was dressed all in black. She looked like a night burglar. All she lacked was a mask and a bag marked *swag*. Her hair was slicked back and her lips pinched in a shade of lipstick no doubt called Deadly Red.

"Erica?"

Erica laughed. "You've gone quite pale. Do you need to sit?"

For some reason Erica carried on laughing. Molly had no idea what was so funny. Erica obviously felt no shame or guilt or anything, it would seem.

"So what on earth brings you to London on a Wednesday evening? Has your little museum loaned something? How sweet."

"No."

"Oh, that makes more sense, after all space on these walls is quite in demand. Have you seen Tracey's latest?"

"Tracey Emin? Her 'Death Mask'? Very briefly, yes."

"And what did you think? I've just told her she's quite the genius."

"She's here tonight?" Molly looked at the few remaining people as they made their way into the lecture theatre.

"Yes, somewhere. I'm not sure how long she'll stay for. She nipped out for a fag, but in fact it wouldn't surprise me if she's gone. Ooh, is that Georgina Wright? Now she's an elusive one. She's taken over as head of the Wright Foundation. It never hurts to make an ally of a funder. And of course her mother is Lydia Wright, tortured *nearly* famous artist and influencer in the art world even today. We had a go at wooing the dashing Georgina Wright a few months back. I even had a colleague attend her father's funeral. To no avail." Erica waved in Georgina's direction.

"Funny you should say that…" Molly paused as Georgina returned to her.

Erica held out her hand. "Georgina Wright? Erica Bell, of Bell and Co. We deal out of St. James's. May I say how sorry I was to learn of your father's death. In fact I believe you recently met a colleague of mine at your father's funeral."

Georgina shook Erica's hand. "I can't say I remember."

Molly leaned slightly into Georgina and whispered, "My ex."

Georgina seemed to stand up straighter.

Erica narrowed her eyes. "Yes, we used to date. We were quite the couple for a while. Couldn't persuade her to settle in London. Quite the local girl. Isn't that right, Molly?"

Molly's cheeks burned. She glanced at Georgina who had visibly flushed at the comment.

"And, of course, as I'm sure you'll understand, Georgina, I found Leicester…limiting. So anyway I won't keep you. Please do let me know if I can be of any help at all." With that Erica offered her business card.

Georgina just looked at it. "I'm struggling to think why I might need it."

Erica's mouth fell open. "Well of course, I wouldn't want you to struggle."

"Well then," Georgina said, her tone guarded. "Have a good evening."

Erica looked at Molly and back at Georgina. "Yes, you too. And Molly, it's nice to see you looking so…" Molly held her breath waiting for the wounding insult. Erica's eyes hovered over her outfit. "Happy."

"Thank you, Erica. Goodbye." Whether or not Erica had wanted to say *happy*, Molly had definitely wanted to say goodbye. For Georgina was right—there was always something that should be said.

Molly stood in silence as she watched Erica walk away.

❖

Georgina whispered, "You okay?"

"Yes. Thank you. I am, as a matter of fact."

Molly looked so proud, and if possible her smile seemed even brighter. "Good for you. Let's go."

Georgina guided Molly along the Lerner Gallery and out into the cool of the stairwell and up the wide, low stone steps. Molly stopped halfway to admire the view of the ornate stonework and leaded windows.

"It's so grand, isn't it?" Molly cast her gaze from the decorative ceiling to the worn stone floors. "It almost has a cathedral-like feel and is so different to the Lerner Gallery. Where are we heading exactly? And more to the point, what happens if we get caught?"

"Don't worry, we're not trespassing." Georgina glanced up the stairwell to the levels above. "The whole building has been hired for the evening."

"The whole building? Wow."

Georgina shrugged. "They're a corporate partner. Third floor."

"You're taking me to the loos?"

Georgina laughed. "Somewhere with a slightly better view."

They climbed until they reached their destination.

"Oh, you mean the restaurant?" Molly said, slightly out of breath. "My mum and I once tried to have afternoon tea, but it was so busy."

"Well, I confirm it's not busy tonight." Georgina led Molly into the elegant dining room which had closed for the night. The space was lit only at the entrance by the light of the landing. Not that it was dark. Light flooded in from the city itself, reflecting against the windows and sparkling in the polished surfaces and glinting against cutlery and glassware. The city spread out before them, illuminated in all her urban splendour. The rooftop restaurant of the National Portrait Gallery commanded one of the most captivating views of London.

Molly went straight to the window. "I always make a point when I visit the museum of stopping for a moment just at the entrance to the restaurant to glimpse the view across the rooftops of Trafalgar Square."

Georgina joined Molly close at her side. There was only one view in that moment that captivated her.

"And there's Big Ben." Molly glanced at Georgina. "I love that they're restoring it."

Georgina dragged her gaze from Molly to look out to her city which had once been everything she needed and was in that moment a distraction from everything she wanted.

Molly pointed into the distance. "And Whitehall and the London Eye. It's such an awesome view."

The city's lights rested on Molly's cheeks before tangling themselves in her eyes.

You're so beautiful. Georgina stood utterly transfixed by the sight of Molly—the enchanting woman from the square, the woman who made her father's death somehow tolerable, the woman who made her laugh, the woman she'd opened up to who had listened to her with such empathy, and the woman who in that moment she just wanted to kiss.

"Does living in London ever become normal?" Molly turned to face Georgina again. "I imagine it never…" Molly's words drifted away as she blinked into Georgina's gaze, her lips falling slightly open.

Georgina hadn't planned to kiss Molly right there and then. She just couldn't not. It was as inevitable as the splash of rain on the windowsill that fell from the night sky above. She leaned down and placed her lips gently to Molly's, and without hesitation Molly rested her palms on Georgina's cheeks and kissed her. Georgina slipped her arms around Molly's waist, drawing her in. It felt so right. Molly's body matched close against hers, as if the separation of their bodies had been the wrong thing in the first place.

Only a passing siren with its wailing brought Georgina back into the room. She found just enough will to step away from Molly at the sound of the soft scuff of feet on the landing announcing the arrival of the waiter with a tray of champagne and canapés.

She found the breath to say, "Thank you, just at this table, please."

The waiter quickly placed the tray beside them. "Shall I lay things out?"

Georgina shook her head. "We'll be fine."

The waiter left, almost as if he had never arrived.

Georgina gazed at Molly's flushed cheeks and at her lips, moist and full with their edges smudged pink by their kiss. Was the room spinning for Molly too? "You okay?"

Molly nodded. She was, it seemed, utterly lost for words.

Georgina glanced at the tray. "I asked for extra pastries. Just in case."

Molly laughed and then quickly bit at her lip as if her laughter had freed emotions that threatened to overwhelm her. "Thank you—for all of this. It's amazing."

"You're welcome." Georgina lifted two glasses of champagne and handed one to Molly. She then raised her glass. "To you, Molly."

Molly lifted her glass. "To us. And to the rooftops of London and the most magical evening anyone could wish for."

Georgina swallowed down the swell of joy catching in her throat. "Yes."

With a clink of their glasses, they drank their champagne, with the city lights sparkling against the windows like starlight in the falling rain.

❖

Molly wasn't certain whether she could feel her toes. Was she sitting there at all? Surely she was floating above everything and everyone. Her lips tingled and her neck felt warm. She placed her palm to her cheek, lightly, briefly, in the hope that the heat of her recent passion would cool sufficiently to get her through dinner. Surely she would give away to her fellow diners how ignited with passion she felt. Had they noticed already but were too polite to comment?

She had tried, with some success, not to stare at Georgina seated opposite her but instead to valiantly concentrate on the thread of dinner conversation.

She was seated between Mr. Oberon and Mr. de Clancy, who seemed content to talk over her. She found their discussions about investment trends and the continued mire of short selling and the future prospects of renewables beyond her knowledge or interest. She smiled in agreement when it seemed appropriate and frowned as a gesture of shared consternation when the need arose. But even if they had ventured onto topics Molly could have contributed to, she feared her brain could not hold a thought beyond *You kissed me.*

"And do you work with Georgina?" Mrs. Oberon had said very little, so when she eventually spoke everyone seemed to listen. Molly couldn't decide whether to be flattered or horrified that she'd been chosen as the focus of her attention.

Molly quickly swallowed her mouthful of petit four and momentarily pressed her napkin lightly at her mouth. "We're not colleagues, as such." She dared not look at Georgina, for surely just the slightest glance would betray her feelings for all to see. "That is, I don't work for Staithe Street. I'm the curator of fine arts at the City Museum in Leicester. Georgina and I have been working together on a couple of projects."

A murmur of interest circled the table in response.

"Oh, thank goodness, the prospect of a change of subject." Mrs. Oberon smiled warmly at Molly. "There is only so much talk of money and politics that one can endure. So tell me, what did you think of the lecture?"

Everyone looked at Molly.

Georgina and Molly had followed their plan to sneak back into the talk in the hope that they would not be missed. They had caught the speaker's last words.

Bugger. She should have found time to research beforehand and been prepared. Evelyn had warned her, hadn't she? And now all she could anticipate was letting Georgina down.

She took a deep breath. "I always greatly value a new perspective on an artist." She gripped her napkin. "And to see together…for the first time"—Molly scrambled to call to mind the blurb from the programme—"over fifty of Cezanne's portraits, provides a real insight." The silence in response was clearly an expectation of more. "Indeed, I always wonder what the artist would have thought, seeing works that they completed on a separate, individual basis and at different periods in their life brought together all at once."

Molly's observation was met with a general rumble of accord.

Buoyed by their response, Molly continued, "I'm certainly very aware that as curators we have the privilege and responsibility of creating new meaning by the choices we make when we bring work together within one exhibition. What we omit and what we add, even the order of display, changes the discourse and ultimately the understanding." Molly took a quick sip of her espresso. Was she making any sense? To her horror, she caught the eye of Erica seated at the table with the speaker who was holding court. Molly quickly looked away.

"It's so easy, isn't it," Mrs. Oberon said, "to imagine that when you visit an exhibition that you are somehow having a direct experience with the artist, but you have reminded us, Molly, that everything is mediated and edited for us."

"But what if the artist explains their work and approach? A self-curated exhibition," Mrs. de Clancy asked, her tone without judgement and her expression one of genuine enquiry. She looked at Mrs. Oberon and then at Molly.

"That's an excellent question." Molly smoothed her napkin flat. A calm of sorts returned as she deliberated upon her reply. "You would think that would help. But in truth, here is where we meet not so much a problem, more the essence of things. If we consider that art is created and belongs in a visual realm, then the moment we try—and that includes the artist—to define it with language, we dislocate it from where it belongs and infect it with the bias that comes with words, and with thought, even."

Mrs. Oberon leaned forward. "So you are saying art is beyond definition?"

Molly took another sip of her espresso. "We need definition so we can share our experience of art with each other. And there is no question that knowledge can add more to an experience. But then we are adding, colouring over the work with what we know. So yes, I am saying art is beyond definition if we are to get close to experiencing it in its purest form."

"Yes." Mrs. de Clancy was nodding. "I do love it when a piece of art leaves me speechless. Words would certainly spoil those precious moments. Hairs on the back of the neck kind of thing."

"Can I add a twist?" Molly risked a glance to Georgina. She was smiling as if amused and Molly hoped not entirely regretting inviting her.

"Yes. Twist away." Mrs. Oberon's eyes shone.

"I'm afraid it is impossible to look at something without defining it." Molly shrugged.

"How intriguing," Mrs. Oberon said. "And is this because of the way we see?"

"Yes. When we look at something, we instantly try to recognize it and to understand what it is. When we seek to understand something, a piece of art for example, we compare it with what we've seen before, and to what we know. In other words, it is inescapable that we will try to define an art piece just by the act of looking at it."

Mrs. Oberon held both hands aloft as if surrendering. "So let me get this straight. Not only is art beyond definition, but we are incapable of not defining it."

"Yes, that's right. Therefore art will always be remote to us, and that is what I think makes it so magical."

"Goodness, what an intriguing evening. Thank you for your company tonight, Molly. I must make a point of visiting your museum." Mrs. Oberon stood, and with that so did everyone at their table. "What a wonderful evening, Georgina, as always." Mrs. Oberon held Georgina by both hands. "And please thank Martin and the team."

"Of course. Let me walk you to the door." Georgina turned to Molly and whispered, "I won't be a moment."

Molly sat back in her seat staring at the tables emptying around her and enveloped in the heady air of conversation and the drifting sound of laughter and heartfelt farewells.

It was an evening she couldn't have imagined and one that, if she could wish it, would never end.

CHAPTER NINETEEN

When Georgina returned to the Weldon Gallery she found Molly alone exploring portraits of Regency era reformers and staring up at large paintings depicting parliaments and reformation committees at work. The tables had already been cleared and lay empty but for their tablecloths and floral centrepieces. A clink of glasses could be heard being carried away down the corridor.

"I'm sorry, that took longer than I thought." Georgina rested her hand lightly on Molly's back. "Estelle Oberon insisted on asking me about our work together. I explained briefly about the Wright Community Room and Gallery and of course about Edith's painting. She was quite clearly fascinated. She wanted to know how long you had worked at the museum and then I realized I didn't know. And then I got caught with the de Clancys." Georgina paused to catch her breath. "Sorry—I ran up the stairs. I didn't mean to neglect you by leaving you so long."

"That's really sweet of you," Molly said with a smile that reassured Georgina all was well. "But there was no need to worry. I have been enjoying the company of kick-arse reformers. Oh, and to answer Mrs. Oberon's question, I've been at the museum about nine months now."

"Is that all?"

"Yep. I guess I'm the new girl keen to make a good impression." Molly rolled her eyes.

"Well, if Estelle Oberon's interest is anything to go by, you have made quite an impression indeed."

Molly beamed a smile. "She seems lovely."

"Yes, she is. And kind and generous to boot. The Oberons support a lot of very good causes, particularly surrounding health and education. Estelle in her own right has done a lot of work around supporting young people, particularly from disadvantaged backgrounds, and raising their self-esteem. I've done some mentoring as part of one of her campaigns."

"Really? I love that you've done that." Molly stroked Georgina's sleeve and she played for a moment with the cuff before catching the tips of Georgina's fingers. "I love everything about you in fact."

Georgina's heart caught at Molly's words and at the sensation of her fingertips, so warm and soft. "Likewise. Having you by my side tonight, and over the last few months knowing you were there…" An urge to cry choked at Georgina's throat.

Molly rested her palm briefly on Georgina's cheek. "I've loved every minute of our time together. Really, I have. And as for our research into Edith's painting, it's just been so captivating, hasn't it? And it feels *so* important. And being here amongst Josephine's and Edith's contemporaries, how amazing is this?"

"Yes, it's awesome." Georgina looked around the room with its silk wallpapered walls laden with portraits with soft pink faces staring out from the depths of oil paint gloom. "I guess they got bored painting this poor fella." Georgina stared at a half-finished portrait of a kindly looking old man.

Molly laughed. "That's William Wilberforce."

"Really?" Georgina leaned in to look at the plaque next to the painting and read, "Parliamentary leader of the abolition movement. 1759 to 1833. Oh, he died the same year as Josephine and William married."

"Yes, and I remember reading that he lived just long enough to hear that the Abolition Act of 1833 had gone through."

"He looks quite a softy. Not exactly the face of an ardent campaigner against slavery." Georgina leaned in again to finish reading the plaque. "It says that he was well liked. Then I imagine Josephine and Edith would have been in awe of him."

"Maybe." Molly tilted her head and frowned.

"You don't think so?"

"It's just…do you remember Edith's logbook?"

"The one with Edith's passionate entry about painting Josephine?"

"Yes. Well in there was also a rhyme she'd written, maybe a poem or a hymn, I don't know. I can't recall the exact title—something about defiance—but it definitely had an angry tone. Anyway, it was about campaigning. I remember it because by the side of it was a cartoon of a man who looked like Wilberforce with the exception of a less than flattering large nose. By the side of the cartoon were the initials *WW*. It was the piece of evidence that led me to think that Edith could draw."

"Wow. Okay."

"According to the rhyme, Edith wasn't keen on him at all." Molly tapped the side of the frame. "It makes me question whether the man didn't quite live up to the figure that history has us remember."

May 1832
Chambers of Brancaster and Lane Solicitors

"They're lighting the new lamps this September, on City Walk. The corporation has finally decided. Just imagine—it will be so pretty, the trees lit in the soft glow of lamplight as if Christmas is every day."

Josephine turned from the window to face Edith. "That's good news indeed. It will be much safer, one hopes, to enjoy an evening walk."

"Will you be my guest, Miss Brancaster, on such an auspicious occasion?" Edith took Josephine's hand and kissed it, finishing the action with a low bow.

Josephine laughed. "I shall be honoured. But now I must work and so, Miss Hewitt, must you." Josephine released her hand from Edith's and sat at her desk. She sighed. "I always feel so behind."

Edith sat on the edge of her desk. "Is this the latest newsletter? What! *Brazen-faced*!" Edith squeezed her lips together as if the words which forced at her mouth were molten and threatened to burst and spurt with fury. She held out the offending article in front of her.

"Edith. Wilberforce is unwell." Josephine glanced up from her writing.

Edith stood straight backed and indignant. "But yet he finds the energy in his state of infirmity to mock our efforts and to call us brazen-faced for taking a stand for ourselves. Does he imagine that the progress towards the freedom of slaves is entirely of his achievement? A male conquest."

"Probably," Josephine said matter-of-factly.

Edith began to pace around the room. "Well, I will write. No, I will compose a hymn and sing it at the top of my lungs. I will call it 'Onward Defiance.' Yes. Its fierce notes of rebuke will carry on the air to London and rest upon ears who will hear and listen and condemn him."

"I doubt such a man will be condemned, Edith, as history will not remember him as the man of your hymn. It will remember him as the man who ended slavery in the British Empire."

"You cannot be sure of that. And why are you so easily persuaded to resign yourself to things? You give in as if all things are inevitable."

"How can you say that? I campaign, I write protests, I have dedicated my life to social justice. I do not just give in."

"Don't you?" Edith moved to Josephine. She rested her hand against her neck, leaning forward to place a kiss on her throat. "You give in every day to your fears of what a life lived with me, as us, would mean."

Josephine sat fixedly in her seat. She closed her eyes. "I will not talk again on this matter. Your delusions are obsessional."

Edith moved in front of Josephine, kissing at her closed eyelids. "If love is delusional, then I am mad indeed." Edith tipped her chin to the ceiling and howled like a dog.

"Edith!" Josephine looked urgently at the door. "If you are seeking to provoke me—"

"I am seeking no more than to love you."

"That is not true though, is it? You have my love. What you seek is a commitment from me that I am unable to give."

"And that is where you give in."

"No, it is where my heart breaks."

Georgina folded her arms. "It's difficult to know what to trust, isn't it? At the end of the day, all you have is your instinct."

"Yes. On the subject of trusting your instinct—a few weeks back now, Fran gave me some research she had done for a previous exhibition some years ago which featured Josephine. It contained a list of Josephine's writing."

"Okay."

"I noticed something a little bit odd, but I'm not sure if it means anything, which is why I haven't mentioned it before now."

"But your instinct makes you think it does?"

"Yes. You see, there's a gap of about two years where Josephine stopped writing completely. She'd been married six months or so by this point. I can't shake off the sense that something happened that made her stop. And I keep wondering as well if that something also affected Edith. What if by answering this question about Josephine, we get new answers about Edith?"

"Yes, I get that—a new way in. Do you think it was William? Could he have somehow forbade Josephine from writing?"

"Maybe. It's possible. But then, why fall for someone only to stop them being the person you fell for? What's more, she started writing again a few years later. I think I need to go back to the records office and have one last look. Just to settle myself."

"Will you let me know if you find anything?"

"Of course."

The noise of the staff closing doors outside their gallery prompted Georgina to reluctantly say, "We should go."

Molly looked at her watch. It was just after ten o'clock. "Yes, I can't really risk missing my train."

They walked in silence down the stone steps. Each step for Georgina was agony because it was a step closer to goodbye. They collected their coats and Georgina's brolly which she opened up over Molly and herself as they stepped out into the busy streets of London. The rain had eased a little, but the air was still wet to breathe and damp in their lungs.

Georgina raised her arm, bringing a passing taxi to a halt. She opened the passenger door and leaned in and said, "St. Pancras, please."

She held the door for Molly who hesitated.

"This evening has meant so much to me." Molly rested her hand over Georgina's.

Georgina tipped her brolly just enough to offer a little privacy as she pressed her lips tenderly against Molly's. "And finding you means so much to me." She took a deep breath and stood back to allow Molly to climb into the taxi and out of the cold.

"Goodnight then," Molly said. "See you soon. I'll text when I get home. Perhaps we can make plans for the weekend?"

"Yes, definitely. Goodnight, safe journey."

Georgina waved back at Molly as the taxi pulled away. The red of its brake lights caught in the puddles as Georgina's heart ached at the sight of the taxi turning the corner and taking Molly away. She stared after the taxi long after it had disappeared, for if she didn't look away, then the spell of their magical night in London would not be broken.

But then the spell would always break, wouldn't it? For Molly didn't belong in London. Erica had said so, and Molly hadn't corrected her. She had simply looked down as if the truth was hard to face.

But then could she leave London and return to Leicester for Molly? Georgina didn't have to kiss her to know that Molly was in every way her future. But then there was her past.

Painful memories of her childhood and thoughts of the cold emptiness of her father's house swept in with the rain, chilling Georgina to her core.

She quickly turned to look out to London. It was more than just a city. It had been her refuge from hurt and in every way the glittering hostess who had clasped Georgina to her heart when her own mother had been nowhere in sight.

Chapter Twenty

Molly, can you pass that rule, the metre rule. I'm not sure whether Vanessa's watercolour of Charleston's gardens and George's photograph of the house from the garden should go together or not. Underneath each other perhaps?" Evelyn's voice bristled with frustration. "A riot of rich colour is one thing—a chaos of gaudiness is another entirely. What do you think?"

Molly quickly placed her hand over her mouth to hide the yawn that had slipped free. Thinking after last night was proving a challenge, let alone concentrating on anything other than *She kissed me.*

Evelyn snapped her fingers and extended her palm in a dramatic display of emptiness.

"Oh, I'm sorry. Here you go." Molly handed the ruler to Evelyn. "Yes, I love those two works together absolutely, but perhaps that space would also be excellent for our introductory panel. It almost has a natural shape for text."

"Yes, you may have a point." Evelyn scratched her head. "I have never curated an exhibition of such diverse pieces not only in their subject matter but in chronology. What possessed George to collect so randomly?"

"Perhaps he didn't think of his work as a collection but just chose objects he enjoyed."

"In my experience enjoyment is always flawed as a rationale for anything."

Blimey. "There are some quite strong themes coming through which may work well with the notion of the room as a community space that will be great for schools and local interest groups." Molly picked up a piece of A1 paper stamped with a dusty shoe print and left over from the final measurements for the cabinet. She found a marker pen that had rolled under a bench and began to sketch out the room. "We could tell a story of war, by grouping the Nash, the Piper, and Hugo Wright's sketch. Georgina was telling me about the tragic history of Hugo's death at the Battle of the Somme soon after he'd completed his drawing. We could highlight George as an important local figure and pair the Leibovitz photo of George with the bust of Thomas Cook, another local of importance, and we could include the John Flower piece as Flower was a well-known local artist who concentrated on the city's history."

Molly wasn't sure what Evelyn's silence meant, and having mentioned the word *community*, she couldn't bring herself to look up to check, so she carried on regardless. "I was telling Georgina how keen I was to display her family portraits from the 1800s together just as they have hung for all those years in George's sitting room. I think there is a real opportunity to engage visitors with the lives of the people in the portraits. We could explore the fashion of the day and highlight customs such as baptism and marriages and notions of love in all its forms. As you know, we've already done a lot of work to uncover the history behind Josephine's portrait—"

"No, no, no." Evelyn all but collapsed onto a bench. "If we progress along those lines then the individual works are lost, subservient to theme. And that is *always* ghastly. This is an exhibition celebrating the work of great artists, not an exhibition focusing on local individuals and the needs of the national curriculum. And given George's notoriously unfortunate history, certainly not an exhibition focusing on marriage. Actually that reminds me—replies to invitations are starting to pick up, but we have a few unknowns. Not that I expected Lydia Wright to be prompt to reply to hers."

What? *No.* Lydia Wright?

"Don't look so stunned—exhibitions arise from the energy of debate and discussion." As she spoke Evelyn's gaze was drawn to outside.

"No, it's not that," Molly said. "It's just, did you say—"

"Oh God, I have five minutes before that awful woman from town planning pours officious scorn on our plans for the grounds. Did I tell you that we've been told we can't separate off the terrace area by the annex and that she doubted the practicality of Italian flagstone. Ignorant woman. After all, the charm in the stones is their natural patina. They are laid now and I'm not taking them up. And I won't be deterred from the plans for the formal rose bush border. And if that landscape design sets itself apart from the rest of the square, then I will consider that a triumph. What was your question?"

"I didn't realize we'd invited Georgina's mother."

"Yes, there was no question that we wouldn't. Lydia was and remains influential, less so in my opinion as an artist more as a, how shall I put it, cultural arbiter, a voice to which key figures in the art world listen. Even though she's always seemed to seek refuge abroad, she cannot be underestimated."

"But as she's divorced from George, I would imagine it might be upsetting for her to attend. And of course there are Georgina's feelings to consider."

"Add to that it was a particularly painful divorce." Fran arrived with a tray of coffees. "Not that any divorce is easy."

"Well, there you are." Evelyn narrowed her eyes at the sight of the councilwoman looking back at them from outside. "I imagine Lydia Wright might wish to attend to lay some ghosts to rest and even seek a closure of sorts. Sentiments, particularly hurtful ones, have a habit of lingering, after all. So we can but hope to tempt her to accept. Molly, don't go anywhere—I want to talk merchandise. And please reimagine the layout chronologically, as I do not want any sniff of a theme. This won't take long."

Struggling to take in the news of Lydia's invitation, Molly stood instead with Fran sipping at their drinks and trying in vain to not watch the woman from the council nod in evident stunned agreement to Evelyn's plans. It was cruel really. The woman was left standing, dazed, as if someone had spun her round and round and she was trying to orientate herself. She walked off unsteadily as if in shock, stumbling against a bin on her way back to the promenade.

"I'm guessing they'll send someone else next time," Molly said, concerned.

"An unmanned device probably," Fran said, without a hint of humour.

Fran looked at the A1 sheet lying on the floor, mapping out how each section of the space would look. "It's coming on."

Molly shook her head. "Too thematic."

"You mean too community?"

Molly shrugged and yawned again.

"I take it that yawn is an indicator of a late night. I honestly thought you were going to burst like a pinched seed pod yesterday afternoon, you were that excited. All you need to say—success or nightmare."

"She kissed me." Molly clutched her mug of coffee to her chest. They both looked to the door to check for the imminent return of Evelyn.

Fran rested an elbow against a plinth in response. "I see. Things are progressing then."

"I was too excited to sleep. I can't stop thinking about her."

Fran smiled affectionately. "Well, that's nothing new, is it?" Fran lifted the empty tray in preparation to leave.

"I'm worried though…"

Fran turned back to Molly.

"It's just, what do I do about Lydia Wright? Georgina doesn't know that she's been invited to the opening. It will hurt her terribly. I need to tell her. But then if Lydia doesn't come, and I've warned Georgina that she's been invited, could it jeopardize the museum's relationship with the foundation? And I would have hurt Georgina with mention of her mother for no reason. But if I don't tell her and Lydia comes, then it will not only jeopardize the museum's relationship with Georgina—it will jeopardize mine. I can't risk it. Can I?"

Fran pinched at her brow. "So basically you're asking me, do I think Lydia will come?"

Molly nodded.

"All I can say, Molly, is would *you* come back to the place where you caused such pain? To endure the humiliation of everyone knowing what you did and wondering what you're doing there? Be given a tour of an exhibition of those belongings on display that could have been yours? To face a daughter who hates you?"

"When you put it like that…"

"Such a cold-hearted invitation for the museum to have sent."

"And reckless," Molly said. "Why would Evelyn work so hard to earn Georgina's trust and respect and then do this? It makes no sense. Georgina will be furious."

"It doesn't make sense, does it?" Fran said, tapping softly at her chin. "Unless in Evelyn's mind she's taken a pragmatic view that if the museum took regard of everyone who didn't get along, then issuing invitations would be near impossible."

"Yes, but even so—"

"Right, where were we." Evelyn returned in a bluster of post combat and without a single battle scar. "Oh yes, merchandise. Time is so pressing upon us that we need to decide today and place our order before the close of play. I was thinking a small supply of glasses cases, cushions, and those long draught excluders." Evelyn paced up and down the room. "Are you making a note, Molly?"

"Oh yes, sorry." Molly ripped a slither of paper from the A1 sheet at the same time mouthing, "Bye," to Fran who quietly slipped away. "Got it."

"In addition, please tell the shop to order our usual stalwarts that always sell so well, mugs, tea towels, fridge magnets, key rings, and of course tote bags. Postcards, notelets, and posters, and unframed and framed prints are a given. But the question for us is which one image from the objects on display in the Wright room will captivate visitors? This will be the exhibition's signature image. They've sent through a photo of the Rodin." Evelyn stared at an empty plinth. "I don't know."

"I really don't think you could do better than Josephine's portrait."

Evelyn replied, "Yes, Josephine's painting, a wonderful work, but leading with fox hunting is such a contentious decision—such a divisive subject. We don't want to narrow our audience."

Fox hunting? She couldn't mean *The Hunt*, could she? Was Evelyn intending to display it in the Wright room? "No, sorry. I mean the watercolour. The one we've been researching. It ticks all the boxes. I can see everyone falling in love with the beauty of it. And its story is so—"

Evelyn lifted her finger in the air as if she'd just remembered something. "We have the acrylic of St. Martin's, but then again, too common. It could have come from the cathedral's gift shop. No, I think I am decided—everyone loves a Rodin."

No. "But isn't the Rodin also generic. I mean, I love a Rodin of course, but we have something very special with Josephine—"

"And with the Rodin we have something exceptional that will bring people to the museum. And as you have raised the subject of the watercolour of Josephine, whilst I admire your passion for the work, it is not appropriate for the space."

Not appropriate? The sting of injustice pierced Molly's heart. She watched dumbfounded as Evelyn turned to leave.

"Thank you for your contribution this morning, Molly." Evelyn peeled off her acrylic gloves and discarded them along with their conversation in the refuse sack by the door. With a half glance over her shoulder, she said, "Please make the arrangements with the shop. Oh, and I want the cushions to have a tweed design on the back. Light in tone, classic rather than Celtic."

"*No.* Please wait. May I ask why?"

Evelyn turned back to Molly with her gaze a terrifying blend of frustration and incredulity.

"Of course." Evelyn's strained tone suggested she was holding on to something that might break, most likely her patience. "We already have a most excellent example with *The Hunt* of the work of George O. Thorpe which captures Josephine in her prime. There really is no need for another work concentrating on her. To exclude *The Hunt* in favour of the watercolour would be unthinkable. It is far superior in maturity of style and composition. Furthermore its full provenance is not in doubt—"

Molly added quickly, "But neither is the watercolour's. You see, Edith Hewitt is the painter of Josephine's portrait. I found evidence in the records office that confirms Edith as the artist." *Oh. Tricky.*

"I'm sorry, it seems I'm missing something, as I could have sworn that when we last spoke on the matter of the portrait we agreed to the conclusion of further research. Did we not?"

"I might have conducted a little more research—but on my own time."

Evelyn narrowed her eyes in reply. "Furthermore, *The Hunt* fits perfectly in the chronology to hang in line with the other paintings from the 1800s. It is meant to be."

"But to omit Edith's painting is neglecting a most important history—"

"But it is *Josephine's* history. It will only serve to distract and derail George Wright's own story."

Molly shook her head. "You're wrong." The words were out before Molly could take them back. Molly's organs squeezed together in panic. "I don't mean you're *wrong*-wrong. Obviously."

Evelyn's neck began to flush pink, as she replied, "Obviously."

Mustering courage Molly continued, "It's just, Georgina said she remembered Edith's painting hanging in line with the other portraits in the sitting room when she was a little girl. It clearly meant a lot to George, and it certainly means a lot to Georgina. So it's the Wrights' history surely."

Evelyn seemed to have aged in the course of the debate as a shadow of weariness cast over her face. Even her voice seemed weaker, as she said, "I have taken everything into consideration and all reasonable argument points to the inclusion of *The Hunt*."

"But—"

"I have made my mind up." Evelyn held up the palm of her hand, stopping like a policewoman the flowing traffic of their conversation. "And please do not mention this matter to Georgina Wright. For I feel sure *she* will understand that final curatorial decisions lie with me."

Molly hung her head. "Of course." When she looked up again Evelyn had left the room.

❖

"Hello." Molly lay with her head on the kitchen table with her phone more or less flat against her ear. She answered the phone without looking at the caller ID.

"Hey. It's Georgina."

Georgina? It was only just seven o'clock. Molly sat up. "Hi."

"So how was your day? Have you recovered from last night?"

"Almost. I'm having to tell myself I didn't imagine it."

"I know what you mean. But then I don't think I could imagine anything quite so beautiful."

Georgina's heartfelt words caught at Molly's heart. "I loved it when you kissed me. I'm sorry, that's very—"

"And I loved kissing you. Really, I did. I felt so sorry when the evening ended. Watching you leave, well."

"It was horrible, wasn't it? I resorted to reading the *Metro* from cover to cover before moving on to a discarded *Times* and a half-completed crossword just to try not to engage with how much I didn't want to leave."

There was a moment of silence of the kind where words offered no consolation.

Georgina cleared her throat. "So did you get a thousand questions from Evelyn?"

"Do you know, she didn't ask me how it went. But then her focus is the Wright room."

"Yes, I can imagine."

"We're making good progress. In all fairness to Evelyn, she's sweeping up all the loose ends. Frankly, I'd hate to be the Tate."

"You're still waiting on the Rodin?"

"Yep."

"Well let me know if you need my help. Have invitations gone out? I sent Evelyn a list at the end of last week."

"Invitations?" Molly swallowed down nausea. "I'd have to check on that for you. I mean, I'm sure they have." *Quick, change the subject.* "We ordered a draught excluder today. That's how organized we are."

"Okay. Not sure I quite understand…?"

"Exhibition merch."

"Oh. Of course."

"And if you think a draught excluder a little random, then wait till you see the glasses case." Molly gave an amused sigh.

"Right. I'm picturing it as we speak. So I'm guessing they'll feature an object from the exhibition?"

Molly's heart ached. Could she mention Edith's portrait of Josephine? Georgina would sort things in an instant, wouldn't she? No. It would be career suicide, for there were surely only so many times she could defy Evelyn, and she would risk embarrassing her and undermining her in front of Georgina. She would make her position untenable and this would show in the next round of museum cuts for sure.

"Molly?"

"Sorry, yes, we'll have postcards of every object. And then we'll use the better-known images across the selection of merchandise." Molly took a deep breath. "Evelyn has selected the Rodin as the iconic image for the exhibition as a whole."

"Okay, that makes sense. Everyone loves Rodin, after all."

Molly said, blankly, "That's what Evelyn said."

"And you don't agree?"

"It's just, well, for example, there's Hugo's lovely sketch from your father's sitting room window into the square. I should have mentioned that, but I didn't. But then it would likely have still not been impressive enough."

"You sound kind of defeated."

"I'm not—well, maybe a little. I love my job but sometimes…I don't know."

"I know the feeling. It can seem frustrating and unrelenting can't it?"

"Yep, definitely. So how about we see each other tomorrow evening? Forget about work for a while? If you can't make it to Leicester, maybe I could come to you? Although I had half thought I might go to the records office on Saturday morning."

"Yes, do that. I'll try to come tomorrow night, but I think it's going to be more likely Saturday lunchtime."

"Sure, no worries. Shall I come to your father's place then, when I'm done researching?"

"Yep, sounds good. I'll text when my train arrives in."

"I can't wait to see you again."

"Me too. Goodnight then."

"Goodnight." Molly held her phone in her lap and lay with her cheek against the table. She closed her eyes and softly whispered, "Goodnight, Georgina Wright."

Chapter Twenty-one

You have to be clear what you are trying to achieve to prevent yourself from getting lost amongst its treasures. As Molly sat at what had become her favourite desk at the records office, Fran's words of warning replayed themselves in her head.

She cast her eye over Josephine's and Edith's archives spread before her once more. The parish registers sat directly to her side. The answer to why Josephine stopped writing between August 1834 and November 1836 would surely be here, hidden somewhere, just waiting to be found with the turn of a fragile page.

Inexplicably, nerves unsettled her. *Everything's fine. Concentrate.* She tucked her hair away from her shoulders to rest at her back. *Right.* She would start with what she already knew.

Molly reached for her notebook. She found the notes she'd made from the portraits on George Wright's wall. There was no baptism portrait for Adelaide Jane. But there would have been a baptism surely?

Molly reached for the baptism register and turned to the pages for 1834. It was unlikely that she would have been born earlier than November given that her parents had only married at the end of the previous December. She traced her fingers down the lines of records. Yes. There it was. Her heart surged at the entry that read, *Baptism 10th December 1834. Adelaide Jane daughter of William Wright, and his wife, Josephine. Born 10th November 1834.*

Why no commemorative painting then? She closed the register. *Think, Molly Goode. Think.* What else did she know for certain? Molly looked at the archives spread about her. She gazed at the scrapbook, remembering the sketches of Josephine hidden like their love. Edith's passionate words written indelibly on the back of the painting flooded Molly's questioning mind. *All my love always, Edith.* Edith had promised to love Josephine for always. Hadn't she? Was Josephine Edith's forever one? But then Josephine married William. Did Edith stop loving her? But then, could you just stop love? Was that what the heartbreaking prayer was about?

Molly lifted the volume of prayers, searching for the entry that had upset Georgina and her so much. The words seemed to resonate from the page, shining out, each letter leaping from the text as if restless and alive with meaning.

Her gaze rested upon the last lines of Edith's prayer. *To speak, to write is to feel pain. I ask no more than tomorrow my burden will be lighter and my grief more tolerable.*

To write is to feel pain. Molly looked up. "Grief," she said into the hushed room. Was that it? Was Josephine grieving? And like Edith just a year earlier, had Josephine felt pain when trying to write and just stopped, her loss too great to endure?

The nerves that had been at the edges came closer with their unsettling breath at her neck.

What had Josephine lost—or rather, who?

❖

"I'm sorry, I didn't quite catch that." Georgina pressed her phone closer to her ear. "Where did you say you were?" As she spoke she rested her weekend holdall at her feet and dug in her pocket for her keys. Her train from London had been on time and Molly's call came in just as Georgina had arrived at her father's door.

"St. Mary de Castro." Molly's voice sounded peculiar and oddly distant. "Will you meet me there?"

"Yes, of course." Georgina dropped her holdall just inside the house and turned around. "I'm setting off now. Is everything okay? You sound strange."

"I think I know why Josephine stopped writing." Molly's blank tone expressed anything but relief at her discovery.

A terrible sinking feeling rose up cold in Georgina's blood. "Okay. It's something to do with Edith, isn't it? Molly?"

"Yes."

Ten minutes later Georgina found Molly standing in the middle of a graveyard under the protective boughs of an oak tree. She was gazing at a sandy coloured gravestone, crumbling a little at its edges and half claimed by the suffocating embrace of the tendrils of ivy.

"Molly?"

Molly seemed not to have noticed Georgina's arrival. Instead she was leaning forward, pulling away at the leaves of ivy to fully reveal the inscription. She brushed with her fingertips at the words that read, *Edith Hewitt, 1808–1834.*

Georgina stared at the inscription and at the name *Edith Hewitt.* "Edith," she said, her name escaping her lips like a prayer.

Up until this point Edith had been a figure of myth. She was just the glimpse of a woman revealed in slim volumes and notes, and sketches in a scrapbook. Her emotional life evoked and brought to life in ink on the back of a canvas with the words *All my love always, Edith.* Her passionate words as proof that her love existed, vibrant and alive. Edith's heartfelt words passing through generations to Georgina, in every way the heir through Josephine of Edith's heart and of her feelings spent and lost.

Georgina turned to Molly and said with a quiet disbelief, "She was only twenty-six. She died so young."

Molly looked at her with a face shadowed with sadness, the smile that always greeted Georgina and that lit her heart with joy now heartbreakingly absent.

"Yes," Molly said. "And the inscription on her gravestone is so cruelly brief, isn't it? I mean, there's no mention that Edith was a campaigner. No words of affection from her family or any loved one. Nothing. With such omissions and such silence they condemned her to be lost forever."

Georgina moved to Molly and slipped her hand in hers and said, "She's found now. You've found her."

They stood silently looking at the grave with their unspoken thoughts, cast against the background rustle of the wind in the surrounding trees, blending in uneasy harmony with the sound of the city.

1st August 1834
Chambers of Brancaster and Lane Solicitors

"Listen!" A flushed-faced William stood at the window with his hat held at his chest. "Can you hear the sound of the city? It is alive! Listen to the church bells. It's St. Martin's, St. Nick's, and St. Mary's. They're in tune with each other. What a sound! And the cheers, Josephine. They are chanting freedom. Do you hear? Such celebrations indeed. We must hurry as we will miss the parade. Jo?"

"I shall wait. Yes, I think that's best. She may yet come. Both letters cannot have been misplaced."

"She will know where to find us. Come, where is your bonnet?"

"No. I am minded to wait." Josephine sat with her gloves in her lap. William bent down in front of her and rested his palm against her cheek.

"I fear you will wait in vain," William said, his kind eyes glistening with compassion.

Josephine shook her head. "Then I shall go to her. Her lodgings are not far. We shall follow on."

"Please, I simply can't allow it. The crowds this day are too much for you to walk alone. You risk being crushed. My responsibility is not to Edith, but to you, both of you." William placed his hand against Josephine's pregnant belly. "Let her come to you when she is ready."

"But it has been almost a year, William. She has not replied to my letters and continues to refuse to see me. But today of all days she may bear to look upon me. I miss her so. And my father has only seen her but just a handful of times, the most fleeting of encounters."

A jumble of voices, male and female, in the hallway called their attention from their discussion to the door. And then they listened as an eerie silence fell before the front door banged too.

"Who is it?" Josephine said. "Can you see, William?"

William leaned against the glass. "There are so many people—I can't quite see, but it was a woman."

"Was it Edith? Could it have been Edith?"

"William, could I have a word?" Charles Brancaster's voice came echoing from the hallway as the door to their room swung open.

Josephine stood with her hand resting on her belly and strained to see into the hallway. "What is it, Father?"

"Dear Jo, please let me speak to William."

"Oh Lord, no. Please no." Josephine placed her hand across her mouth at the sight of her father stepping from the shadow of the hall, ashen faced, holding a painting awash with watercolour. Tucked under his other arm and spilling against his chest were papers and notes bundled loosely together and balancing on top of a scrapbook.

Josephine sat heavily in her chair with both hands now covering her mouth.

"Mrs. Hewitt called. She was very sorry to inform us of"—Charles swallowed—"of her daughter's passing. Just this last week. This Tuesday in fact. There's a note. It is addressed to you, Jo." He gestured to his waistcoat pocket. William dutifully lifted the folded paper and walked with sombre steps towards his wife. He offered the note to Josephine who shook her head and closed her eyes.

"Do you want me to read it to you?" William asked.

Josephine nodded with her eyes clamped shut.

William unfolded the note and with unsteady voice began to read. "It is from Mrs. Hewitt. It is quite short. Let's read it another time."

Josephine opened her eyes, which flooded in the first swell of grief. "No, please. Read it now."

William looked at Charles who gave a simple nod in reply. He took a deep breath and read, quietly, "I have no place for these. Mrs. M. Hewitt."

If anyone spoke thereafter Josephine didn't hear. In fact if life continued in the following months, it continued for someone else, for Josephine felt utterly absent from it. People became shadows, voices. Even the cry of her newborn daughter seemed remote. No doctor could help, for there was no help where there was no hope.

Josephine knew one thing clear and true as the dark clouds of grief shrouded her in black: two lives had been lost the day Edith Hewitt died.

"Let's go back to my father's place," Georgina said, mindful to be respectful to the memory of Edith and of all that she was and all that life took from her.

Molly looked away from the grave with her cheeks streaked with tears and her head bowed against her chest.

Georgina's heart ached at the sight of Molly so distraught, but death was a dragon that no one, not even wearing the armour of love, brandishing the sharp sword of justice, had ever been able to slay. Georgina wrapped her arms around Molly and held her tight against her.

After a few moments Molly moved slightly away. Wiping her eyes she said, "I had a feeling, but I somehow never thought…"

"I know." Georgina touched her hand to Molly's cheek with the back of her fingers softly brushing her cold skin. She then placed her arm around Molly's waist, guiding her away from the gravestone and away from the shadows of the overgrown graveyard, and out into the glare of the streets where no one cared and no one remembered yet another life forgotten.

CHAPTER TWENTY-TWO

Molly stood in George Wright's sitting room staring numbly out into the hallway in the direction of the kitchen where Georgina was making coffee.

"I feel a bit foolish to be so affected." Molly's voice drifted in small echoes into the hallway.

She had tried so hard to keep a professional perspective and to approach all matters relating to the watercolour with dispassionate interest. She had made sure to fix into context each and every discovery as if she were solving a puzzle, the completion of which mattered to someone else.

But then that *someone* was Georgina, and she could sense with each time they met that her emotions, soft and urging, had begun to envelope fact into feeling, muddling her intention and engaging her heart.

As she had stood in front of Edith's gravestone, something had snapped in her. It was the intangible restraint which had held her emotions in place giving way under the increasing pressure of each new discovery. And now Molly felt weak and ridiculous for feeling so distressed, for this was not her grief and not her loss. It felt mawkish and sentimental, and embarrassed her. And yet she could not shake off the feeling that Edith's story *was* her story, a universal one of terrible injustice.

"Here." Georgina arrived at Molly's side and handed her a mug of coffee. "You're not foolish. Edith's story, in so much as we know it, is truly heartbreaking. Please have a seat." Georgina gestured to the sofa. "You'll be pleased to know I saw sense and relegated the law journals to my father's office."

Molly nodded. She couldn't even muster the smallest of smiles as she forlornly patted the sofa cushions into life. She glanced at the floor. Joyful indoor picnics felt a world away. "It's just the cruel injustice of it all that upsets me."

"Yes, I get that." Georgina waited for Molly to take her place before sitting next to her with her legs casually crossed and her body turned towards Molly.

"Thanks so much for the coffee." Molly blew across the hot liquid taking several grateful sips.

"My pleasure." Georgina's smile, warm with affection, seemed to mirror her words.

Molly wanted to kiss Georgina and to feel her body pressed close to hers again, but somehow it didn't feel right. It was almost as if it would be disrespectful to Edith to do so. It would be like they were flaunting their freedom to love as if they did not care.

Instead Molly reached for Georgina's hand and held it tightly. "Thank you for standing in a murky graveyard with me."

"Well, I'll be honest and say that wasn't quite what I'd imagined for our weekend." They both laughed only for their laughter to soon be replaced by a silence that felt reverential and contemplative.

Georgina stared down at her coffee. Quietly and a little tentatively she then asked, "If it doesn't upset you to say—"

"How did I find out?"

Georgina nodded. "Did it have something to do with the gap in her writing?"

Molly turned herself further towards Georgina, settling herself to explain, "Yes. Once I realized that none of the obvious explanations entirely accounted for it, well, it triggered something for me."

"Yes," Georgina said with a tone focused and intense. "I've been thinking about it too. It seemed out of character for such a woman to just stop her work, her *calling* even."

"That's exactly what I thought. Although in truth when I returned to the records office I had no idea where to begin or what I hoped to find, so I began with what we knew already."

"Makes sense." Georgina took a sip of her coffee.

"So I thought about what we'd seen that had struck us as important, even if we didn't know why. I thought about the inscription on the painting revealing Edith's declaration of love, and then of course we have the revealing note in her logbook written as she was sketching Josephine. How passionate she seemed." Molly looked at Georgina whose expression was one of absolute concentration. "This led me to think about Edith's prayer book and how in contrast her words seemed so desolate. It was that prayer, in fact, that unlocked everything."

"Yes, I remember it well." Georgina set her mug beside her on the floor.

"Well, in the prayer Edith had said that she was grieving and it hurt to write. So I made the not unreasonable connection that Edith might have been grieving over the fact that Josephine had become engaged, given the timing of her wedding to William. Edith would have felt that she had lost Josephine."

"Yes." Georgina shifted in her seat slightly with her hand still clasped around Molly's. "That's a reasonable explanation in light of everything we've found."

"So I asked myself, had Josephine stopped writing because of grief too? Had *she* lost someone? It didn't fit that she was mourning over giving up Edith because her writing had continued before and after she had married." Molly paused to take a deeper breath. "So I went to the register of burials and found the records for July 1834. That was the month before she stopped writing. I expected perhaps to find a Brancaster, a much loved relative…" Molly's words choked at her throat. She took a sip of coffee. Georgina held her hand tighter. "I couldn't believe, I refused to believe almost, what I saw. I even checked desperately to see whether there was any note, any sketch, anything from Edith after this date that would suggest I was mistaken. But no. Nothing. I hunted amongst Josephine's later work for an *EH*, for any sign of her. She had gone."

Georgina briefly closed her eyes. "That's heartbreaking."

"I simply didn't want to accept it. I even wondered whether there was a possibility that the *Leicester Chronicle* would have a death notice for that date that indicated somehow that it wasn't our Edith. But rather than contradict my findings, it simply served to confirm my worst fears. For I found two notices related to the passing of an Edith Hewitt. One, presumably from her family, was just a cold line of facts. But then another from a Charles Brancaster—"

"Brancaster?"

Molly nodded. "Josephine's father. I took a photo. Here. It's a bit fuzzy."

Georgina read aloud, "*It is with great sadness that we discharge this duty to notify of the death of our dear colleague and friend, Miss Edith Hewitt. Notes of condolence to be received by Brancaster and Lane, Solicitors, New Street, Leicester.*" Georgina sighed heavily. "So no question of doubt then?"

Molly shook her head. "To be honest I feel really stupid to be so surprised because I knew Josephine married. I'd guessed, given Edith's passion for Josephine, how utterly heartbroken she would have been. How vulnerable that heartbreak would have made her both in body and soul. So given this, I'm not sure what I expected."

"You couldn't have expected her to die so young." Georgina gazed out to the square before looking back at Molly and asking, "Did it say how she died?"

Molly stared at the mug resting in her lap. "Influenza. Infectious disease would have been rife at this time. Flu regularly killed, particularly the young and the vulnerable."

Georgina's hand slipped from Molly's and she pressed her fingers flat against her lips. "Poor Edith," she said quietly as if collecting her words in her palm. "But then I don't suppose a broken heart can be given as a cause of death or, for that matter, betrayal as the weapon that struck the fatal blow."

Betrayal? Georgina's words were so strong and anger clearly simmered beneath them. Was this about Edith at all? Was she thinking of her mother perhaps? Molly rested her hand on Georgina's arm. "We still don't know if Josephine betrayed Edith."

Her attempt at offering solace by finding perspective only seemed to inflame Georgina's anger. She looked back at Molly with sharp questioning eyes and cheeks newly flushed. "But the facts speak for themselves, don't they?"

Molly shrugged. "I guess in truth we don't have that many facts about Josephine and Edith's relationship. All we have is the reasonable interpretation of evidence."

"You sound like a lawyer." Georgina stood and went to the window, resting her shoulder against the glass, and fixed her gaze to the view outside.

"Do you know what upsets *me* the most?" Molly said. "It's the gravestone. I keep thinking about it and in particular the unforgivable absence of any sense of Edith and of her achievements and of her true nature. Add to that her name omitted from her painting of Josephine and the all but buried public record of her brave campaigning. Her love, her talents, and her passion, hidden, invisible. It's like she never mattered. Like women like her never mattered."

Georgina looked back at Molly.

"Well she does matter. Her story matters." Molly's cheeks stung with a rising anger. She thought of Evelyn brushing the suggestion of displaying Edith's watercolour away, dismissing Josephine and Edith's story as a distraction from the narrative the museum would tell and from the story that would be remembered. The preference yet again of the patriarchal voice. "I should have fought even harder for her. I gave up too easily."

Georgina frowned. "I don't understand."

"At the museum, on Thursday. I should have somehow insisted. I should have rung you straight away. You would have put things right in a blink. I'm such a coward. And it's cowardice that always does the most harm, isn't it?"

Georgina returned to sit with Molly. "You've lost me. What happened Thursday?"

"Evelyn has selected *The Hunt* for the Wright room in place of Edith's portrait of Josephine. I tried to advocate for it by explaining that it had hung in your family home alongside the other paintings for as long as you can remember, and that it must have meant a lot to your father, and how much it means to you."

Georgina continued to frown and gave an uncertain, "Okay. What did she say?"

"Something ridiculous about the portrait representing Josephine's history and that it will only serve to distract and derail your father's own story. Which is just nonsense, isn't it?"

Georgina didn't say anything. Her eyes flitted over Molly's face, and yet her expression had become distant as if her thoughts had settled elsewhere.

Molly sat further on the edge of the sofa with her body tense and rigid and with the sense of injustice refuelled with the discovery of Edith's death. "What's more, she is adamant she won't change her mind. She shut me down by saying she'd taken everything into consideration. She said I wasn't to reopen discussion with you on the matter, and that you would understand curatorial decisions rested with her. But how can I not mention it? Not after today. So can you help? We both know Evelyn will do anything if you particularly insist."

Georgina refocused her gaze on Molly. "Molly—"

"The only thing is, though, we need to somehow find a way of it being your idea and not coming from me."

"Molly."

"Hum?"

"I'm sorry, but the thing is when you mentioned your plan to display the portraits, I assumed you meant the bequeathed pieces. And I don't recall now that you mentioned Edith's painting specifically."

"No, but I did say that we could display them as they had been hung all those years, and that of course includes the watercolour." Why hadn't she been clearer and sought Georgina's approval for Edith's painting to be in the Wright room before now, so the run in with Evelyn could have been avoided?

"I'm sorry for any confusion," Georgina said. "And I understand why you would want Edith's painting to be displayed in the Wright room. It's just…"

"What?"

Georgina frowned. "It's not that simple. I'm not in a position to make decisions relating to Edith's painting. Not at the moment anyway."

Molly looked down. "I see." She didn't see. The painting belonged to Georgina. Didn't it?

"Molly?"

Molly looked up.

"What I'm trying to say is," Georgina continued, "as you know the portrait wasn't included in the museum bequest, but it also hasn't been mentioned in my father's will. Something just doesn't feel right about the painting being forgotten. So I am not comfortable to gift Edith's painting or temporarily lend it for display, at least not at the moment."

Molly said, "That's okay, we can work around that uncertainty. You could add to the exhibition label *Lender unknown*. It's not unusual. A good number of the items in the museum we have no clue who gifted them."

"I don't know Molly. I'm not sure that feels right either."

Molly's heart ached in her chest. *You don't know? I don't know*—it was the phrase Erica always used whenever Molly had an idea that was contrary to hers, *any idea* that was hers, it ended up feeling like. Eventually Molly's confidence had ebbed away, the worth of her suggestions and her values undermined with every *I don't know*.

"Molly?" Georgina searched Molly's face as she placed her hand warm on Molly's arm.

"I'm still confused," Molly said with a more defiant tone than she had intended.

Georgina's cheeks flushed. "Okay."

"You seemed as upset as me by what we discovered about the painting. In fact, at times more so. I thought you would care about telling Edith's story. You said yourself that she was *found* now. To display Josephine's portrait with Edith credited as the painter and to tell of Edith's love for Josephine and of her untimely death will spark debate, and—who knows?—other Edith's may be searched for and found as a result. Hidden histories will be uncovered."

"Molly—"

"You see, Evelyn is opposed to this debate taking place. She wants nothing to distract from her vision which seems to me a sanitized, generic reading of your father's history with the focus entirely on the artworks."

Georgina's cheeks flushed deeper and her brow became furrowed as if she was confused or cross or both. "You *know* I care about Edith. But you must understand—in addition to the unresolved issues surrounding the painting, I have to think of my father and try to imagine what he had hoped for the Wright room and how he would wish to be remembered. He has faced such controversy and such public speculation into his private life at the hands of my mother that to actively provoke debate once more at the mention of his name…I'm sorry, but I'm afraid I can see where Evelyn is coming from."

Molly felt sick. In that moment she struggled to grasp what she should feel and what her reaction should be. *I thought you felt the same as me. I thought…* A panic of confusion began to stifle her and pressed the breath from her lungs.

"Molly?"

Molly nodded vigorously. "I understand. Absolutely." She didn't understand. And what was worse, she'd thought she had understood. It felt like the rug had been pulled from beneath her. Had she assumed too much about Georgina? Had she so badly wanted Georgina to care about what she cared about that she had imagined her to be someone she wasn't? But then everything about her had felt so right.

"If I could help, I promise I would. I'd do anything for you, Molly. You believe that, don't you?"

She didn't know what to believe any more. "I'm sorry, I'm not feeling great. I've found this morning a bit too…so I think it might be best if we postpone this weekend." Molly quickly looked down at the sight of Georgina's perplexed expression.

"Can I get you something?" Georgina said, panic at the edge of her voice. "Some lunch perhaps? It might help you feel better."

Molly stood and reached for her coat and bag. "That's very kind, thank you, but I think I need to go home."

Georgina stood to face Molly. She looked as confused as Molly felt. "Of course, if you're sure."

She wasn't sure. She wasn't sure of anything.

Georgina silently followed Molly to the door.

Molly pulled on her coat. Finding the strength to summon her calmest, most professional voice, she said, "I meant to ask if you would feel able to give a speech at the opening of the Wright room. It doesn't have to be very long or anything. Evelyn and perhaps even I or Fran may say something too."

Georgina's voice wavered as she said, "Yes, that's fine."

Molly nodded, her lip aching at the bite of her teeth.

Georgina took a deep unsteady breath. "I'm very sorry again for the confusion over the painting."

"Yes, me too." Molly was unable to meet Georgina's gaze. "Goodbye then." Molly opened the front door and stepped out and down the steps and through the gate, briskly walking towards Daisy May.

Molly felt like everything had shifted. For all that had felt certain was now unknown and all that was once unknown had been heartbreakingly revealed.

❖

Georgina sat on the bottom but one step of the hallway stairs. She focused on the pattern of the tiles, noting the discoloration here and there of the grouting and the slight wear of the patterns faded by years of the tread of people arriving and departing.

A thin shaft of light pierced the glass pane at the top of the door, falling in lengths onto the floor, slicing the black and white tiles into mosaics of grey and lighting the tips of her shoes. She closed her eyes and pressed her hands over her ears, determined not to listen to the sound of Daisy May's engine start or to imagine Molly disappearing around the corner, gone from her.

She'd had such hopes for their weekend. She had imagined Molly at the door, smiling, and then in her arms, kissing her again. Laughing, tipsy, sprawled out on the sitting room floor, their legs entwined and their hearts tangled up in each other. She had imagined the scene with such clarity, that now she wondered whether it had happened.

But no. Edith had happened. She had died and so had the joy in Molly's eyes. Molly had always seemed so in control and professional when it came to the painting and their research. Edith's death had obviously asked too much, and then the confusion with the watercolour... the questioning hurt in Molly's eyes. But what could Georgina do? She had to think of her father. And there was so much uncertainty around the painting. Molly said she understood. But then if Molly had understood why couldn't she look at her? And why did she leave without looking back? Why would anyone leave without looking back?

Was this how it would always be? Molly leaving and Georgina left alone with a sickening, fearful sense that she had somehow disappointed and hurt her without meaning to. Was this because Molly was not the one for her? Had Georgina in fact been right all these years—there would never be a *one* for her.

She stood and numbly went into the sitting room. She sat in her father's chair with her head in her hands. The leather felt so cold to the touch that it seemed to drain her blood of its warmth. She shivered. The room had never felt colder or emptier of life or more full of grief.

CHAPTER TWENTY-THREE

With only a week to the opening, everyone was so busy that a steady purposeful hush had fallen on the museum. Fran and Molly spent more time in the Wright room than in their office and far more time at work than at home. Evelyn had not given Molly an inch of free rein or time to herself in the last few weeks. They had not spoken again about Edith's painting but an unspoken rub remained implicit in the sharpened spike of Evelyn's voice and in the unnerving fix of her eyes. Molly knew she had gone beyond debate to questioning Evelyn. She had crossed the line and now it felt like she stood alone in no man's land, staring out at a threatening horizon.

"You okay?" Fran briefly rested her palm on Molly's back.

Molly shrugged. "Can I say no?"

Fran nodded. "Of course. In fact I always trust a *no* more than I trust a *yes*."

Fran always knew what to say, and Molly loved her for it and for her every cynical life-weary wise word.

"And it's no surprise to hear. I've been putting your unnerving quietness these last few weeks down to work pressure." Fran sat with a groan on a bench against the far wall. "And I can't believe I'm saying this, but I rather miss the regular updates on you and Ms. Wright."

Words choked in Molly's throat. The last weeks of being brave and of pushing to the back of her mind all thoughts of Georgina had taken their toll. What was Georgina thinking at that moment? Why hadn't she rung or messaged? Was she waiting for Molly to be in touch? Was that it? Should she have apologized? But for some reason it felt like she would be apologizing for caring, and hadn't Georgina once said that she should never do that? Then why hadn't Georgina rung? Had Molly lost her?

Fran patted the space next to her. Molly just stared at the empty seat.

Fran shook her head and sighed. "So why am I having to endure your miserable face?"

Molly couldn't help but smile. "Rude."

Fran gave an unapologetic shrug.

Molly reluctantly perched on the edge of the bench and took a long deep breath. "I found out that Edith died just seven months or so after Josephine married. She was only twenty-six."

"Oh, poor Edith and poor Josephine, indeed. Losing a loved one before their time is just cruel. On that note, I'm guessing you've updated Georgina?"

"Yes. She was with me the day I found out. We saw Edith's grave together. Edith is buried in the graveyard of St. Mary de Castro. All that was marked on her gravestone was her name and dates. Nothing else. It was like she'd achieved nothing and loved and was loved by no one. It was properly heartbreaking, Fran. It really upset me. Georgina seemed upset too, but then..." Molly hung her head.

"Why do I get the impression we're about to get to the actual reason for your subdued mood."

"I thought," Molly said, barely above a whisper, "hoped, maybe, that we were on the same page, you know?"

"Nope, I've no clue what you're on about."

"No, not you and me. Georgina and me. You see I wanted to display Edith's portrait of Josephine alongside the other paintings from the 1800s and for it to be a discussion point. It could be the instigator for revealing other hidden histories, couldn't it? Correcting similar injustices even. I naturally assumed, as Georgina had been so involved with uncovering Edith and Josephine's story, that she would want this too."

"And Georgina doesn't?"

"No. It really threw me, and then I didn't know what to say or how to feel. All I seemed to want to do was leave. So I did, and now we haven't spoken since."

"Goodness. I see. Did she say why she didn't want it displayed?"

Molly nodded and repeated Georgina's explanation. "So as things stand, she's not comfortable offering it for display."

"That's so strange, isn't it?" Fran said, frowning. "What was George thinking?"

"It could have been just a mistake. But it's clear Georgina doesn't think it was."

Fran absently stroked the bench. "It's almost like he didn't feel it was his to bequeath. But then it's clearly his family's heirloom."

"So maybe he'd already given it to someone. But then why not let the solicitors know? Why oblige Georgina to have to sort it out? It's like he wanted her to focus her attention on the painting and to solve its mystery. Do you think he'd always wondered about it?"

"It's impossible not to wonder about that painting. It's so intriguing and enticing." Fran looked at Molly. "But I think, Miss Marple, you may be getting a bit carried away."

"Maybe. It was awful, Fran, to feel the mood become tense between us. And it got even worse when I suggested that the painting would prompt debate and how important that was. She was adamant that her mother's infidelity had already invited scrutiny and speculation and that she wanted to protect her father from all that again."

"Look, you've simply hit on a sore spot." Fran gave a slight shrug. "It happens when you're getting to know someone."

"Yep, definitely." A terrible sinking feeling tightened around Molly's chest. "Now that I think about it, during our research Georgina was really upset with what she saw as Josephine's betrayal of Edith. Of course, I'm so stupid, the last thing she would want in the Wright room is discussion involving betrayal." Molly swallowed. "She must think I've never understood what she has told me about her life. And then I walked out on her…Oh God, no wonder she hasn't been in touch since."

"Maybe she's just giving you some space," Fran said. "Because you left, it could be that she's waiting for you to get in touch with her."

"I miss her, Fran. I really miss her." Molly pressed a hand to her chest and a tear rolled down her cheek. "My heart hurts so much."

"Well then, you must make sure you find a moment to tell her all this when you see her at the opening." Fran handed Molly a tissue from her cardigan pocket. "I have a theory that what we feel for someone, they likely feel for us."

"So Georgina is missing me too?"

Fran looked at her and smiled. "I think her heart will be hurting as much if not more than yours. Now I'm going home, and I suggest you do the same before we are mistaken for artefacts with you hung on the wall and me stuffed on a plinth."

Molly's chuckle at Fran's comment soon drifted away as she glumly said, "Sure, I'll lock up. See you Monday."

How could that be possible? How could anyone's heart hurt more? For it was hard to imagine a pain greater or a regret more sorely felt.

Chapter Twenty-four

Molly was right. The annex hadn't lost the poignancy Georgina had felt on that first visit when it was just an empty space yet to be filled with objects. Now that it was completed, it was still without question simply beautiful, and as before evoked a calm peaceful mood. *You would have loved this, Father.*

Georgina was so pleased that by arriving early for the opening she'd somehow managed to slip unnoticed into the annex. She was delighted to have the room to herself if only for a few moments and relieved to notice that Evelyn was now focused on the foyer and the imminent arrival of the evening's guests. Molly and Fran were nowhere in sight. *Molly.* Georgina crossed her arms. What would she say to her tonight? Tears which had threatened every day since she last saw Molly rose again. She mustn't get upset. Not here. Not tonight, for this was her father's evening.

She took a deep breath and walked around the elegant space, taking everything in. Rodin's bronze cast of *Little Eve* and the bust of Thomas Cook sat resplendent on their plinths positioned opposite each other at either side of the French doors. Two explanatory panels had been designed to fit the long column spaces that supported each side wall of glass. One panel introduced the Wright Foundation and the other provided an outline of her father's life and work, just as Molly had anticipated. Georgina peered into the cabinet placed in the centre of the room, smiling for a moment at the memory of laughing with Molly about protecting the porcelain from stray elbows. The light glinted in the soft sheen of the figurine's milky glaze and the patterned blue of the vase shone out like a cloudless sky on a summer day.

"Georgina! How wonderful. Fred said he thought it was you." Evelyn strode into the room with the confidence of someone whose victory in all matters was assured. "Welcome and tell me, what do you think of the room?"

"It's beautiful, Evelyn. My father, I'm sure, would be very pleased indeed. Thank you."

"It has been our pleasure. I hope you can see that we've been at pains to let each artwork breathe." Georgina followed Evelyn to the far wall. "And you will see we have taken a chronological approach. On the left are your family portraits from the 1800s."

Georgina stifled the sensation of hurt triggered by the mention of the paintings.

Evelyn carried on without pausing for breath. "I took the liberty of including *The Hunt* within this series of works, which I'm sure you'll agree fits very well. And then we move left to right into the twentieth century to the present day ending with the Leibovitz and your father's photograph of his charming garden."

Georgina nodded. "It works well."

"Good. Now in terms of the order for the night, as people gather I will give the briefest of welcomes and then hand over to you. I know how much it will mean to our guests to have you speak of your father and for you to introduce them to the Wright Community Room and Gallery. I've asked Molly to say a few words from a curatorial perspective." Evelyn looked out towards the foyer. "Oh, there's the mayor. I hope you don't mind—I made some additional invitations to those persons holding influence both locally and further afield. Oh, wonderful, Mark has seen him. Won't you join us in the foyer as we welcome our guests?"

"I'd rather take some more time with the room before people arrive." Georgina glanced at the dignitaries milling in the foyer. "If that's okay?"

"Of course. When you're ready." Evelyn left with her back straight and her demeanour poised to take the moment the occasion offered to win over hearts and minds and, above all, patronage.

Georgina stood motionless, claiming a final private moment with the objects her family had cherished and loved. Soon all that had been familiar and personal would become unfamiliar and impersonal, for seeking public memory came at a cost, and sentiment and privacy seemed to be the price.

Georgina risked another half glance in the direction of the foyer. More guests had arrived, drifting in from the blackness of the December night and gathering in small groups, their eyes furtively seeking out the refreshments.

She quickly turned away. Could she excuse herself somehow and leave? But they were expecting a speech, weren't they? They were expecting thanks and praise and poignant memories of her father. Did they want her to publicly grieve? As a minimum they were expecting her to impress them and to show them she was the worthy heir to the Wright

Foundation. Tonight she belonged to them, and the thought filled her with rising panic and dread.

"Hi. I figured you might need a drink. I've had two."

Georgina turned at the sound of Molly's voice, so familiar and reassuring. Molly was smiling at her, a tentative smile, uncertain perhaps of Georgina's reaction.

"Thank God for you." Georgina took a glass and a huge gulp of wine.

Molly's smile grew wide, as she said, "You look—"

"Terrified?"

Molly laughed. "Yes. Terrified and beautiful."

Georgina felt herself blush. "Thank you." She brushed nervously at her thighs before running her fingers along the bottom edge of the jacket of her dark grey trouser suit. She was surprised at how self-conscious she felt. It had all of the trepidation of their second meeting and all of the heartache of their last. When she hadn't heard from Molly she hadn't known what to do or what to think. Her doubts about ever having a *one* didn't match how much she missed Molly and how much she hurt. She knew in her heart, she was here this evening as much for Molly as for her father, if not perhaps more.

"You look beautiful too," Georgina said, relieved to feel the warmth of Molly's smile upon her.

But then Molly always looked beautiful. Whether dressed to impress like tonight in a slim fitting navy-blue dress set off with her free-flowing auburn curls or chatting casually in denim jeans with her hair tucked up under a fisherman's hat. Pain stabbed at Georgina at the memory of Molly's heartbroken face that day she found out Edith had died. The same day Georgina had so evidently disappointed her.

Molly's expression became serious as she looked down, her eyes darting as if chasing her thoughts. "I've missed you and...and I'm so sorry about the last time we chatted. I shouldn't have left like that."

Guests were mingling around them. Georgina could hear Evelyn's voice approaching. Georgina rested her hand on Molly's arm. "Let's talk later."

Molly looked up. "Yes, I'd like that."

A high-pitched tapping of pen to glass called everyone's attention to Evelyn. "Everyone. Welcome to the opening of the Wright Community Room and Gallery. This is a space which celebrates a most generous gift from the Wright Foundation of an exquisite collection of fine and decorative art. It is also, we hope, a fitting tribute to the late George Wright, who was instrumental in bringing this gift to fruition. Amongst the works on display tonight are pieces from George's own personal collection, which it is now our absolute honour to treasure on his behalf. Without further ado I would like to invite George's daughter and head of the Wright Foundation, Georgina Wright, to say a few words." Evelyn turned, clapping in Georgina's direction, encouraging the gathered crowds to join her in appreciative applause.

"Good luck," Molly whispered.

Georgina nodded and tugged at the cuffs of her shirt. She joined Evelyn, standing at her side.

"Thank you, Evelyn, and to your hard-working team." Georgina glanced at Molly who blushed. "And thank you to the museum's trustees and to the city council for their kind support in making this evening possible. I know my father would have been so proud to see his artworks and the foundation's collection residing in such a fitting and wonderful space." Georgina paused to allow the murmur of approval to circle the room and rest. "He would be as thrilled as I am to think of the visitors who will be able to enjoy these amazing objects as my family have had the privilege of doing for so many years. I know he would ask you, as I do now, to raise a toast to—" In that instant everything stopped. *No. It can't be. Not you. Not here.* Georgina's gaze was captured by a figure standing at the back of the room. A figure she had not seen for many years but one she recognized instantly. It was the same slender-framed woman who haunted her dreams, waking her night after night, as Georgina tried to stop her from leaving again and again and again.

Georgina glanced at the crowd and at their raised glasses and confused expressions. She briefly closed her eyes and swallowed. Her mouth was dust dry and the sound of her blood pounded in her ears. She could feel the room slide and shift. She opened her eyes, seeking out Molly who mouthed, *You okay?*

"To the Wright Community Room and Gallery!" Evelyn said, with a confidant tone that almost persuaded the onlookers that this was intended, a double act indeed.

The guests all dutifully repeated the words of Evelyn's toast. Their questioning faces leaning like sunflowers tilted to the sun in the direction of Georgina.

Georgina turned to Evelyn and whispered with barely concealed fury, "Did you invite her?"

Evelyn smiled broadly at the gathered audience, at the same time saying with the skill of a ventriloquist, "I thought it might offer opportunities for…My apologies if I am mistaken." Without waiting for Georgina's response she quickly raised her voice to the crowd once more and continued, "Thank you so much, Georgina. We are so very grateful. So everyone, to help you enjoy your evening with us, I would like to welcome Molly Goode, our curator of fine art here at the museum, to say a few words to guide and to illuminate."

"Are you okay? What is it?" Molly whispered as she joined Georgina and Evelyn.

Georgina shook her head. "My mother's in the audience."

Molly swallowed and her face drained of all colour. "Oh."

Evelyn gave a short cough. "And here is Molly to say a few words."

"Yes. Good evening, everyone." Molly gripped her notes. "There is"—she cleared her throat—"perhaps no surer way of getting to know a person than through the objects they have loved."

Georgina couldn't face hearing Molly speak on behalf of the museum that had taken such liberties not only with her feelings but with her father's memory. But even more than that, she couldn't bear the thought that her mother was now looking at her. She quietly stepped back and left the room to find sanctuary in the foyer.

"Would you like a drink, Miss Wright?" Fred was smiling and gesturing to the drinks table in front of him.

Georgina looked at the wine poured out in glasses. "A glass of red. Thank you, Fred."

From the safety of the foyer and with her back to the Wright room, Georgina half listened to Molly's speech, giving an overview of the major items in the collection before wrapping up with, "So everyone, this evening, art is truly celebrated as the past and present come together to remind us of the wonder of art throughout the decades and, indeed, generations. Please do not hesitate to ask questions as you enjoy the works on display."

Without missing a beat, Evelyn added, "And please do take a moment to browse our gift shop and let us tempt you to a little something as a memento of your evening or as the perfect Christmas gift." Georgina's stomach turned over at the sound of Evelyn's voice. "So we welcome you," Evelyn said, "to the Wright Community Room and Gallery."

Applause followed, soon to be replaced by the hushed deliberations of public scrutiny.

"Georgina?"

Georgina turned round at Molly's voice and the feel of her hand on her back.

"I didn't think she'd come. I'm so sorry," Molly said.

"You knew she'd been invited?"

Molly nodded, biting at her lip.

"And you didn't think to warn me? After everything I'd told you about my mother, about what she'd done to me, to my father? How could you have thought that it was okay that she was invited?"

"I didn't think it was okay. I thought it was awful and so did Fran."

"Fran knew? Everyone knew?" Georgina's eyes misted with fury.

"Georgina." Molly attempted to place a reassuring hand on Georgina's arm but Georgina stiffened in response. Molly let go. "By the time we found out, the invitation had been sent. All we could do was hope your mother wouldn't come."

Georgina gasped in disbelief. "No, Molly. That's not *all* you could have done. You could have told me. You should have told me. How could you let me find out this way?"

Molly looked down. "I'm sorry."

"So am I." Georgina turned away from Molly. She looked back at the crowds in the annex, noticing the one person she didn't want to see.

Staring at her with her hand half raised in the suggestion of a wave was her mother. Wearing a billowing white chiffon dress, she was slimmer than Georgina remembered, taller even than the woman of her nightmares. And even from this distance, she appeared fragile, her willowy frame swaying as if blown with the bluster of the crowds.

Georgina felt every muscle tense. *Why are you here?*

"You don't have to speak to her," Molly said quickly. "I can explain that you prefer not to—Georgina, wait."

Georgina shook her head and drained her glass dry, then walked slowly towards her mother.

"I remember these so well." Her mother stood staring at the baptism of James Ambrose. She placed her hand delicately on the frame as if feeling for the threads of a heartbeat in the grains of wood. She frowned and her gaze drifted along the line of paintings. She walked a few steps to stand in front of *The Hunt*. "Such a depressing piece. Don't you think? I always thought Josephine looks so sad in it. I remember suggesting many years ago to your father that we should gift it to this museum." Her mother leaned in to read the label. "Yes, in 1985. And now here it is jostling its way back in again. If I'm not mistaken, it has replaced the beautiful watercolour of Josephine. Has it been stored? Is it here in the museum?" Her mother looked about her. "I would love to see it again."

Georgina could not believe that her mother was attempting to have a conversation with her as if they always talked and as if they'd never spent more than a day or so apart and as if she hadn't ripped their family into pieces and crushed her father, and torn apart her heart.

"You look well, Georgina, if perhaps a little tired," her mother continued, seemingly with no shame. "I try to keep up with how you're doing as best I can through friends. I hoped you might write." Her mother pressed her lips together and for a moment looked down. When she looked up again she had reapplied her mask of cheer. "You're doing well in banking, I believe? May I say, I was relieved when I heard you'd broken with tradition and not gone into the law. Such a combative career."

Her mother tucked a strand of fine grey hair behind her ear. Her eyes had a faded quality to them, as if light and laughter once filled them and all that remained was the suggestion that they were once there. The frown lines around her mouth betrayed a tendency to sadness. Powdery foundation concealed none of this, and rouged cheeks mocked her with the suggestion of youth and joy.

Georgina had not allowed herself to imagine this moment, standing in front of her mother for the first time in so many years. She wished now that she had rehearsed it and that she had at her disposal a series of retorts to counter every possible attempt by her mother to make things right. For there was nothing her mother could say that could undo what had been done. Nothing.

"What the hell are you doing here?" Georgina's every word pinched corset tight with suspicion. "No, let me guess, you have come to pick over my father's belongings. Well, let me make this clear—you are divorced from him and from anything to do with us. I would have thought that was obvious. So I repeat, why are you here?"

Her mother swallowed. "To see *you*. It is what your father wanted."

Georgina let out an incredulous burst of laughter. "Really? And you expect me to believe that?"

"Of course not. In fact I'm relieved you are talking to me at all."

"Well your relief is short-lived. I want you to leave, and that really shouldn't be a difficulty for you—leaving. After all you managed it so well."

"Georgina…" Her mother rested her hand on Georgina's forearm. "Darling, please."

Georgina roughly pulled her arm away. "I'm not your darling, and if you don't leave, I will."

"Wait—I have a letter. You need to see it."

"No, Mother. I don't *need* to do anything. And as for letters from you, I would have thought it was obvious how little they mean to me." Georgina watched her mother step back a little. She suppressed the sensation of guilt and hurt with the knowledge that her last emotional punch had struck hard.

With a voice clearly winded by their exchange, her mother said, "It's not from me. It's from your father to me." She reached into her handbag.

"For the last time, I don't believe anything you say. I am not interested." Georgina walked out of the annex and into the foyer. She spotted Evelyn in deep conversation with Molly and Fran. Molly and

Fran both had their arms crossed defensively, as Evelyn, noticeably more flustered than usual, held their attention. They hadn't seen her, so this was her opportunity to leave. She glanced at her watch. She could catch the nine thirty. In an hour and a half she could be back in London where she belonged.

She risked a last look behind her. Thankfully her mother had not tried to follow. Instead she was chatting with the chairman. She showed no signs of leaving.

Georgina headed for the exit only to slow to a stop at half hearing Evelyn's instructions to Molly.

"I need you to smooth things over with Georgina. We need you, Molly, more than ever. If we lose Georgina, then we are sure to lose Lydia Wright's potential influence and support as well. Is that understood?"

"What *is* understood is that I have been used by this museum in the most deplorable fashion." Georgina's voice had a chilling calmness to it.

All three women turned around in unison. All three jaws dropped.

"Georgina—" Molly reached out only for Georgina to step out of reach.

"It's so obvious now. I've been such a fool. Send in your sweet curator to soften me up. What better Trojan horse than Molly. Was that it, Evelyn?"

Taken aback, Evelyn said, "Really, Georgina, please—"

"And you." Georgina directed her glare at Molly so that it would penetrate right through to her heart. "It was all about your career, wasn't it? And that's why you left the other day—because I said no to your career plan to display Josephine's portrait for maximum effect—I wouldn't play your game."

Like a hawk spying prey, Evelyn turned her head and fixed a steely gaze on Molly, who folded her arms ever more tightly in response.

Without pausing for breath, Georgina continued, "It was staring me right in the face that you were using me, but I didn't see it."

Molly shook her head, her face creased with evident hurt and confusion. "No, that's not right."

"And do you know why I didn't see it? Because I genuinely cared for you." Georgina swallowed down the anger choking at her throat. "You let me think…We even…I *trusted* you."

"That's quite enough." Fran stepped forward blocking Molly from Georgina's fury. "I think it's best you go home, Georgina." Fran looked beyond Georgina to the annex.

"Don't worry, I intend to." Georgina turned to see her mother standing watching them. She quickly looked back, this time her attention fixed squarely on Evelyn. "You're welcome to my mother, Evelyn. Let's hope the infamous Lydia Wright can replace the lost patronage of the Wright Foundation."

Evelyn's neck prickled and flushed pink.

Georgina left, without looking back.

❖

The ceiling spun and the walls rose up to suffocate Molly. She tried to fix on something real, something to hold on to, to stop her falling any further into the blank abyss of shock. She pinched at her leg hoping to feel the sting of pain, for all sensation had become dull and muted. She could hear but couldn't hear. She could feel but couldn't feel.

"Molly? You okay? Molly?" Molly looked down at Fran's hand holding hers tight. "It was just the shock of seeing her mum again." Fran squeezed at her hand. "After all these years. It was shock talking, that's all. She didn't mean the things she said. Molly?"

"She did, though," Molly said. "She clearly meant every word."

"And so do *I* when I tell you this," Evelyn said, with a tone of voice that was so chilling the cold of it brought Molly back into the room with a start.

Molly swallowed. She thought she might be sick. She risked a glance at Evelyn. Evelyn's neck was pink but her face had drained to ashen grey. Her eyes had grown darker than the December night outside.

Evelyn had lowered her voice but her words impacted with all the force of a shout. "There will be no further discussion tonight on what has just happened. You will return to the Wright room and fulfil your duties. Then come to my office first thing Monday morning." Evelyn pinched at her brow and sighed. "I have no choice but to update the chairman. I'm sure I don't need to tell you, Molly, how serious this is."

Fran shook her head. "Evelyn—"

Evelyn raised her hand. "Don't even try, Fran. Professional lines have clearly been crossed. Let's just hope we can rescue this evening." Evelyn stuck her chin out with her chest rising in defiance. She resurrected a smile from what were no doubt the ashes of her aspirations for the night.

Molly stood and watched Evelyn return to the Wright room. Fran was still holding her hand.

"Well, that could have gone better," Fran said, deadpan. "She's got some nerve making you a scapegoat when she invited Lydia in the first place."

Molly nodded, wiping away a stray tear. "She's going to sack me, isn't she? I undermined her and acted unprofessionally with such an important stakeholder."

"Look, let's just wait and see. She has the weekend to calm down, and on a plus note, she hasn't fired you yet." Fran shrugged.

"Only because she needs me to work tonight."

"Well then, you have the rest of the evening to make amends. Impress her with your schmoozing talents. In fact if you can face it, you could start with her." Fran nodded in the direction of Lydia Wright who seemed far more interested in Molly and Fran than Evelyn and the chairman, who were trying to engage her in conversation.

Molly shook her head. "You're kidding, right?"

"Nope."

"Her daughter *hates* me and I think I'm going to puke."

Fran pinched at Molly's cheeks. "Nonsense on both accounts. And Georgina doesn't hate you. That kind of impassioned fury doesn't come from hate. Anyway being on the wrong side of Georgina means at least for tonight you and Lydia Wright have a lot in common. Go on, before she loses interest." Fran placed her hand on Molly's back, shoving her lightly towards the annex.

Lydia had drifted away from Evelyn and the chairman, content it seemed to wander around the exhibition alone. She was not exactly what Molly was expecting. For some reason the name Lydia Wright had conjured an image of a woman who sought attention and coveted the limelight and who always found an opportunity to strike a pose whether a pose was required or not, or someone who might cause a scene without a thought or care. But this woman was quietly taking everything in. If anything you would not notice her other than to remark perhaps on her tall elegance and a certain foreignness of dress.

Lydia Wright had paused at the French doors to take in *Little Eve* when Molly plucked up the courage to say hello.

"Good evening, Ms. Wright. I'm—"

"Molly Goode. I heard your speech."

"Oh, of course." Molly's cheeks stung with embarrassment.

Lydia extended her hand. Her fingers were long and elegant like Georgina's. Molly shook it and gave a polite smile. She then glanced to Fran who gestured for her to continue.

"I hope you are enjoying your evening," Molly said, hoping her voice betrayed none of her uncertainty.

"Very much. And you?"

Having watched Lydia endure Georgina's shock and anger, Molly doubted that Lydia was enjoying her evening very much. She was likely enjoying her evening as much as Molly, which was not at all.

"Uh-huh," Molly said. "It's certainly a…memorable evening." Molly knew that Lydia had seen Georgina shouting at her, so was she being kind by not mentioning it, or playing with her? What kind of woman was Lydia Wright—kind or cruel or neither?

Lydia turned to the bronze figure of *Little Eve* resting on the plinth at her side. "I remember George and I went to see this work at the Tate. That would have been...oh, I don't know, mid-nineties, maybe. We couldn't see it at first in the public galleries, and so when we enquired, we were told it was on display in the members' room. George complained and reminded them in strong terms that it was a loan from a public foundation for public good. If I remember correctly, it was then loaned on by the Tate for a touring exhibition, and I'm not certain it was on permanent display again. It's good to see it here."

"We're really excited and proud to have such a prestigious work on display here." Molly stared at the biblical figure of Eve sculpted with her arms folded across her chest and her face bowed and turned away in a physical expression of embarrassment and shame.

She should say something professional. It was about the details, that's what Evelyn always told her, *Please remember the details.* "This piece was inspired by the larger original 1881 model." Lydia's face seemed to brighten with interest. "If you look closely, you can see Rodin's signature just at her left foot. The name of the foundry—Alexis Rudier, Paris—is on the base."

Lydia leaned in. "Yes, how interesting," she said. "Tell me then, what do you think of Rodin?"

"I enjoy his work very much," Molly said. "I love that he captures the human form in such a sensual way. You almost expect the cast materials, whether bronze or even marble, to give way with your touch, like flesh. I have such respect for how he seemed to master the materials and evoke the human form so beautifully."

Lydia smiled. "Then you must visit the Musée Rodin in Paris. The museums in Paris are my lifeblood. I live right in the heart of the city—I can feel it beat." Lydia rested her hand momentarily against her heart. "I spend my summer in the south but always seem to return to Paris as the seasons change, as it seems to suit my winter mood."

"I have visited the museum, although it was a long time ago." Molly hadn't meant to be enjoying her conversation with Lydia quite so much. It made her feel strange. But then the whole evening had been strange, and nothing about it felt real. Or was it that everything about it was too real, too raw?

"It's always good to return to a museum and to see its collection again," Lydia said. "An artwork must be seen several times over the course of one's life to be truly appreciated. We miss so much at first sight." Lydia's attention was drawn past Molly to the Wright family portraits at the far wall behind them. "It is like seeing old friends again and returning to the comfort of the familiar."

Molly turned in the direction of the paintings, as they came in and out of view as people paused before them, reading the labels and moving on.

Lydia sighed. "You know, I think she is sadder than I remember her."

"I'm sorry?"

"In *The Hunt*. Josephine. I was only saying a moment ago to my daughter what an upsetting painting I thought it was."

Molly's heart squeezed at the mention of Josephine. "Yes. She looks so forlorn."

Lydia said, her eyes narrowing, "I always wondered why."

Had Molly any right to tell Lydia the possible reason? That grief following the death of a love had likely left its indelible mark, casting her expression in the shade of eternal sorrow. But no. This was not the narrative for the Wright room, and that couldn't have been made clearer. Molly closed her eyes, pushing away thoughts of Georgina which badgered with every breath. *Don't think about her. You can't, not here, not now.*

"I guess we'll never know for sure," Molly suggested, swallowing down the nausea pressing at her throat. She glanced away from the paintings. Fran was nowhere to be seen. She caught Evelyn's eye and a terrible rush of self-consciousness made her stomach drop. Was Evelyn pleased she was talking to Lydia, or horrified? Molly couldn't tell.

"There was another portrait of Josephine," Lydia said. "It was a watercolour."

Molly turned quickly back to Lydia at the mention of Edith's painting. Lydia was frowning as if trying to remember a detail.

"Sketchy," Lydia continued. "Yes, of the moment, I would say. It was a charming work. I even wondered whether it might have been displayed?" Lydia looked at Molly as if she would naturally provide the answer.

Feeling flustered, Molly quickly explained, "The pieces chosen for this exhibition have been guided by the bequest and the final decisions have rested with Evelyn Fox."

Lydia raised her eyebrows. "Not you?"

Molly shook her head. "I was part of a team who brought the bequeathed items together. I then helped with their installation in this room."

"I see. And the watercolour? Did you come across it?"

"I'm sorry, but you'd need to speak with Georgina—"

Lydia gave out a pained laugh. "I've spent the last eighteen years trying to speak to my daughter."

"I'm sorry," Molly said, looking down.

"Thank you, that's kind of you to say. And thank you for taking the time to talk to me. I imagine you've heard all kinds of things about me." *Oh God.* "Me? No. I mean not really. Very little." *Quick, move on.* "I've enjoyed our chat. I love talking about art."

"Then you are in the right job."

Molly winced at Lydia's words. She loved her job, for it was more than work—it was her vocation and her life. And soon it would be gone, wouldn't it, and there was nothing Molly could do about it.

Fran arrived at Molly's side.

Molly quickly said, "May I introduce you to my colleague, Fran Godfrey. Fran is the museum's social historian."

"Ah, yes." Lydia held out her hand and smiled warmly. "We have met before, haven't we? You were school friends with George."

"Indeed," Fran said, shaking Lydia's hand in turn. "We've met once or twice at the persuader evenings."

"Oh, such wonderful nights," Lydia said wistfully. "You would have loved them, Molly."

"Yes, Fran has told me about them. They sound just amazing and very glamorous."

Lydia gave a slow nod. "They were."

"If you'll excuse me, I need to borrow Molly." Fran gestured into the foyer.

"Oh, of course. Good evening to you both."

"Good evening, Ms. Wright," Molly said.

Lydia raised her finger. "It is Lydia, please. And let me know if you make it back to Paris."

"I will, thank you," Molly said. Despite such conflicting feelings, she really thought she might.

Molly followed Fran out of the annex, aware that Lydia was watching them leave. She stared ahead, not wanting to see if Evelyn had also noticed their departure. In the safety of the foyer, everything seemed to crash in on Molly as tears forced themselves through the barriers of her bravery.

"I'm sorry," Molly said. "I'll be okay in a minute."

"Go home." Fran looked towards the exit. "I'll cover for you. You went back in there. You've done as Evelyn asked."

"I don't know what to think or do—about work, about Georgina. How could she say those things about me? How could she even think that of me? How has everything gone so wrong? What on earth do I do?"

"I wish I had the answers for you." Fran wrapped her arms around her. "I really wish I did."

CHAPTER TWENTY-FIVE

Molly had worried the weekend away. By the time Monday morning arrived, she'd bitten her nails to the quick and not slept a wink.

Added to the horror of everything, she kept seeing Georgina's face ripped with distress and her eyes clouded in a storm of anger and hurt. And she kept hearing Georgina's voice over and over, recalling her words coiled tight like a cobra about to strike. She'd remained gripped all weekend, barely able to breathe in the shock and agony of the venom of Georgina's accusations.

How could Georgina think so little of her? Yes, she had tried to win her over and to impress her in the hope that she would feel able to have faith in the museum, but she had not set out to manipulate her or to deceive her. And she had certainly not set out to fall for her. She had not set out to imagine that Georgina could be the *one*.

She'd followed no plan, not even Evelyn's. What would Evelyn say? What could Molly say in defence of her actions? She had crossed professional boundaries with Georgina with seemingly little regard for how important Georgina was to the museum. No words of argument could change the fact she had disregarded Evelyn's direct instructions, not once, but twice. She'd carried on researching Josephine's portrait, and then she had raised the matter with Georgina of displaying the portrait in the Wright room. And Fran had warned Molly to take care, for she had seen the standoff coming. And now it had arrived, stark and with nowhere to hide.

Evelyn's door swung open, and Evelyn emerged looking tired and fuzzy at the edges. Her weekend had also obviously offered little rest.

"Molly." Evelyn's voice was weary and her eyes fell heavily upon Molly's face.

Molly quickly stood. "Good morning. I'm so sorry about Friday night, really I am. I—"

Evelyn raised her hand. Molly shut up. "Come in." Evelyn led the way back into her office. "Take a seat."

Molly sat with her knees pressed together and her hands clasped in her lap.

Evelyn sat forward in her chair with her elbows resting on her desk. She placed her glasses on the table and rubbed at her eyes before taking a slow sip of water. She then began, "Can I ask what you spoke about with Lydia Wright?"

Lydia? "Yes, certainly. Well, we talked about the Rodin. She asked me if I liked Rodin and I said I did and that we felt excited and proud to have such a prestigious work on display at our museum. She said I was to let her know if ever I returned to Paris to visit the Musée Rodin."

Evelyn raised her eyebrows. "I see, and was that it?"

"Pretty much. We talked just for a few more moments about the family portraits. She said she remembered them." This was surely not the time to mention that Lydia had asked after Edith's painting.

"Thank you for that clarification. Now to the matter of Georgina Wright. What did Georgina mean during her tirade? What did you let Georgina Wright *think*, Molly?"

Molly pressed her hands further into her lap at the sensation of her stomach dropping. "I'm sorry," Molly said. "I don't quite know what you mean."

"Well it's clear that Georgina had been expecting something from you, and that you had let her down in some way. She had *trusted* you. Those were her words were they not? What had she trusted you with? Molly?"

"I don't know."

"You don't know?"

Molly shook her head. What answer could Molly give? Could she really say *her heart*?

Evelyn sat back in her chair and released a heavy sigh. "I'm sure you appreciate that I cannot ignore the fact that there has been a breach of trust. Not only from the perspective of Georgina Wright but also from my perspective. I trusted you to work with Georgina as a professional member of my team, and I trusted you to follow my instructions. You have shown a wanton lack of care on both accounts."

Molly swallowed hard. "I'm really sorry for any distress and embarrassment I have caused you and the museum," Molly said. "And... and for my lack of judgement." Molly had trusted Georgina as much as

Georgina had trusted her. Georgina was not the only one left hurt and confused.

"Apology noted." Evelyn sat forward again and opened her notepad. She began to make notes. Without looking up she said, "You may as well know that I haven't spoken to the chairman yet. I want to see if we can salvage things, and by *we* I mean me. I want to give Georgina time to calm down. And then I will speak to her."

Molly nodded, "Anything I can do—"

Evelyn raised her hand. "You will have nothing more to do with Georgina Wright. Is that understood?"

"Yes," Molly said quietly.

"And you will take annual leave with immediate effect. I don't wish to see you in this museum until after the Christmas period."

Molly's heart surged in panic. With barely enough breath to speak she gasped, "You're suspending me?"

"You have given me no choice."

"But—" Molly wanted to say *But you invited Lydia Wright, you put the museum at risk, you encouraged me to get close to Georgina. It was all* you.

Evelyn looked up. "You can go now."

Molly stood and turned away only to stop. She looked back at Evelyn and took a deep breath. "Have you used me?" Molly said, finding bravery from who knew where. It was what Georgina had accused Evelyn of and what Molly could not help but think.

Evelyn's neck prickled pink, and this time the rash of colour spread right across her face. "My role is to utilize my staff to the maximum of their potential. Nothing I asked of you was beyond your job description. This meeting is over." Evelyn returned to making her notes. "It is in your best interest for this conversation to end."

Molly knew what Evelyn was getting at. She quickly left Evelyn's office, rushed down the stairs and out into the foyer, and thankfully left the museum before any other staff had arrived. She walked across the square, praying she could make it to Daisy May before breaking down.

Movement outside George Wright's house caught her eye and caused her to momentarily slow her pace. George's furniture was being loaded into a van. Molly watched as the sofa was guided precariously down the steps. And then a man dressed in a suit with his hair slicked back carried out a for-sale board. He looked across at her. Molly looked away and headed for Daisy May.

Safe inside, through half-steamed windows, she stared at the man hammering the board into the ground. It felt like with each blow he was striking at her heart, nailing home the brutal point that all was lost.

CHAPTER TWENTY-SIX

So this was it then? The day that had been arriving since her father told her he was dying. The day she would return for the last time to find the house empty and bereft of everything.

For this was no longer her father's home. It was just a grand beautiful old building waiting to be loved again. A home was made by the people in it and by the objects they cherished. Now it was like an empty shell with its memories tipped up and emptied out like sand.

But then there was the wine cellar where the very last dregs of her father's life were hidden, musty in the dust and darkness. Having a cellar full of wine would be most people's idea of heaven, but for Georgina it was simply the last of many tasks in the emptying of her father's house.

She leaned against the wine rack in the cold cellar, stifling a shiver and a yawn. She was bone-tired. Her train had been delayed and her phone had not stopped ringing with work calls. She'd crammed the next twenty-four hours with meetings and tasks. She would meet with her father's solicitors and the estate agents, and in one hour a wine merchant would come and inspect her father's wine and quote for its purchase.

The removal men had followed Georgina's instructions to leave the bed in her childhood bedroom in place for the last night that she would be here, because on balance a local hotel had managed to seem a lonelier option.

Apart from her bed, all the furniture had been removed, and all that remained was a Mr. Men beanbag that her father had sentimentally kept in his office. Georgina had once asked her father about it and he had said that he liked to have it there, and that it reminded him of her when as a child she would drag the beanbag into his office to read her books, to be with him as he worked late.

She'd now placed the beanbag in the sitting room as something vaguely comfortable for her to sit on in between meetings and tasks.

She gave a heavy sigh at the thought of the work ahead. At least she still had the coffee machine onto which she had placed a label *Do Not Move*. Apart from the bare pieces of crockery that she would need, the rest of the kitchen and bathroom needed to be emptied and the blinds and curtains throughout the house needed to be taken down. The housekeeper had offered to take any items suitable for charity to the local hospice. She'd offered to do these last tasks as well, but the only way Georgina could get through the next twenty-four hours was to keep busy. The last thing she wanted was time to dwell on all that she had lost, and it wasn't just thoughts of her father that simply broke her heart.

For not an hour had passed in the last two weeks without the thought of Molly. Breaks in concentration always led to her, and then it would take all of Georgina's might to stop thinking about her. And when she was tired, Molly filled the spaces where useful thoughts should be. For what was the point of thinking about her? Why couldn't her head and her heart just let Molly go? Why wasn't there a merchant who could come and take broken-hearted thoughts away in a van to be sold on to someone else, someone who knew how to mend them when Georgina herself had no idea.

And what was worse, at some point today Edith's painting would be returned to her as she had requested, marking the end of everything.

She turned and glanced up the cellar steps at the sound of sharp drumming at the front door. It was just after three o'clock. Was the wine merchant early?

Georgina wearily climbed the steps and went to the door, bracing herself for negotiations over the clarity of clarets. She took a deep breath and opened the door.

"Fran?" Georgina's heart caught at the sight of Edith's painting in Fran's arms.

"Good afternoon. I have your painting," Fran said.

"Of course." Georgina gestured for Fran to step inside. "Thank you for bringing it over. Ordinarily I'd invite you into the sitting room, but the only room with a proper seat I'm afraid is the kitchen."

Fran glanced into the sitting room. "Kitchen it is then."

"Great. Please, after you."

Georgina followed Fran into the kitchen. She could do this. Take the painting and say thank you. It would be over in less than a minute. She wouldn't even have to think about Molly. It would be fine.

Fran carefully rested the wrapped painting on the kitchen worktop. She shooed Georgina away when she attempted to offer a hand as Fran struggled onto the stool.

"I always find kitchen stools," Fran said, "require the core strength of an athlete and the balance of a monkey. I am neither. So I shall make this quick. I apologize for any offence I may or may not cause by what I am about to say. I hope you will understand that it comes from a place of concern for both yourself and Molly."

Georgina's chest tightened. "Right. I'm very sorry about what has happened—"

"The poor girl has done nothing wrong whatsoever. If you'd given her half a chance to explain, she would have told you how worried she was about the invitation to your mother. She honestly did not know what to do."

"She should have warned me."

"And see you hurt yet again with mention of your mother? *I* told Molly the last thing your mother would do was come to the opening of the Wright room. *I* discouraged her from telling you. I am certain that if I had told Molly that your mother would likely come, she would have warned you. She would have risked her job for you, and I know that, because she's been doing it ever since she's met you."

Georgina swallowed down the terrible ache in her chest at the continued mention of Molly.

"It was unforgivable of Evelyn to invite your mother, and you were entirely justified in being cross with her. But *only* with her. Molly has never used you. And she did not betray your trust, Georgina—she was simply caught in the most awful position."

Was Fran right? "Well I appreciate your candour, but if you'll excuse me, I've a lot to do."

"And there's one last thing you should know—"

"Really, I do have to get on."

"Evelyn's suspended Molly."

What? No. "I didn't know."

"Well, now you do."

"I'll talk to Evelyn."

"Good, I'm relieved to hear that. Now help me down from this godawful stool." They made their way in silence to the front door. As Georgina reached for the door knob, Fran placed her hand momentarily over hers. "Don't think that I don't know how much you miss your father, Georgina. I also understand that grief is playing its part here. But I can't imagine he would want you to be alone. So now that you know the truth, talk to Molly. Apologize."

"Goodbye, Fran." Georgina held the door open.

"Goodbye then."

Just as Georgina went to close the door Fran shouted over her shoulder, "And look after that painting."

August 1834
Chambers of Brancaster and Lane Solicitors

"What will you do with her things?" Charles Brancaster stared at Edith's scrapbook and notes.

"I have not thought. It has been two weeks now, and still she will not look upon them." William lifted up Edith's painting of Josephine and studied it carefully. "She looks so beautiful in this. Edith has entirely captured the essence of Jo. She has somehow seen her as I see her. Did you know she had painted her?"

Charles stared at his daughter, captured in washes of colour and light. He silently shook his head.

"There is an inscription—can you see, just here by the stretcher." William lifted the back of the canvas towards Charles. "It says *All my love always, Edith*."

Charles looked into the office where Josephine sat silently staring into the distance with her face paler than the sheets of paper crumpled on her desk discarded.

"It is no wonder that she cannot write a word. They were great friends, William, ever since they were children. No, they were like sisters, in fact. And Edith…" Charles's voice broke. "I hoped she looked upon me as a father figure."

"Edith was in your charge?"

"No. I was Edith's father's solicitor and his closest friend. He died suddenly, and poor Edith and her mother were saddled with terrible debt. They were once a wealthy family."

"Goodness."

"Indeed. They ended up living in lodgings not far from here. Jo begged me to pay for Edith to stay on at school. Edith was such a passionate, clever girl and not to finish her education would have been a crime. What a waste of talent and life." Charles's voice caught again, and he cleared his throat. "But I promise, Jo is a fighter, and she will recover from this and return to you, William. It is just the shock of it." Charles placed his hand on William's shoulder. "It may take time. But we have time. And we will wait."

William nodded and said with renewed purpose, "Let's keep these safe. The letter was addressed to Jo, so these are hers. My sense is she would not forgive me if I did not keep them from harm. And I will not let her down. And I would certainly not wish to find myself having to seek her forgiveness on this or any other matter. *For I fear that it is easier to forgive a stranger than a love."*

I need a drink. Georgina returned to the cellar, pulling out a red wine. In that moment she could not face seeing another human being. She found the merchant's number among the long list of calls and texts she had received in the last twenty-four hours. Five minutes later she had rescheduled their meeting to the next day and was retrieving a wine glass from a half-packed box in the kitchen. But she needed one final thing. Where had she seen it last?

She went into the sitting room. "Think. You last saw it here. It's got to be somewhere—surely the removal men wouldn't have taken it?" A growing panic filled her chest at the thought of having lost Molly's corkscrew. She scanned the empty room, lifting through the remaining post piled on the floor by the fireplace. A glint of metal half covered by the curtains caught her eye.

"There you are." Georgina deftly opened the wine and filled the glass to its brim and drank down the contents in one. She immediately refilled it and slumped into the beanbag. She held Molly's corkscrew, closing her fingers tight around its metal wings with her thumb pressed against the curl of its cork-piercing beak.

Molly. Fran's words had ignited all thoughts of Molly to burn ever brighter in Georgina's mind. She could remember every detail of that first magical evening with Molly here in the sitting room, lying on the throw together looking up into the sparkling light of the chandelier. It was the beginning of things that had led to London and to their first kiss and Molly's arms around her and her soft warm body pressed into hers.

Molly had opened up Georgina's heart, letting light flood into its dark chambers and urging warm blood to flow, melting the sharp crystals of sadness that had lined every artery.

She took another large slug of wine, its spicy heat smoking out sense and reason from anger and pride.

Fran was adamant that Molly hadn't used her or betrayed her trust. So why on earth had Georgina imagined she had? Had she allowed her anger to cloud her judgement? Had fury bent and twisted the truth to its own warped design?

How could she be so stupid? For wasn't she the one who instigated everything and not Molly? She shivered as the heat of anger dissipated and the cold truth seeped in. She'd been as intrigued as Molly to want to continue to research Josephine's portrait and pushed to uncover its buried history. So why was she surprised when Molly defended the painting's story and pleaded for it not to be buried again and for it to be told in the space they had created *together*? No wonder Molly couldn't understand, and no wonder her confusion prompted her to leave. And then she blamed her for leaving and punished her with unforgivable silence, forcing an apology Molly hadn't needed to make but made anyway for the sake of them. For *them*.

Georgina felt tears of guilt and regret sting. Molly hadn't used her. She had just cared, not only about the painting, but about Georgina herself. Fran was right and Georgina couldn't have felt more wrong.

She sat forward hugging at her knees. Molly would never forgive her. It was too late. She had ruined things and lost the most beautiful woman she could ever have hoped to meet.

Georgina looked up to the ceiling at the glinting chandelier. She closed her eyes and the fading shapes of glistening glass imprinted on her eyelids. *I can't lose her. There must be something I can do.* As she opened her eyes and dropped her gaze from the ceiling, she caught sight of the empty wall opposite. She stared at the dust outlines made by the absent paintings and at the darker blocks of paint protected behind them for all those years. They were safe now together, hanging in the Wright room. But they weren't all together were they? Georgina looked out to the hallway that led to the kitchen that led to Edith's painting.

Could it be the answer? It was certainly at the heart of everything wasn't it? It would have to be something more though than the display of the portrait in the Wright room. It was too obvious. In any case it might seem too little too late. But what then? Georgina sighed heavily and picked up the corkscrew in her hand once more.

"How do I show her, Penguin, how much I care?"

This was Molly Goode after all, and nothing shining or superficial would truly impress her. The possibility of an idea suggested itself like a whisper in her ear. What had upset Molly the most? It was the thought that Edith had been forgotten by her loved ones and by history. What could she do to correct this? If she could solve that question, then maybe it would mean a chance for them. Even if she could come up with a plan, she'd have to take on Evelyn. But she would do that. She would do anything for Molly. Was this a glimmer of hope?

CHAPTER TWENTY-SEVEN

The bottle of wine had helped Georgina sleep, although it was less helpful in the morning as she squinted at the low winter sun beaming brightly in through Evelyn's office window.

Georgina stood for a moment looking out at the square and at the empty space where Daisy May would wait for Molly. A raggedy man was sitting on Molly's bench talking to something or someone or nothing or no one, except maybe the occasional pigeon who pecked around his feet. She looked across to her father's house standing empty with its proud exterior buffeted by the occasional swirl of dust and drifting litter. Everything looked so desolate. Winter had never felt so bleak.

"Georgina. Thank you so much for calling by." Evelyn bustled in a little breathless, with her pink cheeks matching her flushed neck.

"Good morning." Georgina shook Evelyn's hand. "Would you mind if I lowered this?" Without waiting for a reply she lowered the blind and cast the room in ominous shade.

Evelyn switched on a light. "Not at all. Please make yourself at home." Evelyn hung up her coat and stroked her hair and clothes into place.

It was eight thirty and Georgina had clearly caught Evelyn off guard. "I'm sorry for arriving unannounced." Georgina wasn't sorry— she wasn't sorry at all. Evelyn was on the back foot and that was precisely where Georgina intended to keep her.

"*No*, think nothing of it. Please take a seat." Evelyn settled herself behind her desk and gave a little sigh as if grateful for the protection it offered. "Our door is always open for you, Georgina, anytime. Thank you, Marianne."

Marianne placed a tray of coffee and biscuits on the table. Evelyn poured them coffee from the cafetière. If she was not mistaken, Evelyn's hand was shaking slightly.

"Before we go any further"—Evelyn placed a hand against her chest, whether as a gesture of sincerity or in an attempt to calm her heart Georgina couldn't tell—"I must apologize for the unfortunate confusion at the opening of the Wright room. I trust you have had a chance to read my note of apology and explanation I included in your Christmas card from the museum?"

"I haven't checked my post." Georgina took a guarded sip of her coffee. She'd seen that the museum had sent her a Christmas card, care of her father's address. She'd been using it unopened as a drinks mat.

Evelyn double blinked. "Well I do hope, that is, I trust, that you will forgive this unfortunate"—Evelyn seemed to hold the next word in her mouth as if sucking on a boiled sweet—"misjudgement on our part and accept our sincere apology for any upset we have caused."

Georgina thought that she might have to painfully extract an apology and was surprised when one came so easily. "Thank you for your apology, Evelyn, which I accept."

Evelyn visibly relaxed. "That's a wonderful relief."

"I do, however, seek your reassurance with regards to Molly Goode." Georgina's tone was measured to rest uneasily somewhere between furious and calm.

Evelyn rearranged herself in her chair. "Molly?"

"Yes. I understand she has been suspended."

"That's right. There are a number of reasons—"

"I'm not interested in the reasons. I am interested in her immediate reinstatement."

"May I say I'm a little confused, Georgina. You gave the impression that Molly had misled you in some way. I considered this to be a breach of trust which we will not tolerate at the museum. As a key stakeholder we greatly value your support—"

"And I have greatly valued Molly's. I now have a better understanding of Molly's part in matters, and whilst I understand your confusion, I would greatly appreciate her reinstatement."

Evelyn leaned forward and took a considered sip of coffee. She looked at Georgina with her eyes levelled to hers. "I wonder if this might be an occasion for the museum to seek a little…clarity from yourself as to our relationship with the Wright Foundation, as you see it going forward. Understandably I found your parting words the other night a little disturbing. Notwithstanding my part in that, of course."

Was Evelyn using Molly's reinstatement as leverage for what she wanted? "Of course. And yes, I agree. This is indeed the perfect moment to establish some *clarity*. So let me define for you what the Wright Foundation will be looking for in terms of funding applications going forward. We will want to see museums adhering to their stated aims and delivering upon them."

Evelyn gave a cautious nod. "That sounds entirely reasonable."

"I'm glad you think so." Georgina opened her iPad and retrieved a saved document. "I see that the museum has stated aims which include prioritizing local histories and the acquisition and display of objects which reveal society's progress."

Evelyn gave a fidgety, "That's right."

"I think there is an excellent opportunity here for the museum to show the Wright Foundation in tangible terms that they intend to deliver on their aims."

Evelyn had shifted forward to the edge of her seat. "In tangible terms?"

"Let me put it this way—I would be greatly impressed to see Edith Hewitt's painting of Josephine Brancaster displayed as part of February's LGBT history month. And I would be equally reassured to find the display remains in place throughout March to become part of the celebrations for women's history month. The life of Edith Hewitt is a local history that has not been fully explored before and fits the remit very well. I feel sure this is something both Molly and Fran would be pleased to work on."

Evelyn tilted her head and looked at Georgina, studying her with the care of someone who intended to remember every detail. "LGBT history month?"

Georgina held her gaze. "Yes."

"No."

"May I ask, why not?"

"You may. February is too soon to put together a display of any merit. Even March is asking too much, but then I suppose it will please Fran, who has been hovering like a hornet in my ear about a local focus for women's history month." Evelyn wafted her hand at her ear as if she could hear the soft hum of the hornet still.

"Surely meeting the February deadline would only require the ready assistance of the records office to lend the necessary objects?"

"What is required remains to be seen. And the narrative, the emphasis of the display would be…?"

"The *whole* life of Edith Hewitt. Her work and her personal life."

"I see. And you are insistent upon this?"

"Yes. Very much so. This and something else."

Evelyn raised her eyebrows. "Something else?"

"The Wright Foundation would be interested to sponsor a project to explore the collections for other similar hidden histories. Obviously for the matter of neglected histories to be dealt with properly, the root cause must also be addressed." Evelyn raised her pen. Georgina ignored her and continued, "I understand the problem lies primarily at the point of entry with the cataloguing of the objects. Sensitive contextual data such as sexuality, gender, race, and religion are not required to be recorded and are being lost."

"You seem very well informed." Evelyn's tone implied *not that I need to ask by whom.*

"I make it my business to understand things properly."

"Well, please rest assured that as an accredited museum we meet all the sector standards in this regard. Furthermore I'm sure you appreciate we do not set the standards, we follow them."

"I would have thought this museum would prefer to set best practice rather than merely follow it. Or am I mistaken?"

Evelyn's knuckles grew ever whiter as her grip on her pen tightened. "It goes without saying that this museum regards itself as a leading institution—"

"Excellent. Then I can expect to see the museum leading the way by specifying sexuality, gender, race, and religion as compulsory primary fields in your database."

Evelyn let out a pained sigh. "If only the delivery of your expectations was as straight forward as we would like. Sadly in many respects our hands are tied, for to redesign at will our generic museum database with its prescribed fields and controlling term lists is…" Evelyn waved her hand in the air searching no doubt for a phrase to match her expression of many shades of agony.

"Completely possible?"

"Well, in theory—"

"Great. And rest assured that the Wright Foundation looks forward to happily untying your hands and supporting this museum to make the theoretical entirely practicable. And may I add, I am surprised to find that you allow your curatorial vision to be constrained by the limitations of a computer database." Georgina folded her arms.

"One moment. I just need…" Evelyn stood and went to the blinds, lifting them before sliding a window open slightly. She stood for a moment in the thin cold slice of breeze.

Georgina shivered as the winter air chilled her skin.

Evelyn turned around with her expression newly cooled and her demeanour calmed as she leaned against the windowsill, and the blinds lightly knocked against the glass. "Georgina, I must say how much I admire the direction the foundation is moving in. It is very commendable."

Where was this going? "Thank you."

"But I would like to clarify that not every project the museum needs to undertake will have a local or minority community focus."

"And I understand that," Georgina said. "But let me clarify in turn to say the foundation is more likely to want to work with a museum on the more, shall we say, prestigious applications, if they are making a genuine effort towards meeting the needs and raising the visibility of a diverse audience."

"I can assure you that the last thing the museum wishes to do is alienate any audience member."

"That's good to hear. So we are agreed on the points discussed."

"I didn't say that." Evelyn returned to her seat, tucking her chair firmly under her desk. "Look"—she held her palms up in front of her— "let me think about everything you have highlighted. Why don't we meet again in the new year. Molly will have returned to work by then—"

"Today."

"Pardon?"

"I want Molly reinstated today."

"Today? May I say I am struggling to digest the long list of your requests."

"Why? Surely I have simply offered to fund your museum and to help the museum meet its aims. I am also correcting an earlier error with regard to Molly."

Evelyn sat back in her chair. "The best I can do is promise to think about it."

Georgina stood. "No, I would have thought the best you can do is to put into motion my requests today. Thank you for your time. I'll see myself out."

"Georgina."

Georgina turned back.

With a surprisingly gentle tone, Evelyn said, "Not that I need to say this, but neither of us knows how Molly feels at the moment, and I have come to understand neither do we know what she will do."

Georgina's cheeks tingled at the inference of Evelyn's observation. "Yes. I understand that point."

"The thing is, Georgina—and I mention this not to be cruel but because I greatly appreciate your continued support—I told Molly to have nothing more to do with you. She didn't...I'm afraid she didn't put up much resistance."

Georgina felt her heart contract and ache. "Thank you, Evelyn."

Georgina left with the heartbreaking sense that no wiser word had been spoken by more wily a fox.

❖

"Hello, Molly!"

"Hi, Fred. Happy Christmas! Can't stop!"

Molly ran across the foyer and up the stairs. She then raced down the corridor to her office. "Have you heard?"

Fran nodded and grinned. "Welcome back, Molly Goode."

Molly gave Fran a big hug. "Evelyn rang me an hour ago. Do you think she's banged her head? Reinstating me early is one thing, but I mean, to tell Edith's story for LGBT history month? Next she'll be suggesting we hang a rainbow flag outside the museum for the whole of February." Molly paused. "Oh, maybe we could ask about that?"

"*Maybe* we should be thankful for the amazing gesture and take a breath and ask ourselves if this sounds like an Evelyn decision."

Molly shook her head and perched her hip on Fran's desk. "It sounds nothing like an Evelyn..." Molly paused. In the excitement of being reinstated and with her first task lined up for after the Christmas break to prepare suggestions for a display based on Edith's life, she had simply overlooked the blindingly obvious. "If Evelyn has asked me to be involved, then does that mean art is involved? You don't think...?"

Fran reached behind her and lifted Edith's painting to rest on her desk. "I was asked to collect it half an hour ago. I'd only dropped it off with Georgina yesterday. Such toing and froing, this poor thing and I have travelled further than Michael Palin's sandals."

"I don't understand—why would she?"

Fran smiled affectionately. "For such a bright and talented woman, you can be really quite stupid."

"Rude. So, what, this was your idea and you persuaded her when you saw her yesterday?"

Fran shook her head. "Granted, I was rather frank with Georgina and put her straight about you. And I did get the impression she might ask for your reinstatement. I honestly didn't expect all this, though."

Molly spoke her thoughts aloud. "She's the reason I have my job back and that Edith's painting will feature in a display?"

Fran nodded. "If I didn't know better, I would think that girl might have fallen in love with you." Fran turned back to continue her work.

Love? Molly's heart missed a beat. "You think she loves me?"

"That's the only explanation that makes any sense to me."

Molly looked at the wrapped painting. But then Georgina hadn't been in contact—what if this wasn't love but just sorry and goodbye? And how could you love someone and say the things she did?

"Did she mention me when you saw her today?"

Fran shook her head. "No, but I got the impression she wanted to ask after you but was hesitant to. Instead she apologized to me for putting me out. I thanked her for what she'd done, and she just nodded. I think she was a little embarrassed. And then some silly man kept disturbing us to ask her questions about wine, so I left her to it. You never know—she may call in before she goes back to London."

"She's going back today?"

"The house was certainly very empty. She kept saying yesterday that she had to get on. I rather got the impression she was trying to get things over and done with."

Molly bit her lip. "Right."

"I'll cover for you if you want to try and catch her."

Molly shook her head. "I'm not ready to. I need to think about things. Anyway, playing truant in the first hour of my reinstatement to see a woman I've been forbidden from seeing may be just a little bit risky."

Fran smiled. "You don't say. Don't overthink things, though. Sometimes things are just as they seem."

If that was the case, then things couldn't be clearer, could they? Georgina was continuing to empty her father's house, which was now for sale. She had obviously decided that Edith's painting would be best cared for by the museum, and as far as Molly was concerned, Georgina had given Molly what she wanted. Was it an apology of sorts, or an easing of conscience? Either way it was likely that as far as Georgina would be concerned, everything was concluded.

"Oh, Molly. Wonderful, you've arrived so promptly and in jeans." Evelyn appeared at the doorway, not quite managing to venture in.

Molly quickly stood. "I rushed over."

"Clearly. Anyway, I'm glad I caught you both. I wanted to let you know that the Wright Foundation has expressed an interest in supporting a project related to identifying histories within the collection that have yet to be revealed."

Molly and Fran looked at each other.

"Minority histories—that sort of thing. Give this some thought, would you. Georgina Wright seems very keen on this. I was surprised to find that her keenness even extended to correcting, as she saw it, omissions in the cataloguing process. A remarkable amount of insight for a banker, wouldn't you say?"

Molly looked down at the floor. She could feel Evelyn's eyes boring into her.

"Fran will be the lead on this project. Anyway, as you were." Evelyn turned sharply and walked away. The sound of Evelyn's heels tapping against the floor disappeared down the corridor.

Could she be dreaming? Georgina had raised all of Molly's concerns with Evelyn *and* she was planning future projects with the museum. That didn't sound like goodbye.

❖

Georgina sat on the bottom but one step of her father's stairs. It was five thirty. Her things were packed up all around her. Her meetings were completed, and it had been agreed that any tail-end matters she would deal with from London. It was hard to imagine that this was likely the last time she would sit on this step or make coffee in the kitchen or bend at the mat for the post or walk through the front doorway to be greeted by the imposing familiarity of it all. It was hard to imagine that the end could come and feel so small. All that was left to do was stand and walk a few paces and open the front door and leave. No one would see this, and no one would care.

Certainly not Molly, it would seem. Georgina checked her phone for one last time, suppressing the sensation that she was a hopeless fool for imagining that Molly could forgive her.

It was time to leave because wasn't that what happened when there was no reason to stay?

Autumn 1840
City Walk, Leicester

"So what do you think? Shall we buy it?" William looked at the house, his face lit with excitement.

Josephine stared up at the beautiful building with its grand and yet refined exterior. She glanced along the tree-lined promenade towards the south fields and the race course. "Can we afford it? And what about the new railway line?"

"You're not to worry about such things." William rested both hands on her shoulders. "But yes, my client list is full, and your father has agreed to help us, should we need it. And really, in spite of the railway, City Walk is considered to be a most desirable residential area."

"You've spoken with my father?"

"Yes, of course. We have agreed that this could be a fresh start. It has broken both our hearts, Jo, to see you so sad for so long." William reached for Josephine's hand and held it against his heart. "And we have so much to be thankful for. This is the place where our family can take root and where generations of Wrights can thrive and flourish."

Josephine watched the future glint in William's eyes, like half-buried gold, as he stared wide eyed at the house.

"Yes, this is the place. I shall ask for a viewing." He turned to Josephine and said with a voice thick with emotion, "Let's bring Adelaide, even James—we shall make our final decision as a family."

Were decisions hers any more? Had they ever been hers? An unblemished reputation of good works, a husband of standing, a beautiful family, and now a home of stature. It was what she had chosen. Wasn't it? This should have been a day of such excitement with the thrill of her future beating alive in her heart. But all Josephine could think about was that this was what she had chosen over Edith, over love. This life, her future, felt so empty in comparison to her time with Edith, which had felt so full. Love would have been enough. Edith had been right. *And now everything in all its perfection felt so wrong.*

With her head down, Georgina hurried past the museum with her eyes fixed at the leaf-trodden ground.

"Georgina!"

She slowed her pace in surprise. She stopped and turned with her eyes seeking after the sound as if to catch it. There was something in the tone of the shout, something fervent, that it was almost like Georgina was lost and the person shouting was trying to find her.

"Georgina, wait!" Molly shouted again as she ran towards Georgina, stopping with a breathless gasp in front of her. "Are you leaving?"

"I don't know." Georgina shook her head. "I honestly don't know what I'm doing any more. All I know, all I can think about, is how sorry I am. I can't believe how I have hurt you, the terrible things I said."

"I hadn't known what to do myself. And all I know is how panicked I felt when I saw you leaving." Molly raised her palm to Georgina's cheek, resting it briefly there. "Does knowing that help at all?"

Georgina nodded and then looked up at Evelyn's office, at the movement of a shadow, at the sense of her. Molly turned to look as well, dropping her hand from Georgina's cheek.

"Thank you for going in to battle with her, for Edith, for me," Molly said.

"That's just it—I would do anything for you."

Molly's eyes filled with tears. "Then don't leave, as least not tonight." Molly inched the bags from Georgina's hold to carry them for her and gestured in the direction of George Wright's home.

Georgina followed her gaze. "It's empty."

Molly shook her head. "It won't be empty. We'll be there."

Chapter Twenty-eight

Without turning on the light, Molly stood in the sitting room looking around at the space furnished only with echoes. The light and movement from the promenade cast shadows onto the bare walls. The features of the room, which were once so familiar with their soft curves and angles, had become foreign, exiled from the context of the life they were once part of.

Only a beanbag resting in place of the armchair offered a suggestion of life. Molly turned in the direction of the kitchen at the sound of the boiler firing and of the pop of the cork from a wine bottle.

"The beanbag's a nice quirky touch to welcome the new buyer." Molly joined Georgina in the kitchen.

"What? Oh, yeah." Georgina shook her head and ripped at the tape securing one of the boxes set aside for charity. She pulled out two glasses and filled them with wine. "There was a brief moment where I wondered whether I could take it on the train with me, but thankfully sense prevailed. Here." Georgina handed Molly her glass and leaned against the worktop opposite. "I kept a couple of bottles for myself from the wine merchant's grasp."

"Good idea. Thank you." Molly rested her wine on the counter and climbed up onto a stool. "And I see Penguin's still coming in useful."

"Oh God, yes, I'm sorry, I should have returned it to you. I promise it wasn't going to charity—there's no way I was letting it go." Georgina hung her head. "It was all I had of you." She looked up at Molly with her eyes swimming with tears. "I can't tell you how ashamed I am by my outburst and by my complete inability to see sense. But most of all I shudder at the thought of the things I said to you. In fact I don't deserve for you to be talking to me."

Molly shook her head. "I want to talk to you, and I can see how sorry you are. And in fact what you didn't deserve was what happened to you at the opening. I'm not surprised you lost it—anyone would have done." Molly paused. "It's just, well, I thought…"

"You thought what? Tell me, please."

"I thought you knew me," Molly said. "More than that, though. I'm not sure I know how to explain. You see, for me everything about you felt right. When we kissed, it was like your lips were somehow meant for mine, it was so…I hoped you felt the same about me, and for a while I thought you did." Molly fell silent with her gaze resting on her hands clasped together in her lap.

Georgina joined Molly, taking a seat on the stool next to hers. She rested her arm across the worktop, closing the gap between them. "I did. I *do*, Molly. Please believe me."

Molly nodded. "I want to."

"Then I have a confession."

Molly's stomach tightened at the word *confession*.

"I'd seen you many times in the square before we met." Georgina glanced out to the hallway that led to the promenade and the square beyond. "You were the beautiful woman who in those last few weeks of my father's life I found myself looking out for."

"You did?" Molly tried to think of herself in the square and tried to imagine what Georgina might have seen and what she might have thought of her.

Georgina's cheeks flushed with her confession. "Yes. One day you'd be feeding the birds or looking up into the sky. The next you'd be chatting away to a random person or Fran, of course. One time even"—Georgina smiled—"you were sitting in a circle with a group of schoolchildren drawing daffodils. They were utterly captivated by you."

"I remember the daffodil day. It had been really wintery weather until then."

"Yes, that's right. My father had me open his bedroom window to let in the air. I brought up from his office the photo—you know, the one that he'd taken of his garden—and hung it in his bedroom so he could see it. He died a few days later."

Molly rested her hand on Georgina's knee. "I'm so sorry."

"Don't be, because it was the sight of you that brought me such comfort, and just the thought of you now keeps me believing that the world isn't entirely bad. So"—Georgina's voice broke—"not only does everything about you feel right, but you fill my life with hope. Hope and joy."

Molly's voice caught in turn as she swallowed down the emotion tightening her throat. "You know, when I first saw you, I swear my heart stopped beating." Her cheeks tingled with the memory. "You were so striking. You were stunning. I almost didn't think you were real. I've never wanted to reach out and touch someone so much." Molly shook her head. "From that moment I couldn't get you out of my head. And as we began to spend time together, I couldn't wait to see you again, and then I swear I began to miss you even before we parted. I kept hoping you'd kiss me. Willing you to. So when you did…Thank God for Edith's painting and for the Wright room for keeping you here."

"*You* kept me here. I returned each time for you," Georgina said with a calm and certain tone. "The painting was the excuse. You were the reason. You will always be the reason for me."

Molly struggled to say, "No one's ever said things like that to me before."

"And I've never cared about anyone enough to want to say them." Without another word Georgina kissed Molly with such urgency and passion that it left Molly in no doubt of the integrity of Georgina's words and the conviction of her heart.

Georgina's kisses were perfect, just like everything about her. Her lips, soft and urging, left Molly desperate for the taste of her, for the feel of her, craving Georgina with the madness of addiction. She broke away to ask, "We could go to my place? Now. If you wanted?"

"Yes," Georgina said without a moment's hesitation. "Or…" Georgina glanced out into the hall. She shook her head. "No, it's a crazy idea."

"I'm a big fan of crazy, just so you know." Molly squeezed at Georgina's hand, encouraging her to finish her thought.

Georgina laughed. "Okay, well, it's just…I have a bed, not that I'm suggesting or indeed presuming—"

A bed? "What *here*? Really?"

Georgina nodded. "I should add it's the bed from my childhood. It's not quite a single and not quite a double, that kind of thing."

"I don't care."

"I should probably add it creaks terribly."

"I still don't care," Molly said, her heart drumming with excitement.

Georgina's eyes sparkled in the brightness of her broad smile. "And I'd need to retrieve the sheets, pillows, and duvet from the charity bag."

Molly laughed. "Fine. I'll grab the wine. You grab the linen. Meet you up there."

Molly waited in Georgina's room lit only by the landing light. Even though the space was, all bar the bed, emptied of its furniture, Molly could still feel the presence of the teenage Georgina.

Had her father kept the room as Georgina had left it? Maybe with its posters of pop stars or a corkboard with its rash of pins hung above a desk and stickers perhaps on the wardrobe peeled off, the torn strips of sticky white paper left behind. And had a favourite teddy, love-worn and dusty, waited on the bed in vain for the return of the child who had loved it so?

Molly sighed at the thought of Georgina finding sanctuary in these four walls, distressed at her mother leaving, mistrusting and hating the world beyond.

She moved towards the window, her gaze tracing the curve of the crescent moon. A long garden stretched out into the darkness of early evening with its shape formed of shadows caught by the moonlight. It was grand and formal, and just like the house, silent and withdrawn with winter and no doubt grief.

Molly imagined Georgina as a young woman looking out from this window. Had she dreamed of her future and of who she might become and who she might one day—

"No curtains, I'm afraid." Georgina leaned against the doorframe, her body silhouetted in the landing light.

"Right, noted," Molly said, feeling slightly caught off guard at Georgina's arrival. "I was just picturing you when you were young being in this room."

Georgina stared into the space of her youth. Her attention seemed to have been caught by the light from the hallway which fell as it would likely have always fallen in long rectangles against the same wall. "My parents would leave the landing light on for me because I couldn't fall asleep in the dark," Georgina said, her voice hazy in the mist of remembering.

Molly moved to Georgina, reaching for her hand. "I won't let the monsters get you."

Georgina smiled. "Thank you. Although it was a long time ago." She briefly looked away to the bed, and when she turned back to her, Georgina's eyes seemed to sparkle with more than just moonlight. "I'm all grown-up now."

"I can see that," Molly said. "You did a good job of growing up, by the way. Perfect body." Molly smoothed her hands along Georgina's shoulders with her fingers catching at her collar. "Perfect features." Molly lightly kissed Georgina's cheeks. "Perfect everything. You're so unbelievably beautiful."

Her thoughts, let alone her words, evaporated into heady mists of arousal as Georgina leaned in to kiss her neck, the warmth of her cheeks pressing against Molly's skin.

Molly held her close to her with her palms flat against the top of Georgina's back as Georgina's hair softly fell against her.

Georgina then awkwardly, with frustration it seemed, pulled at the sleeves of her blazer in an attempt to release her arms.

"The curse of the tailored suit, eh?" Molly teased, adding, "Let me." Molly slipped Georgina's blazer off her shoulders, her sleeves unrolling from her arms, leaving the blazer to fall to the floor. In a seamless motion Molly ran her fingers down Georgina's shirtsleeves, pausing to unfix the button at the cuffs.

"Wait, just a sec." Georgina switched the light off in the hallway, leaving the moonlight to light her way back to Molly.

"Good thinking." Molly reached out her hand, guiding Georgina to sit with her on the bed. She turned her attention to the line of shirt buttons rising and falling against Georgina's chest. She slowly released the top button. Georgina took a deep breath with her breasts rising against the edge of Molly's hands.

"Tell me if you don't want to," Molly whispered. "If you're not ready."

"I'm so ready." Georgina drew Molly ever closer. Their bodies pressed against each other. "I've wanted you for so long."

Molly swallowed down the overwhelming sense of relief at finding the woman she'd longed for was here with her now saying the words she once could only dream of hearing.

One by one Molly slipped the buttons free to reveal soft white skin newly lit in the moonlight's glow. "I can't believe I get to do this to you."

Georgina smiled. "That's such a sweet thing to say when you could have anyone."

Molly giggled. "Yeah, right. In any case I don't want anyone. I want *you*." She pulled her jumper over her head and brushed her hair away from her face.

Georgina ran her fingertips lightly down the straps of Molly's bra, tracing the thin line of material from the curve of her shoulder to the lacy cups enclosing Molly's breasts.

Molly trembled at Georgina's touch as waves of arousal swept in, breaking ever more strongly against the shores of her control. It felt like her heart had swollen to fill her entire chest and that she might at any moment suffocate and drown in the swirling depths of sensation.

"Let's…" Molly attempted to say as she guided Georgina to lie down with her, only to find that the exquisite weight of Georgina moving on top of her and the slide of her bare skin against hers stole the words from her lips.

Molly arched her back and gave a small gasp of pleasure as Georgina unclasped her bra, the material slipping away to be replaced by the warmth of Georgina's mouth caressing her breasts and Georgina's tongue teasing her nipples. An uncontrollable ripple of pleasure travelled along her body, igniting every nerve to fire and to burn with engulfing need.

She gripped Georgina's body tight against hers, chest against chest, skin against skin, hips against hips, her hands slipping from Georgina's back to the button of her trousers.

She paused breathless to ask, "Okay?"

When Georgina breathed, "Yes," Molly eased her hand between Georgina's trousers and underwear and over the dip at the base of Georgina's spine to the swell of Georgina's bottom. She squeezed the warm soft cotton of her underwear, feeling the shape of Georgina beneath.

Georgina gave a soft moan in response, pulling open Molly's jeans, and in one unspoken action they slipped their hands between the other's legs.

With her forehead buried into Molly's neck, Georgina released a muffled whimper as they rocked their hips, hands underneath underwear, fingers pressing deeper with every movement.

Georgina's breath became ever more ragged before her body tensed and shuddered. A warm wetness flowed against Molly's palm as Georgina cried out. And then Molly stopped hearing anything. She was caught in a whiteout—engulfed in a blizzard of desperate need. She squeezed her eyes tightly shut, intense rhythms of arousal vibrating through her again, again and again, taking her to the edge, closer and closer.

The merciful sharp sweet pain of the bite of Georgina's teeth at her nipple broke through the whiteness and sent her over to fall free with a cry of relief.

"Molly?" Georgina's voice came into focus.

She opened her eyes. Georgina was looking at her, stroking away Molly's damp hair from her forehead. Molly nodded, unable to think, let alone speak.

Georgina gently rolled away, her weight easing from Molly.

Eventually Molly found the breath to say, "That was…intense."

Georgina held her close. "I want you to know it wasn't just sex for me."

"Me neither. It was…" Molly's cheeks burned. "I want to say…"

"Yes?"

"Everything."

"Then say it." Georgina's voice broke. "Say it, knowing I feel that way too."

❖

Georgina felt a ray of sunlight fall upon her face with its soft glow caressing her skin in a gentle embrace. She moved her arm, expecting to feel the warmth of Molly against her just as she'd been all night, her soft cheek resting against Georgina's chest and her arm tightly wrapped around her waist, but instead she felt the coolness of the empty sheet.

She sat up and looked around her and blinked at the golden winter sun rising through her window, washing the white winter sky in hues of orange. She could just make out a brushing noise from the garden.

Molly?

She climbed out of bed and pulled on her clothes and went to the window.

What? Molly was sweeping garden debris into the middle of the lawn.

She unclipped the sash window and lifted it open. A shock of cold took her breath as she shouted down, "What are you doing?"

"I've made a Christmas star. For you. See!"

Molly stood back to fully reveal the shape of a star made up of leaf litter and finished with evergreen clippings of cedar and fir. Sprigs of holly with their bright berries had been placed at the tip of each point. It was so clever and so beautiful, just like Molly.

"What do you think?" Molly stared up at Georgina, her face bright with unmistakable joy.

"It's amazing!" Georgina shouted down. "We need a photo."

"Yes, good thinking. Come down and be in it with me. Oh, good morning, by the way!"

"Good morning!" Georgina turned back inside and hunted in her pockets for her phone. She could hear Molly begin to hum "We three kings of Orient are."

Carols meant Christmas, and just the thought of it filled Georgina with a cold dread. Tomorrow was Christmas Eve. The day of the year eighteen years ago when the light somehow became duller and the rain wetter and the wind chill like never before. And from then on, joy was always tinged with sadness and laughter always ended too soon.

Georgina shouted down, "Sorry! I'll be there in a sec." In the last pocket she checked she found her phone only to be distracted by the symbol of a missed call. It was a Leicester number, and Georgina recognized it as her father's solicitor. It seemed that he had tried to reach Georgina late yesterday when her attention was fixed on Molly. Only Molly. Georgina retrieved her message and held the phone against her ear. *Georgina, this is Henry Fothergill. Sorry to disturb you so late on a Friday. We have been contacted by your mother with regards to the painting omitted from the bequest. I wonder if you could give me a ring back to discuss. Thank you.*

Edith's painting?

Molly arrived in the bedroom with cheeks apple red and her hair as wild as the garden. She went to the window and stared down. "On second thoughts, I think the photo may be better from up here." Turning to Georgina she asked, "What do you think?" She looked at the phone in Georgina's hands. "Bad news?"

"No." Georgina hadn't meant to sound so emphatic. She moved to Molly and retrieved a stray leaf caught in her curls. "No, not at all. Just my father's solicitors. Loose ends and all that. I'll ring them Monday."

"You plan on ringing them back on Christmas Day?" Molly said with an amused frown. "Before or after the Queen's speech?"

"Oh, right." Georgina shook her head. "I'm so used to ignoring it."

"You didn't celebrate with your father?"

"He hated it just as much as me. We agreed long ago to keep things low-key when it came to Christmas."

"So no turkey?"

"No lunch. After I moved out, we didn't see each other over Christmas. All the Christmases before that we just made ourselves miserable thinking about my mother. So we made a pact to forget Christmas existed."

"Blimey. Well"—Molly slipped her hand into Georgina's—"I was thinking how about rather than ignoring it this year would you like to spend Christmas with me? We could have Christmas Eve at my place. I can't believe you haven't even been to mine. Anyway, it's a tiny terrace. Think the house version of Daisy May."

Georgina laughed. "I can picture it perfectly."

"And then if you could bear it perhaps Christmas lunch with my mum and dad? I know it's way too soon for you to meet the in-laws, but it's not fair to change my plans with such short notice..." Molly shrugged.

Georgina choked back the tears of joy threatening like a swollen river from her heart. How long had she tried to convince herself that being alone at Christmas was a good thing? How long had she pretended that she didn't care? "Yes," she said. "I'd love to spend Christmas with you. Thank you."

"That's settled then," Molly said, with a broad smile that left no room for sadness.

"Since we're on the subject of plans." Georgina stroked Molly's cheek misted with early morning dew. "I wonder, do you have plans yet for New Year's Eve? It's just the Oberons invite me each year to their home to celebrate. If it fits for you, would you like to come with me?"

Molly said, with a voice bubbling with excitement, "Yes, please. That sounds amazing. Will there be dancing?"

Georgina nodded. "There's supper, followed by a live band. And everyone at the party stops to listen for Big Ben and to watch the fireworks at midnight over the Thames."

"You can hear Big Ben from their house?"

"Yes they live in an apartment on the South Bank overlooking the river."

"Okay, as plans go, that's properly awesome," Molly said, wide eyed. "Thank you. I can't wait to start the new year with you."

That might have been the sweetest, most unguarded thing anyone had ever said to her. She struggled to say in response, "Me too."

Molly reached for Georgina and kissed her. She smelled of the garden and of all that was natural and good.

Molly drew her lips away slowly. "It feels like there's fireworks exploding in my heart right now in fact." She rested her palm against her chest. "I'm so excited. Oh, wait, I nearly forgot my Christmas star. I hope the breeze hasn't redesigned it. Oh no, we're good."

"I've got it." Georgina took several shots.

"Fab! Shall we go for breakfast? And by breakfast I mean a Mr. Brown's special." Molly headed for the stairs and shouted from the landing, "Thoughts on me sliding down the banister?"

Georgina laughed. "Go for it. What the new owners don't know won't hurt them."

In that instant Georgina's heart ached and her whole body felt winded by the casual mention of the life of the house after her. She swallowed down the pain and instead thumbed through the photos. Her eye was caught again by the symbol of the missed call. Her thoughts turned once more to the message and to the question of what the solicitor had to say.

What are you playing at mother? Whatever it is it won't work.

CHAPTER TWENTY-NINE

Please stop smiling, Molly." Fran let out a pained sigh.
Molly turned to Fran, who sat next to her at the long table in the small airless room that had been set aside for them in the records office. She leaned her elbow on the tabletop and rested her cheek in the palm of her hand. "Fran, really," she said with a chuckle. "I'm annoying you by smiling?"

"Exactly. I think you'll find excessive happiness is far more irritating than excessive sadness. And what's more, smiling in your case tends to lead to humming. And don't think I don't recognize 'Auld Lang Syne' in the tapping you've been doing on your notepad."

"Oh." Molly dropped her pencil flat against the table.

"I think you'll find Christmas and New Year's are over, thank God." Fran gave a slight shake of the head. "And so is my seasonal goodwill."

"You had seasonal goodwill?" Molly bumped Fran's shoulder. Fran let out a noise that sounded not dissimilar to a growl. "Just kidding. I know I've probably been a bit unbearable. Sorry." Molly winced at the memory of what must have seemed like endless excited chatter about her Christmas break and her time with Georgina. How magical it had been in every way. How Georgina had just fit seamlessly into her family. How Big Ben had chimed out across the rooftops of London at New Year's, and how they had walked along the South Bank that same morning as the sun rose. And how she was sure she was still walking on air.

"Forgiven. And if anyone is going to annoy me with their happiness, then I would prefer it to be you. But at least try and concentrate. So is this everything?" Fran gestured to the gathered collection of Edith's archive.

At the sobering sight, Molly's mood dispersed and drifted from joy to melancholy. "Yep, I think so. I have a list somewhere…"

"This one?" Fran tugged at a sheet of paper Molly was leaning on, lifting it away and forcing Molly to sit up straight. With a face furrowed with purposeful focus, Fran read aloud, "First item, Edith's scrapbook." Fran placed a pointed forefinger on the cover. "This contains the preliminary charcoal sketches for the watercolour. Is that right?"

"Yes." Molly eased the scrapbook towards her, carefully releasing one of the sketches to show Fran, who gave a slow reverential nod in response. Molly softly smoothed the brittle paper flat, its surface aged to the texture of sugar.

"I think it's just beautiful," Molly said. "So full of movement with each stroke a line of energy, of life. I'm so pleased we have them, Fran, not only as evidence that Edith painted the watercolour, but that we can show the development of the final piece and engage the visitor in the artistic process, maybe even have them imagining how the painting came to be."

March 1832
Chambers of Brancaster and Lane Solicitors

"You keep so much, Edith. That scrapbook is nearly full. Surely your memory will not fail you to the extent that you require to keep and press each flower we come across."

"I would keep the clouds that shaded you in my arms today, pin the wisps of white like cotton seeds, if I could. And your soft kisses I would fix forever on my lips if only there was a way. Don't you see, for me the memory of you is not enough."

"Edith…"

"It makes me want to mark you on this very page, so I can look upon you every day. In fact…" Edith grasped a stick of charcoal and began to sketch with her eyes darting to and fro from the page to Josephine's face. "Wait, don't turn away."

"I am working and so should you be."

"But I am yet to fully capture the shape of your neck as it sweeps to your shoulder. It is no good—I am at a loss as to how to mimic the way the light catches on your collarbone and the blush of your skin. It is no good." Edith dropped the sketch on the floor and bent down in front of Josephine with her chest pressed against her legs and her cheek resting on her lap. "What do I do if memory is not enough and no mark upon the page can capture you? What do I do?"

Josephine could feel the push of Edith's sobs against her legs. She placed her hand to Edith's hair and stroked gently, hoping that her touch, this time at least, would be enough, but knowing in her heart that nothing would ever make it right. That all she could offer Edith would be the memory of them that would one day fade and surely be gone.

Josephine lifted Edith's chin to see her face fully. "One day this cruel world will open its eyes, my dear Edith, and see how blind they have been, and love in all its forms will be celebrated as equal and free." Josephine brushed away the line of Edith's tears which merely found a new path instead.

With a voice bruised with feeling, Edith replied, "You truly think that?"

"I truly hope for it, my dear Edith, with all my heart."

"Well I imagine"—Fran raised her eyebrows in thought—"that neither artist nor sitter could have foreseen these sketches would be on display nearly what two hundred years later. Such a private moment exposed for all to see."

"You think it's intrusive?" Molly had been so sure that Edith would have felt aggrieved, that she hadn't stopped to reflect on whether she would wish to have her story told in public. "Am I being presumptuous to think that Edith would want the sketches and her painting—not to mention her heartfelt inscription—revealed?"

"We'll never know what Edith thought. We can only speculate about what she might have thought possible within the cultural constraints of her time. It strikes me that what is most important is what your intention is."

"My intention?" Molly instantly thought again of Edith's grave-stone. The absence of her achievements or mention of who she might have loved or been loved by. Molly took a deep breath. "I want visitors to know that love between women exists throughout history. I want to correct the omission of this truth in the museum and in our public consciousness." Before Fran could comment, Molly continued, with the rising sense of injustice filling the chambers of her heart. "What's more, I want Edith to be able to recognize herself in her display. For her to say that's me—that is my work, that is my passion, that is my love. You have captured me as I see myself."

"That's asking a lot Molly, don't you think?" Fran ticked off the scrapbook from the list. "After all can anyone truly see us as we see ourselves? Impossible."

Molly sighed. "I suppose not."

"As I see it the best you can do for Edith is to present her life in context and with those facts you can have confidence in. The visitor will then form their own impression. Some will get it right and some will get it wrong. And let's face it, most just come to the museum because it's raining."

"Fran Godfrey!" Molly glanced at the half-open door.

"Don't look so affronted—we both know it's true."

"Well then, this is our opportunity to engage visitors and have them return even when it's dry. In fact, do you know what? I'm going to propose that we have the display in the foyer. Even the most reluctant visitor will see it. We could have images of Josephine's portrait blown up as posters for outside to entice people's curiosity, and then from the display itself we can signpost people to the annex to explore the Wright room. Yes, now I think about it, it makes total sense."

"Inspired. But what makes *most* sense is for us to hurry up. Evelyn wasn't exactly thrilled to release us both at once. So where were we?" Fran returned her attention to Molly's list. "Edith's logbook, check, volumes of prayers, check, and…" Fran squinted at the remaining loose page.

"The petition." Molly held it up and pointed to the long list of names. "It was signed by thousands of local women asking for the immediate abolition of slavery in the British Empire. I wondered whether you might wish to write a short history of local women's contribution to the abolition movement to give a sense of context. One of our panels in the display could be devoted to campaigning. What do you think?"

"Yes," Fran said, staring at the petition. "That works."

"It's great that it shows how passionately and effectively Edith and Josephine were as campaigners. Vitally, here are Edith's initials. It evidences Edith working alongside Josephine."

"Good. So is your plan then for all these objects to go in a display case with the portrait and the explanatory panels hung alongside?"

"Yep. I checked, and we've got spare plastic rests, book cushions, and sleeves. So we are officially good to go." Molly gave a small clap. "I'm excited."

"Uh-huh, you don't say." Fran smiled. "Let's get these safely wrapped and packed into that container. Can you hand me some tissue?"

"Sure." Molly's heart sank at the sombre sight of the parish registers overlooked in all the excitement. "Bugger, I forgot about the registers. I was going to take photos of Edith's entries. It's great that we've been able to track down her baptism entry from her burial record."

Fran looked at her watch and frowned. "Definitely. Although it's almost lunchtime, so please be quick."

Molly meticulously took a photo of the front of each register. She began with Edith's baptism record photographing the whole page of those who were born in more or less the same time period as Edith. Heartbreakingly Josephine's baptism recorded in May was at the top of the page, and Edith's July record was the last but one on the bottom. It was perfect in a terrible way. Molly leaned in to take a focused snap of Edith's individual record: *Baptism 31st July 1808. Edith daughter of John Hewitt, Businessman, and his wife, Margaret. Born 29th June 1808.*

Molly released a heavy sigh.

"You okay?" Fran narrowed her eyes at Molly.

"Not really."

"Try not to think. Just do."

Molly nodded. She took a deep breath, pausing before opening the register of burials. But how could she not think or hope? She had the ridiculous notion that just maybe if she opened the register, this time Edith's name would not be listed for that untimely date. That if she managed to find her again at all, then she would be a feisty old lady who died of old age, worn out by a life full of joy. Yes, she could have been mistaken. Couldn't she? Mistakes happen, after all? In fact if she went right now to the churchyard, could it be possible that she would find the date on the grave corrected, or the words *Loved for always* hidden beneath the ivy? Or could she wish it, cross her fingers tight behind her back, that there was no grave at all, only grass browning in the shade of the trees, stillness in place of bones? Was Edith Hewitt merely a figment of Molly's deep-seated dread of not mattering to anyone?

Molly opened the heavy leather binding, feeling the familiar weight of the cover and the brush of the musty pages against her fingers. She hesitantly turned each page. *Don't be there, don't be there…*

Her heart sank at the sight of the record she dreaded to rediscover: *Buried 5th August 1834. Edith Hewitt, daughter of John Hewitt of Leicester (deceased) and Margaret. Age 26, Influenza.*

Molly rested her hand on the fading line of ink, before reaching for her phone and taking a photo of the entry and then of the page. Molly closed the register.

She slowly shook her head. "This entry is not the sum of her, or the gravestone. I won't let it be."

"Good for you, Molly," Fran said. "Good for you."

With their work complete and Edith's archives stored away in their travel container, Molly drove back to the museum, doing her best to avert her gaze from Fran's strained expression and tight grip on the dashboard. There was nothing she could do about the potholes. Swerving to avoid them didn't seem to be helping either.

"For goodness' sake, I would be most grateful to arrive back at work with at least one bone unbroken."

"I'm so sorry." Molly wiped watery streaks of condensation from the front window. "Look, we're here. Well done, Daisy May."

Molly carried the archives into the museum, and Fran led the way with their bags over her shoulders, opening the sliding entrance doors.

"Coming through," Molly said. "Hi, Fred, I need to rest this here at reception for just a second."

"Morning, ladies." Fred cleared space for the container.

"I've left the store keys on my desk," Fran said, looking exhausted.

"No probs. I'll get them."

For some reason Fran then blinked at the stairs and her mouth fell slightly open.

"What?" Molly turned round to see Evelyn descending the stairs with Lydia Wright by her side. They were chatting as old friends might do. Lydia was dressed from head to toe in a cream fur coat which shimmered under the museum lights. Wait, was she carrying a painting?

"Ah, Molly, you've arrived back at last," Evelyn said. "Of course you have met Ms. Wright at the opening of the Wright room."

Molly gave a wary, "Yes." She stared at the wrapped painting in Lydia's arms. It couldn't be, surely?

"Molly. It is good to see you again." Lydia held out her hand, greeting Molly with a warm smile. "I hope I find you well. You look a lot better than when we last met."

Molly shook Lydia's hand. "Yes." *Yes* was all Molly could seem to manage.

Evelyn quickly stepped in. "Well, it is with great relief all round that the mystery of the full provenance of the beautiful watercolour has been solved. I wish you every happy enjoyment of the piece."

What? Molly struggled to pull together her thoughts. Full provenance? Was this something to do with why it was missing from the bequest? Was Lydia claiming that it belonged to her? Why on earth would George gift the portrait to the woman who broke his heart?

"Thank you, Evelyn, for its safe care." Lydia held out her hand which Evelyn shook with the care of someone who was trying not to leave a fingerprint.

"It has been our pleasure, such a charming work. Safe journey home to Paris." With that Evelyn turned and headed upstairs.

As Lydia proceeded to leave, Molly reached out and lightly held her arm. "Please don't take the painting." Molly cast a quick eye up the stairs to the disappearing figure of Evelyn.

Lydia turned slowly to Molly. Molly dropped her hand to her side.

"Why would you ask such a thing?" Lydia said, her tone curious rather than offended.

Molly swallowed. Lydia Wright wasn't just one of the most influential critics and arbiters of modern museums—she was Georgina's mother.

"Answer me, please." Lydia looked over to Fran and Fred, who quickly looked away.

"It belongs here." Molly swallowed. "With the other paintings. You see, it belongs to Edith—that is, it used to." Molly knew she was making no sense as her words choked in her mouth, thick and cloying.

"Who is Edith?" Lydia gestured to the foyer bench where she took a seat, resting the painting beside her. "I don't understand."

Molly perched next to Lydia. "Edith Hewitt. She was the painter."

Lydia raised her eyebrows. "A woman called Edith Hewitt painted the watercolour of Josephine?"

"Yes. But she wasn't just any woman. We think, we're certain—well as certain as we can be—that she was Josephine's lover. The painting has survived alongside the other family paintings from that period for many years."

"I see. And you don't think it can survive in my care?"

"Oh God, no. No, that's not what I'm saying."

"Then what is it that you are saying, Molly, for I am no clearer."

"We're having a display of Edith Hewitt's work and life. She campaigned alongside Josephine on so many matters of social justice, but she is hardly known, let alone remembered. And what's more her gravestone has no inscription, as if she did nothing, loved and was loved by no one."

Lydia looked down. "How sad indeed."

"You see, the watercolour was going to be the focus point. It has an inscription hidden underneath the frame. It says *All my love always, Edith.* And then Edith died, at just twenty-six, we think of a broken heart, only a few months after Josephine married."

Lydia looked up. She stared out beyond the sliding doors to the promenade, and her face had fallen with what Molly could only assume was the weight of her thoughts. Could she be reconsidering?

Lydia turned back to look at Molly. "I had no idea that such a tragic story existed behind the work. George's solicitors mentioned that it was due to appear in a display, but I hadn't appreciated that it was to be the focal point or that it had such meaning to you."

"So please don't take it." Molly rested her hand briefly on Lydia's arm. "At least not until after we have displayed it. Until after we've told Edith's story. Please."

Lydia stood and swept the sides of her long fur coat together with her belt. "I admire your passion, and also I am convinced of your plea."

"Really? That's wonderful. Thank you so much."

"But if I agree to lend the painting to the museum, I'd be most grateful for something in return."

"An exchange?"

"Quite."

"I would have to check with Evelyn. There's a possibility of a Cezanne—"

"I want to see my daughter. I want you to arrange a meeting for me." *What?* "I can't do that. Sorry."

"Why not? You haven't made things up with her? Oh, please don't tell me that my daughter has inherited her father's stubbornness."

"No. I mean, yes, we've made up. Look, I'm sorry. I'm really not sure how I can help."

"You don't need to be sure of anything. All I ask it that you try. Please." Lydia gathered the painting tighter in her arms and moved to walk away.

There was something oddly undemanding about Lydia's demand. It seemed so heartfelt and more like a plea than a threat. "How will I contact you? Through Evelyn?"

"I'm staying at the Belmont."

"The Belmont Hotel just off the promenade?" It was just a few hundred yards away. So close.

"Yes, sentiment got the better of me." Lydia turned away. From over her shoulder she added, "You should know, I leave for Paris in a couple of days. So until we meet again." And then with a swish of her coat she was gone.

Without waiting another heartbeat, Molly rushed back to the reception desk and rummaged in her bag for her phone. She dialled Georgina's number. "Come on, pick up."

"You have reached Georgina Wright. I am unable to answer your call. Please leave a message."

"Georgina, it's me. When you have a moment, can you ring me back? Thanks. Bye."

"Well there's a turn up," Fred said.

"How much did you guys hear?"

"Enough," Fran said. "I don't understand—what right does Lydia have to take the portrait? Do you think Georgina knows?"

"I don't know—on both counts. Hopefully she'll ring back soon. There's no way Georgina's going to meet with her. Do you think Lydia will be so hurt that she'll refuse to lend the painting?"

"Well, let's put it this way." Fran shrugged. "We didn't think she'd turn up to the opening of the Wright room, did we. She's unpredictable."

Fran was right. Who knew what Lydia was capable of. The only thing Molly felt sure she could predict was an unimpressed Georgina. Molly couldn't ask Georgina to do this just for the painting, just for Edith, just for her. Could she?

CHAPTER THIRTY

H ey."
"Hey." Molly checked her watch. It was just after ten when she answered Georgina's call. She had even wondered whether Georgina would ring that night. Just because they had spoken every day since Christmas, and just because Georgina seemed to take every opportunity to return to Leicester to see Molly, this in no way committed Georgina to a daily routine. In fact she hoped that Georgina didn't feel obliged to ring out of an established habit, but that she wanted to ring her, and like Molly, she could not bear the thought of a day passing without hearing her voice.

"Sorry I couldn't get back to you straight away."

"That's okay." Molly closed her laptop and folded her arms resting them against her kitchen table. "It was hectic at work anyway. We collected Edith's objects from the records office. And then I had an after-school visit. Oh, and I wanted to mention that we're going to put Edith's display in the foyer for maximum impact and footfall."

"Okay, makes sense."

"Although we've been squashed up a corner half under the stairs, so we don't block the exit. But I'm going to get some artwork blown up for the wall. I was thinking maybe a copy of Edith's handwriting to provide that personal connection to reach out to visitors."

"Good idea."

"Thanks. The opening is scheduled for the first of Feb to coincide with the beginning of LGBT history month. Wow, that's just over three weeks away."

"The first. Okay. I'll get it in my diary."

"Fab." Molly couldn't bring herself to mention Lydia, at least not for a few more precious moments. "So enough about me. How's your day been?"

"The usual. Although I did manage to grab lunch with Estelle Oberon. She really has a particular soft spot for you. I was to be sure to send you her best wishes and to thank you for your card. I didn't know you'd sent her a card."

"Just a thank-you notelet for having me at New Year's. I felt bad because I'm pretty sure I might have been the reason they ran out of cheese."

Georgina laughed. "You'll be relieved to know it didn't come up in conversation. I was telling her about Edith's display, though. She was impressed."

"That's encouraging." She couldn't put it off any longer. She would have to tell Georgina about what happened today. She would keep it low-key. "There's something else I wanted, well, needed to talk to you about."

"Sounds ominous."

"It's just we had an unexpected visitor at the museum."

"Okay."

Keep it breezy. "Your mum, as it happens."

"My mother? Today?"

"Yep. This morning. It was quite a surprise in that she had come to collect Edith's portrait of Josephine." Molly felt herself tense. "It seems she's under the impression that it belongs to her. I don't know how she convinced Evelyn—"

"Really?" Georgina let out a long deep sigh. "I'm so sorry. She's used the letter. The one from my father."

What, you knew? "I'm sorry, what letter? I don't understand."

"Do you remember I had that phone call just before Christmas from my father's solicitor? I rang them back last week. They said my mother had been in touch with them and explained that she has a letter from my father gifting the painting to her."

"But that doesn't make sense."

"Nope."

"If he'd done this, why would your father not mention it to you, why make it such a mystery? And for that matter, why gift something so precious to someone who hurt you so much?"

"I have absolutely no idea."

"What did the solicitor say?"

"He said there was nothing to suppose that the letter wasn't genuine. At the opening my mother did mention something about a letter from my father that she wanted me to read. At the time I didn't think it meant anything. I'm sorry, Molly."

"It's hardly your fault."

"I promise, I tried to make it clear to the solicitor that she couldn't just take the painting, and that it was part of a museum display, but as she's the legal owner, I guess she can do as she pleases, as she always has. I didn't mention this to you before because it is such a magical time for us, and everything to do with my mother brings drama and upset. For some reason I thought she wouldn't just turn up out of the blue and take the painting, and that I would have time to find the right moment to tell you."

"As it happens, I asked her not to take it."

"You did?"

"I begged her actually. I explained about the painting's history and how much it meant. She said she knew about it featuring in a display but not how important it was."

"Right. And I take it that didn't change her mind?"

"Well, not exactly."

"Okay, why do I sense a catch?"

You have to tell her.

"Molly?"

"She is prepared to lend the painting for Edith's display in exchange for—"

"What does she want?"

"To see you. I guess she's worked out we're together, and I suppose she thought I might be able to persuade you."

"And if I don't see her, what then, she'll take the painting and walk away without looking back?"

Molly could feel Georgina's anger resonating on the line.

With her voice newly inflamed Georgina said, "Did she honestly imagine that she could use the painting and how much she now knows it means to you to get to me? Well she can keep it. I won't play her games and I certainly won't be blackmailed."

Molly didn't know what to say.

"I'm sorry. I hate that you have been affected by this," Georgina said, softening her tone. "You know that, don't you?"

"Uh-huh." *Don't make her feel bad, not like last time.* "It's okay. Really. I wouldn't expect you to speak to her. In fact I've already reimagined the display to feature the sketches in place of the portrait, so no probs." It was a small white lie. At least now she knew that she would have to.

"Right, well, that's good to know."

That was enough heartache for one phone call. She just wanted to focus on them. Just them. "Do you have time to meet at the weekend? I know it's Monday and we only saw each other yesterday—"

"I was thinking tomorrow evening? I'll work on the train back to London the next morning."

"And I'm thinking that's awesome."

Georgina laughed.

"I miss you." Molly didn't care if that sounded needy—she simply couldn't end the call without saying it.

"Me too."

"See you tomorrow night then."

"Yes, I'll text with times. Goodnight."

"Goodnight." Molly heard the phone signal drop. "I love you," she whispered, entrusting her words to the confidence of her softly beating heart.

Chapter Thirty-one

Georgina's train pulled in to Leicester at just after four. She had given up on work at about midday, just as she'd given up on sleep the night before.

For a few hours earlier the searching first light of dawn had seeped into her London apartment, ebbing up the walls like an insidious tide. She had felt such relief to be packing to be with Molly again and to see her smile and to hear her laughter and to feel her close.

She had thought that work would help see her through the day, but it seemed that nothing could distract from the many questions that ate away at her concentration. Why on earth would her father write to her mother, the woman he hated, and gift her the portrait of Josephine? Was it not the very painting he had held, protective, in his arms after they rowed, just before she left for good? And why didn't he warn her that he had done this and that her mother would likely return spectre-like into Georgina's life? Georgina's heartbeat began to gather pace. Her skin prickled with the rising heat of irritation and her muscles tensed and gripped with fury.

She texted Molly. *In town early. Meet you in the foyer about five? Food at mine?* Without waiting for the reply she hurried out of the station. She knew where her anger was taking her. For she had questions she needed to ask, even if the answers would always be out of reach.

She could hear the bells of her destination ring out. As she approached the city's cathedral she could see people spilling out from its main door. A service had obviously ended and the priest stood in the doorway with his white cassock billowing about his calves. He was shaking hands with each member of the congregation as they filed past, hoping no doubt that his earnest farewells would encourage a return visit.

Georgina found the side entrance and sought out the quiet corner where brass plaques glinted with the sheen of polish and formality.

"Father how could you?" Georgina whispered. She lightly placed her fingertips to smudge the surface of a plaque that read, *In memory of George Wright, 1955–2017, barrister of this parish, who faithfully served this community for thirty-two years in the noble pursuit of justice and truth.*

Truth. Georgina shook her head. It seemed to her now such a duplicitous word with so many angles and so many shades that it remained entirely illusive. And *justice.* There was nothing *just* about life, certainly not if Georgina's mother could march back into hers with such ease. And where was her father's faithfulness to her?

Georgina pressed harder into the metal with her fingers whitening at their tips. "Why?" Why would he do something that would inevitably bring her mother back into her life when her leaving had brought such pain? How could he betray her? "I put you first. I risked losing Molly for you."

As she dropped her hand, another plaque caught her attention. It was carved in stone and hung half shaded in the darkness of the corner. She stared hard at it as she read, *This tablet is erected to the beloved and blessed memory of William Wright, barrister and loyal servant of the law, born 1803 died 1875, by his devoted wife Josephine, parishioner of this church.*

Georgina had seen this plaque before and had casually noted that it was a relative and that her father was remembered in a place of his heritage. But now the plaque had a whole new meaning, and as she reread the inscription it felt as if the edges of each word grazed her heart. The *beloved memory* of a *devoted wife?* Georgina's already simmering anger bubbled up to boil indignant in her blood. Where did that leave Edith? Was she that easy to forget?

26th December 1833
St. Martin's Church, Leicester

Charles Brancaster held his daughter's hand, tighter in truth than was necessary, for she was his only daughter and giving her away felt like a loss of almost unbearable degree. It was ridiculous because he greatly admired William, and a better son-in-law he could not have imagined. A more kind man he could not have wished for Josephine. If only she were happier, and if only he felt that this was the day that all she had been was leading to. It should have been her beginning—then why did it feel like an end? Why did she hang her head beneath her veil?

"Look tall, my darling." Charles squeezed gently at Josephine's slim gloved hand. "Today is the beginning of a most wonderful chapter and your mother and I could not be prouder."

"Thank you, Father," Josephine said, with a voice that lacked the conviction of her words. "I will be right in a moment."

Charles wished there was someone who in that moment could help. He instinctively looked for Edith. Where was the familiar frame of the wriggling young woman he had known since a child who could not sit still or walk like a lady? She always made him smile. Edith would know what to say, but she was not there. He remembered now that the last time he had seen her, she was walking with her mother in the street, and she gave her apologies but was unable to attend. He'd wondered for some time if there had been a disagreement between Edith and his daughter discernible by the noticeable absence of Edith from their lives. They were taking a break from writing together, Josephine had said. He thought it might have something to do with Josephine meeting William. But what would he know? And it did not feel like his place to ask.

The congregation stood and the organist began to play. William turned and glanced behind him with the glint in his eyes of emotion caught in the candlelight.

Josephine lifted her head as one who bravely faces that which they fear most. "I am ready."

It was Charles who found his feet reluctant to move forward. He wanted to say, *I am not*, but he would not default in his duty and walked Josephine slowly towards the altar, each step a peculiar anguish towards his daughter's fate.

Releasing Josephine's hand into William's, he quickly looked away knowing that William would now see the tears beneath the veil and feel her sadness at his side.

He felt some relief to hear William whisper, "I love you," and Josephine solemnly reply "I know."

The heavy oak main door closing followed by the soft swishing of a cassock reminded Georgina to check the time. It was just before five.

❖

Molly stood on the promenade outside the museum wrapped up and rubbing her hands together waiting excitedly for Georgina. She was looking towards the station, and Georgina was practically beside her before she turned with a start. "Where'd you come from?" Molly placed her hand against her heart.

"I'm sorry, I didn't mean to sneak up on you. Have you been waiting long?" Georgina glanced at Fred who was leaning down to lock the sliding glass doors. "You'd think they'd let you wait inside. You look freezing." She reached out and softly touched Molly's cheek.

"I was too excited to see you to wait inside." Molly wrapped her arms around Georgina, squeezing her tight. "I suspect however I may now be part snowman."

Georgina laughed.

"I had this mad notion," Molly confessed, "that I would run up the promenade into your arms."

Georgina pressed Molly into her. "And I ruined it."

"No." Molly released her hold sensing a sadness in Georgina's tone. She shook her head. "In fact my glasses always steam up when I run, so I'd probably miss you altogether and end up hugging some random person, you know, like in the Specsavers advert." Georgina laughed again. "Do you fancy Pizza Express? Emphasis on the *express*. I forgot to mention that art club is at seven. Sorry. But as soon as it's over, I'll rejoin you. Is that okay?"

"Sure."

Molly slipped her arm into Georgina's, snuggling close again as they walked the few hundred yards to the restaurant. "It's so good to see you."

"You too. I've been thinking about everything. About the painting, about my mother, about Edith, us..."

Us? Molly held her breath.

"And the thing is, I'm sorry I didn't say yes to speaking to my mother."

"That's okay. You have reasons. I get that."

"It's not okay."

Molly stopped walking. She gazed at Georgina, trying to guess from her expression what she might say next.

"It's not okay that I'm letting you down again by letting my parents' toxic drama affect me so deeply."

"Georgina—"

"I should be putting you first and not just because I..." Georgina paused.

Molly swallowed. *Because you...?*

"Because you've been right all along."

"I have?"

"I've just been to St. Martin's to tell my father off for inviting my mother back into my life. As you may remember, he has this plaque there. Anyway there's another plaque dedicated to William Wright by Josephine. She's described as his devoted wife and the plaque records her beloved memory of him. It is just like the gravestone. Edith has been totally forgotten."

Molly shivered. "How about we chat it through over a glass of red?"

"How about two glasses?"

"How about drunk in charge of art club?"

"Oh, right."

"Come on. Let's go in and you can tell me more."

"I think we got here just in time." Georgina looked around as reserved notices were placed on the tables around them.

"So you were saying about the plaque?"

"Oh, Molly, I felt so cross about Edith, angry for her. And then I thought about her painting, that it was so symbolic of her feelings for Josephine and of their love. It struck me that the painting is in every way Edith's plaque that deserves to be displayed in memory of them. And then I thought about you, and how you'd always known how important it was, and how you'd stuck up for the painting, risking everything. And how bad I feel for not sticking up for her with you."

"But you have—the whole reason there's a display for Edith at all is because of you. It's not your fault that your mother—"

"I'm going to speak to her."

"You are?"

Georgina nodded, taking a large mouthful of wine.

"That's awesome." Molly reached out, placing her hand over Georgina's. "Thank you. But only do it if you're sure and if you're doing it for you."

Georgina nodded. "How about I do it for us?"

"For us?" Joy bubbled in Molly exploding into laughter. "Yep, that works for me." Molly raised her glass. "So a toast. Here's to fighting for Edith and the really large bowls of spaghetti coming our way."

Georgina's face seemed to relax with relief as she raised her glass to Molly's. "To Edith and spaghetti."

A silence fell over their table while they devoured their supper. Sucking up a last flick of pasta, Molly said, "I meant to say your mum's at the Belmont, but only for tonight."

Georgina wiped at her mouth with a napkin. "The Belmont?"

"Yes." Molly added hesitantly, "She's goes back to Paris tomorrow."

Georgina drew in a deep breath. "Okay. That's settled then. I'll go to her while you're at art club. Meet me back at my father's place?"

"Deal."

They lingered over coffees until it was nearing seven.

"I best go over. I've got to open up the side door and set up. Will you be okay? If you like, we can always go together to see her first thing."

"To be honest, I'll lose my bottle if I don't go now, and I don't want you dragged into things any more than you have been. It's not fair."

"I don't mind." Molly left money on the silver tray with the bill. "My treat."

"Thanks. But you should mind, you know. We should just be enjoying each other, planning cinema trips or holidays, just normal stuff."

Molly nodded. "Yeah, eating in Pizza Express is not normal at all. Freaky."

"You know what I mean."

"Anyway, those things can wait." Molly stood and pulled on her coat. "My students, however, cannot. Walk me over?"

"Sure." Georgina walked Molly back to the museum. Unsurprisingly she seemed to drag her feet and had gone quite pale.

Molly reluctantly let go of Georgina's arm. "Good luck then."

CHAPTER THIRTY-TWO

The lights from the Belmont Hotel's conservatory illuminated the promenade in blocks of gaudy yellow light that cast the moon in eerie contrast, stark and haunting, white-grey in the dark winter sky. The Belmont Hotel had a faded Victorian grandeur to it which lent a mood of formality tempered by the soft easing of age.

Georgina climbed the short run of steps shaded at their top by a small stone portico. She hesitated at the door, holding it just open. The warm air from the hotel's reception blew perfumed against her cheeks.

It was not too late to turn around and would be entirely forgivable to say to Molly that her mother had left early and that they had missed each other, no doubt only by minutes, and that it was a sign that it wasn't meant to be. But she couldn't lie to Molly and look her in the eye and see the disappointment quickly retracted so as not to make Georgina feel bad. No. She wanted to see Molly's face shine with pride and her eyes light up with admiration, the warmth of her smile melting Georgina's heart.

She took a deep breath and adjusted the cuffs of her coat, and tucked her hair behind her ear. She lifted her chin and said under her breath, "You can do this. Just think about Molly. Just Molly."

"Good evening, madam. How can I help?" The receptionist beamed an empty smile at Georgina.

"Good evening. I would like to speak with one of your guests, please, Lydia Wright."

"Let me see. Yes, I have a Lydia Wright. Is she expecting you?"

Was her mother expecting her? That was the very question. Was she honestly expecting that Georgina would break a habit of a lifetime and engage in conversation? Listen to her attempts to make excuses for herself? But then her mother still believed in cursed hope, didn't she? So maybe she was. "I don't know. I mean, no."

"One moment, I will try her room for you."

Georgina turned away from the receptionist and leaned against the desk facing the conservatory and the diners taking coffee after their meals.

"I'm sorry, madam. There's no reply. Can I leave a message for you?"

"No. Thank you anyway." Georgina expected to feel relief, but instead she felt strangely peculiar and upset at the thought of her emotions wasted. At least she wouldn't have to lie to Molly. She walked back down the steps, pausing to tighten her belt around her waist. It had begun to rain and droplets fell in dark spots on the pathway ahead.

She stepped out onto the promenade, stopping to allow a bike to whoosh past with its tyres spraying a swirl of rain at her feet. She pulled her collar up and glanced to check for any more cyclists, and as she did so a figure caught her eye. A woman in the conservatory had stood and was staring out right at Georgina.

Georgina turned away and continued walking, and then a voice called out her name and she could hear feet splashing after her.

"Georgina. Please, wait."

Georgina turned around slowly.

Her mother was scowling up at the night sky as if holding it responsible for everything. "This damned British weather. Always so wet. Won't you come inside? Please. After all, you have made it this far. Yes?"

Georgina gave a guarded nod, determined not to betray an ounce of feeling.

"I need a cigarette. Before we go in." Her mother slipped a thin silver cigarette case from her pocket and squinted towards a shelter. "There."

Georgina stood with her mother under the wooden shelter with her height sheltering her mother from the worst of the night. She watched the blue haze of cigarette smoke drift down the promenade.

"Thank you for seeing me," her mother said. "I feared you might not come."

Georgina remained silent. She was here to listen for as long as she could stand to, and then she would firmly request that her mother lend the painting for Edith's display. And she would make it clear that she considered her mother's actions deplorable. And then she would leave.

"I've sat waiting in that chair for most of today." Her mother nodded towards the corner seat in the conservatory. "There were so many people who looked like you from a distance because I so wanted them to be you.

I even called out and banged on the glass at one poor soul. How I must have looked." She took a long drag on her cigarette. "Turns out only you really look like you."

"I'm surprised you can recognize me, Mother. I mean, what would you have done if it weren't for Evelyn's introductory speech that night identifying me? Asked around? Have you seen my daughter Georgina? She was that young girl I left without giving a damn eighteen years ago." Georgina hadn't wanted to be cruel, but the bitterness was so overwhelming it forced out the hate from her heart.

Her mother took another deep drag, holding the smoke and then blowing it away in one long slow wisp. "There is no point, is there, in me speaking if you are unable to listen, if all you can hear are your words condemning me." She threw up her arm. "No point. I thought I might have been talking to an adult. Someone mature enough to understand that the world is made of many shades of grey. That none of us is perfect. None of us. But it seems you have not grown up."

"What do you know of my growing up? You were not around. Remember?"

Her mother pointed to her heart. "I was with you."

Georgina stabbed with her forefinger at her own heart in reply. "I was *twelve*."

"Yes, and I have counted every day I have not been with you."

"Funnily enough, *me too*. Hundreds upon hundreds of hours of lost sleep, wondering what I had done so wrong for my mother to leave and never return."

Her mother reached out. "Georgina."

Georgina pulled her arm away. "I demand you return the painting to the museum. That is where it belongs, not with you. That is the only reason I am here."

"I will not have you demand things of me."

"And I will not be blackmailed."

"For pity's sake, Georgina, I just wanted to speak to you, to have a chance to explain. Look—please read this letter from your father. It will help you understand."

"For the last time, I am not interested in that letter and what it may or may not prove or explain. For what it's worth, I am certain the last thing my father would have wanted to do was hand the painting over to you."

"Your father gave that painting to me as a wedding gift. It is *mine*."

"Just keep it then. And I hope that every time you look at it, you remember how much I hate you."

Her mother gasped, *"Georgina.* Please wait—" She tried to reach out, her hand catching at Georgina's pocket as Georgina wrestled free and left with all the speed and might she could muster.

❖

Molly discreetly checked her watch. Art club would be over in ten minutes. Had Georgina returned home? Had she somehow managed to find a peace of sorts with her mum, or at least begun the process? Perhaps she'd even returned with Edith's painting. A student's pencil rolled from their desk to the floor with a dull plink and reminded Molly she should be concentrating and wrapping things up.

"So let's bring our thoughts together." Molly swept over the next sheet of paper on the flip board. She looked back at the eager faces young and old with their pencils and pens poised as they began to jot down the key points from the evening's lesson on self-portraits. "So in summary, we all agreed that the eyes are important to how an image of a face is received and how we read a face to help us know how to respond."

Molly paused. Georgina stood just outside the education room. Her face was pinched with unmistakable pain and she looked utterly broken. Molly's chest tightened as Georgina bowed her head and began to cry.

Molly took a deep breath. "Next week we will be painting our own self-portraits, so think about how you might adopt some of the techniques we have chatted about tonight. Thank you for your attention, have a lovely rest of the evening, and see you next week."

Molly rushed out to Georgina and wrapped her arms around her.

Georgina mumbled through her tears, "I shouldn't have gone."

Molly felt the most terrible guilt. Georgina had faced her mother for them hadn't she? She had gone into battle and returned with what Molly desperately hoped was not a mortal wound. *Say something to her. Anything.* "I just need to lock up," Molly said. "Why don't you head home. Maybe rescue the coffee machine from the packing box again. I'll raid Marianne's biscuit stash, and if she asks I'll say one of my students had an attack of low blood sugar."

Molly felt Georgina's sobs subside. She moved away, nodding.

"I'll be five minutes, max," Molly said. "I promise."

Molly arrived at George Wright's door with her notes in one hand and two packs of Bourbon biscuits in the other. "Got the biscuits. I'm officially a criminal."

"And I'm officially ridiculous. Come through."

"No." Molly slipped her arm around Georgina's waist. "You're officially brave. And you're my hero."

Sobs overwhelmed Georgina again. She forced out, "I just need a minute."

"Sure." Molly finished making the coffee and placed a mug on the worktop next to Georgina. "I've put a couple of scoops of sugar in, just to warn you. I'll be in the sitting room—oh, and if you hear a hissing noise, it's me on the beanbag, not an angry adder."

A laugh escaped Georgina. She shook her head and said, "Don't go anywhere." She reached out for Molly's hand and pulled Molly in to her. She whispered into Molly's ear, "Sorry about the painting."

"What painting? Oh, that old thing. I've forgotten about it already."

"You're a terrible liar."

Molly shrugged. "I guess if it's hers, then we have no right to keep it."

"Actually I told her she could keep it, and that I hoped when she looked at it…"

Molly could feel Georgina's chest shudder. "Georgina?"

"It would remind her how much I hate her."

Molly squeezed Georgina as tightly as she could. She wanted to take her pain away and bear it for her somehow.

"I'm so tired." Georgina wiped at her eyes.

"I bet. Let's finish our coffees and go back to my place."

"Can we stay here?"

"Yes, of course. I love being with you here—you know that."

Georgina looked intently at Molly. It was like she wanted to say something but didn't dare. She chased the thought away with a smile. "Then I'll see you up there." Georgina walked away up the stairs to her room with the not quite double bed and the shadows that fell as they'd always done against the wall.

Molly rinsed the mugs at the sink while looking out at the garden. The moon shone brightly in the sky. Was Georgina looking out at it too?

April 1832
Edith's lodging, Cank Street, Leicester

"Do you think the moon looks like a holy wafer?" Edith turned to Josephine, naked at her side, her skin ice-white in the moon's glow.

"Maybe. Although rather than holy, I always find the moon rather ominous."

Edith traced her paint-smudged fingers along the line of Josephine's collarbone. "Ominous? And not beautiful?"

Josephine leaned up on her elbow. "No. It is the black shadows it casts. Sometimes I feel that blackness upon us."

"You do?"

"Yes. As if our love exists in moon shade rather than sunlight." Josephine lay back into Edith's arms.

"I love you with all my heart," Edith whispered. "No shade, no doubt. My love for you couldn't be brighter."

"And I love you too, Edith. Always."

Edith held her tightly, staring out at the moon, wondering if somewhere in the world there were two women loving each other freely—on a continent far away perhaps—and *looking up at the moon like them, but with their hearts open to admire it fully without sadness to dull its light.*

Chapter Thirty-three

Molly's cheek lay against Georgina's shoulder and her hand curled in a loose fist resting just under her chin. She looked so peaceful.

Georgina rubbed at her tired eyes. She didn't remember falling asleep. Molly had been telling her about the troubled life of Frida Kahlo, and Georgina had drifted off.

Molly stirred warm at Georgina's side. "It was a picture of a watermelon," Molly said sleepily. She opened her eyes and smiled. "Frida's last painting. It had the slogan *Live the life*. Super inspiring. Just so you know."

"I *was* listening honestly." Georgina placed a kiss on Molly's lips. "Well, until I wasn't, obviously. Coffee?"

"Yes, please, to coffee. Just two gallons will be fine." Molly stretched, arms out wide, expanding her chest beneath the sheet. "Are you going back to London today?"

Georgina climbed out of bed and at the same time checked her phone, staring at the emails and messages that had filled her inbox. "I bunked off yesterday, so I've no choice but to make an appearance at some point today."

"You've just flashed your boobs to the robins in the garden by the way," Molly said with a chuckle.

"What?" Georgina glanced up and out the bare window to the garden busy with birds bravely facing the cold morning. "I dread to think how many times in recent weeks I've done that." She pointed at Molly. "And you can stop smiling. It is your fault that I am naked more often than I'm not. I once had some dignity you know."

She picked her coat up from the floor and rested it back across the bottom of the bed frame. It was still a little damp from the rain the night before, and she shivered at the cold material as it brushed against her skin and with the sudden recollection of the row with her mother. She could still taste the bitterness of their exchange, inky on her lips.

"I tend not to worry about dignity myself, mainly because I've never really had any." As she spoke Molly was leaning down under the bed to retrieve something. She made a straining noise and said, "Got it. This fell out of your coat pocket just then." Molly frowned at the envelope in her hand. "Lydia Wright. Wow. Is this the letter from your father? I'm sorry, I'm being really nosy. Here." Molly attempted to hand the letter to Georgina. "Georgina?"

Georgina sat heavily on the bed tucking the end of the duvet around her. "I honestly don't know how it got there. She was trying to get me to read it."

"It's understandable that you don't want to."

"Will you read it to me?"

Molly raised her eyebrows.

"It's a silly idea." Georgina shook her head. "You don't have to—"

"I don't mind. So, what, shall I read it now?"

Georgina nodded. There would never be a good time. Now was as good as it was going to get.

Molly took a deep breath and tugged the letter from its envelope and rested it against the sheet. "Ready?" Molly said softly.

Georgina nodded and clasped her hands together in her lap.

Molly began. "*Dear Lydia, I have drafted and discarded this letter many times. I am now too tired to keep rewriting so this draft must do.*"

Georgina could sense Molly looking across at her. "I'm fine," Georgina said. "Please go on."

"Right. Okay. *I will dispense with pleasantries, which is best all round, and get straight to the point. As you no doubt are aware I am*"—Molly paused and gave a hard swallow before quietly saying—"*dying. I mention this for context, not to elicit sympathy. Dying forces one in rather sharp terms to assess one's past behaviour and to set one's affairs in order. To this end I have two matters I wish to raise with you.* Still okay? Georgina?"

Georgina nodded.

"*Firstly, I wish to confirm that I consider the 1832 watercolour of Josephine Brancaster to be yours. Having earlier gifted this work to you, it follows that I have no right to keep it. I ask that as its rightful owner you accept the portrait into your care. I am sorry for the delay in this regard. Please present this letter to my solicitors Fothergill and Lowe as proof of ownership.*"

Georgina looked at Molly as she stared back at her. "There we have it in the clearest terms," Georgina said. "Edith's painting belongs to my mother."

Molly stared at the letter and nodded.

Georgina squeezed her eyes closed, refusing to recall her parents rowing and the image of her father nursing the portrait in his arms.

Georgina felt Molly's hand on her arm. "We can always finish reading this later."

"Let's finish it. What else does it say? He mentioned two matters?"

"Let me see, where was I? Oh yes." Molly read ahead silently only to pause and double blink.

"What is it?"

"Nothing." Molly folded the letter. "Your dad was just a bit worried about you. Thought you'd like to see your mum again. That sort of thing. Are you hungry? I'm starving."

"What do you mean he was worried about me? I know you're only trying to protect me by paraphrasing, but read it fully, please. I need to hear it."

"Okay." Molly nodded and reopened the letter. She cleared her throat and read, "*The second matter relates to our daughter. I wish to be frank and to tell you that I worry that she has developed a habit of self-reliance which excludes the need for others. I fear that my death will only increase her emotional isolation. I request your help with this and ask that you make contact with her. It is likely Georgina will not be receptive. Indeed you may have to insist. She knows nothing of this, so she will not feel hurt if you decide you cannot fulfil my request. I earnestly hope you do. For the simple fact is that she has always needed you, and I sincerely regret that I made it difficult for you to maintain a relationship with her. For what it's worth, I will carry this regret to my grave. George.* I'm sorry." Molly rested her hand on Georgina's leg.

What on earth? He'd kept her mother from her? How? Why? Georgina stood up. "Well that explains the secrecy. He obviously couldn't face her and was covering up while he was alive all the shameful things he'd done. In fact I bet you...What's the postmark?"

"Oh, weird—the letter's dated 20th February 2017, but the postmark on the envelope is 21st August 2017. But your dad died in March. So who posted the letter?"

Georgina gave a heavy sigh. "My guess, the same person who left bloody lilies all the time."

"You think the housekeeper knew?"

"No, I don't think so. He would routinely leave correspondence for her to post on the console table. Come to think of it, he was always precise about when he wanted things to arrive with people. He would leave Post-it notes to say post this on that date and so forth. She would have thought nothing of it. I can imagine the letter was probably part of a collection of post she was no doubt told to send when probate was complete. A calculating mind for you."

"Blimey."

Georgina rummaged in her holdall and pulled out her running gear. She quickly got dressed.

"I guess at least," Molly said, tentatively, "he was trying to make things right."

"More like he was easing his conscience. This is all about him. He clearly never cared about me or my mother."

"Georgina—"

"I thought the world of him. I looked up to him." Her voice broke. "I feel so stupid."

Molly quickly climbed out of bed and held Georgina by her arms. "You're *not.* Understood?"

Georgina nodded and sat on the edge of the bed to put on her trainers.

Molly quietly said, "Maybe this changes things for you and your mum. It sounds like he behaved badly."

"So did *she.* They're obviously as bad as each other. And for him to invite her back into my life…" Georgina shook her head. "I've got to run or I'll explode."

"I get that. I'll leave the letter here on the side for you."

"Thanks for reading it. And for last night. For everything, in fact. Look, how about I get breakfast on the way back?" Georgina gave Molly a quick kiss.

Molly grabbed her by her collar. "You're welcome. I think you're quite a bit smashing, by the way. Just so you know."

"You're just saying that because you're hoping I'll fetch a Mr. Brown's."

"I promise that's not the only reason."

"Uh-huh." Georgina made for the door.

Molly blurted out, "And by smashing, I mean I love you."

I can't. Instead she said, "Thank you. I won't be long."

Molly's cheeks flushed pink. "See you in a bit then." Molly couldn't have sounded more crestfallen. Georgina knew she needed to hear *I love you* in return, and even though she couldn't have loved Molly more, the words just wouldn't come. She could feel everything closing down and the defences to her heart rising once again.

Without waiting another second Georgina bounded down the stairs and out the door. A blast of cold January air caught her breath, forcing her to stop and cough. Bent double with her hands resting on her knees, something made her look up. Something familiar.

"I've been standing outside for twenty minutes. I couldn't bring myself to knock, and I couldn't bring myself to leave." Her mother tightened the scarf around her neck. "I'm hoping against the odds, that you can bring yourself to care."

Georgina straightened up and glared.

"So on all accounts I am quite the fool." Her mother's voice caught and she seemed to sway slightly.

"Go back to Paris, Mother," Georgina said. "You've fulfilled *his* wishes."

"You read the letter?"

Georgina dug in the pocket of her joggers to find her phone and proceeded to place earphones in her ears.

"Then you'll know that your father regrets his behaviour towards me. That we have both been victims."

Georgina pulled out her earphones. "Victims? In what way are you a victim? That he divorced you? That you didn't get everything you wanted?"

Her mother leaned heavily against the railings. She hung her head. "All I wanted was you."

"Really? Then tell me this—why didn't you fight for me?"

"I did!" She threw her arms in the air. "With all my might. But he was always mightier. He created this image of me as morally wayward and unstable. His rhetoric convinced the judge I was unfit. He all but convinced *me*. And then when you chose to stay with him, it broke my heart. It broke me." She reached again for the railings. She looked so frail with her translucent skin and her eyes sunken with what seemed like fatigue deepened with decades of despair.

Passers-by dragged their feet to listen and watch.

"Everybody's staring at us. For God's sake, come in." Georgina supported her mother loosely by the elbow through the gate and up the steps. She felt her hesitate at the door.

"Demons," her mother said quietly. "I relive the moment I left each day."

"You do?"

She nodded. "I am afraid to go in."

"Don't worry, the place is empty."

Her mother stepped inside. "So you're selling? Oh, of course, the board outside."

"I can't see how that's any of your business, Mother." A smell of soap drifted down the stairs and they could hear a tap running. "Molly," Georgina said in the direction of the landing.

"Then the place is not empty at all." Her mother loosened her scarf. "I like her very much."

"I'm not seeking your approval."

"Of course not. It is merely a statement of fact. You have good taste. I am glad that you have made things up with her, and that you are not alone, Georgina. I have been alone all of my life, and I do not want that for you."

"And yet you left me. Despite all your loneliness." Georgina's voice broke. Her mother went to comfort her and Georgina stepped out of reach.

Her mother sat on the stairs with a weary sigh. "I begged to see you. Your father told me you didn't want to see me, and that I had forfeited my right to you. That I had made my choice."

"Hadn't you? You chose that man. You cheated on us."

"And not a day has gone by that I haven't regretted it. The affair was over before it began. It was more a cry for help than anything."

"Help? With what? Your awful privileged life with a husband and child who loved you? How you must have suffered."

"Your father didn't love me or at least not in a way that can be recognized as true love. He owned me like the artwork on his walls." Her mother pulled at the collar at her neck. "I couldn't breathe. I couldn't work. I couldn't remember who I once was. Jean Claude gave me a glimpse—"

"I don't want to hear about him. All of this *My husband controlled me* and yet you still waited for his written permission before you came to me? You're pathetic. I've wasted so much of my life…" She wouldn't cry. Not in front of her.

"But *you* refused to see *me*. He must have poisoned your mind."

"I was a teenager. The facts spoke for themselves. Everything he said about you was the truth."

"No, this was when you were in your twenties. I came to the house one Christmas. I was determined to see you. I stood on the doorstep and he repeated that you wanted nothing to do with me. He said you didn't celebrate Christmas because of me. I was horrified. He told me that if I really loved you, I'd stay away."

"So you gave up on his say-so."

"*No.* I never stopped writing. And when you never replied to my letters, I could only think—"

"So, what, your absence from my life is my fault somehow?"

"No. I am just trying to explain. It took all my strength to keep writing, knowing you'd never reply."

"Then you should have stopped."

"Never. It was all I had." Her mother shook her head as if steeling herself once more. "Look, I am not expecting miracles or for everything to suddenly be all right—"

"Good, then you won't be disappointed."

"Georgina?" Molly stood at the top of the stairs. "I'm so sorry to disturb. I have to go to work. Lydia—hello again."

"Molly," her mother said. "How lovely to see you."

Molly gingerly descended and Georgina held out her hand to her as she reached the bottom step. Molly whispered into Georgina's ear. "Do you need me to stay?" Georgina shook her head. "Will you come and see me before you get your train?"

"Yes." Georgina kissed Molly, stroking softly at her cheek.

"Are you sure?"

"I'm fine. Go."

Georgina watched Molly close the door behind her. She hated watching Molly leave. The wrench she felt was almost unbearable.

Georgina rubbed at her forehead. "I need a coffee."

Her mother followed her to the kitchen and continued to the French doors and looked out to the garden. "My how the cherry tree has grown. I used to love to see the blossoms, and that lavender has such a beautiful fragrance when it flowers. How everything has changed and is yet the same."

"Nothing's the same. Everything changed the day you left." Georgina handed her mother a coffee and leaned back against the worktop, studying her mother as she studied the garden with her focus fixed rigid upon the outside. "You ruined our lives. Just to be clear."

Without flinching her mother just stood there staring out. Had she said all she could bear to say? A heavy silence rested between them. It was a silence where there was too much to be said to be able to say anything at all. When the only way to speak was to try to find questions that would hurt the least to answer.

"He never mentioned to me that he'd gifted the painting to you." Georgina looked at her mother.

Still staring out, her mother said, "We had just gotten engaged. It coincided with your grandfather's death. We inherited this house and began to prepare for the move from London to here. There was no question of George renting or selling it. I found leaving London hard. It felt like I was leaving a part of me behind. It turns out, I was leaving all of me." Her mother took a sip of coffee. "Your father did his best, I suppose, to help me see that this could be home. We moved a lot of items into the attic to make way for our belongings, and that's when I found her hidden away up a corner, facing the wall as if she should be ashamed somehow."

Edith's painting was in the attic? "Sorry, are you telling me that Edith's painting hasn't always hung with the other portraits?"

Her mother walked over to a stool and took a seat. "I obviously don't know about its past. Your father had not seen her before. I fell in love with her immediately. I felt a kind of kinship with her. So he gifted her to me on our wedding. I encouraged George to replace *The Hunt* with Josephine's portrait. It fit, as it helped with inheritance tax to gift *The Hunt* to the museum. I felt so sad to see Josephine's portrait absent from the Wright room."

Georgina winced at the memory of Molly begging her to display the portrait with the other paintings. What would Molly think to learn that the portrait had been buried away in the attic?

"Right," Georgina said. "That explains why it hung out of chronological order. Hold on, why didn't you claim it that night at the opening, there and then?"

"I hadn't spoken to your father's solicitors. In many ways I was still taking everything in. If you remember, I was trying to ask about it. I tried with you and Molly, but you were both so vague, and then, well, we both know how that night ended. For what it's worth, I didn't come to the opening for the painting or to succumb to Evelyn Fox's fawning. I came to see you."

"Yes, because my father told you to. We've already been through this, Mother."

"No. When I heard that your father had died, I felt such a sense of liberation. I knew I must see you, but for some reason I couldn't. I couldn't even write to you. I think I was frightened to be rejected again." Her mother swallowed hard and paused to finish her coffee. "And then the letter came, and something burst in me, something angry and defiant. It made me sick to my stomach because I knew this would make it seem that he was the good guy making everything right."

"I don't understand. You've been divorced from him for so many years. Why would you suddenly feel liberated?"

"Not my liberation, Georgina. Yours."

"That's nonsense. I wasn't captive to my father."

"No, but you loved him, and there is no greater bond or hold on a person than love."

"So, again, you're trying to blame me—"

"No, I'm not. I'm trying to explain that while he was alive we would never have had a chance."

"What makes you think we do? You seem to overlook all the years that have passed. The memories that have haunted me and that haunt me still. I watch you leaving again and again in my nightmares."

"When did you see me leave?"

"That night. The Christmas Eve you left and never returned."

"You saw that? I'm sorry you had to witness that. I didn't know you were there."

"I found my father in the sitting room with Josephine's portrait in his arms, sobbing."

"We were rowing over the painting. He had been telling me that he would see that I would be left with nothing. Which he very nearly did. I reminded him that he'd gifted Josephine's portrait to me. I tried to take it, and he snatched it from me and held it tightly to make the point that he would never let me have it. Your father was crying for himself, Georgina. Not for our relationship. After all, we mostly cry for ourselves, don't we? One might even say tears are selfish."

"Selfish. Really? So when I cried myself to sleep every night for years after you left, I was being selfish? You know, on second thoughts, can you leave? I've heard enough. You know the way out, after all, don't you?" Georgina left the kitchen and went into the sitting room, closing the door behind her. She slumped down with her back against the door. She could sense her mother standing on the other side.

"Georgina. Please. I cried too. Every day. My grief for you has made me ill. I have missed you so much."

Georgina felt tears sting and blur. "Please leave."

"I have told you the truth. Not a version of it. The truth." Georgina heard the door open, and then a moment of silence fell, shortly broken by her mother calling out, "I love you, Georgina, whatever you may think. I always have."

As the door closed, Georgina looked out to the promenade to see her mother walking away, her tall fragile frame bracing against the British winter she hated so much.

❖

"Georgina—hi, how did it go?"

Georgina stood at Molly's office door. She arrived unannounced and couldn't have looked sadder or more forlorn. "I didn't get the painting for you. I failed. I'm sorry."

Molly rushed to the door and hugged Georgina. "You haven't failed me. It doesn't matter about the painting. All that matters is that you've survived seeing your mum again." Molly gestured into the office. "Come in and have my seat. Can I get you anything? Some water perhaps?"

"No, thank you." Georgina sat on Molly's chair. "I just needed to see you."

Molly perched on her desk, and Georgina turned her chair to face her and rested the side of her head against Molly's thigh.

Molly stroked Georgina's head in a slow comforting action. "I'm here."

Georgina mumbled, "As much as I struggle to understand my mother, I feel certain that she will care for the painting."

"Me too."

"She found Josephine's portrait in the attic, would you believe? She fell in love with her then and there, apparently."

Molly momentarily stopped stroking. "The attic? Really? So she wasn't hanging on the wall with the other paintings?"

"No. According to my mother, she hung Josephine there in place of *The Hunt* which was given to the museum."

"I feel a bit silly now, as I had this romantic notion that Josephine had the painting framed and hung, maybe after her husband had died, and that it had remained on the wall with the other family portraits unchallenged until you brought it to the museum. It just underlines again how little one ever knows about the past."

"It's still a romantic story," Georgina said softly, "in that it has survived all these years."

"Yes." Molly entangled her fingers in the hair falling at Georgina's neck. "I reckon Josephine's so beautiful, no one would want to cover her up."

"My mother says that she found her all but hidden away and facing towards the attic wall. She made some melodramatic comment about that making Josephine look like she was ashamed."

"Oh no. I hate the thought of that." Molly swallowed down the sense of loss. She would have to find a way to accept that she would likely not see the original work again, and that her part in caring for Josephine was done. She took a deep breath. "Anyway, I think you've been really brave to face your mum. And maybe it's even good that you've had this chance to get things off your chest and to tell her how you've felt all these years. I think it will help."

"Molly's right, Georgina." Fran bustled into the small room with her arms full of Victorian costumes. She dumped them in the dressing-up basket, and then all but collapsed into her chair with a sigh.

Georgina quickly sat up straight and fussed with her hair clearly embarrassed at their intimacy exposed.

Fran didn't seem bothered in the slightest. "It may not feel like it now of course. I'm interfering—I'll shut up."

"No," Georgina said. "If it wasn't for your earlier intervention, I might never have seen sense. Thank you."

"Nonsense," Fran said. "You would have gotten there eventually."

"I don't know. When it comes to emotions, I'm not very good at seeing my way through."

"What you're going through's hard." Molly gave Georgina's hand a quick squeeze. "Anyone would find it tough."

"My mother's trying to say my father was controlling and poisoned my mind against her. She even said I had been captive to him just by loving him. I mean, that can't be right. Can it?" Georgina looked at Molly and Fran in confusion. "And the stuff she said he said to keep her away was true. She did ruin our lives and I didn't want to see her. And surely if my father was trying to prevent contact between us, he would have destroyed her letters, wouldn't he?"

"But then he knew you never replied to them," Fran said. "Am I right?"

Georgina nodded.

"Sometimes," Fran said, "and I'm not saying your father did this, although I do know that he was understandably bitter, by not defending someone and by not building bridges between those who cannot build their own, you conspire to perpetuate hurt. All your father had to do was nothing—just repeat the truth as you both saw it. And do not misunderstand me—I am not defending your mother's actions, and I am not accusing your father of being malicious."

"But he was. I mean, you've explained perfectly what he did." Georgina shook her head. "And he used the fact that I loved him—that's what my mother was getting at—so I wouldn't even question things."

Fran raised her voice slightly to say, "No, Georgina, I knew your father as a young man and he was a good man. In my opinion he just met and married a passionate girl he couldn't entirely handle. They were ill-suited and hurt each other and unfortunately you, as a result. But do not begin to doubt for one moment their love for you. The sad truth I'm afraid is that human beings are far from perfect."

"That's what my mother said, that none of us is perfect." Georgina turned to Molly. "She even said that whether I believed it or not, she loved me."

Molly swallowed the lump in her throat. "She did keep writing to you and stood in the Wright room that night, facing everything, which must have been pretty hard. I think you'd only do that for something as strong as love."

Georgina smiled. "You're just saying that because you like her."

"No, I only *say* things for a Mr. Brown's breakfast." Molly rested her palm to Georgina's cheek and Fran coughed.

They smirked guiltily.

"Molly." Marianne's head appeared round the door. "Lydia Wright is in the foyer asking for you."

"She is?" Fran and Georgina looked at each other and then at Molly. "Okay, I'll come down now. Thank you."

Georgina turned ashen and shook her head. "If she's looking for me—"

"Don't worry, I'll tell her you've already gone back to London. I'll be straight back."

Molly ran down the stairs trying to anticipate what Lydia might want. Was she hoping to strike another deal perhaps? Georgina hadn't said how she left things, but it didn't take a genius to guess not well. Molly couldn't have been more surprised by the sight that greeted her.

Lydia was standing in the middle of the foyer with Josephine's portrait resting beside her.

"I'm sorry to take you from your work," Lydia said. Molly hadn't thought it was possible for Lydia to look any frailer. "But I wanted you to have the painting. After all, I promised."

"That's awesome. Thank you so much. If you can wait one moment, I need you to fill in an object entry form. It's the process we have to follow when someone lends an object to the museum." Molly leaned over the reception desk trying to find the forms. "They should be here somewhere."

"I'm not lending it to the museum."

Molly slipped down from the desk. "You're not?" *Here we go.*

"I'm gifting the work to you."

"You are?"

"I want you to have it. You seem to feel the passion that I felt for it, and that is what is important to me." Lydia lifted the painting into Molly's arms. "I know you will love it and care for it, just as you are clearly loving and caring for my daughter." Lydia glanced beyond Molly to the stairs.

Molly turned round to see Georgina walking towards them.

"Your mum's returned the painting to us," Molly said, wondering what had made Georgina join them and what she might be thinking.

"To be precise, I've gifted it to Molly," Lydia corrected.

Georgina raised her eyebrows and her face lightened with surprise. "I see."

"I thought you'd approve." Lydia tilted her head slightly as if to gauge Georgina's reaction.

"I do. Very much."

"Good. Well, trains won't wait. My best wishes for the display, Molly. Perhaps you might let me know how it goes?"

"I will. Thank you."

"You're welcome." Lydia glanced at Georgina. "Goodbye then." Lydia took a deep breath and turned to walk away.

"It opens on the first," Georgina said. Lydia stopped without turning round.

Molly looked at Georgina. *Good for you.* Her heart drummed in her chest. "Yes," Molly added. "If you let me have your address, we can send you an invite."

Lydia cleared her throat, and still without looking back she said, "You'll find my address in my next letter."

"Great." Molly said, all but bursting with relief. She hugged the painting to her chest and felt Georgina's arm slip around her waist. They stood in silence together, watching Lydia leave.

As the doors slid closed, Molly said softly, "I'm so glad you came down."

"I just had to. I was sitting in your office." Georgina looked out towards the exit. "And I felt a terrible sense of panic. It came from nowhere. But I knew what it was. It was the thought of her leaving. That I wouldn't see her again."

"I get that," Molly said. "She's your mum."

Georgina nodded and then looked at the floor. "I can't believe I've got to go now. I hate leaving you."

"I hate you leaving." Molly swallowed down the urge to cry. "Although I've got to go too. I'm amazed Evelyn hasn't sensed that I'm not working. Ring me tonight?"

Georgina looked up. "I'll ring every night."

"Yeah, that's a bit clingy."

Georgina laughed. "What can I say—I've got it bad." Georgina kissed Molly with the painting pressing between them, resting against their hearts.

Chapter Thirty-four

Down a bit, left a bit. Stop. That's it. Perfect." Molly leaned forward and reached behind Edith's painting, which was being held up by a perspiring Fran. Molly carefully marked with a pencil the areas where the fixings would be hammered to the foyer wall.

"Hurry up, Molly. Whilst I'm in favour of perfection, I'm less in favour of a hernia."

Molly mumbled through a mouthful of nails, "Nearly there." She hammered the hooks to the wall, fixing the painting securely. "All done." She stepped back, placing her hands on her hips, and exhaled a deep breath of relief.

"The blue for the title banner works really well." Fran gestured to the strip of navy vinyl lettering stretching along the wall above the display case. "I see now what you were saying about wanting to pick out the deep blue background of Edith's painting."

"Yes, I'm properly chuffed with the final result." Molly gazed up at the title of the display. Her heart caught as she read aloud, "Edith Hewitt, 1808–1834. Radical campaigner and artist, a life remembered." Molly shook her head. "I can't quite believe we've got to this point. That Edith's story is being told. And tonight."

Fran stood beside Molly and gave her a squeeze. "Yes, the day has come. Well done, Molly Goode. The display looks great. You've done Edith proud."

"I hope so. I really do. Thanks for everything, Fran, and sorry I've dragged you into drama now and then."

"Nonsense. What is life after all without a little bit of drama? And I mean it when I say you should be very proud. Your determination is impressive. Nearly as impressive as these panels, which are certainly hard to miss."

"They're fab, aren't they? I *love* them." Molly rested her hand against one of three brightly coloured explanatory panels hanging alongside Edith's painting and filling the entire corner space with interest and energy. "My aim was for them to be visible pretty much from the entrance."

"I suspect that they're pretty much visible from space," Fran said with an amused smile.

"Well that's even better." Molly glanced at her watch. "Bugger. It's nearly one. Now have I forgotten anything? So we have the *Campaigning* panel. Check." Molly moved along the wall with her arms outstretched as if directing a plane to land. "Then *Edith the Artist* on this panel. You know, the photos of the sketches have worked even better than I'd hoped. Then we have Edith's painting, followed by the summary panel. Super-dupes."

"Is this the final version of the portrait's label?" Fran lifted the strip of thin white board that would accompany Edith's painting, from where it rested forgotten on top of the display case.

"Oh, bugger, yes." Molly carefully peeled off the backing tape and pressed the label into place. "I kept it factual." She tilted her head, wondering if she should have written more. "It's a bit depressing how facts seem to hide more than they reveal."

Fran nodded in agreement and narrowed her eyes to read aloud, "*Miss Josephine Brancaster, 1832, Watercolour. Painted by Edith Hewitt. Donated by Molly Goode, January 2018. Accession number: 2018.01.*"

"But then that's where explanatory panels come in." Fran pointed towards the final summary panel. "And that couldn't be clearer."

Molly had blown up the image of the inscription hidden beneath the frame to become the title of a panel dedicated to a narrative about the importance of revealing our hidden histories and uncovering truths untold. The words *All My Love Always, Edith* shone out radiant for all to see.

"Knowing that poignant inscription is behind that frame," Molly said, "sharing that secret with the visitor, there's something magical about that, don't you think?" Molly rested her hand at her throat with the thought of how much it meant.

"Certainly." Fran stared at the painting. "I can't help thinking that whoever covered that inscription over in the first place couldn't have foreseen this day."

"No," Molly said with a sigh. "That's for sure."

Summer 1876
Josephine Wright's House, City Walk, Leicester

Had it really been forty-two years since she'd last been able to bring herself to look at Edith's painting? It had been a month or so after Edith's death when William asked where she would like him to store Edith's things. She'd glimpsed the inscription and vowed never to look upon it again. She'd made a space in a cabinet in what had been their office, and they remained in there hidden away until William retired. And then they came to the house where she found she could still not look fully upon them, and she stored them away under her bed. It wasn't the right time was it?

Even now, unwrapped from its hessian covering, she thought it might be too much. And it was in many ways. The sight of Edith's handwriting and the words *All my love always* hurt so terribly to see again. It was like a wound reopened, sorer than first inflicted and now more difficult to heal. In the birds chattering in the trees lining the promenade Josephine could swear she could make out Edith's voice as if she was with her right then and there, kneeling in front of her with her head resting in her lap, declaring all her love for always.

"Who's Edith?" Adelaide Wright leaned over her mother's shoulder to see what she was staring at.

"Nobody. It's nothing." Josephine brushed away a tear, quickly turning the canvas over.

"Oh, goodness, is that you?" Adelaide touched at the painting and at her mother's face awash with colour. "You look so young."

"Yes." Josephine reached over to wrap the protective hessian cloth around the painting once again. She then turned her attention to finishing the note for the framer.

Adelaide rested a hand on the back of her mother's chair. "Are you having it framed?"

"Yes, I thought I would." Josephine gazed across at the wall of portraits, fixing on her wedding day. She was so young then too.

"Are you thinking of hanging it next to father's painting?"

"Yes."

Adelaide hovered at her mother's side, fidgety with questions. It took no guesswork to imagine that she wanted to ask again who Edith was and what she had meant by inscribing *All my love always*. But it seemed she couldn't find the words. Instead she asked, "Why didn't you frame it while Father was alive?"

Josephine's cheeks stung. "There are many things I now must do without your father because, whether we choose it or not, life goes on. Now please, Adelaide, let this matter be."

"I didn't mean to upset you, Mother." Adelaide turned and left. Josephine could sense her daughter's eyes upon her right until she closed the door.

Josephine stared out to the promenade. The lamps were lit and the rain had begun to fall, misting the window in droplets of light. For a moment she watched the hypnotic blur of passers-by. How much life she had seen over the years passing by her window. How many more years would she have to carry the burden of regret.

With a weary sigh she laid her cheek against the painting's hessian covering, and with words that hurt to speak, she said, "I cannot promise our painting will hang here forever, Edith. *But I promise you this, with all my heart, that my love for you will be forever, for always.*"

"Is it your intention for people to guess what is in this case?" Evelyn arrived in a gust of perfume and criticism. She squinted into the display case.

Not entirely sure how to respond to that question, Molly said cautiously, "No."

"No? Well then, may I suggest cleaning the glass?"

Embarrassed, Molly said, "We were just about—"

Evelyn raised her finger in the air. "Are we sure that's straight?" Evelyn tilted her head towards the painting.

"Yes, definitely," Fran said with a defensive frosting to her voice. "*We* have checked several times using a spirit level."

"I see. I often think the eye more accurate. Still," Evelyn said with a tone that suggested her sentence continued with *nothing we can do about it now*. "And you're changing for this evening, Molly, of course."

Molly looked down at her smock top. "It matches my…I'll change."

"Wonderful. I think you'll find it better to complement than match when it comes to one's outfit. Oh, and as a rule of thumb, if one is comfortable in one's clothes, then one is likely to be underdressed. Thank you, ladies."

"Ignore her." Fran scowled at the shape of Evelyn making for the stairs. "Remember, you are not her clone. You are you, and that is exactly how it should be."

"She's always so glamorous, though."

"She always looks like a stick's up her arse."

"*Fran.* I think she can hear that."

"Let's hope so."

"You're a bad influence."

"I'll think you'll find that's the best kind. Grab the duster. Don't be surprised if she returns wearing white gloves."

Molly laughed. "She wouldn't. Would she?" Molly watched Evelyn disappear out of sight. Despite everything that had passed between them, she wanted to impress her and for her to see that Molly could be trusted with the museum's reputation. And that she was indeed the curator Evelyn evidently so hoped she could be.

Chapter Thirty-five

Before Molly knew it, she was standing under the elegant columns of the portico greeting guests with a warm smile and a hug or a handshake. "Thanks so much for coming tonight. It's lovely to see you," Molly said to each eager face. "Please help yourself to a drink." Molly's entire art club had turned out, and there was talk of ending the evening at a local pub to celebrate. "Of course, I wouldn't miss it for the world," was the answer she gave each time she was asked if she'd join them.

But in that moment the only thing Molly didn't want to miss was Georgina. Georgina had messaged to say she was sorry but that she was running late and to start without her if need be. Molly stepped further onto the promenade looking out for Georgina.

"Georgina!" Molly ran towards her, then straight into her arms. She hugged her so tightly, wanting nothing more than to absorb Georgina into her.

Georgina laughed. "Managed not to miss me then."

"What? Oh no." Molly giggled. "Although I am a bit steamed up."

Georgina cupped Molly's hands. "You're also freezing again."

"I've been welcoming guests as they arrive."

"Oh, right. So you weren't standing in the cold waiting for me again?"

Molly nodded vehemently and at the same time said, "Absolutely not."

Georgina slipped her arm around Molly's waist as they walked back to the museum. "I'd like to say a few words tonight, if that would be okay?"

"Yes, that would be awesome. Thank you."

Georgina slowed her pace. "It just feels right to."

Molly stopped and looked up into Georgina's eyes. "I'm so pleased you feel that way. I really hope you'll love the display."

"I know I will. I love everything you do."

The sensation of pure joy tightened at her throat. She could have sobbed her heart out with happiness. Instead, she looked away to compose herself, only to notice the last stragglers going into the museum. "Oh, bugger, we're late. Come on." Molly tucked her arm into Georgina's as they quickened their pace towards the museum.

Reaching the door and slightly breathless, Molly said, "I'll let Evelyn know that you want to speak. The format is fairly straightforward. Evelyn will welcome guests on behalf of the museum and give a brief introduction to the display, and she'll then likely direct people to me and Fran for any questions they have. A lighter touch than the Wright room, but nonetheless a similar occasion to last time really." Her stomach dropped as she realized what she'd just said. "Well, not exactly like last time, obviously."

Georgina was looking nervously at the entrance. "Has she arrived?"

"I haven't seen her. She could of course be with Evelyn." Molly squeezed Georgina's hand. "Georgina, whatever happens tonight, remember how smashing you are."

"Oh, Molly." Georgina quickly stole a kiss as if oblivious to the curious stares from the promenade. "Thanks for the pep talk," she whispered close to Molly's ear. She seemed more than reluctant to step away as she eventually took a deep breath and pulled at the cuffs of her shirt. She brushed her jacket flat against her and fiddled for a moment with the buttons. "I'm ready."

No sooner had they stepped into the museum than Evelyn approached with Lydia at her side.

"Molly, thank goodness." Evelyn rested a dramatic hand at her chest. "I thought you had decided against joining us this evening."

"I was running late, Evelyn," Georgina said. "Molly kindly waited for me."

Evelyn's neck flushed pink. "Of course." She promptly shook Georgina's hand. "It is a pleasure to see you again, Georgina."

"The display is beautiful, Molly." Lydia smiled warmly and took Molly's hands in hers. "I had a feeling you would donate Josephine's portrait."

"It wasn't for me to keep it," Molly said. "It has a job to do."

"Well." Lydia turned towards the throng of visitors gathered in the corner of the foyer reading the panels and staring transfixed at the painting. "It appears it's working hard."

Molly felt Georgina's hand briefly rub, in silent praise, at her back.

"Georgina. How are you?" Lydia asked, with a note of caution in her voice.

"I'm well, thank you, Mother. It's…it's good to see you again."

"Excellent," Evelyn said, visibly exhaling. "Let's get things under way."

"If you'll excuse me." Lydia slipped a cigarette from its thin silver case and went outside.

"Oh, Evelyn." Molly lightly caught her arm. "Before we begin, Georgina would like to say a few words. I said that would be fine."

Evelyn looked at Georgina with unconcealed surprise. "Yes. Wonderful. I'll bring you on after I've done my welcome." Without missing a beat Evelyn then raised her hands in the air in a manner not dissimilar to the Pope welcoming the devoted. "Everyone. Welcome."

An obliging hush fell upon the foyer as Evelyn began to speak.

Lydia returned to Molly's side in a cloud of sweet tobacco. She leaned in and whispered, "May I be honest and say I've never been a great fan of speeches."

Molly sensed Georgina stir and shift her weight from one leg to the other before folding her arms.

"Yes," Molly said, mustering diplomacy. "But when the right person is speaking on a topic they particularly care about, they can be truly inspiring."

"Indeed." Lydia seemed to concede the point with a smile.

Evelyn began her speech by expressing the museum's gratitude to the Wright Foundation for its recent investment in future projects that would focus on correcting past injustices. "We are delighted," Evelyn said emphatically, "to be uncovering further hidden histories just like the display before you, telling the moving story of local activist Edith Hewitt, whose contribution to history has been up to now shamefully neglected. We hope that tonight's display will be the first of many." The audience, led by the chairman, applauded.

Evelyn's speech should have been inspiring. After all she was promising to meaningfully address the need for a more diverse museum. But Molly struggled to see past the museum's initial reticence, so much so every word felt hollow and akin to paper-thin rhetoric easily torn and defenceless against the slightest ill wind.

Lydia had clearly lost interest and was looking across to the painting all alone in the corner, relieved for that moment of the scrutiny of prying eyes.

Lydia turned to Molly. "What will the museum do with the painting after your display?"

"Care for it with its other artworks," Molly said. "It's a valued part of the museum's permanent collection now, even though it may not be exhibited."

"I see." A disconcerted frown fell across Lydia's face. "Such a shame for it to be stored unseen again and with her face no doubt facing another wall."

"The paintings are hung on specially designed racks in a controlled environment," Molly said gently. "I promise she won't be looking at any walls. In fact I shall ensure she faces a beautiful landscape painting."

"And it will be catalogued properly, Mother," Georgina said. "People will be able to find her."

"I rather prefer the notion of being seen rather than having to be found, don't you?" Lydia's gaze drifted away to the Wright room. "Such a depressing painting, *The Hunt*." Lydia turned to Georgina. "Wouldn't you agree?"

"Yes," Georgina said. "Certainly."

Molly could sense something pass between them, a private understanding perhaps that required no words to be understood.

"Oh, Georgina, you're up," Molly said, feeling nervous for Georgina but determined not to let it show. She clapped loudly, joined by Lydia, as Georgina moved away to stand next to Evelyn.

Georgina began a little hesitantly, thanking the gathered crowd for attending. She then expressed her gratitude to Evelyn and the chairman and to the museum's trustees and stakeholders for supporting the work to highlight an important aspect of her family's history.

"I cannot tell you as a Wright how proud I am," Georgina said, "to make claim to this otherwise forgotten history of brave campaigning, friendship, and love."

Molly caught Georgina's eye and gave an encouraging nod.

"I have to confess, I was not a fan of museums," Georgina said, sharing a brief wry smile with Molly. A murmur of interest rose from the crowd. "But I stand before you with a change of heart. These last few months, I have felt for myself the magic of museums. Very few civic spaces seem to engender such trust and have the authority and purpose to truly inspire. For this reason I believe the museum is uniquely placed to uncover social injustice, to foster inclusivity, and to champion the diversity of our shared history."

Georgina was so impressive. Lydia's face, animated with unmistakable pride, made it clear that she felt the same way too.

Even Evelyn stood stock still as if transfixed. In fact if Molly was not mistaken Evelyn had yet to draw breath.

"Edith Hewitt's story revealed to you in this illuminating display is in every way our shared history." Georgina's voice broke a little and she paused to swallow. "For it is a story we can all recognize—one of determination, of bravery, of love, and of loss."

Molly could see that Georgina was speaking without a script and that every word seemed to flow directly from her heart.

"We will never know for sure what Edith meant when she inscribed *All my love always*. But we all know what it is to want to say that to someone." Georgina looked across at Molly.

Could Georgina be talking about her? Please let Georgina be talking about her.

Georgina took a shaky deep breath. "I can tell the woman I love that I'm sorry if I ever let her down."

The gathered crowd shifted slightly, their attention held to every word Georgina spoke.

"We will never know whether Josephine had regrets, and if so whether she had the chance to tell Edith in time. I can tell the woman I love that I miss her terribly when we are apart. Edith's words must have felt pointless. I can tell the woman I love that I want to spend my life with her…" Georgina's voice broke. She looked down.

Molly heard Lydia encourage, "Go on, darling."

Georgina looked up again and took another deep breath. "That I want to spend my life with her in front of anyone who cares to hear. Josephine and Edith's love went unheard, hidden until today." Georgina turned towards Molly with her cheeks blushing pink. "We all owe a debt to the passion of one curator, the woman I love, Molly Goode."

She loved her? *You love me.* The audience turned their heads sharply to look at Molly.

"To Molly." To Molly's utter amazement, Evelyn had raised her glass and the audience dutifully held theirs aloft. Molly could feel tears run down her neck to dampen her collar.

Lydia leaned in to Molly and said, "Now that's a speech."

Molly laughed only for her laugh to become a cry, prompting Lydia to place an arm around her and squeeze her tight.

"Oh, my dear," Lydia said. "Love is such sweet distress. Here, have a tissue."

"Molly?" Molly looked up to find Georgina balancing two glasses of wine and a plate of nibbles.

"Well, I shall leave you in the hands of the woman who loves you." Lydia walked off in the direction of Evelyn, who had somehow found herself newly pinned between an enthusiastic visitor and the foyer corner. At the refreshments table, Fred was handing Fran a large glass of wine and a hanky.

"Hi," Molly said, drying her eyes.

"Hi." Georgina swallowed hard. "I thought you might think talk was cheap, so I've backed things up with nibbles."

"Thank you," Molly said, with the wine glass shaking in her hand. "I wouldn't have believed you without a prawn vol-au-vent."

"Knew it." Georgina rested her cool palm against Molly's hot cheek. "I imagine you thought I'd never say…it," Georgina said. "It's not that I didn't want to before—" Molly placed a finger to Georgina's lips.

"It doesn't matter. As I figure it, all that matters is that the woman you love couldn't love you more."

Georgina's eyes flooded with tears. "I love you so much."

Molly hugged Georgina close. From over Georgina's shoulder, she caught sight of Lydia talking with Evelyn. She was pointing to Josephine's portrait and then to the Wright room. Molly could just make out that Evelyn's neck was prickling pink.

"I don't know what your mum's saying to Evelyn, but I'm not sure it's going down that well."

Georgina dried her eyes and glanced across at the two women deep in conversation. "My guess is she's suggesting that *The Hunt* be replaced by Edith's painting."

"In the Wright room? Really? It would certainly match her flustered expression." Molly looked down hoping to avoid Evelyn's attention. "Is that okay with you?"

Georgina lifted Molly's chin. "Yes. I can't believe given what I now know that I defended my father, and that I put him above everything." Georgina shook her head and looked across at Edith's painting surrounded still by curious visitors crowding in to take a closer look. "When it is so clear that the portrait needs to be seen and that it belongs in the Wright room."

"There's a chance," Molly said, a little hesitantly, "that Evelyn won't want to change her mind. Curatorial pride and all that."

"Maybe. Except I'm pretty sure my mother hasn't written her review of the Wright room yet."

"Of course. I doubt Evelyn saw that coming."

"I don't know, she's a wily old fox. I doubt there's much she doesn't anticipate. Anyway, enough of museums, paintings, parents. How about after this, pizza at mine?"

"Oh no, I promised I'd go to the pub with the art club. And given your speech, I think they'll be expecting us both. I promise they're a lovely bunch."

"It's fine. Sounds fun. Although I'm not posing naked for them. That privilege is entirely the robins'."

Molly laughed with her heart so full of love she could have sworn it would soon spill onto the floor, a hazard of emotion, glistening for all to see.

CHAPTER THIRTY-SIX

"Morning," Molly whispered into Georgina's ear, only for Georgina to pull the duvet over her head with a groan. "I'm leaving some paracetamol and a coffee here for you."

Georgina slipped the duvet slowly from over her face and without opening her eyes croaked, "I had the most crazy dream that I was standing in front of everyone declaring that I love you."

Molly sat on the edge of the bed and smoothed a hand along the line of Georgina's arm beneath the duvet. "Imagine that."

Georgina opened her eyes and gave a sleepy smile. "Don't go to work."

"Weren't you once a workaholic?"

"Weren't you once a rebel?"

Molly laughed. "The most rebellious thing I've ever done was run across the road before waiting for the pedestrian crossing lights to flash."

Georgina sat up and rested the duvet at her lap. "You risked everything to correct injustice. That's pretty rebellious, if you ask me."

"None of that was planned. Isn't rebellion planned? And stop tempting me with your breasts."

Georgina laughed only to quickly hold her head. "Ow."

"Yep, ow's about right. My head feels like rhinos are disco dancing inside it."

"Then don't go."

"I'll come back for lunch."

"I'll have left for London by then."

"You're going back today? But it's Friday."

"I've got meetings just after lunch, I have no choice. I'm sorry."

Molly gathered Georgina's hand in her lap. The thought of not waking up with her tomorrow morning caused a dull ache in her chest. "I hate not waking up with you."

"Even in this ridiculously creaky bed?"

"I shall miss this bed." Molly pressed the mattress and heard the bed frame creak. "It's been fun."

Georgina studied Molly's face for a moment before nodding. "Lots of fun."

Molly gazed around the room. Her attention drifted out to the long garden beyond. "I can't believe that you haven't had buyers snapping off your hands for this place." Molly walked over to the window and stared down at the beautiful grounds. She couldn't have envied anyone more. The new buyers would be so lucky. Molly thought of the memories they would make. Of the laughter. Of the return of life this house had so longed for.

She leaned her head against the cold glass. "I wonder if they'll put an arbour over the path, just there where it divides, and more seating to catch the evening sun, perhaps?"

"I have had offers."

Molly looked at Georgina. "You have? You didn't mention anything." It looked like Georgina wanted to say something as her eyes flitted over Molly's face, but then she looked down to the duvet in her lap. Molly quickly added, "Not that it's any of my business, obviously. So when do you think you might return?"

"Look, I have an idea—why don't you come over, say, Sunday evening. We could have a picnic in the sitting room. What do you reckon?"

Molly returned to sit on the edge of the bed once more. "You're not coming back until Sunday night?"

"It's just there are some things I need to do."

"Sure." She must keep it breezy, not needy. Georgina had to leave. It wasn't her choice—it was just how things were. "And so have I lots to do. I am a very busy woman, I'll have you know. What time on Sunday? I may just be able to squeeze you in between *Countryfile* and *Antiques Roadshow*."

"Six?"

"I've pencilled you in." With their hands entwined, Molly kissed Georgina goodbye. Reluctant to move away she said, "See you Sunday then."

"I hate waking up without you too. Just so you know."

Molly traced her fingertips to the tips of Georgina's fingers before their hands parted.

Leaving Georgina was sweet agony. As Molly rushed the few hundred yards to work, she couldn't help but wonder: Would it always be this way?

"Good morning, Molly." Evelyn's voice startled her back to the day ahead. As ever, Evelyn looked immaculate. Even the tips of her stilettoes shone as she paused under the portico with her coat resting over her arm.

Molly felt instantly unprepared. Had she even brushed her hair? She hoped she wasn't wearing the tights with the ladder. "Morning."

"Could you join me?" Evelyn carried on into the foyer before Molly could reply.

"Yes, of course." Oh God. Was this about last night? Had they guessed right and Lydia had obliged Evelyn to remove *The Hunt* from the Wright room? Evelyn would hold her responsible wouldn't she? Would she think that she had gone behind her back yet again?

Molly hurried after Evelyn giving a breathless, "Hi, Fred," as they passed by reception.

"Molly. Ms. Fox." Fred stood up straight.

"I'm expecting the chairman, Fred. Please send him straight up."

Fred smoothed his shirt against his chest and gave a dutiful nod.

The chairman? "Is this about Edith's painting?" Molly tried to recapture the breath that was escaping her with every step.

Evelyn's breath remained steady and alarmingly calm as they reached the corridor. Without breaking her stride Evelyn said, "I have agreed with Lydia Wright's request in that regard if that's what you're asking about. And now as far as I'm concerned that matter is concluded. Understood?"

"Yes, absolutely. So does that mean by any chance…"

They stopped outside Marianne's office.

Evelyn let out an exasperated sigh. "*The Hunt* will return to the Victorian gallery and the watercolour of Josephine Brancaster will hang at the beginning of the family portraits in the Wright room. And as we are evidently continuing to discuss it, please make this adjustment with the conclusion of the Edith Hewitt display."

"At the front of the family portraits?" Molly's heart skipped with how right that felt. For Edith should be first in every way. "Did Lydia request this?"

Evelyn looked at Molly as if she had completely lost all sense. "No. There is simply no question of me hanging a series of works out of order." Evelyn popped her head into Marianne's office. "Three coffees and two further copies of the letter from Estelle Oberon. We're meeting in the conference room."

"Estelle Oberon?"

"Yes. Before we come to that. Please shut the door behind you and take a seat."

Molly sat on the edge of her chair, for nothing about this meeting suggested it would be relaxed.

Evelyn sat back in her seat and folded her arms.

Molly held her breath.

"I would like to share something with you. Take from it what you will." Evelyn smoothed her hand over her notebook pressing it flat against her desk.

"Okay." The thought of Evelyn sharing with her couldn't have been more unsettling, and it certainly wasn't helping that the voice of the chairman arriving could be heard through the door.

"I was married once." Evelyn closed her eyes to add, "A long time ago." She swallowed as if the thought was less a memory and more a regurgitation of something acidic burning in her throat. She pinched at her brow and reopened her eyes to fix on Molly. "I mention this because I was doing very well in my post. There was even talk of promotion. But my husband was offered a job, and well, I dutifully resigned, followed him. It was what you did. And then less than a year later, he left me for some silly girl with a crush on him. Men are so weak, don't you think? Their egos demanding to be stroked like a cat in heat."

"I've not really given much thought to that question."

Evelyn shook her head. "Right, yes, of course. But here is the point." She lifted her palm from her notepad and poked her finger into it stabbing the cover as she said, "Is *your* job, *your* career worth less than your partner's? Are you meant to sacrifice everything and follow them?"

"Is this about Georgina and me? Because if it is, then you're mistaken. Georgina hasn't asked me to do anything. Certainly not to leave—"

Evelyn leaned towards Molly slightly. "They don't ask, Molly. Come in!"

Molly jumped at Evelyn's raised voice and felt a shudder at her insinuation.

Marianne's head appeared around the door. "The chairman's arrived."

"Marvellous. Shall we?" Evelyn pushed her chair back and gathered her papers.

"Sorry, I still don't quite understand what you're implying."

"Well then, let me put it this way—when someone stands in front of their partner's friends, colleagues, and employers declaring their love as Georgina saw fit to do last night, then that to me is a clear statement of intent."

"Is it not just a heartfelt declaration of love?"

"Molly, in many ways your naivety is charming and in many ways blinding. I've said all I can."

Molly's head spun. Georgina wouldn't ask Molly to leave her job and move to London. Would she? No, of course she wouldn't.

Evelyn paused and stood behind her desk with her hand on the back of her chair. "Before we meet with Mark, I want to briefly mention the next matter of interest. As I said, Estelle Oberon has been in touch. I only know of the Oberons by reputation as generous philanthropists. How is it *you* know them? You see, Estelle mentions you personally in her letter."

"I met them at the National Portrait Gallery."

"Networking?"

Was that the same as chatting? "Sort of."

"Well, you'll be pleased I'm sure to learn that they wish to donate a not insubstantial amount of money to a project here at the museum related to encouraging young women to engage with their own particular history."

"Really? That's awesome."

"They want the focus on using those histories to empower and underpin the young women's confidence and well-being. Apparently there is a need, a *gap* in our programming. I wasn't aware we had a gap?"

Panic gripped Molly in a tight embrace. "I only mentioned the idea in passing, very briefly. Estelle, Mrs. Oberon, didn't mention her intention to run with it."

"Well not only has she run with the idea, she has positively sprinted with enthusiasm. The chairman is delighted. He tells me he has been trying to entice the Oberons for some time. Well done."

"Oh, it was nothing, really."

Evelyn placed her hand lightly on Molly's forearm. "What you achieve is not nothing. Please remember that. Right, let's go."

Molly began to follow Evelyn. She could see through the open conference room door the chairman sipping at his coffee with a stray smile on his lips. Evelyn stopped at the threshold to the conference room. In a half whisper she said, "Can we, though, do you suppose, allow the chairman to believe it was his doing, the fruits of his labour, if you will? I think it best."

It was clear to Molly in that moment that if Evelyn Fox mismanaged one relationship with a man, she had clearly determined never to mismanage another. She had become a master of conceding everything and nothing all at once.

"Of course." Molly gave an understanding nod.

And then Evelyn did the most peculiar thing. She smiled. It was as if she forgot herself for a moment, because no sooner had her face relaxed into a warm expression, than she quickly turned away to the chairman, her face re-fixing, as if for battle.

"Mark. How wonderful to see you. And you've a copy of Estelle Oberon's letter. I've invited Molly to join us. She's the perfect choice to lead this project. I feel you agree…"

❖

"I've never known the museum, or the square for that matter, so quiet." Fran ushered Molly to move along the bench to make room for her. "I have had the most pleasant peaceful morning. Not one person asked me where the toilet was or if the embalmed mummy was real."

"The morning-after phenomenon," Molly said. "It was such a good night, wasn't it?"

Fran gave Molly's hand a quick squeeze. "A very good night. I'm impressed you made it in."

Molly grimaced and rubbed her forehead. "I was tempted not to. I have the hangover from hell. Thank God I did go in though. Evelyn pounced on me for a meeting with her before I'd even gotten through the door. Honestly I have so much news to tell you."

"Excellent. Although I've never found you lacking in that department."

"I aim to please. Item one—Edith's painting will hang in the Wright room after the temporary display has finished."

"Molly, that's wonderful. So which Wright threatened Evelyn into that decision?"

"Lydia."

"Goodness. I love it. Next item please."

"Do you remember I spent New Year's in London with Georgina at a party held by the Oberons?"

"How could I forget."

"Yes, *anyway*, the Oberons are important patrons—think the Wright Foundation but much, much bigger. It turns out Estelle Oberon is funding a project here at the museum aimed at helping young women engage with their history."

"That's excellent. Was this something you'd been hoping for?"

"No, that's just it—it was a complete surprise. I do remember chatting with Estelle over a glass of wine, and her asking me what my next project was. I said that I wanted to keep developing a diverse museum where every visitor could see themselves reflected. I also mentioned our aspirations for extending our outreach work. It obviously struck a chord with her."

"I take it Evelyn is pleased."

"She smiled at me."

"No? Now that *is* news."

They both laughed. Molly gave a whimper of pain and clutched at her forehead.

"I'm never drinking again. The last thing I remember clearly was arriving back with Georgina to her father's house and sliding down George Wright's banister."

"Molly Goode. That's original woodwork." Fran's scolding words did not match her amused expression. "And Georgina? How was she this morning?"

"She could barely open her eyes."

"Aha. Very telling. I see the for sale sign's gone. Don't tell me you're responsible for that too?"

"What? It has?" Molly shielded her eyes, straining to look for the board. "Georgina didn't say anything. You know, I could have sworn I narrowly collided with it first thing. It must have been taken down this morning at some point."

Molly looked at Fran, who just shrugged.

"Come to think of it, Georgina let slip only this morning that she'd had offers." Molly bit forlornly into her sandwich.

Fran frowned. "Except wouldn't they just put up a *sold subject to contract* banner over the for sale notice? Maybe Georgina's decided not to sell after all."

Molly shook her head. "I don't think so. She told me that she literally has nightmares about what happened in that house."

"Well you know her best. It's just…"

"What?"

"What puzzles me is if she hates the house so much, why do you both spend so much time there?"

Molly shrugged. "It's convenient for my work and the train station."

"It's practically empty. Trust me, there's nothing convenient or comfortable about that house. Want an apple?" Molly shook her head. Fran continued, while rooting round in her bag, "My sense is that it means a lot for Georgina to be there, whether she would admit it to herself or not."

Could Fran be right? But then what if it was Evelyn who was right? And London was all that Georgina had in mind. Maybe it was a private sale that had just gone through and that was that. No more beautiful sitting room to admire, no more stairs to want to dance down, no more coffee in the glamorous kitchen, and no more bedroom where the morning light fell upon the bed where she woke in Georgina's arms.

"You okay?" Fran stared at Molly with an expression of concern.

"Yes. I was just thinking how much I'll miss the house."

"But then you have the girl to compensate, eh?"

"She honestly means everything to me. My work also means the world to me, and I will never stop doing what I do and caring about what I care about but…I know this is going to sound terrible, but I just want to be with her wherever that is, wherever she needs me to go. Is that really weak of me to put her first?"

"No. It's not weakness." Fran put her arm around Molly and gave her a squeeze. "It's love."

Chapter Thirty-seven

Sunday arrived with merciful speed. They'd ended their Saturday evening call with Georgina saying that she was still on schedule for six the next day and that she couldn't wait to see her. She sounded excited—not that she could be more excited than Molly herself. And now it was time to meet again, and as she stood at Georgina's door, she thought she might burst.

"Georgina. Hi, it's me." Had Georgina intended to leave the door ajar?

Stepping gingerly inside, Molly's feet caught at a newly laid mat. Her gaze tripped along the length of the hallway, resting on a vase of sunflowers placed on George Wright's console table. What? How could that be? The house was empty. Wasn't it?

The house smelled warm and full of life rather than its usual sense of emptiness which had always clung like grief to its floors and walls.

"Is anyone there?" Molly pushed the sitting room door to slowly open and peeked inside. "No way." She turned in a slow circle, staring in wonder at each familiar piece of furniture. There was the sideboard decorated with another vase of flowers, this time yellow roses. And then there was the leather armchair by the fireplace with its soft material so familiar to her touch. She looked at the mirror rehung, to find her breath catch by the items framed in its reflection.

She turned sharply to face the wall behind her where the family portraits once hung, to find in their place a series of three framed pictures.

"Wow." Molly moved to them. The first image she recognized immediately as the view from the restaurant of the National Portrait Gallery. She touched the edge of the frame. It was their first kiss.

Molly held her hand against her heart at the sight of the next picture, a photo of the Christmas star she had made for Georgina that magical morning.

And then the last image, so familiar, so evocative of everything, Edith's portrait of Josephine.

"It's a print, obviously." Georgina stood at the sitting room door.

Molly brushed away tears. "You've done all this? Does it mean...?"

Georgina moved to Molly and took her hand in hers. "The last time we were together, we'd come back here the night before from a wonderful evening, and I'd watched you skip from lamp post to lamp post down the promenade. It felt so right. And then in the morning everything felt so wrong. We were talking about how the new owners would make the garden their own, and you were leaving, and then when your hand slipped from mine, I knew in that instant what to do. It became so clear what I wanted..." Georgina's voice caught.

"You wanted?"

"I wanted to come home, here, to you, every day, forever. Could this be our home, do you think? We can replace the furniture of course."

Molly squeezed Georgina's hands tightly. "*Yes.* Yes, please. I love you so much. And I love this house and everything in it—you know I do. I couldn't imagine anything more perfect. Except you, perhaps. There is nothing more perfect than you."

Georgina kissed Molly. It was a passionate, complete kiss that filled every space in Molly's heart and soul. It was a kiss that spoke of the memories they shared. And a kiss that spoke of the memories they would make and of the thrill of their future, full of joy and love, unhidden, for all to see.

About the Author

Anna is an English literature graduate with a passion for LGBT heritage. She has Master's degrees in museum studies and the word and the visual imagination and has written and curated a permanent exhibition of LGBT voices and memorabilia, based at Leicester's LGBT Centre.

Anna's debut novel, *Highland Fling*, was a finalist in the 2018 Golden Crown Literary Society Awards and was recommended as one of the Top Ten Summer Reads of 2017 by *AfterEllen*. Her short story "Hooper Street" can be found in the BSB anthology *Girls Next Door*. Her poems have been published with Paradise Press and the University of Leicester's Centre for New Writing.

www.annalarner.com
Facebook: @anna.larner.writer
Twitter: @annalarnerbooks
Instagram: @anna.larner.writer

Books Available from Bold Strokes Books

Dangerous Curves by Larkin Rose. When love waits at the finish line, dangerous curves are a risk worth taking. (978-1-63555-353-6)

Love to the Rescue by Radclyffe. Can two people who share a past really be strangers? (978-1-62639-973-0)

Love's Portrait by Anna Larner. When museum curator Molly Goode and benefactor Georgina Wright uncover a portrait's secret, public and private truths are exposed, and their deepening love hangs in the balance. (978-1-63555-057-3)

Model Behavior by MJ Williamz. Can one woman's instability shatter a new couple's dreams of happiness? (978-1-63555-379-6)

Pretending in Paradise by M. Ullrich. When travelwisdom.com assigns PR specialist Caroline Beckett and travel blogger Emma Morgan to cover a hot new couples retreat, they're forced to fake a relationship to secure a reservation. (978-1-63555-399-4)

Recipe for Love by Aurora Rey. Hannah Little doesn't have much use for fancy chefs or fancy restaurants, but when New York City chef Drew Davis comes to town, their attraction just might be a recipe for love. (978-1-63555-367-3)

Survivor's Guilt and Other Stories by Greg Herren. Award-winning author Greg Herren's short stories are finally pulled together into a single collection, including the Macavity Award nominated title story and the first-ever Chanse MacLeod short story. (978-1-63555-413-7)

The House by Eden Darry. After a vicious assault, Sadie, Fin, and their family retreat to a house they think is the perfect place to start over, until they realize not all is as it seems. (978-1-63555-395-6)

Uninvited by Jane C. Esther. When Aerin McLeary's body becomes host for an alien intent on invading Earth, she must work with researcher Olivia Ando to uncover the truth and save humankind. (978-1-63555-282-9)

Comrade Cowgirl by Yolanda Wallace. When cattle rancher Laramie Bowman accepts a lucrative job offer far from home, will her heart end up getting lost in translation? (978-1-63555-375-8)

Double Vision by Ellie Hart. When her cell phone rings, Giselle Cutler answers it—and finds herself speaking to a dead woman. (978-1-63555-385-7)

Inheritors of Chaos by Barbara Ann Wright. As factions splinter and reunite, will anyone survive the final showdown between gods and mortals on an alien world? (978-1-63555-294-2)

Love on Lavender Lane by Karis Walsh. Accompanied by the buzz of honeybees and the scent of lavender, Paige and Kassidy must find a way to compromise on their approach to business if they want to save Lavender Lane Farm—and find a way to make room for love along the way. (978-1-63555-286-7)

Spinning Tales by Brey Willows. When the fairy tale begins to unravel and villains are on the loose, will Maggie and Kody be able to spin a new tale? (978-1-63555-314-7)

The Do-Over by Georgia Beers. Bella Hunt has made a good life for herself and put the past behind her. But when the bane of her high school existence shows up for Bella's class on conflict resolution, the last thing they expect is to fall in love. (978-1-63555-393-2)

What Happens When by Samantha Boyette. For Molly Kennan, senior year is already an epic disaster, and falling for mysterious waitress Zia is about to make life a whole lot worse. (978-1-63555-408-3)

Wooing the Farmer by Jenny Frame. When fiercely independent modern socialite Penelope Huntingdon-Stewart and traditional country farmer Sam McQuade meet, trusting their hearts is harder than it looks. (978-1-63555-381-9)

A Chapter on Love by Laney Webber. When Jannika and Lee reunite, their instant connection feels like a gift, but neither is ready for a second chance at love. Will they finally get on the same page when it comes to love? (978-1-63555-366-6)

Drawing Down the Mist by Sheri Lewis Wohl. Everyone thinks Grand Duchess Maria Romanova died in 1918. They were almost right. (978-1-63555-341-3)

Listen by Kris Bryant. Lily Croft is inexplicably drawn to Hope D'Marco but will she have the courage to confront the consequences of her past and present colliding? (978-1-63555-318-5)

Perfect Partners by Maggie Cummings. Elite police dog trainer Sara Wright has no intention of falling in love with a coworker, until Isabel Marquez arrives at Homeland Security's Northeast Regional Training facility and Sara's good intentions start to falter. (978-1-63555-363-5)

Shut Up and Kiss Me by Julie Cannon. What better way to spend two weeks of hell in paradise than in the company of a hot, sexy woman? (978-1-63555-343-7)

Spencer's Cove by Missouri Vaun. When Foster Owen and Abigail Spencer meet they uncover a story of lives adrift, loves lost, and true love found. (978-1-63555-171-6)

Without Pretense by TJ Thomas. After living for decades hiding from the truth, can Ava learn to trust Bianca with her secrets and her heart? (978-1-63555-173-0)

Unexpected Lightning by Cass Sellars. Lightning strikes once more when Sydney and Parker fight a dangerous stranger who threatens the peace they both desperately want. (978-1-163555-276-8)

Emily's Art and Soul by Joy Argento. When Emily meets Andi Marino she thinks she's found a new best friend but Emily doesn't know that Andi is fast falling in love with her. Caught up in exploring her sexuality, will Emily see the only woman she needs is right in front of her? (978-1-63555-355-0)

Escape to Pleasure: Lesbian Travel Erotica edited by Sandy Lowe and Victoria Villasenor. Join these award-winning authors as they explore the sensual side of erotic lesbian travel. (978-1-63555-339-0)

Music City Dreamers by Robyn Nyx. Music can bring lovers together. In Music City, it can tear them apart. (978-1-63555-207-2)

Ordinary is Perfect by D. Jackson Leigh. Atlanta marketing superstar Autumn Swan's life derails when she inherits a country home, a child, and a very interesting neighbor. (978-1-63555-280-5)

Royal Court by Jenny Frame. When royal dresser Holly Weaver's passionate personality begins to melt Royal Marine Captain Quincy's icy heart, will Holly be ready for what she exposes beneath? (978-1-63555-290-4)

Strings Attached by Holly Stratimore. Success. Riches. Music. Passion. It's a life most can only dream of, but stardom comes at a cost. (978-1-63555-347-5)

The Ashford Place by Jean Copeland. When Isabelle Ashford inherits an old house in small-town Connecticut, family secrets, a shocking discovery, and an unexpected romance complicate her plan for a fast profit and a temporary stay. (978-1-63555-316-1)

Treason by Gun Brooke. Zoem Malderyn's existence is a deadly threat to everyone on Gemocon and Commander Neenja KahSandra must find a way to save the woman she loves from having to commit the ultimate sacrifice. (978-1-63555-244-7)

A Wish Upon a Star by Jeannie Levig. Erica Cooper has learned to depend on only herself, but when her new neighbor, Leslie Raymond, befriends Erica's special needs daughter, the walls protecting her heart threaten to crumble. (978-1-63555-274-4)

Answering the Call by Ali Vali. Detective Sept Savoie returns to the streets of New Orleans, as do the dead bodies from ritualistic killings, and she does everything in her power to bring them to justice while trying to keep her partner, Keegan Blanchard, safe. (978-1-63555-050-4)

Breaking Down Her Walls by Erin Zak. Could a love worth staying for be the key to breaking down Julia Finch's walls? (978-1-63555-369-7)

Exit Plans for Teenage Freaks by 'Nathan Burgoine. Cole always has a plan—especially for escaping his small-town reputation as "that kid who was kidnapped when he was four"—but when he teleports to a museum, it's time to face facts: it's possible he's a total freak after all. (978-1-63555-098-6)

Friends Without Benefits by Dena Blake. When Dex Putman gets the woman she thought she always wanted, she soon wonders if it's really love after all. (978-1-63555-349-9)

Invalid Evidence by Stevie Mikayne. Private Investigator Jil Kidd is called away to investigate a possible killer whale, just when her partner Jess needs her most. (978-1-63555-307-9)

Pursuit of Happiness by Carsen Taite. When attorney Stevie Palmer's client reveals a scandal that could derail Senator Meredith Mitchell's presidential bid, their chance at love may be collateral damage. (978-1-63555-044-3)

Seascape by Karis Walsh. Marine biologist Tess Hansen returns to Washington's isolated northern coast where she struggles to adjust to small-town living while courting an endowment for her orca research center from Brittany James. (978-1-63555-079-5)

Second in Command by VK Powell. Jazz Perry's life is disrupted and her career jeopardized when she becomes personally involved with the case of an abandoned child and the child's competent but strict social worker, Emory Blake. (978-1-63555-185-3)

Taking Chances by Erin McKenzie. When Valerie Cruz and Paige Wellington clash over what's in the best interest of the children in Valerie's care, the children may be the ones who teach them it's worth taking chances for love. (978-1-63555-209-6)